FORTIFIED

A NOVEL

PAUL ELMORE

FORTIFIED

ISBN: 9781731589989

Original Cover Art by: Ellen DeVrieze

The virtue of adversity is fortitude
Cicero [Roman statesman, orator, and philosopher]

That which does not kill us makes us stronger
Friedrich Nietzsche [German philosopher, poet, composer, and Latin/Greek scholar]

CHAPTER 1

Autumn in eastern Washington State is frequently spectacular. Days are sunny and pleasant; nights are cool, but not cold. The apple harvest in the rolling hills along the eastern slopes of the Cascade Mountains all the way to the Columbia River is in full swing. Grapes are coming in from the vineyards too. Table grapes are headed directly to market and wine grapes to the presses. At the wineries, previous years' vintages are loaded on to trucks to make way for the new wines. From the outside, the Spring Rain Winery was bustling with positive energy like other local wineries, bringing in the last of what might turn out to be a record crop of exceptional grapes. On the inside, the mood was decidedly different.

"Why the fuck don't you act like the owner of a business and carry your goddamned cell phone when you're out of the office, so we can track you down when we need you? We've been trying to get a hold of you for three hours."

Without a word in response, William St. James set his backpack by the stairs and backed his antagonist into his office with a stare. He then closed the rarely shut, eight-foot-high, solid wood doors behind him. Calmly setting his briefcase on the massive oak desk, he glanced out the bay window overlooking the three-hundred-acre operation before leaning his muscular upper body forward on the desk and saying, "After all the time we've known each other, Jack, you know damned well I take everything regarding the operation of this winery very seriously. So, stop talking bullshit. Take a deep breath, act like the competent manager I know you to be and tell me what's wrong."

"We found contamination."

"What kind of contamination?"

"Chemical, biological, or maybe a combination of both. We haven't been able to pinpoint the agent or its source yet. Tests on wines bottled just prior to this and immediately after were all negative. So, whatever the problem, it's specific. We've used the same barrels and vats since so that's at least one possible contamination source off the list. We're still looking at bottling machinery, bottles, and corks. I'm fairly sure all the grapes came from our vines, but I'll double check to make sure we didn't buy any to make up for a shortfall. I haven't heard of any other wineries having any problems," Jack said.

"How many bottles?" St. James asked as he sat in the heirloom, century-old, high back leather chair.

"At least two hundred cases. The entire Merlot vintage is questionable. We haven't had any reports prior to this, but I think we should try to get all the Merlot back especially all the recent shipments."

St. James turned his chair to look briefly out the window then turned back again. "Why are we just finding out about this now. Didn't any of it get tested?"

Pulling one of the straight-backed, hardwood chairs up to the desk, Jack still had to stretch to toss the lab reports onto the blotter. "Every required test was done. I've reviewed all the lab work. There is nothing to make us suspect anything would be wrong. Frankly, we just stumbled onto it. A week or so ago, while we were moving cases to a shipping pallet, workers found a case where all the bottles had either blown corks or were shattered." Holding up the bottle of wine he had brought, "This is the only bottle from that case that was intact. Only the label had come off. It ended up on

Kevin's desk in the lab. At the time, they thought that the case had somehow gotten overheated or frozen. Kevin was here early to finish up some reports that needed to get to the ATF today. When he was done, he opened the bottle out of curiosity more than anything. It smelled odd to him, so he called me and started testing samples. I came in, looked over all the paperwork and even tasted some. It's really bitter, I had to spit it out. Even at that, I got a bit nauseated. This wine is bad!"

Taking the bottle, Bill pulled the cork and winced as the odor hit his nostrils. "What's the definition of bad?"

"People could certainly become ill and it may have the potential to kill. We just don't know for sure," Jack answered.

Turning his chair, Bill briefly stared out the window again. Without turning back, he calmly said, "Let's get that wine back or have it destroyed. Hopefully, it's all still in distribution warehouses. Do we know exactly where the wine was sent?"

Responding with confidence, Jack said: "Yes, it's all on the West Coast, one hundred fifty cases in Southern California and twenty-five cases each in Oregon and Washington."

Turning back to face Jack, St. James, in the self-assured tone that was typical said, "OK, let's get on this and do some damage control at the same time. Call the truck lines and distribution warehouses directly. Tell them we'll incur any expense involved in returning or destroying the wine. I want to account for every bottle with written confirmation showing case and GS1 barcodes. I'll write up a press release and contact the FDA myself. Let's get going on this right now. If anyone gets sick or, heaven forbid, dies, the liability could drive us into oblivion. Exactly when did we ship?"

Jack shuffled papers until he found one listing the dates and names of trucking lines, looked at it briefly, then handed it across the desk. "Well, the good news for California is that those shipments just left last Friday, so chances are they're still in the warehouses. Hell, some of it might never have gotten off the trucks. Unfortunately, the Oregon release was a week ago and the western Washington shipment almost two weeks ago."

"Those Oregon and Washington shipments could easily be out on market shelves by now. Well, let's get on those calls." Speaking in a loud voice and looking past Jack, St. James called out to his secretary.

The heavy doors creaked like fingernails on a blackboard as Janet opened them just wide enough to step through, then stood motionless in the archway with a frightened look on her pale face, nervously twisting a lock of hair in her fingers.

St. James's tone softened when he noticed her standing there. "Janet, I know you heard what we were talking about. We'll need phone numbers for the trucking lines and distribution warehouses, then get me someone at both the FDA and ATF. I want every trucking firm and distribution warehouse contacted immediately. Get Kevin in here to help with the calls. I want follow-up e-mails sent to everyone on that list requesting confirmation that they received the email and then confirmation after the wine has been destroyed. Document everything; who you talked to, what they said, and when they say it happened. I'll also need the phone numbers of the ABC, NBC, and CBS affiliates in Seattle. I don't want to go public if I don't have to, but if even one bottle is unaccounted for, I want to be ready."

The small office was in a frenzied mode for almost an hour, reviewing and confirming case and lot numbers. By noon, open phone lines began to appear. St. James hung up from his third call to the FDA and came out into the waiting area smiling at the work of his tenacious staff.

"Well, Jack, what's our status?"

"We've had mostly good news. All the cases in California and Oregon have been accounted for and destroyed before leaving the warehouses. The twenty-five cases in Washington went to two distributors in the Seattle area. They did distribute some, but we've contacted the retailers directly. As far as we can tell, we've had all of it pulled and destroyed. It appears none was sold. I believe we've dodged a bullet."

There was a moment of silence, and then a nervous chuckle that turned into full-blown laughter as the tension of the past hours disappeared.

"Thank you, everyone, for your hard work." Looking at his chemist, St. James continued, "Kevin, just in case we missed something, I want you to send out some samples of the bad wine to a toxicology lab for analysis. I also want random samples from every lot we've bottled six months before and after the bad wine. Let's not ship anything until we have a better understanding of what we're dealing with."

Chair legs screeched against hardwood flooring, as Jack and Kevin stood then stretched. Standing at the office doorway, St. James met each employee with a firm handshake, a pat on the back, and a heartfelt thank you.

Looking St. James in the eye, Jack said, "Sorry about saying that stuff about you not caring what goes on here. I know you do. I was just anxious and worried."

"No problem. You only said it because you care too. If you didn't, I wouldn't have you working here."

The office was quiet now. Bill sat down again in what was once his father's chair and gazed out the window. A slight breeze filled the room with the fragrance of grapes.

Glancing to the left, he looked at a picture of his father and himself standing next to an old farm tractor. It was just down the hill from the three-story, white Victorian farmhouse that serves as the Spring Rain office. The picture had been taken over a year ago, just a few weeks before his father's death. At six feet two, Bill was several inches taller than his father. Five years earlier, before cancer struck, they could see eye to eye. Both had gray hair, Bill's several shades darker. Bill was trim, his father gaunt. The smiles were identical, a family trait. "How'd I do, Pa?"

CHAPTER 2

The day's weather in Seattle was common for early October. Skies were gray and rain was threatening, but because it was a Monday, the streets were alive with activity.

At the Corner Market, a small mid-town grocery store, the owners, Mr. and Mrs. Son Kim, received a phone call that morning from their local distributor to pull some Spring Rain wines. They were surprised and skeptical but a call ten minutes later from the winery near the eastern Washington city of Pullman, convinced them the request was genuine.

The most common buyers of Spring Rain wines were local office workers. Since they don't work weekends, none of the wine delivered the previous Friday had been sold. Recording the case and lot numbers as requested, Mr. Kim called to instruct the only non-family employee to dispose of the tainted wine.

Jim Stacy had been working at the market part-time for about six months to supplement the income from his other job for an online taxi service. Working both jobs allowed just enough money to support himself, his wife, and their new baby. At twenty-three, six feet tall, with dark brown hair, soft blue eyes, and a trim athletic build, Jim got lots of attention from female customers and gay males. He was, to their deep dismay, devoted to his wife.

Using clear, but slightly fractured English, Mr. Kim called out to Jim. "I put two boxes of wine next to the sink in the storeroom. Please open each bottle and pour them out."

After emptying eighteen out of twenty-four bottles, Jim stopped and put the last six in his backpack, covered it with his coat and returned to his cleaning and stocking duties. The market closed at nine p.m. Jim was the last to leave, as usual, his backpack over his shoulder.

Being fall, the air was cold but not freezing, a light rain had started a couple of hours earlier emptying the area of even more people than usual. Outside, those too young or broke to get into the local clubs were standing under awnings in pairs, individually stuffed in doorways, or ignoring the rain and sitting in groups on benches in the open.

Jim approached one of the larger groups made up of young adults, both male and female, ranging in age from about seventeen to twenty-five. "Anyone interested in buying some wine?" he asked.

As if choreographed, the group looked at Jim in unison. The biggest and probably the oldest member of the group turned and spoke. "What have you got?"

Jim responded, "I've got some good wine here for only four bucks a bottle, or six for twenty bucks."

"Let's see it." Looking over the bottle, the young man showed it to the other members of the group. "How 'bout fifteen?"

"I'll give you five for fifteen."

"Done," said the young man. Then turning to the group, said, "Ok, we need fifteen bucks." Each member of the group pulled a couple of dollars from jeans pockets and dropped them on the corner of the bench where they were congregated while Jim pulled the wine from his backpack. Pocketing the money, Jim said, "Have fun," then walked toward a darkened doorway where the faint outline of a person could be seen silhouetted against the light coming through the glass doors of the building.

In the doorway, Jim could see what appeared to be an old man. He was dressed in army surplus coat, jeans, heavy work boots, and a black stocking cap pulled to just above his eyes. A backpack leaned against the wall beside him.

"Hey man, you interested in buying a bottle?" Jim asked him.

The dark figure didn't move. Jim thought that the person might be dead. Repeating the question in a slightly louder voice, he saw movement and a head raise and turned to face him. Later, Jim would tell police the guy was in his seventies. Really, he was a fifty-two-year-old named Harold.

Through bloodshot eyes, Harold stared at Jim trying to focus. Then in a very clear, soft voice ask, "What do ya got?"

"I've got a bottle of real good wine for three bucks," Jim said.

Harold shook his head no and laid it back down on his

crossed arms that were resting on his pulled-up knees.

Jim took a quick look at his watch. It was almost nine thirty, and he wanted to go home to see his wife and get something to eat before he took the midnight to eight a.m. shift driving. He didn't have time to go looking for another potential buyer.

"Ok, listen, how about two bucks?"

Harold didn't even raise his head. Reaching into an inner pocket, he pulled out a single dollar bill and held it over his head.

Taking it, Jim said, "Shit. this isn't even worth the effort." He handed the bottle to Harold, who put it in his backpack without even glancing at it.

As Jim started jogging away, Harold slipped his hand under his coat again, this time to feel the warm soft fur of a puppy he had snuggling against his body.

~*~

The first group of people that Jim had approached, consisted of a boy and two girls in their teens, and three young men in their early twenties. They hadn't even waited for Jim to get out of sight before attempting to open the bottles. The youngest guy produced a Swiss Army knife and handed it to one of the older boys. Using the corkscrew that the Swiss Army incorporates into their tools, all but one of the bottles were opened. With the group in a roughly formed circle, the bottles slowly made their way around one at a time. It took about three rotations before a new bottle was needed.

Although the taste was bitter at first, no one in the group wanted to be the first to complain and the bottles were soon empty. A discussion then began whether or not the remaining bottle should be opened. The guys voted to drink the last bottle, while the girls both shrugged indicating they didn't care. So, the corkscrew reappeared, and the last bottle was opened and consumed quickly, then the group disbanded.

The three teenagers, Mike, Michelle, and Joan had been friends since grade school. Mike and Michelle had been dating each other exclusively for almost a year. Walking through town, they were indistinguishable from the hundreds of teens who comprise the growing population of street people.

Mike was eighteen, six feet tall, with dark hair and eyes. His muscular build had come from several years of weightlifting in preparation for football, at which he excelled. Unfortunately, in a late-season game the previous fall, he suffered a severely broken and dislocated leg. Months in a cast and weeks of working with a physical therapist had left him with only a slight limp, but playing football was no longer an option. He managed to get through his junior year, but without football's academic and attendance requirements now only six weeks into his senior year he was missing a day a week.

Michelle was a five-feet-five-inch blonde beauty with emerald green eyes, long flowing hair, and a perfectly proportioned body. Had she been a few inches taller she could have easily been a fashion model. She was very popular in school, but her main interest was Mike. When he wasn't in school, she frequently chose not to be either.

Joan was beautiful in a different way. Her hair was dark and short, eyes brown, and her five-feet three-inch body was firm and muscular from years of sports; including cross-country running, volleyball, and softball. She was popular and dated often but no one guy in particular. She was a good student and still very much interested in sports, so her attendance record was spotless.

They needed to go about a mile to the apartment of Rob Packard where both Mike and Joan's cars were parked. Joan and Michelle would drive home from there. Laughing at the oddly worded strip club marquees and the assortment of people milling around in front of them, the walk became a moving comedy routine. Walking so fast they were nearly running, all three seemed to have an unusual amount of energy. Three-quarters the way to their destination, Mike and Michelle started having stomach cramps and pain in their right sides just below the ribs. Joan was a little nauseous and slightly dizzy, but not in any particular discomfort. By the time they reached the apartment, Mike was carrying Michelle.

Believing they were suffering the effects of excessive alcohol, Rob encouraged them to lie down. It was ten-forty when they went into the bedroom. Joan fell asleep in a recliner in the living room. When Rob woke Joan forty minutes later, she was disoriented and began vomiting. When he went to wake Mike and Michelle, he found their corpses.

A frantic 911 call produced a small army of police, fire department, and medical personnel, but nothing could be done for the pair. In the few minutes between Rob's call and the arrival of emergency crews, Jane had started complaining of abdominal pain and had fallen to the floor, unconscious. As paramedics slid the gurney with Joan into a waiting ambulance, the apartment was sealed off as a crime scene. Rob was taken to the local police precinct to be interviewed, then was released three hours later. Not allowed to return to his apartment, Rob called his sister for a place to stay.

~*~

The almost constant construction in downtown Seattle requires the city to frequently buy and tear down buildings to make way for wider streets. The basement of one of those vacant, but yet to be demolished, buildings was the current home to the three young men who had been with Joan, Mike, and Michelle earlier. Noisy from the nearly constant traffic nearby, foul-smelling from excretory habits of the occupants, and dangerous by nature, it still provided relative comfort during the cold and wet fall and winter.

Living on the streets for a couple years, each had earned the three young men the dubious badge of being street smart. Forsaking their given names for Gopher, Blue, and Crazy Larry, they managed to adapt to their chosen lifestyle.

Gopher was really Jason Nevers, a twenty-two-year-old community college dropout, who had been ostracized by his family after impregnating his sixteen-year-old cousin. He was the longest continuous resident in the building and thus the name Gopher. Having had some college education, and usually resourceful, he was the unspoken leader of the trio.

Blue was Arron Stevens, a twenty-year-old drug addict. At seventeen, he got expelled from school and followed that with a series of brushes with the criminal justice system. Two of those resulted in short stays in the county jail. His mother was powerless to intervene in his destructive behavior and eventually needed a restraining order to protect herself from his drug-induced physical attacks.

Then there was Larry Jantzen, a.k.a. Crazy Larry, a twenty-four-year-old with the intellect and impulse control of a ten-year-old. His mother had put him in foster care when he was seven and never returned. He ran away at fifteen and lived on the streets ever since.

Heading north, they needed to walk nearly a mile to the building they'd shared for the last three months. They had each consumed far more than any of the teens. They were less than halfway there when they began developing symptoms similar to what the others had experienced. Severe nausea was the first to appear. Crawling through the surrounding chain link fence, they finally reached the once-boarded entrance to the space they shared. Each laid on his dirty sleeping bag hoping the sickness would ease.

"It must have been that damned wine," said Gopher. "Do you think that guy poisoned it?"

"I don't know, but we've got to get to a hospital," responded Blue.

Crazy Larry was facing a wall vomiting forcefully. If the others could see him, they would have seen their own future. He was deathly pale and shaking in the throes of a seizure that ended with Crazy Larry gasping for air. Death came moments later.

The bodies would be found a week later by state Department of Transportation workers inspecting the structure.

Of the six, Jane was the only survivor and she was in a deep coma. Reaching the hospital totally unresponsive, she stayed in the emergency room just long enough for a breathing tube to be placed in her lungs and to start her on a ventilator.

Taken to the intensive care unit in critical condition, she was diagnosed with a possible drug overdose. Her prognosis was poor, considering the fate of her two friends. Doctors hoped the lab results would reveal much-needed clues. All they could do in the meantime was contact her parents.

Joan was the daughter of Edward Leahy, a twenty-two-year Boeing Aviation employee, and Carol Leahy, an elementary school teacher. They were seen by others as a model family and in many ways, they were, but in the past two years, Joan had become more independent and distant from her parents for no other reason than the lack of time their individual schedules allowed. They continued to be a loving, concerned family.

Ed and Carol began to worry when Joan had not arrived home by eleven and they couldn't get through on her cell phone. When the police came to the door at one-thirty a.m., their worst fears were realized. They rushed to her side and one, or both, remained there always.

CHAPTER 3

Harold Pearson was the last person to buy wine that night. Under his army surplus coat, he was five feet eight and one hundred sixty-nine pounds. He had a solid build but was not seen as muscular but rather lanky. Black frame glasses sat on a twice-broken nose. Thick salt and pepper hair sat uncombed above green eyes and a soft, barely used, voice. Sitting in the doorway where Jim Stacy had first approached him, Harold remained almost motionless until the square was nearly empty. Rising slowly due to joint stiffness, he walked with a slow deliberate gait that became more fluid with each step. Passing a row of buildings, he took a quick look around and disappeared down a narrow, unlit, dead-end alley. Reaching in his coat, he gently lifted out the little fur ball puppy and sat him down on the pavement. The pup yawned, stretched, peed on the first three items his nose encountered and trotted off down the alley after Harold.

"We're heading to a very historic place," Harold said to the pup. "In the 1800's, almost all the buildings in Seattle were made of wood. But on June 6th, 1889, a cabinetmaker named Jonathan Back, knocked over a glue pot and started a fire that eventually burned between twenty-five and thirty-one city blocks depending on which reference book you read. After that city leaders made two decisions. One, that all the new buildings would be made of stone or brick to prevent another big fire and two, that the streets in this area would be raised one or two stories high. That was because buildings around here were built on sandy tide flats close to Elliot Bay. High tide would often make toilets back up and the streets flood. So, they built concrete walls on both sides of the street and then filled that in to raise the street level. Shop owners kept using the original first floors for a while. People had to go down ladders to get to them. Some brick archways were addded later with amber-colored glass blocks put in to act like skylights. Hardly any of those original first floors are still used. They do give tours around some of it. We're going to a part that isn't seen on the tours."

At the end of the alley, a few dumpsters overflowed with refuse. Cardboard and other miscellaneous rubbish lay around various trash cans. On the ground, a metal storm drain grate lay partially covered. Using a four-foot-long piece of iron pipe hidden behind a downspout, Harold lifted the grate and moved it sideways before replacing the pipe in its hiding spot. In the nearly complete darkness, he lowered himself two feet into the opening until his foot reached the top rung of a built-in ladder. Calling the pup to him, he slipped the pup back into his coat and lowered himself further into the drain. Once totally inside, he reached up to slide the grate back to its original position. Climbing down eight more rungs, he turned his body one-hundred-eighty degrees and stepped off into the darkness.

His foot landed three feet away from the ladder in a shaft running perpendicular to the drain. This horizontal shaft was six feet in diameter and pitch black. Using a small flashlight, he was able to walk unimpeded for another twenty feet down that shaft to where it came to a branch. Going left, he walked another thirty feet toward a spot of filtered light coming from what appeared to be the front entrance of a building.

The stone and mortar were as sound as when they were set some one-hundred-twenty years before. The wooden window and door frames had, for the most part, lost the battle to moisture and parasites. Inside, the buckled and split wood floors were generally sound. The room was twenty-feet square with a twelve feet high ceiling. A wall at the far end of the room seemed out of place. The bricks, although old, were several decades younger than the originals. On the other side of that wall was a walkway used during tours. Harold could hear the people coming and was especially quiet as they passed. A single bare light bulb hanging in a corner gave reasonable light to the entire room. This was Harold's home and, at this time, no one either knew or cared about it or his existence there.

It had taken more than a year, but Harold had accumulated a bed, small table, two chairs and hundreds of books, along with a multitude of odds and ends scattered around a room that was relatively clean. He had read a vast majority of the books, but the poor light made reading difficult as his sight slowly weakened. He rarely read underground now, choosing to read only when outside.

Walking to the table, he unloaded his backpack; a half-eaten sub sandwich, three cans of dog food, a bottle of wine and some other odds and ends. Moving to a makeshift shelf against one wall, he got a bowl and can opener. Opening the dog food, he put half the contents into the bowl and set it down for the pup.

The little black pup was soaking wet, shivering and sending out a pitiful little whine when Harold found him in a parking area across the street from the waterfront. He'd waited and watched for someone to come looking, but after three hours with the pup warm and dry under his coat, he headed for a nearby rescue mission. Both got something to eat and Harold asked the mission workers what he should do. Advised to turn the dog over to county animal control, Harold considered it as he made his way through town but instead decided they should be together. He gave him the name Auggie and thus began a mutual admiration society of two.

Finishing his meal in seconds, Auggie began to explore

the surroundings while Harold kept a watchful eye as he opened the bottle of wine. Finding a sock, Auggie was thrashing it around while Harold watched and laughed before sitting on the floor to play tug-o-war and fetch until both Auggie's and his energy waned. The wine remained on the table, open, but untouched.

Flashlight in hand, he walked back into the tunnel with Auggie on his heels. Going past the cutoff to the entrance, he headed straight for thirty yards. There was another storefront. Stepping through a wall where a window had been, he walked to a corner and opened a rickety oak door revealing an old bathroom. Water was running at a rate slightly more than a trickle from the cold-water tap on a rust-stained sink. The hot water tap did not function nor did the water to the toilet. Attaching a small hose to the facet he started to fill a two-gallon plastic container sitting on the floor. While that was filling, he relieved himself in the toilet then pulling the hose from the container and used the water to flush.

Starting back down the tunnel, he stopped in a small alcove and encouraged Auggie to relieve himself. Auggie obliged and the two retraced their steps back to the living space. Removing most of his clothes, Harold got into a well-used sleeping bag. Auggie jumped up on the bed and snuggled next to him and together they were soon asleep. The overnight temperature was in the upper thirties outside, but in this space, the temperature was rarely above sixty-five or below fifty-five.

Morning came for Harold in the form of a wet nose pressed firmly against his own; then it moved to his ear, neck, chin, then back to his nose. Barely opening one eye, he gazed at a bright-eyed, open mouth, tongue-wagging, nearly smiling face of Auggie anxious to greet the new day.

Initially startled, then fully awake, he started his day. A quick trip to the bathroom for each was followed by breakfast. Auggie's meal consisted of leftover dog food from the night before. Harold started the day with a drink from the bottle of wine he had opened the night before. He never bought wine for the taste, but this was peculiar.

Half an hour later, with a third of the bottle gone, Harold was feeling drowsy. His coordination was non-existent as he stood. He stumbled backward, jarring the table, and knocking the bottle to the floor where it spilled but did not break. Trotting over, Auggie sniffed briefly then licked at the wine. Harold shooed him away but could not get to the bottle before the remaining contents had emptied into the deep cracks of the wood floor. Barely able to maintain his balance, Harold literally fell into the bed and covered himself up. Auggie joined him and both fell into a very deep sleep.

Waking to the extreme discomfort of an overextended bladder, Harold's muscles ached, and his memory was cloudy. Auggie, sitting in the middle of the room, appearing to be twice as big as before. Heading toward the bathroom, he looked at his watch. Seven o'clock. He guessed he'd slept an additional ten hours. After relieving himself, he started back down the tunnel but stopped in front of the exit tunnel. There was a faint light coming in that he followed to the exit. It was early morning sunlight. How could that be unless he had slept nearly twenty-four hours? Heading back to his living space, he was completely confused.

Auggie had been following at his feet and began to search the room as soon as they returned. Harold realized if he had, in fact, slept one whole day, then Auggie had not eaten since the previous morning. Another can of dog food and the half-eaten sub sandwich from two days earlier seemed to satisfy the pup.

Putting on his clothes and picking up his coat, he headed for the tunnel exit. At the exit, he told Auggie to stay as he stepped over the void and climbed the ladder. Pausing to listen for activity and hearing nothing, he pushed with hand and shoulder to move the grate sideways, then went back and found that putting Auggie in his coat was more difficult than before. There was barely enough room. Ascending the ladder again, he took a quick look around before setting Auggie on the ground and climbing out himself. He replaced the grate and headed off in search of something to eat.

Coffee shops and restaurants were open, catering to the working community flowing into the downtown center.

With all the traffic and confusion around him, Auggie stayed close to Harold's heels. He rewarded the pup by frequently bending down to pat his head. Stopping at a fast food restaurant, Auggie waited impatiently as Harold went inside. Returning with egg and sausage biscuits and coffee, he sat on a brick planter in front of a commercial building and ate while feeding Auggie. Polishing off two biscuits each, took only ten minutes.

They started walking again. This time toward a series of conjoined buildings on multiple levels housing hundreds of vendors selling fresh vegetables, seafood, baked goods, handmade items and much more.

Harold made one more stop. Going into a small market, he bought a bottle of cheap wine and stepping outside, took his first drink of the day. Putting the bottle into an inside pocket of his coat, he and Auggie continued on their way. Down to about five dollars, he was hoping to replenish his money supply by panhandling. He always liked to have at least twenty.

Stopping at an intersection a few blocks from the market, Harold waited for traffic to clear. Unfortunately, Auggie did not stop and stepped off the curb into the path of the oncoming cars. Harold called out and stepped into the street.

A late model Ford, moving at about thirty miles an hour down one of Seattle's many steep hills, struck Harold. The forty-year-old insurance adjuster could do no more than hit the brakes, close his eyes, and brace for the inevitable contact. The impact threw Harold about ten feet and caused significant damage to the front of the car. Harold got up, picked up Auggie and headed off. The driver was left stunned, but all right, trying to peel the airbag from his face. The car was immobile, in middle of the intersection, with fluid draining from its radiator. By the time the driver got out, Harold was down the street and around the next corner. Witnesses told police that the man and his dog appeared to be unhurt.

The red neon market sign came into view from two blocks away. In an open area just outside the entrance, Auggie's playful nature and energy were on display. People walking by smiled at the scene and commented to the playful pup. With Auggie as a drawing card, Harold was able to panhandle more money in a few hours than he usually got in a whole day. It was a beautiful fall day, and by noon the temperature was in the mid-sixties under bright sunny skies.

Buying food from the market vendors, Harold and

Auggie walked to the north end of the market, then across the street to a small park that features a beautiful view of the waterfront, Puget Sound, West Seattle, and the snowcapped Olympic Mountains. After eating lunch at a picnic table, Harold dozed, waking occasionally to drink from his brown bag-wrapped bottle.

Wandering around the park, Auggie planted his nose in the butt or crotch of people who were trying to ignore him. Some children played with and petted Auggie briefly before he moved on to a different group. This time, it was five young men sitting on a concrete wall bordering the street.

Harold had been watching the pup but was fifty feet away when one of the men roughly grabbed Auggie by the back of the neck and tossed him several feet to one of the others. Auggie tried to fight but was no match for them at this point in his young life. Harold began yelling loudly and struggled to his feet as Auggie snapped and snarled trying to break free. Others in the park yelled at the young men to leave the pup alone but no one approached the young men, except Harold.

"Put the dog down," Harold said, in a low, soft voice.

"Get away old man. We just adopted this dog," one of them replied.

Harold reached for Auggie and grabbed the young man's wrist. The four others surrounded Harold, pushing and shoving him from all directions. As Harold's anger increased, his grip tightened and could not be loosened by the pushing, which had escalated to punches.

"He's breaking my arm," said the young man in obvious pain as he dropped Auggie.

All six combatants heard a dull crack as Harold twisted

the arm into an unnatural position before letting go. Swinging wildly, even the glancing blows Harold delivered, resulted in painful injuries or large open wounds, ending the fight for three more of the young men. The only one left, had his arm firmly around Harold's neck from behind. Freed, Auggie bit as hard as he could on that young man's right ankle. Blood began flowing immediately, and the intense pain was obvious to the ten or so bystanders. Harold pulled free, spun, and landed several punches. The last one landing squarely on the young man's jaw, sending him sprawling to the sidewalk, unconscious. Harold quickly picked up Auggie and looked him over for any signs of injury but found none. Comforted, they just walked away.

The police report of the incident included eyewitness testimony of an older, homeless guy defending a small puppy and the five young men being the instigators. Of the men, one was hospitalized with a compound fracture of the forearm, a second with a broken jaw and ruptured Achilles. The other three were treated and released. No charges were filed due to the inability of the police to find the old man who could press charges.

Napping for an hour or so in the doorway of an abandoned building, Harold and Auggie wandered the streets for several more hours, had dinner at another fast food restaurant and stopped at a small grocery store before reaching home. They spent the next three days underground, with Harold teaching Auggie basic commands like sit, stay, lie down, and heel. There was also time to teach games like fetch, and novelties like roll over, play dead, and shake. Auggie was a very quick study and Harold had the feeling that, at times, Auggie could read his mind.

CHAPTER 4

Joan's first full day in the hospital was spent unconscious and unresponsive in the intensive care unit. Blood tests showed a high white blood cell count indicating an infection, but no infected site could be found. Her brain showed a small amount of swelling but no trauma. Drug and alcohol tests were negative. A continuous dextrose drip was necessary to keep her blood sugar levels up, even though her parents said she was not diabetic. The doctors were baffled.

The autopsies of both Mike and Michelle showed extensive brain swelling and severe liver damage. No bacterial or viral sources could be found. Results were still pending for toxic substances. A call to the Center for Disease Control in Atlanta gave no other clues.

The neurologist in charge of Joan's care, Dr. Roberta Thompson, found facing her parents a difficult task when she had no answers to offer.

Rereading notes taken by paramedics, Dr. Thompson noted that Joan had told Rob Packard that she and the others had been drinking wine earlier in the evening. Looking over the autopsy reports of Mike and Michelle, Dr. Thompson noted both had high blood alcohol levels, but Joan had none.

Calling the local health department, Dr. Thompson asked about any reports of tainted alcohol. Her call was passed several times from one extension to another until a staffer remembered some problem at Spring Rain Winery, but he was sure that had been all taken care of.

"Spring Rain Winery, how may I help you?" Janet answered the phone in her always professional tone.

"Hello, my name is Dr. Roberta Thompson. I'm calling from Seattle. I'd like to speak to Mr. St. James please."

"May I ask what this is in reference to?" Janet asked.

It's about a possible case of poisoning from contaminated wine," responded Dr. Thompson.

"Please hold, Doctor," said Janet with a slightly higher pitch in her   voice.

Placing the doctor on hold she buzzed St. James.

"Yes, Janet," he inquired.

"There's a Dr. Roberta Thompson from Seattle on the line for you," Janet said and put the call through.

"Dr. Thompson, this is William St. James, how can I help you?"

"I have a very sick patient who may have been drinking wine just prior to becoming ill. The health department told me that there may be an issue with some of your company's wine recently. I can't say for sure if this is a case of tainted wine poisoning, and to tell you the truth, I'm just grasping at straws, but I wanted to talk with you anyway."

Bill mouthed to Janet to get Kevin and Jack and to bring in the appropriate file, while he continued to talk with the doctor. "If you don't mind, I want to put your call on the speaker. My chemist Kevin Williams, and manager Jack Adams are with me now. Please go on."

Dr. Thompson began, "I have a 17-year-old female patient who is currently in a coma. The only positive diagnostic tests are a CAT scan showing brain swelling, abnormal blood values associated with liver function, an extremely low blood sugar level, and a white blood cell count well above normal. Whatever the infective agent is, it's not responding to antibiotics.

I was wondering if you could tell me about the agent

found in your wine that stimulated the recall?"

"Dr. Thompson, this is Kevin Williams. My tests here show the probable toxic agent to be a strain of mutated yeast. As long as the bottle was sealed, the yeast was very toxic but once exposed to oxygen the toxins break down rather quickly. Half-life is only a couple of hours. Ultimately, you would probably end up with wine that doesn't taste very good, but not dangerous."

The phone was silent for a moment, then Dr. Thompson spoke again. "That's interesting. We found an odd-looking yeast in some of our lab work but thought it was a contaminated specimen. I realize you are not doctors, but would you have a recommendation for treatment if someone were to have ingested this wine?"

Kevin spoke again, "Since the yeast seems to break down rapidly in the presence of oxygen, could using a hyperbaric chamber be helpful? Forcing her body's oxygen saturation to one hundred percent for a couple of hours might be enough to kill the yeast. I'd also do blood cultures for yeast and see if any of the current anti-yeast medications might be effective. But remember when you do your testing, this yeast doesn't last long in the open air."

"Thank you for your input, gentlemen," said Dr. Thompson, then continued, "at this point, I'm willing to try almost anything."

Bill broke in, "I was under the impression that we had accounted for all the questionable wine. If you find evidence that leads you to believe this girl's illness is from our wine, I would appreciate a call as soon as possible."

Dr. Thompson said in a decidedly more solemn tone, "Well, there've been two fatalities linked to this incident. If your wine is thought to be the cause, I'm sure the police will be contacting you. It appears from my discussions with FDA and the ATF, that you handled this matter by the book, but in the end, it may not shield you from liability. But yes, I will certainly call if I find any connection."

"I don't believe I'll wait," responded Bill. "I'm leaving for Seattle as soon as possible. I'm sure I'll be there by tomorrow morning. Can I meet you someplace, Doctor?"

"How about here at the hospital? Say, about ten o'clock? Just have me paged overhead from the lobby."

"That sounds great, Doctor. One other thing, do you by chance know the name of the police officer handling this case?"

"Yes, it's Detective Randall Pepper," she replied.

"Would you mind if he met with us at the same time? I'd like to find out as much about this tragedy as I can, as quickly as I can."

"That would be fine. In fact, I'll call now and try to arrange it. It will give me an opportunity to ask him some things about the other victims. Well, I've got to get on this. Thank you, gentlemen, for all your information," Dr. Thompson said.

"You can call here anytime, Doctor. My staff will always be completely candid with you."

"Thank you again and goodbye. Until tomorrow, Mr. St. James."

Bill, Kevin, and Jack were staring at each other in disbelief when Janet walked into the room holding a trip itinerary just off the printer. She handed it to Bill and said, "If you leave in the next hour or so, you'll be in Seattle by five. You'll be staying at a moderately priced hotel not far from downtown. Any questions?"

Smiling broadly, Bill said. "Damn Janet, this is impressive." Looking at Kevin and Jack, he asked rhetorically, "How long ago did I tell Dr. Thompson I'd be coming to Seattle, five minutes?"

Looking back at Janet, he asked, "Do you know what I'll be having for dinner?"

"I know what you should eat, but I don't have any idea what you will eat," chuckled Janet.

Bill turned his chair to look out the window. After a brief pause, he turned back saying, "For that young girl's sake, I hope we helped the doctor. For our sake, I hope our wine is not the problem. But I don't want to be the last to know if our wine is involved. So, the sooner I get to Seattle and get some information, the better I'll feel.

I don't think there is anything coming up here that you three can't handle while I'm gone. I'll call if I find out anything either way in Seattle."

With that said, Bill picked up his briefcase, emptied some items onto his desk and added some files regarding the winery's liability insurance information, wine distributor and retailers lists, and his cell phone.

"I'll try and keep the hotel's front desk updated on where I am if you need to get in touch with me, and I'll take my cell phone, even though I hate those damn things. Be back soon. Hold down the fort."

Bill left the Spring Rain offices and went upstairs to change and pack. He was on the road before eleven, and even with the unusually heavy traffic, was in Seattle by five, just as Janet predicted. During the long drive, he kept going over the steps he had taken to recall the wine, and where he might have made a mistake. He couldn't think of any.

His arrival in Seattle was uneventful. After dropping his luggage off in his hotel room, he walked the downtown streets for an hour or so, ate dinner at a small second-story restaurant, and returned to his hotel by six-thirty p.m. Watching the national and then the local news broadcasts, and a few unfunny situation comedies, he turned out the lights at ten but didn't fall asleep until after two in the morning.

CHAPTER 5

Joining the Seattle Police six years ago, at the age of thirty-eight, Randall Pepper was much older than the average rookie. He'd spent the previous twenty years in the military, with the last half of his service in the military investigative branch. As one of Seattle's newest detectives, he was on his way up, aided by a bravery citation and medal of valor for saving a mother and two small children from a husband and father intent on murder.

A black male with the last name Pepper made growing up difficult at times, and the military system of salutes and sirs along with his physical size of six foot one, two hundred pounds hid a surprising personality. His amiable manner and sense of humor didn't surface until years after leaving the army.

The death of two teens, with a third lying comatose, was Randy's first case as a lead detective. The call from Dr. Thompson regarding the Spring Rain recall gave him a place to start digging. When Dr. Thompson also told Randy that Mr. St. James was sure all the wine had been pulled from store shelves, it looked like a dead end. Meeting St. James would likely turn out to be just a formality.

Arriving at the hospital at nine forty-five, Bill had to wait thirty minutes until Dr. Thompson was free. They had just shaken hands when Randy Pepper walked in.

"Detective Pepper, I'd like you to meet William St. James, owner of Spring Rain Winery. Mr. St. James, Detective Pepper."

Introductions and handshakes over, Randy asked. "Any news?"

"I was just about to tell Bill when you came. The young lady is responding to new medications and a treatment suggested by Bill's staff. She's awake and talking," said Dr. Thompson, smiling broadly.

"This may not seem like good news to you, Bill. It kind of implicates your wine," Randy said, watching Bill's face for a reaction.

"It certainly is a mixed blessing. I couldn't be happier for her and her family, especially knowing that her recovery might have been aided by treatment suggestions from my staff. But, yes, I am very concerned that my company's wine might have played a part in the initial illness."

"So, Bill, tell me about this wine," the detective invited.

Bill gave Randy and Dr. Thompson an outline of events starting from when the wine was first found to be contaminated, including all recall efforts, ending at the current meeting in the hospital lobby.

Dr. Thompson had been listening but a beeping pager in her coat pocket got her attention. Looking down at the numbers illuminating the top of the pager, the doctor excused herself. "I need to return this page, gentlemen, if there is nothing more I can do to be of help?"

"I'd like to talk to the young lady as soon as possible if

it's okay with you and her parents," said Randy.

"I wouldn't want you to talk with her today. We still want her to get stronger and we'll be doing follow up tests to check for residual damage if any. Let's give her a day or so to recover. I'll give you a call."

"That will be great. Thanks, doc," said Detective Pepper.

After shaking hands with Bill and Randy again, Dr. Thompson walked over to a bank of elevators and disappeared into a small crowd as she entered one of the upward bound cubicles.

After watching the doctor leave, Randy turned to Bill and asked, "Did you, by chance, bring the names of the local distributors with you, Bill?"

"Better than that, I brought the list of retail outlets that had the wine on their shelves." Rummaging through his briefcase, Bill pulled out a sheet of paper with several typed lines and handed it to Randy.

"Could I get a copy of this?"

"You can have it."

Scanning the paper, Randy noted a familiar name and knew of its proximity to Pioneer Square. "This Corner Market, did they respond to your notice, Bill?"

"Yes. We had phone contact with the owner the same day we found the contamination. The owner assured me the bottles would be pulled from the shelves and destroyed. A follow-up email confirmed lot and case numbers, which corresponded with the distributor's records. Why are you interested in that particular outlet?"

"Are you familiar with Seattle?" Randy asked.

"No, not really," responded Bill.

"That market is in an area that is a popular spot for young people, street people, and transients. The other outlets are across town. If this is truly a case of poisoning, that market is the most likely source. I think I'll go over and have a talk with the owner."

"Would you mind if I tagged along?"

"No, not at all. Do you want to leave your car here or follow me?"

"I don't mind letting you be the chauffeur since I've never been here before," Bill said.

The temperature was in the high sixties with a slight wind that made it seem a little cooler in the shade but standing in the direct sunlight made it feel several degrees warmer. It was a beautiful fall day. There was a hint of ocean in the breeze, the trees were displaying their spectacular fall foliage, and the sky was clear enough to see the Olympic Mountains to the west. The Cascades and Mt. Rainier dominated the eastern horizon.

The streets were not particularly busy; the morning rush hour was well over, so the drive from the hospital only took about fifteen minutes, with half the time spent looking for a parking space. Frustrated, Randy just parked in a loading zone. During the drive, Bill had given Randy an overview of winemaking and in particular, the fermentation, testing, and bottling processes.

While walking from the car to the market, Randy pointed out the number of street people within one block in either direction.

"This is what I meant about this being a congregation spot, Bill."

"Yeah, I see what you mean, and it's only a quarter till eleven."

Randy touched Bill's arm, and they both stopped just

outside the market. "When we're inside, I'd like to do the talking, but if I seem to be missing something let me know."

"This is definitely your show, Randy. I'm just here as an interested observer," Bill assured the detective.

With that said, both men walked into the store and after identifying himself, Randy asked to speak to the owner. The request caused a momentary silence, then the man behind the counter spoke.

"I am Kim Son. I own this store," the man replied.

Randy introduced Bill and began the interview. "Mr. Son, do you remember talking to people from Spring Rain Winery earlier this week about some wine that may have been contaminated?"

"Yes, I remember. We talked, and I told them the case and lot numbers of the wine.

I wrote those numbers down too and sent an email confirmation." Bill smiled, nodded his head, and confirmed he had received the information from Mr. Son.

"Then what happened to the wine?" asked Randy.

"I took the wine from the shelf and put it in the back room. My stockboy came in and I told him to pour the wine out."

"You're sure none was sold."

"Yes, I'm sure. We just got that on Friday. There was very little time to sell it."

"Did you watch your stock boy pour out the bottles?'

"No, but he's a good boy. He works hard and does what I ask."

"Is he here now?"

"No, he only works here part-time. He also does taxi driving. He may be doing that or he's at home."

Mr. Son's tone was changing to one of suspicion and he

finally asked, "Why do you need to talk to him? What's the problem?"

"We just need to be sure all the wine can be accounted for. Can you give me his name, address, and home phone number please?"

Going through a small file box, Mr. Son pulled out a three by five index card and handed it to Randy.

"He drives an older blue Honda," said Mr. Son, without prompting but sounding more reluctant with each word.

Randy copied the information and handed the card back to Mr. Son along with his business card. "Thank you for your cooperation, Mr. Son. If Mr. Stacy comes in before I have a chance to talk to him, please call me."

On the way back to the car, Randy heard the police radio call his name. Jogging closer, Randy opened the door and grabbed the handset and responded.

"Detective Pepper," a firm low female voice said. "A Doctor Thompson called and said a patient named Joan wants to talk to you," she informed the detective.

Randy was just ending the call as Bill caught up. "Well, Joan Leahy must be doing better than Dr. Thompson expected because she is asking to talk to me. Are you interested in doing more detective work?"

"Sure, why not? If my winery goes belly-up, I might need a new profession. Besides, this might be very interesting."

The discussion while riding back to the hospital, consisted mainly of small talk and a guided narrative of the areas they could see as they drove. They stopped talking when the car was parked and didn't speak again until they had arrived at the appropriate floor. Randy had the unit clerk page Dr. Thompson who arrived a few minutes later.

"I mentioned to Joan that someone from the police would be talking to her in a day or so about what happened. She said she wanted to talk to you as soon as possible so no one else would get sick. She's only been off the ventilator about ten hours and her voice is very low. Her mother tried to talk her into waiting another day, but she insisted. She knows her friends are dead and is genuinely interested in lessening the danger to anyone else. Joan seems to be a very intelligent, sensitive young woman," Dr. Thompson said.

Randy looked at Bill, "When we go in, I'll introduce you by name only. If you need to ask anything, or someone asks directly, tell him or her who you are, but I suggest you don't offer much information. Remember, this is still a possible product liability claim waiting to happen."

Bill nodded in agreement and the three walked down the hall towards the room.

"Her parents are with her. It's been a really emotional day for them getting their daughter back from near death. The parents of the dead kids have called to check on her. I suspect they'll be coming here as soon as they know Joan is better to find out for themselves what happened to their children. Maybe it's better that she's seeing you so soon. She can get her story out before outsiders start to influence what she recalls," said Dr. Thompson.

Entering the room, Dr. Thompson made introductions as Randy and Bill shook hands with Joan and her parents. Joan's mother was in a chair on the far side of the bed away from the door, and her father was standing behind the chair, virtually in the corner. Joan and her mother were holding hands.

The room itself was your typical hospital room with the

bed just off center with a nightstand, rolling tray table, and two sturdy high-backed chairs. The off-white walls gave off a hospital disinfectant smell. A small tv mounted high on the wall opposite the bed was on but muted. Joan looked pale but otherwise good. Her parents were somewhat disheveled from a night with little sleep.

Dr. Thompson spoke again looking directly at Joan. "Detective Pepper would like to hear what you told me earlier about the wine and what you know about the others you were with on Monday night."

Joan spoke in a soft voice made raspy by the breathing tube that had kept her alive during her first hours in the hospital. "There's really not much to tell. We were hanging out and this guy came up and offered to sell us some wine. We pooled our money and bought the wine for a couple of dollars a bottle."

"Did you buy all he had?" asked Randy.

"No, I don't think so. We got five bottles and the guy went looking for someone else to sell to. I think he only had six bottles altogether because that's how many he offered to sell us when he first came up."

"Did you see who he sold the other bottle to?" Randy asked.

"He was talking to someone sitting in a doorway, but the light was bad, and they were at least a hundred feet away," Joan answered.

With a quick glance at her parents, trying to gauge their level of discomfort, Randy continued, "Can you describe the guy who sold you the wine?"

"He was about six feet tall, dark hair, kind of good looking and trim, but not too thin. Early twenties, maybe twenty-five."

"Had you ever seen him before?" the detective continued.

Joan had started to answer but was interrupted by the overhead paging of a doctor. Waiting briefly until she was sure the message had ended she began, "I think he works at that little market just off the square."

"Are you sure?"

"We'd been in there earlier, and I'm pretty sure I saw him there."

"Did he say his name?"

"Not that I remember."

Randy had been writing in a palm-size spiral bound notepad. He'd continued writing for about thirty seconds after Joan had finished talking. Then he stopped, took a deep breath, and asked one of his final questions, anticipating an emotional response. "Who was with you that night?"

Joan's eyes began to tear, and she held her mother's hand more firmly. She let out a slight cough and said, "Michele, Mike, and three guys we met at the square."

"Do you know their names?"

"Just street names; Crazy Larry, Blue, and Gopher."

"Do you know where they live?'

"I don't think they have an apartment or anything. I think they just live on the streets. We had just met them earlier that evening, so I can't tell you much about them." Joan described each of the three and told as much about them as she could remember. She had been sitting very upright initially but in just the few minutes she had been talking, she appeared to weaken and was now lying fully back on the bed with her head buried in the pillow.

Her physical frailty was not lost on Randy, who was torn between needing to ask questions and wanting to let the sick child in front of him rest. "I see you're getting tired. If I can ask just one more question for now, then I'll go and stop by another day. Can you tell me what brand of wine it was and what happened after the group started drinking?"

Joan was starting to struggle to keep her eyes open and her voice would tail off to a whisper with each statement as she continued, "I don't remember even looking, except to say the bottle was green with a multicolored label. I don't remember the name at all." Joan paused while her mother stood and wiped her face with a wet washrag. Joan continued without opening her eyes. "I only had one or two sips and stopped drinking because the wine tasted bad to me. The others kept drinking until all the bottles were empty. We separated pretty soon after. Michelle, Mike, and I started walking to Rob's apartment. We'd only gone a few blocks when Mike and Michelle started to get sick. By the time we got to Rob's, they were both looking really bad and went to lie down. I think I fell asleep in a chair but really don't remember anything that happened from the time we got to Rob's house until a few hours ago."

"You've been very helpful, Joan. Thank you," said Randy as he leaned over and squeezed her hand. If I think of any other questions, I'll either stop by or give you a call."

Joan returned the pressure on Randy's hand and didn't let go. She opened her eyes and looked directly into Randy's and asked, "Was the guy who sold the wine trying to kill us?"

Randy put his notebook and pen on the bed and took Joan's hand in both of his, moving his face to within a foot of Joan's. "I honestly don't know right now, but I fully intend on finding out. When I do, I'll come to see you myself and tell you all I can."

Joan produced a weak smile and said, "Thank you."

Randy said goodbye to Joan and her parents. Bill and Dr. Thompson nodded and smiled. As they turned to leave the room, Joan rolled toward her parents, pulled her mother's hand to her chest, and began to cry.

In the hallway, Dr. Thompson said, "She is lucky to be alive. The weird thing is, the same agent that caused her blood sugar to drop and put her in a coma might have protected her brain and other organs from harm. She doesn't seem to have any residual damage."

"Unfortunately, it seems inevitable that everyone else that drank that wine is dead. They just haven't turned up yet," Randy said without expecting a response.

CHAPTER 6

Jim Stacy had just picked up a well-dressed couple at the airport and was heading back to town when his phone rang. The police officer asked for his location and destination.

"I'm going north on I-5 about twenty minutes from downtown, heading for the Lincoln Hotel."

The static-filled response came back, "We'll meet you there."

Jim's mind raced, palms began to sweat, "What's this about?"

The phone reception was bad and the road noise so loud the fare couldn't possibly hear, let alone understand the discussion. The trip was uneventful, traffic was heavy but moving well. Relieved that no patrol cars were in view, Jim unloaded the luggage onto a porter's cart and collected his fare.

The doorman was about to assist a guest into Jim's car when two men approached, one with a badge in his hand and spoke to the doorman, "Please find him another ride, I need to speak with this driver. James Stacy?"

"Yes."

"My name is Detective Pepper. This is Mr. St. James. I want to talk to you about your other job."

"What about it?"

"Before we go any further, I need to read you your rights." Jim was rocking from side to side as Randy finished. "Do you understand these rights as I've read them to you?"

"Yes, but what's this all about?"

"Do you work part-time at The Corner Market?"

"Yes."

"Did you work this past Monday night?"

"What did I do?"

"Did you work Monday night?" the detective repeated.

"Yes."

"I spoke with Mr. Son. He said you poured out some wine as he directed."

Jim hesitated. "Yes, I did."

"All of it? Before you answer, I have a young woman who says you sold wine to her and some friends Monday night."

"It wasn't me!" Jim said, fighting the urge to run.

"I'm afraid you'll need to come with me to the station," said Detective Pepper.

"All this because some teenagers drank wine?"

"Who said anything about teenagers, Mr. Stacy?"

At the station, Jim was led to a bleak gray room with a heavy steel table and four chairs. Handcuffs off, he looked briefly out a barred window, then sat with his elbows on the table, head in hands.

Bill watched through a two-way mirror as Randy began the interview. "Jim, I'm going to be asking questions about the deaths of two people and an assault on a third. Do you want an attorney here before we continue?"

The words had thoroughly shocked Jim, the blood drained from his face and it seemed he would pass out at any moment. "Damned right I do. I don't know what you're talking about?"

With a sympathetic tone, Randy asked, "Do you have money for a lawyer?"

"No, man."

"Okay. I'll call the public defender's office and see if someone can come over. If it's going to be a while, you'll have to go to lock-up while we wait."

Getting up, Randy stared into the mirror and pointed to the door, then exited. Bill met him in the hall, both shaking their heads. "I sure feel sorry for that kid," Bill said.

"Yeah, another victim. Listen, this is going to get tedious for a while. I'm going to make a call to the public defender's office, then run over to the hospital again and show Joan a picture line-up to try to get a positive ID. I'll drop you off at your car. I was thinking of wandering the streets later tonight to see if I could get a lead on the others. If you're interested, I'll pick you up at about seven-thirty," Randy offered.

"Not a thing in the world better to do. This will just further my investigative education."

The trip to the hospital and back didn't take long. Joan

was able to identify Jim's picture from the half-dozen Randy showed her. Some small talk about her health and his investigation took up about five minutes, and then it was back to the station.

Yvonne Jackson was sitting at his desk, flipping through a file folder. Her hair was loose and touched the shoulders of her navy-blue business suit. The jacket looked to be perfectly tailored as did the skirt that stopped just above her knees and tapered down to her long legs and sensible but stylish shoes. The thirty-six-year-old had been with the public defender's office for about five years and had handled a wide variety of cases, including murder. Being one of only three women and the only person of color in her office, she received more than her fair share of minority clients. Randy was thrilled to find her assigned to Jim Stacy's case.

Hand extended, Randy spoke first. "Ms. Jackson, nice to see you."

"Hello, detective. How are you?" responded Yvonne as she lightly shook Randy's hand.

"Great thanks, and you?"

"Fine. Say, this file you have on Mr. Stacy is pretty thin," she said in a humorously sarcastic tone.

"I'm sorry about that. I haven't had time to write it all up. Most of this happened just in the last few hours. I'd show you my notes, but they're illegible to anyone but me. The condensed version is this: A few days ago, your client sold wine to some people. The wine was tainted and at least two of those people died. A seventeen-year-old just out of a coma, positively identified your client as the seller. We believe at least one bottle is missing which could lead to more deaths if it isn't recovered."

Randy and Yvonne looked at each other silently for ten seconds before Yvonne spoke, "Are you saying my client poisoned the wine?"

"No, not at all. The wine was contaminated at the winery. It'd been recalled. Your client works at a store and was told to pour it out, but instead, he sold it. To teenagers no less."

Yvonne had started taking notes and stopped to ask, "Has he admitted to this?"

"No, he denied everything, but I'm sure of my facts. That's why I called your office so soon. He's facing some very serious charges and it might get worse. I need his help to find the rest of the wine, if any, before anyone else gets sick or dies."

Standing with notes in hand, Yvonne asked, "Can I offer him a deal?"

"I haven't spoken with the district attorney's office, but the two known deaths are teenagers. I don't think your client can avoid jail. But, I'll be very kind to him on my paperwork if he'll help me a little."

Yvonne got up, smiled and said, "No matter how well-meaning your intentions, I want someone from the district attorney's office here before Mr. Stacy makes any statements. While you make the necessary phone calls, I'll talk to him."

After calling to have Jim moved back to the interrogation room, Randy escorted Yvonne and as they walked, he noticed her perfume and the tapping of her leather soles on the tile floor.

Even though she'd done it a hundred times before, sitting in the interrogation room was uncomfortable. The odor of the unclean and the aura of pimps, hookers, drug dealers, and murderers permeated the concrete walls. Occasionally, she would meet someone here who truly did not belong in the situation in which they'd found themselves. Seeing Jim Stacy, head down, shuffling walk, eyes welling with tears, Yvonne knew he was one of those people. He was afraid.

Standing up to pull out the nearest chair, Yvonne motioned to him. "Mr. Stacy, my name is Yvonne Jackson. I've been appointed to act as your attorney, have a seat."

"Hello, Ms. Jackson. Could you tell me what's going on?" he asked, while nervously manipulating an empty soda can.

"Detective Pepper said he already ask you about selling some wine."

With his voice high and cracking, "I told him I didn't do it! I dumped that wine!"

"Jim, they have a witness." Dipping her head toward the table to make eye contact. "Remember, anything you tell me is privileged information. I could lose my license for repeating anything without your permission."

"Ok, ok. I sold some wine. What's the big deal?"

Sitting back Yvonne took a deep breath. "You have no idea why you were told to dump that wine?"

"I just figured maybe we got a complaint about it like maybe it had turned to vinegar or something."

Shaking her head Yvonne said, "If only it were that simple. That wine was being recalled because something had gone wrong at the winery. Whatever it was, made the wine toxic. Two of the people you sold to are dead."

Standing bolt upright, knocking the chair over in the process, Jim said, "Oh shit, I didn't know that! Jesus! I'm fucked."

"Listen, Jim, I'm not promising anything yet, but the police need your help. They can't account for all the bottles. If you help them find the missing wine, maybe it'll help you in court."

Pacing the room, Jim stopped directly across from Yvonne, leaned forward, and in a whisper asked, "If I help, isn't that like admitting I did it?"

"They already know you did it. Remember, they have a witness. If anyone else dies because of that wine, it just gets worse for you," Yvonne said.

"I really don't know much."

"Well, tell me what you do know, and I'll see what I can work out."

Sitting again, Jim proceeded to tell the story, ending with his arrest. He then watched her face hoping for a positive reply. She remained stoic.

With no response, he started pacing from door to window. Finally, unable to handle the quiet, his fear exploded and from across the room, he shouted, "What's wrong?"

"Don't you see? They only have three victims. There should be at least seven, maybe more. We don't know if the last guy shared his bottle."

Randy came in to find Jim sitting with his head buried in his arms, weeping uncontrollably. Tears streaming down her face, Yvonne was hugging him from behind. With a choked voice, Jim asked. "Can I call my wife?" Not waiting for a response, he pleaded, "Please."

Yvonne pulled a cell phone from her purse and handed it to Jim. As he dialed, she and Randy left the room.

"The DA will be going for involuntary manslaughter and

assault, minimum time. They're typing it up now," said Randy as they leaned against the wall just outside the door.

Looking relieved, Yvonne asked, "What if other victims turn up? Will the deal still hold?"

"The DA is aware of that possibility. They also know if a bunch of people die because we couldn't find that last bottle it will look like the DA's office was trying to play hardball at the risk of more deaths. So, yes, the deal's good. But only for the seven people that we know Jim had contact with. You'll have to take a chance that the last guy didn't pass his bottle around and we end up finding twenty corpses in some abandoned warehouse somewhere. But think about it. How many winos share their bottles? I think whoever bought the last bottle either still has it or is already dead. For your client's sake, I hope it's the former not the latter."

"Me too," Yvonne said, looking back over her shoulder as she walked down the hall before disappearing into the women's restroom.

Watching through the reinforced glass in the interrogation room door, Randy could see Jim, sitting with his elbows on his knees, facing the window, head not much higher than the tabletop, shoulders shaking as he cried. It made him appear small.

Yvonne returned a few minutes later to find Jim standing in a corner staring out the window. He smiled when he saw her. "Thanks for the phone."

"How'd it go with your wife?"

"Every bit as bad as I imagined. How'd it go with the DA?"

"I won't bullshit you. It's bad, but it could have been much worse and, in fact, still might be. Come, sit down and

I'll tell you the offer and my recommendation," said Yvonne as she herself sat.

The next twenty minutes were spent discussing the limited options and ended with Jim agreeing to tell the police the whole story and answer questions. He seemed calm. Yvonne figured during that brief call to his wife he resigned himself to his fate.

With a tape recorder running, Yvonne, Randy, and representatives from the DA's office listened to Jim's story. When he finished, Randy began his questioning.

"Tell me what you remember about the last guy."

"Not much. He was sitting, so I don't really know how tall he was, and I only saw his face for a second, so I can't say what he looked like. At the time, I thought he looked old, maybe seventy." Describing the man's clothes and backpack Jim said, "He looked like a thousand guys that hang around down there."

Randy tried again. "White guy or black."

"White, I think. I'm not trying to be evasive, but I don't think I could pick him out if he were standing next to me."

"Do you remember which doorway he was sitting in?"

"I think it's called Seattle Fine Art or something like that," Jim answered.

Turning off the tape recorder, Randy said. "That will be all for now. You'll be arraigned tomorrow. The media will be there for sure, so if your wife can stay with family or friends it might save her a little grief."

As he was being handcuffed for the trip back to his cell, Jim asked. "Will you call my wife, Ms. Jackson? Tell her what's coming up and that I love her."

"Sure, I'll call her as soon as I get back to my office. Anyone else, parents or other family?"

With tears forming again, he said, "No, just my wife."

The room emptied quickly, leaving only Yvonne and Randy. "Well, Ms. Jackson, I'm sure glad I don't have to make that phone call," Randy said as he held the door for Yvonne.

"I wish I didn't. Changing the subject, let's make a deal. You call me Yvonne, and I'll call you Randy."

"Best offer I've had all year."

Laughing, Yvonne said. "Boy, have you had a slow year. Well, gotta go. Bye, Randy."

"Goodbye, Yvonne."

CHAPTER 7

Half an hour spent doing paperwork and another thirty minutes reviewing the case with his supervisor, got Randy out of the station just after five. Bad timing. The streets were clogged with rush hour traffic inching from one intersection to the next. Originally planning to go home for dinner, Randy changed his mind and started maneuvering towards a small, hole-in-the-wall Vietnamese restaurant he frequented.

Commuting disaster struck as two city buses simultaneously pulled away from the curb, mid-block, side-by-side cutting off any escape. Their dark exhaust and the accompanying noxious fumes engulfed the car. Cursing silently, he fought the urge to use siren and lights to get through town.

Finally, able to turn west, he was greeted with an amber-red sky. The distant Olympic Mountains soon to be silhouetted by the setting sun. Purposely parking several blocks away from the restaurant, he walked, just to help clear his head.

A leisurely-paced dinner followed by a call to Bill St. James got him back to the car at ten to seven. By seven-thirty, he and Bill were walking the streets.

"This is a nice area," said Bill, as they walked lamppost-to-lamppost, light to dark. "Randy, I don't mean to second guess, but have you checked the hospitals and morgue?"

"Hospitals, clinics, home health agencies, drop-in centers, soup kitchens, homeless shelters, and every county morgue between Canada and Oregon." With a deep breath, Randy continued, "I've talked to dozens of doctors about transients with gunshot wounds, stab wounds, hypothermia, drug overdoses, and a few other ailments. So far, no admissions or contacts with anyone that has symptoms like Joan's."

"I apologize. I should never have asked that. It would be like you asking me if I know when grapes should be picked. It's basic to the job. Sorry."

Stopping in front of an art shop Randy laughed, "In my life, I've suffered through many indignities. I wouldn't put that question in the top million. Forget it." Pointing to the shop he said, "I think this is probably where the guy was sitting who got the last bottle. Hours are nine to six, so no one was probably here to see what happened. I'll give them a call tomorrow to see if they might have a closed-circuit camera with video of the guy or at least to keep an eye out for him."

Walking a three-square-block area, the two talked with a half dozen men and women wearing military coats and pants. No luck. Flashing his badge to a group of young men standing outside a coffee shop, Randy said, "Good evening gentlemen. Anyone know some guys named Crazy Larry, Gopher, or Blue?"

From behind a cloud of cigarette smoke came, "Yeah, I know 'em. What'd they do this time?"

Randy moved closer to the speaker, a Native American man about twenty-five. Tall, skinny, and well on his way to looking fifty. "They didn't do anything. They were with some people who got sick on some bad wine and we're just trying to see if they're all right. Have you seen them lately or know where they stay?"

The young man dropped the cigarette and crushed it under the toe of a well-worn hiking boot. "Haven't seen 'em lately. They pretty much hang together. Don't know where they stay."

Handing out a business card, Randy said. "If you see them, give me a call or have one of them call me."

The whole group started laughing as Randy and Bill walked away. Randy's business card landed next to the crushed cigarette.

Things went about the same for the next three evenings. Vague references. No real information.

Joan went home that Sunday. Jim Stacy was still in jail. Bail set too high for him to afford a release. With no talk yet of survivors suing, Bill made plans to return to Pullman. Media interest was fading.

Then Monday morning, just before noon, and a week since a manager at Spring Rain first reported a problem, Randy got called to a site where the bodies of three young men were found. And the pot boiled again.

CHAPTER 8

While zipping up the last of three body bags, the assistant coroner said to Randy, "Their pockets have been gone through. Someone knew they were dead long before the city workers found them this morning."

Briefly removing the handkerchief that was partially blocking the stench from his nose and mouth, Randy responded. "I don't doubt it a bit. No Mother Teresa's living here."

After one last look, Randy turned and left the confines of the building and walked out into the bright sunlight, not removing the handkerchief until he was well past the yellow police crime tape and through the hole in the chain link fence. Watching others emerge pulling body laden carts and fighting the urge to vomit, some unsuccessfully, he laughed to himself. News crews were forming pods just outside the police lines. Questions were yelled at anyone who appeared to be in authority. Randy wished all the newshounds could be given a guided tour of the death scene, just so he could watch them vomit. He didn't hate the media, but the intrusive nature of their business frequently irritated him.

With a hand on the car door, Randy stopped. Another media van was pulling up. That made five. This story would be on the national news for sure. Any chance of a quiet investigation was gone. That last bottle would have to be found.

Randy's mind raced as he drove back to the station. He'd write up an outline of the events and push for a news conference.

Supervisors and city leaders would deliver the message, as was customary, although he might be called on to clarify some points. This was going to hit Spring Rain hard. Pulling into a one-way alley to park, with the car faced the wrong direction, Randy took out his cell phone and called Bill, hoping he hadn't already checked out.

"Bill, this is Randy. Listen I don't have much time. The bodies of three young men were found today. From Joan's description, I'm fairly sure they're the ones we've been looking for."

"I was packing and saw a breaking news report about finding bodies in an abandoned building or something," Bill responded in a dejected tone. "I had a feeling that was them."

With his hand over one ear and nearly shouting over the traffic noise, Randy continued, "I'm going to request that the department release a statement to the press. In it, your winery will be named. I had a faint hope we wouldn't find more bodies. Or maybe that the dead kids, Mike and Michelle, had taken something in addition to the wine and others wouldn't be found. I've got to be even more aggressive now in trying to find that last bottle."

Bill had been pacing the room, but now sat on the edge of the bed.

"Do you think it would help if I offered a reward? Say, twenty-five thousand dollars."

"Can you afford that?"

"I'll talk to my insurance carrier. They'll probably go in for at least half. Even if they don't, I'll put the money up myself." After a brief pause, Bill continued "I can't afford not to."

"That would be great. You could make the announcement at the press conference. Someone will call you with the time and place."

"One last thing." Stopping momentarily to choose his words, Randy said, "You've been very helpful, and I've enjoyed your company, but this might be our last personal contact. I don't want the press to attack the department, or you, because of a perceived conflict of interest. Hindsight being twenty-twenty, I wish we would have called the press conference a couple of days ago."

"I appreciate the call. Thanks for letting me play a part," Bill replied.

Back on the road, Randy reflected on the conversation, then on how to best tell Seattle what had taken place the past week. Before any of that would happen though, he was going to see Joan, as he promised, and tell her his suspicions.

~*~

Harold and Auggie had spent several enjoyable days underground, but with supplies running low it was time to go out. For some reason, Harold's vision had improved over the last several days. He could see better now than ever. Glasses became unnecessary.

Auggie had also changed. In those few days, he'd gone from twelve pounds to fifty. Eyes shining and alert to everything around him, his dark coat like velvet over the lean muscular frame of a full-grown dog, but still with the face and mannerisms of a puppy. Harold watched in awe as the pup consumed everything edible, and several inedible things, in sight. Thankfully, the growth seemed to have stopped. Oh, and those eyes. Harold marveled at how Auggie's eyes glowed red in the dark. Auggie also learned a new game. Every time a group would pass by in the

Underground Tour, Harold would say, "Quiet as a mouse." Soon, without prompting, Auggie would hear the groups and lay very still. Realizing what was happening, Harold would sit next to Auggie, pat his head and whisper, "Quiet as a mouse."

Trying to carry Auggie out of the storm drain the day before, Harold found he couldn't handle climbing the ladder while holding the now large pup. To overcome this, he found a still-solid plank and used it as a bridge between the horizontal tunnel and ladder. With that in place, Auggie could easily leap the remaining eight feet to street level. Once out, Harold would replace the grate and the duo could head down the alley and toward the sounds of traffic and another beautiful fall day.

The nice weather brought out a lot of people. Auggie greeted as many as possible with a wagging tail and lolling tongue. Sitting on the sidewalk, knees pulled up, back against a building, Harold's upturned hat filled with coins and bills as happened before when passersby watched the effervescent pup. Soon, he and Auggie had more than enough for several days' meals. Pausing, as he frequently did, at a newspaper stand Harold scanned the headlines: death and destruction as usual.

With Auggie patiently watching through the glass front doors, Harold made several purchases at a small grocery. Food for him and the pup, and a new, fire engine red, collar and leash. After a five-minute fracas, Auggie accepted the new limitations. Walking along the waterfront, Harold stopped to briefly to watch the action two blocks up a hill. There were emergency vehicles, lights blazing, and media vans with satellite dishes positioned to send picture and story around the world. The small crowd was growing by two or three people every five minutes, but Harold did not take part. Instead, he and Auggie continued north on a great day for exploring the city.

CHAPTER 9

Bill called Spring Rain and his insurance company to let them know the ax was about to fall. Without prompting, the insurance agent agreed to put up the twenty-five-thousand-dollar reward and to let Bill make all comments to the press with advice from the company's legal team.

Fifteen crumpled pieces of hotel stationery later, he had a three-paragraph account of events. The last paragraph announced the reward with the bottle description and means of collecting the reward should it be found, full or empty. All the local newspapers and television stations covered the event. In a windowless conference room just down the hall from the mayor's office, a large bouquet of microphones had been duct taped to a small lectern, threatening to topple it over. Glare from high-intensity lights in the back of the room obscured the cameras to which they were attached. Reporters either sat in the twenty chairs set up in the small conference room or stood along the walls.

The whole thing lasted about half an hour start to finish. Brief statements from politicians, police, and the owner of Spring Rain Winery were followed by a question and answer period. The end came mercifully when previously answered questions were reworded and asked again. Bill figured the inquisitors were trying to find inconsistencies.

Back at the hotel, Bill was having a hard time deciding on a plan of action. Not wanting to interfere with the police, he wished he could use Randy as a sounding board. Instead, he made another call to Spring Rain. As expected, Janet answered. Fifteen minutes of discussion resulted in the decision to have flyers announcing the reward distributed to the transient population and posters placed in businesses they frequented.

Winding up the call, Bill was about to hang up when Janet cut him off. "Have you considered contacting the victims' families?" The silence was answer enough. "Bill, you've got to do something."

"You've managed, with one sentence, to make me feel like shit. I've spent all my energy trying to figure out how to stop any more people from dying and limiting the damage to Spring Rain. I don't know why, but I never even thought about the families. Please tell me you have a suggestion?" he entreated.

"Maybe you could have a counselor contact them and offer services like airlines do after a plane crash. If the families use it, great; if they don't, at least you tried."

"Thank you, Janet. That sure seems like a reasonable option. Well, I'd better get going. Apparently, I've got more work to do than I thought," Bill said, ending the call.

Wording for the flyer was easy, as was finding a print shop willing to take the project on such short notice, considering the urgent nature. Flyers would be ready in an hour and the posters the next day. Bill had dinner in the hotel and was at the print shop by seven.

REWARD $25,000.00, in two-inch block letters across the top of the bright pink page, was followed by a picture of the bottle, along with a detailed description of it, and how to collect the reward in bold type below.

Like a carnival barker, Bill caught the attention of everyone within earshot as he walked the dark streets. Pausing at doorways to pass flyers to the huddled groups of people, he persevered as temperatures dropped and the wind picked up. Just ahead, a figure wearing army surplus, carrying a fully-loaded backpack and in stride with a black dog, turned down a street just in front of him. Bill jogged to catch up. The man and dog turned with a start as Bill called out. With his pitch well rehearsed by now, Bill spoke as he handed the man the flyer. It was glanced at before being put into a coat pocket, no words exchanged.

Local merchants were generally agreeable to posting the flyers, but many were closed. One still open was called Curbside Counseling. A notice on the door said a social worker and lawyer were available to assist the homeless and others in need, free of charge. The windows had been painted black three-quarters of the way up. Bill assumed to provide some level of anonymity. The door was solid wood in a frame that had been replaced or repaired a few times. Hinges creaked loud enough that no other signal was needed to alert staff of clientele entering. A half-dozen hard plastic chairs and a couple of mismatched coffee tables littered with miscellaneous magazines made up the waiting room furniture. A few landscapes of local mountains along with different thumbtacked notices hung on white walls which were in urgent need of painting. Three rows of five, eight-foot-long fluorescent lights extended past the waiting area, over four cubicles -- two on each side of a central hall -- in the middle of the office. Along the back wall, a card table and four metal folding chairs sat off-center in front of a small television. A six-foot-high bookshelf obscured the rest of the back room.

No one was in the waiting area. One female voice could be heard, and then a head appeared above the top of the closest cubicle. With a phone to her ear, she waved Bill back, finishing the call just as he got to her desk.

Bill guessed her to be in her late thirties or very well-preserved early forties. She had short, sandy hair styled for easy care, blue eyes, a little makeup, and a striking smile. She wore a heavy gray wool sweater, gray jeans, and running shoes. He could picture her as a model in some outdoor recreation sales catalog, and he found the look very attractive.

Handing her a flyer before sitting down, Bill asked, "I was wondering if I could put some of my flyers in your waiting room?"

After a quick glance at the content, the smile reappeared, and she responded. "Certainly, Mr. St. James."

"I'm afraid you have me at a disadvantage, Ms....?"

"Baker, Jessie Baker. I'm a counselor here.

I just got done watching you on the news for about the twentieth time in the last three hours. You presented yourself very well," Jessie stated.

"I just hope the message got to the right ears," Bill commented. Looking around the office, he asked, "In the last week, you haven't by chance had an older guy come in for help looking seriously ill?"

"If he did come in, I would have called for medics. But no, he didn't, and I haven't," Jessie said as she sat further back in her chair.

"How about your co-workers?" Bill pressed on.

"I doubt it. I'm sure I would have heard about it, but I'll ask." Standing again and calling toward the back of the office, "Yvonne!"

The sound of leather soles on the worn tile floor announced Yvonne's approach. Stopping next to Jessie's chair she asks, "Yes?"

"Yvonne, this is Bill St. James. He wants to know if we've had anyone very ill here in the last week."

Yvonne shook her head not in response to the question, but to the situation. "No, we haven't. Before you ask anything else I have to tell you, I only come here a few hours a week to help Jessie. The rest of the time I work for the public defender's office. I'm Jim Stacy's lawyer. So, we'll have to be careful with our discussion. Conflict of interest and all that you know."

Bill let out a chuckle. "Then you're Ms. Jackson?"

Yvonne looked at Jessie inquiringly and got a shoulder shrug and head shake in response. "How did you know my name?" she asked Bill.

"Detective Pepper spoke very fondly of you while we were discussing this case."

"He did? Well if you speak to him again, you might have him direct some of that fond discussion my way. Now, did you have any more questions for me?"

"No, I don't think so. Apparently, we both have a vested interest in finding that last bottle. So, asking for help seems unnecessary." Looking at Jessie again, Bill asked, "Do you do private counseling?"

The quizzical look on her face showed the question took Jessie by surprise. "Yes, I do have a few private clients. Why?"

Bill had been sitting back in the chair but moved to the edge and leaned forward towards Jessie. "It's been pointed out that I haven't been as sympathetic to the needs of the victims' families as I should have. I would like fill that void and make some counseling available to them."

Leaning back in her chair, flipping a pencil end to end through her fingers she asked, "And if I said yes. What then?"

"I'll get you a list of family names, addresses, and phone numbers. You'd make at least one face-to-face contact with each and be available for any follow-up, be it individual or group sessions. That's up to you. All bills would be sent directly to me."

"It seems like a generous thing to do," Jessie said, a hint of interest in her voice. "How long a commitment?"

"Say, three months. Then you can let me know if a need still exists," he answered.

Handing Bill a pad and pencil, Jessie said, "I believe I would like to be a part of this. Give me the information on how to contact you. I'll have Yvonne write us up a little contract to make it legal and send it over."

CHAPTER 10

Finishing the last of the pint bottle he'd nursed all day, Harold had not expected to have any more to drink before morning since all the stores in the area were closed. Out of habit, he pushed on the door of The Corner Market; it gave way. Some lights were still on, but the store looked deserted. Auggie tried to follow as Harold went in. Told to *stay*, Auggie complied but remained at attention. Hair rose from neck to tail.

Like he'd done a hundred times before, Harold walked straight to the cooler at the back of the store and picked a bottle. Second shelf up, third row from the left. As the cooler door closed, Harold felt a pressure on his back.

Turning, he faced a man dressed head to toe in black, including the gun in his right hand. Grabbed by the collar, Harold was pushed into the back room, dropping the bottle as he stumbled. The store owner and his wife were already there. Tied to chairs, mouths gagged, a second man was holding a gun to the woman's head. A third chair was pulled to the center of the room in line with the others. After being seated by force, Harold's hands were tied behind the chair.

Growing impatient, Auggie pushed the door open and slipped in unnoticed. Moving silently down the center of three aisles, he crouched at a spot where he could see Harold and waited.

"Go lock that goddamned door and turn off the rest of the lights before we have half the fucking city in here," the larger of the two men said.

The sound of running, then of locks being engaged could be heard. Only the humming of a fan in the cooler was left. Neon beer signs and a single bulb above the back-room sink was the only light. With his partner back, the first man stood directly in front of Mr. Kim pulling leather gloves tight against his knuckles.

"We told you when you bought this place, that if you're going to do business here, you have to play along and do what the boss says. This is what happens when you don't." Mr. Kim's face was struck four times in rapid succession; the last blow powerful enough to knock the chair over backward causing Mr. Kim's head to strike the floor. Kicks to the body got no response. He was unconscious.

Then his attention turned to the sobbing Mrs. Kim. From behind, hands moved down her neck to her chest, then pulled hard on her blouse, sending the buttons scattering across the floor as they fell. With her bra pulled up to her neck, those hands now kneaded her bare breasts.

Other hands moved up her bare calves and thighs, pushing her skirt along. With her ankles tied to the chair legs, she could not resist. Fingers hooked the waistband of her panties on each side and they were first pulled to her knees, and then cut free with a knife. Fully exposed, she was forcefully fondled while belts were unbuckled. "You're going to do both of us. If you do a real good job maybe the three of you will live."

Glowing red eyes caught Harold's attention. Smiling, he twisted his wrists to get free. To his amazement, the rope broke easily.

A loud, deep growl stopped everything. Turning toward the sound, gun in one hand, the waistband of his pants in the other the first man said, "What the fuck was that?"

"Auggie!!!" Harold stood and struck with a solid right uppercut. The punch landed just below the jaw, its upward trajectory lifted the assailant off his feet and propelled him across the room. A sound like a watermelon being dropped on concrete came from the corner of the room where he came to rest, face down, head wedged between the wall and a cast iron drain pipe, pants around his ankles.

Auggie moved with the speed of a cheetah. Lunging at the second man, he crushed the man's gun hand in his jaws. As the two fell, a single shot harmlessly struck the ceiling. The attack continued unmercifully. Flailing didn't help as gaping wounds appeared on his arms, legs, and head.

"Auggie, stop!" With those words from Harold, Auggie froze jaws to the man's throat, about to deliver what could be a fatal injury.

Mrs. Kim's eyes were wide and her breathing short and irregular, as Harold stood in front of her. She closed her eyes tightly as Harold moved behind her. She opened them as his hands touched her shoulders and moved down to her wrists. He untied first her, then her husband. Picking up both guns, he handed them to Mrs. Kim. A trip to the cooler for a bottle -- second shelf up, third row to the left, then Harold and Auggie left. Payment for the wine was on the counter.

Crying hysterically, Mrs. Kim was on the phone to the police, her husband moaning as he struggled to regain consciousness.

Slightly disoriented and exhausted, Harold followed Auggie to a familiar alley. Forgetting the board, he lifted the fifty-pound grate easily with one hand, then with Auggie tucked under one arm, Harold went down the ladder and through the tunnels toward home.

It had already been a long day for Randy Pepper. Corpses, news conferences, and reams of paperwork had managed to occupy him until after nine. Finally, on his way home, he heard a call to The Corner Market. Already well past it, he continued on. Three traffic lights later, curiosity got the better of him. He turned around.

The whole side of the street for half a block was filled with police cars, medic units, and ambulances, the strobe lights on each flashing to a different cadence, outshining the streetlights. Parking across the street, Randy dodged some traffic and walked past sentries, badge in hand. The front of the store looked unchanged from when he was here a few days ago.

The back room was jammed. Mrs. Kim, wrapped in a gray wool blanket, sat on a stool, quietly rocking back and forth. The female police officer beside her had an arm over her shoulder. Mr. Kim was being wheeled out on a stretcher, awake but clearly dazed, behind a glassy-eyed stare. Across the room, a group of fire department personnel was partially hidden in a shower of sparks and smoke as power tools with ear-splitting noise cut the drain pipe that held a young man hostage, head to the wall. A group in the center of the room worked to stop bleeding and bandage multiple wounds of another young man.

Finding the officer in charge, Randy listened to the story. Pointing to the two young men, the officer said, "We're familiar with these guys. They're part of a gang working a couple of scams. They buy food stamps debit cards on the street for drugs or cash at fifty percent of face value; make the store owners buy them at ninety-five percent. Sometimes the gangs push the store owners to sell them large quantities of cold medications used to make methamphetamines. This owner is relatively new and didn't want to be involved. These two are enforcers are here to deliver a message."

"So, who did all the damage?" asked Randy. "Mrs. Kim is the only one not physically hurt."

"Some transient wandered in and got caught up in it. Mrs. Kim has seen him here before but doesn't know his name."

Pointing to the far side of the room, the officer said, "He's the one responsible for that guy being stuck behind that pipe. Apparently, he had a dog with him who mangled the shit out of the other guy."

Looking around the room Randy asked. "So, where's that guy and his dog?"

"Mrs. Kim said the fight lasted like ten seconds, then he

just grabbed a cheap bottle of wine, put some money on the counter, then he and the dog left. According to her, he only said a couple of words the entire time, sounded like 'doggie'. I've got cars out looking, but so far, we haven't been able to find him."

CHAPTER 11

The morning started as a media dream day; bodies, poisonings, a large reward, a guy, his dog, and quiet heroism. Where's the last bottle? Who is the man with the dog? Tragedy, mystery, and money. What a great news combination.

The phone lines to talk radio stations were jammed with calls from people sure they'd seen the guy and his dog the previous day. At stores, city parks, fast food restaurants, and dozens of other locations within a few miles of downtown. No one had spoken to him. No one knew his name.

With a police composite drawing in hand, reporters wandered the streets, going into homeless shelters, abandoned buildings, and relief missions. Lots of people thought they recognized the picture. None could recall a name. Transients were interviewed like expert witnesses on behavior patterns. Where to look? Who to talk to?

At the police station, Bill had been given the use of a small room. People holding green wine bottles with no labels were trying to collect the reward. Bill was able to dismiss most within seconds. Trashcans outside overflowed with rejected attempts.

The phone started ringing at Joan Leahy's house at just past seven and rang continuously until it was unplugged two hours later. Out of the hospital for only two days and still weak, she refused interviews. Relatives of other victims did appear, tearfully telling of their loss and demanding police give a full accounting of events. Parents of the three men found the previous day, made little mention of the lack of recent contact with their sons.

Jessie Baker had already read the paper and was following the TV news reports all morning. When the composite sketch was shown, she called Yvonne Jackson. "Don't you think that looks like Harold Pearson without his glasses?"

Staring at the image on her small television, Yvonne said, "It could be. But I can't say for sure. I only saw him once for about ten minutes. You've spent a lot more time with him than I have. Besides, I don't remember Harold having a dog." "So, do you think I should call the police or not?"

After letting the lawyer part of her brain review the options, Yvonne said, "It probably won't hurt anything, so might as well."

In a playful tone, Jessie said, "I could call your boyfriend, Randy and talk to him."

"You can talk to whomever you what," Yvonne countered sharply.

Jessie put off deciding for so long, her counseling appointments started to arrive. Three one-hour sessions later she was again free and made the call. Working her way through a myriad of phone systems and staff, she finally got to talk to Randy Pepper. After introductions, Jessie told Randy her suspicion. Listening to the story, Randy finally said, "I'm not really working that case. How did you decide to contact me?"

"Your name came up recently in separate conversations I've had with both Bill St. James, from Spring Rain Winery, and Yvonne Jackson, who works with me. Both of whom said they knew and respected you."

A long, exhaled breath provided the needed break before Randy responded. "Do you know where this guy Harold is now?"

"No, but I thought if you wanted to cruise the streets, I could go with you and point him out if he happened to be out and about. Besides, part of what little I know about Harold is that he really keeps to himself. I'd rather help you find him than have the media ambush him. I think he'd hate that to no end."

With no leads on the last bottle of wine, and autopsies still pending on the men found yesterday, Randy didn't have much to do anyway. "Like I said before, I'm not really involved with this case, but maybe I could spend my lunch hour driving around. It's not like this guy is a wanted felon or something. The only reason the police want to talk to him at all is that he was a witness to a crime."

Jessie was having trouble with the ambivalence and playfully confronted him. "Yvonne was right. You sure seem to have trouble speaking your mind. Do you want to go or not? If you do, pick me up at the Curbside Counseling office at one o'clock."

Laughing, Randy gave in. "OK, OK, I'll be there."

~*~

Having slept nearly twelve hours, Harold woke to the familiar wet nose pressed against his ear.

Reeling backward, Harold hit his head on the wall and

rubbed the spot vigorously to ease the pain. As he did, he noticed deep red circles around each wrist. Walking down the tunnel to the bathroom area, Auggie close behind, Harold stopped at the exit tunnel junction. Rain was falling through the grate and dropping to the stormwater pipe twenty feet below on its way to Elliot Bay. The sound was comforting, like rain on a tin roof. He was planning to go out today and hoped the rain would stop. Fifteen minutes later, dressed and ready, he slid the plank across to the ladder and started up.

Waiting just out of sight on the ladder for several minutes while someone from one of the shops above dumped trash into the dumpster next to the grate, he was finally able to get out with Auggie bounding out behind him. The sun was breaking through scattered clouds and the air smelled fresh. Even the scent from the waterfront was, for the moment, gone. So, too was a good portion of the traffic, both automotive and foot.

Headlines caught his eye from a discarded newspaper. Harold read for a few minutes with no realization of the significance. He and Auggie were about to be on their way when a line above the newspaper's banner caught his eye. *FLOWER SHOW OPENS AT NOON FOR SIX-DAY RUN AT THE CONVENTION CENTER*. Harold knew that attendance was usually good, even mid-week. It would be the perfect place to panhandle.

The rain had become intermittent and Harold was able to keep dry by staying close to buildings with awnings as he and Auggie, who was oblivious to the rain, walked. Cars honked and the people in them waved they passed. Not one or two, but dozens. Harold was baffled. Historically, if any attention was paid to him at all it was negative. "Get a job, you lazy bastard." He'd heard that one a million times. Most often he was ignored. Now standing outside the convention center, people smiled as they went by or stopped to pet Auggie and hand him money. Not just spare change but dollar bills, sometimes several.

~*~

Jessie was standing in front of the Curbside Counseling office when Randy pulled up. The car was unmarked, but it was surely a police car, big and white with a radio antenna sticking out from the middle of the roof and a cage separating the front seat from the back, as well as a small computer taking the middle third of the dashboard space. Introductions were made through the open passenger side window and Jessie got in. "The office is closed for the rest of the day, so I spent the last hour cruising by myself. I've been all over here and along the waterfront but haven't seen him. We can try further uptown maybe."

Randy began speaking while looking over his left shoulder and pulling away from the curb. "He's going to be hard to find today. The rain will probably keep him tucked into a doorway. How did you come to know him anyway?"

With her window lowered to eye level for an unobstructed view, Jessie examined every sheltered spot they passed. The street noise presented uninterrupted background sounds, to the beat of windshield wipers, as she continued the conversation in a volume just a few decibels lower than a yell. "He came into the office about six months ago wanting to know if we could find his son. Apparently, he hasn't had any contact for a very long time. Yvonne and I both did computer searches but got no place. He kept coming in every few weeks just to talk. He's a very nice man once you get to know him."

Randy asked, "So, do you think this nice old man is capable of beating up twenty-year-olds without breaking a sweat?"

Jessie turned and looked straight at Randy. "I don't know much about his background. Maybe he was a Green Beret or SEAL. In any case, he's done nothing but good so far, and that's the Harold I know."

Forty-five minutes of driving around produced nothing until, while sitting at a light; four cars back from the intersection, Jessie said, "That's him!"

The figure had just reached the curb and was headed down a one-way street opposite of Randy's direction.

"I'm going to try and catch him," said Jessie as she got out of the car just as the light changed. "Go around the block and meet us."

Cars honked as Jessie darted through traffic. Managing to get to the sidewalk without injury, she jogged half a block, slowed to a fast walk with Harold twenty feet ahead and called out, "Harold! Harold Pearson!"

Auggie turned first, then Harold just as Jessie caught up. "Hi, Harold. Do you remember me?" The questioning look said no. "Jessie Baker from the counseling office."

"Oh, yes, Ms. Baker. How are you?"

"Fine, thanks. You're a hard person to find."

Excited, Harold asked, "Have you found my son?"

Seeing his face light up at the possibility made Jessie feel bad. "No, I'm sorry I haven't, but I do need to talk to you." Pointing to the white sedan that had just pulled up to the curb, Jessie said, "The gentleman getting out of that car is Detective Pepper of the Seattle Police." Putting her arm through his she said, "Could we get out of the rain and talk?"

A small restaurant/bar three shops down was nearly empty of its usual lunch crowd and they were able to find a booth next to the front window where Auggie could be seen. Randy and Jessie sat on one side, Harold, the other. A gray-haired waitress, old enough to be Harold's mother greeted them quickly, passed out menus and glasses of water, then left.

Jessie smiled, reached across the table, and took Harold's hand, trying to decrease the anxiety level as Randy started.

"First off, I want to say, you're not in any trouble. In fact, you may be a hero." The confusion showed on Harold's face. "Could you tell me what you did last night say, between eight and ten o'clock?"

Mouth too dry to speak, Harold took a sip of water then cleared his throat before answering. "I scrounged some money, bought food for me and the dog, got a bottle and went home."

"Did you get the bottle at The Corner Market?" "Yeah, I think so."

The waitress had returned, and Randy waved her off. "You don't remember anything unusual happening while you were there?" "No, can't say that I do."

Jessie told the whole story as Harold sat clueless and bewildered. "Why do you think it was me?"

Showing a copy of the police sketch, Randy said. "The owner's wife described you, and your dog very well." Pointing to Harold's exposed wrist he said, "How did you get those marks?"

Sleeves pulled back, Harold examined each wrist. "I don't know."

Jessie offered lunch and the discussion stopped while the three ordered. Harold got a meal for himself, and a double cheeseburger and fries to go for Auggie.

By the end of the meal, Harold had agreed to meet the store owner after some gentle persuasion from Jessie.

CHAPTER 12

A white truck had circled the block twice before. Its enclosed bed contained a dozen compartments with vented doors. On the third pass, it pulled to the curb almost directly in front of the restaurant. No one inside noticed. The twenty-something young man that got out wore heavy work boots, jeans, and a navy-blue jacket with his name and picture on an ID badge pinned to his shirt. He put on heavy leather gloves and took a six-foot aluminum pole with a rope loop at one end from its rack on the side of the truck.

Auggie's tail wagged but he didn't budge as the young man called in a soft, friendly voice, "Here boy." Again, no resistance as the loop was dropped over his head and tightened. But, when the young man began to pull toward the truck, Auggie resisted. The young man was nearly pulled to the ground as Auggie jerked back. The restaurant's front door swung open when struck by Auggie's rump. His barking and growling filled the room. Thrashing side-to-side, Auggie caught the pole in his jaws and snapped it cleanly. With half the pole dangling from his neck, Auggie, fangs bared, advanced slowly. The young man's back was against the side of the truck. He swung the remainder of the aluminum pole wildly as his only defense, terror in his eyes.

Having sat closest to the door, Randy was the first one out. Auggie ignored his calls. The same happened as Jessie got to the street. Fearing the worst, Randy pulled his gun. Other patrons had moved to the windows and saw Harold push Randy aside and with a calm, quiet voice say, "Auggie."

Like turning out a light, Auggie stopped, turned, and trotted to Harold, tongue hanging out and tail wagging. The mangled pole dangled from his neck, scraping the sidewalk as he moved.

The color had started to return to the young man's face, but his breathing was irregular and, although his lips formed words, he was initially speechless. Leaning against the truck, he bent over and put his hands on his knees, took a couple of deep breaths then stood up again.

"I'm from Animal Control. That dog is vicious and needs to be impounded."

Harold had removed the noose from Auggie's neck and slid it across the sidewalk in the direction of the truck. In a quiet voice that was uncharacteristically harsh, Harold said. "You started this, you piece of shit. The dog wasn't doing anything until you tried to drag him away. He didn't even hurt you, all he did was growl, you baby."

Practically screaming, he responded, "I've seen hundreds of dogs and know a violent one when I see him. Besides, I'm just doing my job. He doesn't have a license. So, go to hell, you old fuck."

Jessie looked at Randy. The stare and head jerk had an unmistakable meaning. Randy moved forward, saying, "Listen, gentlemen, let's try and settle this calmly." Pointing at the young man, he asked, "Do you sell licenses?"

"Yes, but that's a dangerous animal."

Randy pulled out his badge and said. "I'll be responsible for the conduct of this dog. Just sell us the tag."

A non-stop monologue about the criminal and civil penalties involved with dangerous animals lasted as long as it took to fill out the paperwork. Jessie and Randy were nearly laughing. Harold just looked pissed off.

Slapping the tags into Harold's palm he said, "Twenty dollars."

Harold paid.

Throwing the pieces of his broken snare onto the floor of the truck he got in and managed one more, "Fuck you," before squealing the tires as he pulled away. The smell of burnt rubber and white smoke filled the air.

Fidgeting and whining Auggie stared at Harold. Looking down Harold and said, "I don't know." Then split a second later, "OK."

Moving like he'd been shot from a cannon, Auggie caught up to the truck in less than thirty yards and sunk his teeth firmly into the right rear tire.

As Auggie trotted back, the high-pitched sound of escaping air could be heard. The dozen or so pedestrians and restaurant patrons that had congregated began to clap and cheer. Knees weak from laughing, Jessie slid down the front of the building and sat on the sidewalk, then rolled to the side holding her ribs. Back against the wall, Randy wiped tears from his eyes but couldn't stop laughing himself. Harold just smiled and petted Auggie who was back at his side, tongue lolling and tail wagging.

As the crowd dispersed, Harold received handshakes and Auggie head pats. Jessie had righted herself but still sat against the building, Auggie trotted over and licked her face, in return getting a big hug. Randy helped Jessie up.

Their waitress was standing just outside now, cigarette dangling from her lips. Handing a brown paper bag to Harold and smiling through stained teeth. "Here's the burger and fries for your dog. His lunch is on me. That's the most fun I've had with my clothes on in a long time."

Rarely chewing, Auggie inhaled the food as it was given. Harold tossed the soon empty bag into a nearby trashcan. Jessie watched the two and finally had to ask, "Harold, can you read Auggie's mind or something? You seemed to know he was going to bite that tire."

Looking into the dog's brown eyes Harold grinned, "I didn't know exactly what he was going to do, I just knew he wanted it really bad. Kind of like if he needs to go outside or wants a bite of whatever I'm eating. Since I'm sure he would never hurt anyone unless he had to, I said OK. If there's any repercussion about this, it's my fault. He would never have done it if I hadn't said it was all right. That guy just made us mad."

"When I get back to the station, I'll make a call. If I mention the profanity and tire squealing in front of witnesses, I doubt the punctured tire will come up," Randy said. "I've heard about dogs biting tires, but it's a usually a Rottweiler or Mastiff, not a lab mix, and not on a moving truck with heavy duty tires. Seeing it with my own eyes, it's still hard to believe."

Harold shrugged his shoulders but said nothing. They all got into Randy's car and started laughing again as they passed the white truck parked against the curb a block and a half away, driver cursing and kicking the flat. The rain had stopped, and bright sunshine made sunglasses necessary for the ten-minute drive.

The Corner Market was open. Harold, Jessie, and Auggie waited outside while Randy went looking for Mrs. Kim. After introducing himself, he was told other members of the Kim family were tending the store and that Mrs. Kim had just returned from visiting her husband at the hospital.

As a pretty young girl went into the back-room, Randy waved the others in. Harold, hands in pockets, stared at the floor and shuffled his feet trying to relieve his anxiety. He'd had more personal contact in the last hour than he'd had in the last two years. Auggie sniffed the nose level racks of candy bars. Jessie returned the smile of the young man behind the counter. Randy stood by silently.

Halfway down the aisle, Mrs. Kim recognized Harold and nearly ran. Randy made the introductions as Mrs. Kim took Harold's hand, kissed it, then held it to her face. In English, mixed with Korean, she told the others the story of how he had saved her and then thanked him profusely.

Blushing, Harold produced an awkward smile and said, "You're welcome."

Tears streaming, she said that her husband was doing well and would soon be home. The mayor, other city civic leaders and members of the local business community had already been in, pledging support in the fight against gang crime. Business had been very good.

Taking a beef jerky stick from a counter display she gave it to Auggie, watched as he ate, then hugged him. As the others talked, Harold wandered through the store picking a few items from the shelves. Back at the front counter, he put the things down, pulled some money from his pocket, and waited for the bill to be totaled.

Bagged, the items were handed to Mrs. Kim who

presented them to Harold, putting her hand up to stop him as he tried to offer payment. After another round of 'thank you' and 'you're welcome', Harold and the others left.

Back on the street, Randy asked, "Jessie, can we use your office for a while?"

A nod in the affirmative and the group started walking the three blocks to Curbside Counseling. Once inside, Jessie and Randy walked to her cubicle, while Harold sat reading a flyer from a pile that sat next to the magazines.

Randy started, "That was certainly a positive identification on Mrs. Kim's part. So, do you think Harold is lying or do you believe he really doesn't remember?"

Sitting back in her chair, Jessie didn't hesitate. "I believe he's sincere. I was watching him the whole time. He didn't show even a remote sign of recognition when she told the story. Unless he was just too drunk to remember, I can't explain it. He seems to be with it otherwise."

"So. What, in your professional opinion should we do now? We can't just leave him to the media."

Jessie stood and looked over the top of the cubicle. Harold was slouched in a chair asleep, while Auggie was busily shredding a three-year-old copy of *National Geographic*. "Well, I guess if we got him cleaned up and quizzed him a little, he might do all right."

Standing, Randy surveyed the waiting area then asked, "Can you handle that?"

Shooting back him a look of disbelief, Jessie asked, "Why me?"

"Because you're the social worker."

Returning to their seats, the two devised a course of action. Jessie pulled out a yellow legal pad and began to take notes. Harold would need clothes. Jessie would tap some emergency funds she had access to. Auggie would need to be seen by a vet so no one could claim he carried disease. Randy would see if the police department would pay for the vet visit in recognition of the dog's heroism.

Finally, was the need for a place for Harold and Auggie to stay while the transformation took place. Hotels were out of the question since there wouldn't be anyone to run interference in case the press showed up. Jessie agreed, after a few minutes of good-natured ribbing from Randy, to allow the pair to stay with her. "You won't have to worry about burglars," he quipped.

Stepping over the mound of paper next to Auggie that was once a magazine, Jessie sat on the coffee table in front of Harold. Randy stood behind her.

Lightly tapping Harold's leg while whispering his name, she woke him. He yawned, stretched, then gave her his undivided attention. The plan was discussed, and Harold reluctantly agreed but was not convinced of the necessity. "Even if I did help that lady, and I don't think I did, why don't I just tell the reporters I don't remember and be done with it?"

Randy moved over and sat next to Harold. "Remember what Mrs. Kim said. The mayor and everyone else in town that owns a suit had been to see her. That means it's already a big story. It's not just about a couple of thugs beating up a store owner. It's gangs, fraud, and intimidation. Maybe it won't last long, but as soon as your name gets out, you'll be on everyone's A-list. Not just news people either. Local radio and television talk shows too. Maybe even some national attention."

Dejected, Harold sat back in the chair. Auggie came over

and put his chin on Harold's leg and received a pat on the head in return. "You both seem to be very nice people, and I'm sure you have my best interest at heart. But my goal is to regain my anonymity as soon as possible without me having to leave town. With that in mind, I'll take your advice, and do as you suggest."

CHAPTER 13

It was agreed that Randy would make a preliminary statement to the press. The hero and his dog had been found but name and whereabouts would not be released. Harold would meet the press in a couple of days at a time and place to be arranged later.

Back at the police station, Randy laughed when told by his superior to work closely with Bill St. James to locate the missing bottle, a union he had thought best to avoid.

Jessie's first stop was at a strip mall barbershop. A young mother struggled at one end of the room with a whining toddler while trying to watch the progress of her six-year old's haircut. Harold sat in the extreme opposite end of the room.

While waiting, Jessie flipped through styling books. Harold thought the scene comical and observed without comment. When his name was called he followed a heavily made-up young woman with rusty-red dyed, teased, and sprayed hair to the shampoo station. The warm water felt good and Harold relaxed and enjoyed the view of braless breasts, barely confined in a tank top that swayed inches from his face in rhythm with the scalp massage.

Hair wrapped in a towel, still wet, Harold moved to the barber chair and watched as hair fell away in three-inch lengths. He tried to ignore the noxious-smelling chemicals that were being applied to each of two-dozen tightly wrapped curls on the head of a white-haired seventy-year-old woman in the chair next to him.

The two stylists carried on a rambling conversation that had something to do with the job prospects of their out-of-work boyfriends. The whole event lasted a mercifully short twenty minutes. Harold's salt and pepper hair now cut well above the collar it had brushed.

Auggie had craned his neck to watch every bit of the action through the shop's glass exterior from the front passenger seat of Jessie's car. He leaped into the back seat when Harold and Jessie returned.

The next stop was a discount retail store where Jessie helped picked out three pairs of pants and four shirts, underwear, socks, shoes, and miscellaneous personal care supplies.

It was dark when they made one last stop at a grocery store for dinner supplies and a forty-pound bag of dog food. The drive to Jessie's house was a brief twenty minutes. They pulled into her garage at seven forty-five.

It only took Jessie and Harold two heavily laden trips to move all the purchases to the house. Auggie did his part carrying two plastic bags in his mouth. Back outside Auggie marked every shrub on the perimeter in a matter of minutes.

The house was bigger than Harold had expected. The living room was about four hundred square feet with a cathedral ceiling that made it look even larger. The furniture consisted of a dark brown couch, love seat, and chairs all overstuffed and comfortable-looking. A big, red brick fireplace dominated one wall. On the mantel, framed pictures of what were probably family and friends. Paintings of wildlife and outdoor scenery decorated the other walls.

In the formal dining room, a three-tiered crystal chandelier hung above an oak pedestal table that was surrounded by six matching chairs. A doorway led to the kitchen. Bright and clean, it was proportionally as large as the other rooms with a small breakfast nook at one end.

Jessie was just finishing putting the food into the cupboards and the refrigerator. "Grab your stuff and I'll show you your room." A moving tour of the laundry room, den, and a bathroom ended at the second to last door of the hallway. That room, dominated by a queen size bed, had its own television, and attached bathroom. "I think everything you'll need is here but, if something's missing, let me know."

Harold walked into the room, set his bags on the bed, and looked around, "This is very nice. Thank you."

With a not so subtle hint, Jessie said, "I'll start dinner while you get cleaned up."

She was nearly out the door when Harold asked, "Why are you doing this?"

Turning in the doorway and leaning against the frame, Jessie asked, "Doing what?"

"All of it. The haircut, buying Auggie and me stuff and, most of all, bringing a pathetic loser into your home."

"It's kind of complicated. The short story is that I believe you're a decent, honest man who for some reason lost his way in life. If, by investing some time and money I can help you, I want to do it." Choking back tears, Jessie walked across the room and back. "Twenty years ago, my brother was living on the streets because of his dependence on drugs. He was a very talented artist. He painted the pictures in the living room. But he couldn't get past the drug use. I was going to college back east and hadn't had much contact with him for a couple years. My parents had gotten burned by his lying and stealing and had given up on him. His body was found in a dumpster, the needle still in his arm. I'm fairly sure he intentionally killed himself."

She was crying now and pulled tissues from a box on the nightstand, wiped her eyes and blew her nose. Another moment to clear her throat, then she started again. "After all this time, I still cry when I talk about him. He was a decent, kind person who needed help. He was also my twin."

Auggie was leaning against her leg, looking up with sad eyes. Jessie smiled and patted his head. "When I got back to school after his funeral, I changed my major to psychology and sociology. After school, I came back to Seattle and with financial help and blessings from my parents, I was able to open Curbside Counseling. On the occasion someone nice comes in who's not trying to work a scam, or get something for nothing, and might benefit from a little help, I do it, in my brother's memory."

"I'll try not to disappoint you," Harold said.

The sounds of pots and pans clanging and silverware against dishes made their way to Harold's room as he closed the bathroom door. Twenty minutes later, he walked into the kitchen, showered, shaved, and wearing new clothes.

Busily filling plates, Jessie didn't hear him come in. Auggie, lying inconveniently in the middle of the room, sprang up. That motion caught Jessie's attention and she turned, plates in hand, to face Harold.

He'd always seemed small to Jessie. Usually bent under the weight of a backpack, hidden under a hat, or shoulders pulled up against the weather. Standing in front of her now without a heavy coat and layers of clothes, he looked trim, nearly athletic. "Oh my god, Harold, you look great."

Blushing, he took the plates from her and set them on the little table in the breakfast nook. Requesting and receiving two large plastic bowls, Harold put down food and water for Auggie before sitting down to his own meal.

Halfway through dinner, Harold stopped and reached into his pocket. He pulled out a piece of pink paper, unfolded it and slid it across the table. "I had this in my pocket and saw others like it in your office this afternoon. Is this for real?"

Jessie recognized the Spring Rain reward flyer immediately. "Yes, it is. Why? Do you know something about this?"

Harold had started to eat again, so there was a pause while he finished a mouthful of food. "Yeah, this was just last week. I was out one night, and some young guy sold me a bottle. Practically gave it to me. I only gave him a dollar."

Excited, Jessie leaned forward. "Did you drink it?"

"Some, but most of it got spilled."

On her feet, looking ready to explode, Jessie said, "If you still have the bottle, you could get twenty-five thousand dollars."

"I think I know where it is. Maybe tomorrow I'll check and see if I can find it."

Back in her chair, Jessie said, "Oh, that would be great for you. I can't wait to see Randy's face when we tell him."

"What's Randy got to do with it?"

"You haven't been reading the newspaper or seen any television lately, have you?" Jessie told as much of the story as she knew. Spring Rain, the recall, Jim Stacy, dead teenagers, dead street people, and a big reward.

"Now that you mention it, I did read about this the other day."

Meal complete, they were cleaning up as Jessie finished the tale. Harold was wiping off the table and, without missing a stroke asked, "So, why didn't I die?"

Jessie stopped washing the dishes and turned toward Harold, arms bare to the elbows, dripping soapsuds on the floor. "I don't know. Maybe the bottle you had wasn't as toxic or you didn't drink enough. Whatever the reason, Mrs. Kim and I are both happy you didn't."

Towel in hand, Harold started to dry the dishes. "Seems like this Jim Stacy fellow is in some big trouble. What's his story?"

"As I understand it, he's just a kid looking to make a little money and screwed up. He's not malicious, just stupid. Too bad too. He has a wife and new baby."

With the last of the dishes put away, Harold sat back at the table and looked out the window but couldn't really see anything but his own reflection with a dark background.

"If this reward thing turns out, what would you think about some of the money going to Jim Stacy's wife and child? In honor of your brother," Harold suggested to Jessie.

Jessie sat down and just stared at Harold. He became uncomfortable and started to squirm in the chair, only momentarily returning her gaze until she finally broke the silence. "Are you trying to build up points for sainthood or something? Unconsciously, you save lives, and now, apparently totally awake, you want to give away enough money to set yourself up for six months or more. Now I get to ask the question. Why are you doing this?"

Head down and fingers laced together as if praying, he

didn't look up. "I've done some things in my life that, although not illegal, harmed people, I'm ashamed to say. This would be a bit of penance toward cleansing my soul."

"It's a beautiful gesture but why don't you sleep on it and we can talk again tomorrow."

They watched television until the evening news was over. Randy had indeed been in a featured segment about the hero being found. The piece lasted about two minutes. Harold took Auggie outside one more time. Goodnights were said in the living room, and then Jessie and Harold went to separate bedrooms.

In bed, the only light in Harold's room came through the window from the half-moon on a clear night. The only sound, the faint ticking of a grandfather clock in the hallway. Uneasy due to unfamiliarity with his surroundings, he fell asleep in twenty minutes, Auggie on the floor by his side.

Sleep for Jessie took a little longer. Relying on instinct was OK in some circumstances but having a virtual stranger in her home was different. She hoped he hadn't heard the lock on her door engage. If he did, she wondered if he would be offended.

CHAPTER 14

Morning brought light rain with a cloud cover that promised no change for the rest of the day. Just after seven a.m., Jessie walked past Harold's room and heard the small whine of an uncomfortable dog. Listening for a minute and hearing nothing else, she opened the door just enough for Auggie to creep out.

Picking up an umbrella on the way out of the garage, she watched from under its canopy as Auggie visited several trees then moved behind some bushes just across the street. Business complete, he covered a hundred yards in a couple of seconds then back again, running and leaping like a gazelle, for no logical reason other than the sheer joy of movement. A trip around the house for good measure and he was back at her feet, barely panting.

In the back corner of the garage, Jessie found an old tennis ball. Returning to the door, she threw it with arm strength barely diminished from her days of high school softball.

Auggie was fast. So fast, that he could catch the ball in midair no matter how far it was thrown. Returning it to her in seconds. Reverting to trickery, Jessie would fake a throw then sail the ball in an opposite direction. Even being briefly confused, Auggie would still rarely need two bounces of the ball before he caught up.

Disheveled and barefoot, Harold watched from the back of the garage. Jessie was laughing as the strong throws began to take a toll on her arm. Facing the house, her last throw sent the ball over the roof.

"You can't beat him. I've tried," said Harold suddenly.

Startled, Jessie paused then smiled. "We'll see. Good morning, Harold." The sound of a wet ball bouncing on the concrete beside her foot interrupted the conversation. "My God, Harold, Auggie has to be the fastest dog in the world."

"I wouldn't know, I haven't seen all the other dogs in the world. But I agree, he's very fast and smart."

"Think about it, Harold. Yesterday, I watched him bite a moving truck tire; today, I see him running so fast he's nearly a blur, both effortlessly. Don't you think it's odd?" she asked.

"Yes, but so what? He seems healthy, he's not mean, and he's a great companion. What would you do if he were your dog? Take him to the vet because he's as strong as a bear and can outrun most cars. Then what?"

Jessie watched as Auggie used his front teeth to pull the green felt cover off the ball. "You have a point."

"Frankly, what I'm most concerned about is someone seeing his abilities and trying to exploit them. Kind of like a child protégé in music or science or something who gets thrown into an adult world and never allowed to be a kid. He's happy, and I love him. That's enough."

"You're probably right. Say, can he do anything else?" Jessie wanted to know.

Being outside barefoot, Harold was getting cold and opened the door to go inside. "Not that I know of. But I haven't really tested him. I'll just wait until something happens and be surprised."

Furious shaking sent a spray of water six feet away as Auggie dried himself. Using old towels, Jessie finished drying the crafty canine and the three went into the house. Harold offered to cook breakfast. Jessie accepted and used the time to shower and dress for the day.

A full meal of pancakes, eggs, bacon, coffee, and juice was on the table when she returned. Looking at the buffet she said, "I was expecting cereal and toast."

"If you're still hungry after this, I'll be glad to make some for you," Harold said proudly.

The meal was consumed with a minimal conversation. Auggie had eaten another large bowl of dog food and was sleeping on a throw rug next to the sink.

Harold had cleared his throat a couple of times and put down his knife and fork. "I thought about it and, if I'm given the reward, I still want to give a chunk of it to Jim Stacy's family. I'll keep some to pay you back and make sure I can take care of him," he said, pointing toward Auggie. "But the majority will go to the lady and child. Can you make the arrangements?"

"Oh, Harold, that's very nice of you. Yes, I think I know just how to handle it. When can you get the bottle?"

"Later today, say about five. If you don't mind, I could just go with you when you go to the counseling office. Auggie and I will wander a bit then go get the bottle and met you back at the office later." Auggie's head popped up when he heard his name but drifted back to the floor as the conversation continued.

"The winery owner is here in town. I'll call and have him meet us at the office. I doubt that he's carrying twenty-five grand with him, but at least he can verify if the bottle you have is the one he's looking for. Maybe I'll invite him and a couple other people to the office for a late dinner tonight. If the bottle is the real deal, he can bring the check with him then."

Jessie watched the local news, then a few minutes of CNN while Harold got ready. The rain had stopped briefly, and Harold looked around as the car pulled out of the driveway. He hadn't been able to see much the day before since they had arrived after dark. In the daylight, he saw that the house, a barn, and two small outbuildings sat on about ten acres that were probably once the center of a farm or ranch. The surrounding property had been sold, then developed into several subdivisions, eight houses to the acre. Harold figured Jessie's property was probably worth at least five million dollars to a developer.

As they pulled away from the house, Harold asked, "Get many offers to buy your place?"

"Nearly every day I have either a message on my answering machine or a letter, sometimes both. But I'm pretty comfortable, so I never return the calls or respond to the mail. Besides, this property was part of four hundred acres cleared by my great-grandfather in the late 1880's. My grandfather sold off about half of it when he got too old to farm. About five years ago, my father sold all but what I have, made a ton of money. He and my mother have a condo in Seattle and a place in Phoenix. That's where they are now. Anyway, I grew up here and have a lot of great memories. So, as long as I can, I want to hang on to it."

"Well, it sure is a nice place."

The drive into downtown Seattle was slow even for mid-day. The notorious traffic congestion was made worse by a series of fender bender accidents. A twenty-minute drive the night before lasted nearly an hour now. A couple of times they came to a complete stop on the freeway. Once out of the slow areas, Jessie got up to highway speed.

Except for the day before, Harold hadn't been in a car in a couple of years. White knuckles appeared as he gripped his knees, cars going by bumper to bumper at sixty miles an hour, vision blurred by rain and road spray. Once on city streets, it wasn't quite so bad, but when they parked a half block from Jessie's office, Harold was glad to get out.

"The office doesn't open until later, but I still have some paperwork I want to finish. After that, I have errands to run. I'll meet you back here around six?"

"That will be great."

They were in front of Curbside Counseling now and Harold started to walk away. He was wearing the same old coat over his new clothes and Jessie made a mental note to get him a new one. He also wasn't wearing a hat and the rain, although slowed to a drizzle, was still falling. "Harold! Why don't you take my umbrella? I have another one in the office."

Looking almost distinguished as he walked away, Jessie was proud of the makeover. She made a mental note to talk to Harold again on the way home, just to be sure he was comfortable with the plan so far and keep him involved in the decision-making.

CHAPTER 15

In her office waiting for the jury to return a verdict in a burglary case, Yvonne Jackson was happy for the distraction Jessie's call provided. "Can you stop by the office for dinner tonight? I have someone I'd like you to meet."

Responding with skepticism, Yvonne asks. "Is this a blind date?"

"No. It's someone you already know, Harold Pearson. Randy and I found him yesterday. He is the one that stopped that grocery store assault. Anyway, he has a surprise and you'll probably want to be there."

"What time, and should I bring anything?" Yvonne wanted to know.

"Say, seven o'clock and no, I was just going to order some Thai and make a little buffet."

"O.K. see you then."

A quick call to Randy got another confirmation. She didn't mention Yvonne would be there, or that Harold might have the missing wine bottle. "Is Bill St. James still hanging around down there?"

"Yeah, they set him up at a desk with his own phone. I'll transfer your call. See you later."

A series of clicks and hums eventually resulted in a ring, then an answer. "William St. James, how can I help you?"

"Bill, this is Jessie Baker from Curbside Counseling."

"Jessie, nice to hear from you. To what do I owe the pleasure of your call?"

"I know you've probably heard this a few times recently, but I met someone who says he can produce the missing bottle. He's very reliable."

Bill exclaimed, "That's great! When can I get it?"

"Come to my office at six-thirty. I figured you could confirm it then. I'm having some people come to the office for a very informal dinner. You're invited, and you could bring the check."

"Sounds great. I can't tell you what a load off my mind it will be to have that bottle," Bill said.

"O.K., I'll see you then and if you don't mind, don't tell anyone about this until tomorrow."

"Whatever you say. See you later."

Satisfied that her plan was falling into place, Jessie ordered the food for later then went out to pick up a few things before Harold got back. Her errands complete, she was back in the office at ten to two. She typed up some hand-written notes of counseling sessions and worked on a grant proposal for money to hire additional counselors and pay a stipend to the student interns that worked there from the local universities.

Engrossed in her work, she hadn't noticed the sun had set behind nearby buildings an hour before. Most of the office was dark. Except for the lamp on her desk, she hadn't turned on any other lights. It was six-twenty by her watch; the others would be coming soon. Unlocking the front door, she flipped switches lighting the entire office. On the way back to her desk, she heard the doorknob turn and door creak as it opened. Turning back to the door she said, "Someone's early," thinking it was Bill or Harold.

Rhonda Jean Williams a twenty-eight-year-old drug addict and prostitute was standing in the doorway. She'd been in the office before and Jessie had set her up twice in drug treatment programs. Both times Rhonda Jean had walked away after just a few days. The last time was three months ago. Today she looked different, worse. She'd lost weight. She probably weighed about a hundred pounds. On her five-foot-seven frame, she was gaunt. Her facial bones were prominent, and her eyes bloodshot and protruding. Makeup didn't help. She was wearing her working clothes. Short skirt, spike heel shoes, bare legs, a leotard top, and coat too light for the weather. No signs of underwear.

Jessie hid her reaction to Rhonda Jean's appearance well. "Oh, hi, Rhonda Jean. I was expecting someone else."

With rapid, slightly slurred speech, Rhonda Jean said, "Ms. Baker, I saw the light come on as I was going by. Can I talk to you?"

"I have an appointment in a few minutes but, sure, come on in."

Rhonda Jean locked the door behind her and followed Jessie back to her desk, looking all the way to the back room and glancing into the other cubicles before going into Jessie's area.

"What can I do for you?"

The story was a familiar one. A john beat her up and

took all her money. She hadn't eaten in a couple of days. Planned to start rehab again next week. Just needed enough cash to get through the week. She couldn't sit still, and the story was disjointed. She spoke fast and didn't make eye contact. Had she changed her drug of choice? Looked like she went from heroin to meth.

Meth users were unpredictable, and Jessie was uncomfortable being in the office alone. The tale went on another few minutes before Jessie broke in.

"We always tell people right off, the first time they come here, but as a reminder, we don't give money here. We arrange for things like food, clothes, a place to stay or, in your case, rehab. Another thing we don't do is work with people who are obviously high like you are now. It always ends up being a waste of time."

Jessie stood and started to walk toward the door. "Why don't you clean up a little and come back. We'll see what we can do then."

Rhonda Jean's hands were trembling, her skinny fingers fumbling in a small black handbag. "Can't you just front me some money? I'll pay you back tomorrow."

"I'm sorry, I can't," Jessie said.

She hadn't had a history being violent, but Rhonda Jean pulled a steak knife from her purse.

Bill St. James had parked just a few doors down from the counseling office and was at the front door when he heard Jessie scream mixed with the sounds of glass breaking and furniture moving against the floor. He tried the locked door. He pounded with fists but got no response.

Harold was being pulled across the street at nearly a dead run by Auggie. Bill had backed up preparing to hit the door with his shoulder. Jessie screamed again. Auggie pulled the leash from Harold's hand. Bill charged, his eyes closed the last few feet. Auggie and Bill hit the door simultaneously; it splintered. Bill stumbled and fell covering his head as pieces of door and frame cascaded down. Harold was stopped at the doorway by debris. Auggie had barely slowed.

Standing in the center hallway, Jessie struggled to control Rhonda Jean's hand that held the knife as she scratched and slapped with her free hand.

Auggie, at nearly full speed, struck Rhonda Jean's rib cage with the top of his head sending her into the wall. Sheetrock collapsed, leaving a perfect outline of her body, and held her upright briefly before she slumped to the floor. She might have fared better being hit by a car.

Pushing off pieces of the door then scrambling to his feet, Bill ran to Jessie. "Are you all right?"

Blood was oozing from a wound on her left hand. "Yes." Pointing to Rhonda Jean, "Please check on her. I'll call 911." Harold took the phone from Jessie's shaking hand and completed the call.

Rhonda Jean was hurt badly. Her breaths were short and irregular. A jagged bone protruded from the right side of her chest. Blood ran from her nose and mouth.

Jessie held her hand. Bill took off his coat, rolled it up, and put it under her head. The place was a mess. "What happened?"

"She came in saying she wanted to talk but pulled a knife and decided to rob me. Then you guys came. By the way, Bill, I'd like you to meet Harold and Auggie."

Eye contact and a nod completed the introduction. "How'd she end up against the wall?" Bill asked.

"You didn't see?"

"No, I didn't see anything after I broke the door down."

Harold was standing behind Bill and started to answer before Jessie could begin. "This young woman was distracted by the door breaking." Still kneeling and holding Rhonda Jean's hand, Jessie looked up to see Harold staring straight into her eyes, smiling as he continued. "She lunged with the knife and Jessie was able to grab her by the wrist and throw her into the wall. Used her own momentum against her."

As emergency crews arrived Bill, Harold, and Auggie backed off as medics took over. Jessie went to a sink in the back to wash the cut on her hand. Police were interviewing Bill and Harold in the waiting area. Static and voices from the two-way radios hanging from the belts of various personnel just added to the chaotic atmosphere.

Twenty minutes after the 911 call, Randy walked in. Hand bandaged, Jessie joined Bill and Harold and told her story, using Harold's version of the ending, once to police and again to a couple of reporters eager to get a quick version back to the stations for the eleven o'clock news.

A small parade moved through the office as Rhonda Jean, surrounded by medics, was wheeled out. By seven-thirty, the place was nearly quiet again. Harold, Bill, and Randy were cleaning up. Jessie was forced to sit and supervise at their insistence, Auggie at her side.

"What the hell happened?" Yvonne said, nearly shouting. When she saw Jessie's hand wrapped to mid-forearm in gauze, she picked her way through the rubble and sat taking her friend's hand. "Oh, my God, are you alright?"

The men had stopped working and watched while Yvonne crossed the room, then continued. Jessie and Yvonne spoke quietly and nearly didn't hear the sixteen-year-old at the door holding plastic shopping bags in each hand. "Did someone order food?"

Except for the broken door, the place was orderly again in fifteen minutes. Yvonne had laid the food and drinks out on the waiting area coffee table, chairs pulled up around it. Mismatched plates and utensils were brought from the small lunch area in the back room.

Jessie excused herself, then asked Harold to join her in the back room, Auggie followed. "Were you able to find what you were looking for?"

Reaching into his inside pocket, Harold pulled out a bottle wrapped heavily in brown grocery bags. As he began to unwrap it, Jessie yelled to the group up front, "Bill, could you come here a minute?"

Grinning ear-to-ear, Jessie handed the bottle to Bill. Harold was pleased that Jessie was happy.

Moving to a small light, Bill leaned over to examine the label, looked through the glass at the label's back, and finally at some code numbers on the bottom. Turning back Bill was stone-faced. When the beaming grin left Jessie's face, Bill felt bad about playing the brief trick and smiled. "This is it!"

With a skip and a yell, "Yes!", Jessie hugged Harold, then Bill.

Yvonne and Randy came running back to find Jessie between Harold and Bill. Her arms were over their shoulders, theirs around her waist, all three laughing. Auggie was spinning, hopping, and barking in the middle of the room.

Caught up in the contagious laughter, it took a while before Yvonne could ask, "What's going on?"

"Harold found the bottle; Bill's bottle. That's not all, Bill doesn't even know this." Looking at Harold she said, "You tell the rest."

"I've decided to give a portion of the money to Jim Stacy's family."

The group moved through the office to the front, sat and started dishing food from paper cartons onto their plates. The discussions were lively. Auggie trolled the perimeter getting handouts at each stop.

With the meal nearly complete, Bill unfolded a money order and was poised to write. "What's your last name, Harold?"

"Pearson, but don't make it out to me. Make it out to Curbside Counseling."

Everyone looked at Harold, but nothing was said. "If you give me the money, our government will want thirty percent. If it's donated to a nonprofit agency to be distributed, then more of it will be available to the people for whom it's intended. Besides, you might be able to deduct in on your taxes as a charitable donation."

Bill started to write and said, "Good plan."

Pieces of the door had been stood up to cover the entrance. Randy looked it over and asked, "What do you want to do about this door?"

"No hope for the door and the frame's not in good shape either," Jessie said, standing next to Randy. "I doubt the landlord will agree to fix it. Frankly, he's a nice guy, but not all that thrilled with the clientele here. I don't want to give him a reason to kick me out, so I guess I'll replace it."

Randy had been closely inspecting the frame and spoke when Bill joined him. "I think the whole thing should just come out. If I get a heavy-duty prehung door, I can have it back together tonight. There's a building supply place across town that just started staying open late."

Jessie stepped in." What's this 'I' stuff?"

"You guys shamed me into it. Bill gives Harold twenty-five grand. Harold gives it to you. You'll give it to someone else. The least I can do is put up a couple of hundred and some labor."

"I'm in for half," said Yvonne from across the room.

Fingertips to her lips, Jessie's eyes filled with tears. "My god, I'm surrounded by angels."

After Jessie went around the room giving hugs and kisses to everyone, Yvonne and Randy left. They would stop first at Randy's house for tools then, get the door, and be back by ten. Bill would stay and try to remove the knob and locks with the meager assortment of tools Jessie had in a little toolbox at her desk.

With Jessie's blessing, Auggie cleaned up the leftovers. Harold made himself busy moving an ornamental tree across the room to hide the hole Rhonda Jean left in the sheetrock then cleaned the blood from the tile floor.

Watching Bill, to be sure they wouldn't be overheard, Jessie whispered to Harold, "Why did you tell everyone I put Rhonda Jean into the wall?"

"It was what I was saying this morning about Auggie's power and not wanting people to exploit it. Bill already thought he broke down the door. Then he said he didn't see anything, so I figured I'd just shield Auggie a little. Thank you for going along with it."

Auggie had trotted over when he heard his name and stood between the two. Jessie squatted and hugged him and in a soft voice said, "Your secret's safe with me."

By eleven-thirty, the door had been replaced and the

group stood back to admire Randy's work. At Jessie's request, Randy made an official police call to the hospital to check on Rhonda Jean. She was still being treated in the ER and then off to intensive care, but the doctor believed she would recover.

Bill would contact the media in the morning to announce the last bottle had been found and the reward donated to a local non-profit social service organization. Jessie and Yvonne would work out a plan to get the money to Jim Stacy's wife with a minimum of fanfare.

The gathering broke up at midnight after another round of hugs and handshakes.

CHAPTER 16

On her way out the night before, Jessie had put a sign on the new Curbside Counseling door, they would be closed the rest of the week. She was expecting a couple of new interns to start orientation Friday, but she'd call to reschedule the start of training for next week and mail them packets of information about Curbside Counseling. The weather was going to deteriorate over the next few days to constant showers, which inevitably cut the drop-in rate to near zero. She'd stop in at some of the local homeless hangouts just to make sure someone wasn't in dire need.

The ringing phone woke her up. Through one blurry eye, she saw it was nine-thirty. She hadn't slept that late in years. Without getting up, she grabbed the phone but winced with pain. The hand cut last night was throbbing. She changed hands and rolled onto her back. "Hello."

"Good morning Jessie, it's Randy." He asked how she was doing and said he'd called the hospital about Rhonda

Jean. "She did spend the night in intensive care but will probably be transferred to a regular floor in a few days. She won't be out of the hospital for at least a week then she'll go to jail. Remind me not to give you any shit. I wouldn't want to end up like Rhonda Jean."

Fighting the urge to tell him what really happened, she said. "Yeah, I'm hell on anorexic drug addicts. So, what do you think they'll charge her with?"

"Could be anything from assault and battery to attempted murder. She does have a rap sheet but nothing violent until now."

"If I ask the prosecutor's office, do you think that they'd offer her a plea bargain for less jail time if she completed a drug program?"

"Since you're the victim, I'm sure your request would carry a lot of weight. Why don't you give them a call?" Randy gave Jessie a couple of names to ask for at the prosecutor's office then changed the subject. "The department's veterinarian agreed to check Auggie out for free any time, just stop in. Finally, the main reason I called. I just came from a meeting with the Chief of Police and the Mayor. They want The Corner Market hero and his dog to come to a black-tie dinner tomorrow night. They want to give him a citizenship award or something."

Wide-awake now and sitting up, Jessie looked out her window. In the backyard between the house and barn, she saw Harold on his hands and knees taunting and wrestling with Auggie. It was raining hard and both were soaked. "He's outside right now. When he comes in I'll talk to him and let you know."

"This dinner is a five-hundred-dollar-a-plate fundraiser

for the governor's reelection. The list of attendees is a who's who of Washington State. It's political as hell but a nice controlled environment. He could talk to the media before the dinner then get the award. It'd be one step closer to having him back on his own."

The last sentence caught Jessie off guard. In just a couple of days, she'd grown to like Harold and Auggie's company. "I'll talk to Harold and call you back."

She watched the duo intermittently for another ten minutes while she brushed her teeth, combed her hair, and dressed in a T-shirt and sweatpants. Harold had thrown a stick in the direction of the barn. It hit the barn roof and slid down until it was half over the edge but didn't fall off. Looking for the stick, Auggie circled the barn once, picking up speed as he came around the last corner. He leaped first to the top of a fifty-five-gallon steel drum sitting next to the barn, then launched himself the remaining ten feet, grabbed the stick on the way down landed in full stride and returned the stick to Harold.

Donning raincoat and rubber boots, Jessie joined Harold and Auggie outside. As she walked across the lawn, Auggie bounded playfully over to meet her. Squatting to greet him, she ended up on her butt when Auggie failed to stop in time. Auggie licked her face as she tried to push him away. Unsuccessful, she rolled to her stomach and covered up as best she could while laughing hysterically. He got his nose under her collar and pressed his wet tongue to her neck. Saying, "I give, I give," she struggled to her feet.

Having come over to intervene, if necessary, in the mayhem, Harold said, "Good morning."

"Good morning, Harold."

Wiping wet hands on pants nearly as wet, Jessie said, "I

saw Auggie jump to the barn roof and grab that stick. Guess we can add unbelievable leaping abilities to the list of things he can do."

Bending down to pet Auggie, Harold said, "I saw him jump over a parked car once, but I've never seen him jump that high before. That was cool."

"I agree. Way cool. Say, I just got off the phone with Randy. He gave me the name of a vet who'll see Auggie for free any time. We could do that later today."

"That would be great, I'd like him to get shots and stuff."

"Another thing. The mayor wants you to come to a political fundraising dinner tomorrow to get an award for helping Mrs. Kim. It's black tie, very upper crust. Do you want to go?"

"Doesn't sound like something I'd really be interested in. What do you think?"

As they walked to the house, arguments for and against going were discussed. When Jessie repeated Randy's observation that Harold would be closer to being anonymous again, Harold's pace slowed slightly, and his shoulders slouched but he didn't say anything immediately.

Once inside he said, "You've been a gracious host but Auggie and I should be getting out of your hair. Tell Randy we'll go. Do you think it would be out of line to ask to bring a few guests? Maybe Randy, Yvonne, Bill, and you could come with Auggie and me?"

"Only way to find out is to ask. I'll call Randy back and have him check into it."

In the twenty minutes, it took Harold to shower and change, Jessie had made and received several phone calls. Guests were welcome. Yvonne, Randy, and Bill had accepted the invitations. Yvonne suggested renting a limousine for the evening. Jessie loved the idea and was thrilled to be able to rent one on such short notice. Harold would need a tux, and Jessie wanted to take her one good evening dress to the cleaners, but the first stop would be at the vet's. Showered and changed, Jessie grabbed her briefcase and cell phone and they left the house about eleven after a quick breakfast.

The waiting room in the vet's office was small. The floor was tile, in a gray and white checkerboard pattern. Gray, vinyl-covered bench seating lined the walls on two sides. They had only been in the office a few minutes when they were led into an exam room. A short, overweight, balding man about forty-five stood on the far side of the exam table. He wore a light blue dress shirt under a thigh length lab coat, his name embroidered over the left breast pocket. Pants were navy blue. Extending a hand, he said, "Mr. Pearson, it's nice to meet you. I'm Dr. Remy. I've heard a lot of good things about you and your dog."

Harold introduced Jessie and thanked the doctor for offering to see Auggie for free.

The doctor was brief but thorough, asking questions as he examined Auggie. A one-sided struggle ensued when the doctor attempted to look in Auggie's mouth. Nearly breaking into a sweat trying unsuccessfully to open the tightly clamped jaws, the vet said, "He's a mighty strong boy, isn't he?"

"Yes, and a little willful too," said Harold. "Auggie, open."

After fifteen minutes, he announced Auggie a perfectly healthy specimen with one reservation. "I think you might be mistaken about his age. He's certainly more than two months old. I'd guess at least a year."

Harold had realized the blunder just as he said it a few minutes earlier and recovered by saying, "What I meant to say was, I've only had him a couple of months."

After Auggie got three injections covering half a dozen canine diseases, they were on their way. Harold thanked the doctor again as they left.

Halfway across the parking lot, Harold looked around to see if anyone was within hearing distance. "I've got to be careful when I talk about Auggie. It's a good thing Dr. Remy didn't pay any attention to me about Auggie's age."

"You mean he really is only two months old?" Jessie said in complete surprise.

"Yeah. Two weeks ago, I could carry him in my coat."

CHAPTER 17

At the bank, Jessie deposited the check Bill St. James had given her the night before into the Curbside Counseling account. She also got several hundred in cash and transferred several thousand into a new account for Harold. "Haven't had enough money to open an account in a long time."

"You'll get a debit card too. Lots of places prefer debit to cash. In the meantime, here's $400.00. Hope this is enough to tide you over for a while."

"This is plenty for now. Especially, since Auggie got to see a vet for free." Counting off eight twenties, he handed them back to Jessie. "Will this cover what you've spent on Auggie and me so far?"

"Yes, more than enough. But you don't have to do this."

"If we want to keep our credit good, we do. I'd also like

to buy you dinner tonight. Any place you want."

"Well, I like the seafood restaurants at the pier."

"Seafood it is."

Harold and Auggie waited in the car while Jessie dropped off her dress for cleaning. She also stopped briefly at a homeless shelter and then a rescue mission. Back on the road, the conversation was light. During a lull, Jessie realized Harold had gotten her to talk about herself again. He knew far more about her than she did him. "Can I ask you a personal question?" she ventured.

"Sure," Harold replied.

"You're articulate, well read, and generally healthy. How did you end up on the streets?"

Harold heaved a sigh before saying, "It's a long story. Are you sure you want to hear it?"

They had just gotten on the freeway and gone about a mile when traffic slowed to a crawl due to the near-constant congestion. Brake lights were lit as far as the eye could see. Traffic came to a complete stop a moment later.

"Absolutely. It looks like we'll have plenty of time," Jessie answered.

"When I was a kid I wasn't athletic or popular. I was what people now would call a nerd. I read a lot and went to the movies. My parents were distant, and although I had my basic needs met, there was never any outward show of affection in our home."

With traffic still stopped, Jessie had turned in her seat, so she could look directly at Harold.

Harold's eyes wandered from the windshield to the side window to his hands folded on his lap, only occasionally looking at Jessie.

"I finished near the top of my high school graduating

class and got a scholarship to Stanford. During my junior year, I had to do a group project in a speech class. I got to know this beautiful girl in my group. She was nerdy like me. We fell in love and married right after graduation. With my degree in architectural engineering, I got a great job in San Francisco. We had a boy a couple years later. Everything was wonderful."

He was looking around less now. Mostly just looking down at his constantly moving hands.

"Then just past our fifth anniversary, my wife was diagnosed with cervical cancer and died within six months. I fell apart. I took a leave of absence from work and never went back. My wife's sister took my son in while I spiraled down.

People tried to help me, but I just couldn't get myself together. I lost the house and everything else. I didn't care anymore. With my son safe, I just started wandering. I came to Seattle a few years ago and, for no particular reason, stayed. That's it."

Traffic was starting to move again but at not much more than a crawl. Taking the closest exit, Jessie headed for the tux shop. Wanting more information, Jessie asked, "When was the last time you had contact with your son?

"I would call or write every few months for several years but when he was around about eight they moved, and I haven't talked to him since. That's why I ask you to see if you could find him. Though I doubt he'd even talk to me after all this time."

Only the sounds of traffic kept the car from being totally silent for several moments. Then Jessie said, "Maybe we could ask Randy to do a search for your son. He has access to a lot more information than I do. For all we know, your son might be trying to find you. Your address isn't on the Internet either."

"Well, I guess it wouldn't hurt to ask."

"Exactly. While I'm being nosy, I have more questions."

"Shoot."

"It doesn't sound like you were ever in the military. Did you ever have any martial arts training that would account for your fighting ability?"

"No military or martial arts training unless you count watching Bruce Lee movies. Besides, I don't even remember the fighting part. Next question."

"You told me you were an alcoholic, but I haven't seen you have a drink in two days and I haven't seen any withdrawals. That's not what I would expect from an alcoholic."

"I guess I misused the word. I use alcoholic to describe my lifestyle more than my drinking habits. I drink cheap wine. But, in an effort not to drop out of society completely, I only allow myself to drink two weeks a month. Sometimes I go a little longer without. Sometimes I drink every day for three weeks. It depends on the circumstances at the time. But I think it all averaged out over time, two weeks on, two weeks off."

"If you can stop, why drink at all?"

"Until I found Auggie, I didn't care about anything. Drinking was a way to dull my senses. I'd stop just to have a brief, clear look at life. Disappointed in what I saw, I'd return to the bottle. Since I found him, I've had three bottles in two weeks and one of those was Bill's bottle that mostly spilled," Harold explained.

Auggie had been staring out the side window at children

in the car next to them making faces. He moved to the center and stuck his head between the seats to watch as that car pulled ahead.

"I don't want to sound negative, but I've had hundreds of people in my office over the years who said they could stop drinking any time, without help, but couldn't. I hope you're the exception."

"I guess I'll just have to show you."

"OK, one more question then I'll stop. Where do you live?"

"It's a very interesting place but kind of hard to describe. I was at the library a while back reading a book about the turn of the century architecture. The book had some old Seattle maps in it. Using copies of them, and some diligent searching, I was able to find a very isolated spot right downtown. Maybe I'll show it to you sometime," he offered.

"That sounds great," Jessie enthused.

The conversation became less personal as traffic got back up to speed. At a small neighborhood park, Auggie was allowed to roam a bit. The rain had stopped but no one else was there.

They spent nearly an hour at the rental shop getting Harold fitted in a classic style black tux including shirt and shoes. Both Jessie's dress and Harold's tux would be ready by noon the next day.

Parking across the street from the restaurant was easy with the lot only half full. Harold took Auggie for a quick walk around then encouraged him to get back into the car.

"They really need to work on the lighting in this lot. Except for the first few rows of cars, you can't see anything," said Jessie.

"Yeah, it is kind of creepy. Glad we're going in the opposite direction."

The restaurant was a local favorite, but it, too, was barely half full. Jessie and Harold were seated quickly at a table with a full view of the bay. The setting sun was a light gray in an otherwise dark gray sky.

Service was fast. Salad and bread followed by the main course, all within thirty minutes. Jessie had glanced at the wine list but ordered iced tea to drink.

As the waiter placed the entrees on the table, Harold said," We'd also like a half carafe of your house white wine please." Responding to the surprised look on Jessie's face, Harold said, "The house wine here is the same as the bottle in your refrigerator. So, I'm sure you'll like it."

The waiter returned promptly and poured each a glass. Jessie slowly drank hers during the meal. Harold did not.

They split an overindulgent dessert as Harold filled Jessie's glass with the last of the wine. His initial glass still untouched.

Raising his glass, Harold said. "I'd like to propose a toast. To a beautiful friend, a magnificent dog, and hope for the future."

Jessie raised her glass to his. As the rims touched, she smiled her stunning smile then finished her glass. Harold's glass was just half full as they got up to leave.

They could see Jessie's car in the fringes of light provided by a streetlight as they crossed the street. It was rocking side-to-side, Auggie howling inside.

Fumbling in her pocket, Jessie found her key fob and unlocked the car's doors from thirty feet while she and Harold ran.

When Harold opened the back door, Auggie bolted. In his now common blur, he disappeared behind a building forty yards away. Blood-curdling screams in both male and female voices exploded from the darkness, barely louder than the sounds of the attacking dog.

Reaching the corner of the building together, Harold put his arm out to stop Jessie. "Let me go first." The rear of the building was completely dark except for a single low watt bulb above a door. The fixture was directed back towards the building, so little of the surrounding area was visible. Sounds of Auggie still on the attack came for the opposite end of the building.

Halfway to the illuminated door, Harold stumbled over something. With his eyes adjusting to the dark, he could barely make out the silhouette of a body tightly curled in a fetal position. Leaning over to touch the shoulder he asks, "Are you all right?"

Uncurling slightly, the person called out in the trembling voice of a young woman, "Ashley! Ashley! Where are you?"

Jessie followed the voice and knelt next to Harold, reached out, found the hand of the young woman, and gave it a comforting squeeze. "Oh sweetie, what's your name?"

"Kari."

"You're safe now."

Pushing herself to a sitting position, Kari hugged Jessie and asked, "Please find my friend Ashley."

Harold advanced again until he came into the small circle of light. He couldn't hear Auggie anymore. A moan came from the darkness and Harold, still in partial light, moved cautiously around a dumpster to investigate.

Dialing 911 from her cell phone, Jessie looked up to see what Harold could not. As he passed the dumpster a shadow appeared from inside. "Harold, look out!"

The figure leaped with the agility of youth and landed on Harold's back, getting one arm around Harold's neck in a chokehold, bulldogging him to the ground. The two rolled in and out of the light as they wrestled for control.

The two women were standing now, but only Jessie was watching as she gave directions and a blow-by-blow account of events to the dispatcher. The young woman's face was buried in her shoulder as they hugged tightly.

The next time Harold and his attacker appeared in the light, Harold was on his back, his attacker, kneeling above him ready to deliver a savage blow to Harold's face. Jessie screamed.

But Harold struck first with a blow to the attacker's sternum that forced every ounce of air from his lungs and drove him backward, eventually hitting the building ten feet away. Coughing blood and struggling to breathe he tried to crawl but collapsed before going three feet.

Scrambling to his feet, Harold continued his search and found a second young woman, partially clothed, lying halfway to the corner of the building, just starting to regain consciousness.

"Jessie, come here." The two clinging women slowly approached, then hurried by the prone attacker, Jessie still on the phone talking to police.

The dumpster rolled twenty feet away after a one-handed push from Harold. With the obstruction gone, a little light got to the scene. Kari cradled Ashley's head in her lap and stroked her face. She didn't notice the glowing red eyes come from the far corner of the building and stop at Harold's side. The light returned Auggie's eyes to their usual brown. His fur was heavily bloodstained, but Harold couldn't find a wound.

Sirens seemed to be coming from every direction, converging on their location. Moments later, flashlights and shouts filled the dark area. An army of dark blue, with guns drawn then holstered as police swarmed. Jessie thanked the dispatcher and hung up.

More cars arrived and drove directly to the back of the building, headlights on high beam until the entire area was as light as day.

Jessie talked with the police while Harold excused himself. "I feel kind of tired, I think I'll wait in the car." Auggie followed. Both seemingly unhurt.

While Jessie held her hand, Kari told a police officer that she and Ashley were new to the area and had spent the day walking around town. On their way back to their car they had gotten confused in the dark and couldn't find the walkway that leads from the pier up the hill and into the center of town. "We saw this guy by the corner of the building and asked him for directions. He said the stairway going up to the market was right behind the building and offered to show us. As soon as we got around the corner, at least three others grabbed us. I was pushed face down to the ground and held by the first guy. The others pulled Ashley away." Kari had been composed to that point in the story but started to cry as she continued. "Ashley tried to yell but they were hitting her and telling her to shut up. I tried to scream but the guy holding me pushed my face down hard into the pavement. I'm not really sure what happened next because it was dark but, I heard a dog's loud growl, a thud, and a grunt, like football players colliding. Then just like that, the guy wasn't on me anymore. I don't know what happened to him. That's when I started to scream. The guys were yelling too, then screaming and running. The dog must have been taking on all of them at once, but I couldn't see anything." Pointing to Jessie she said, "The next thing I knew, a man was asking me if I was OK and this lady was holding my hand."

She said she was sure Harold had fought one of the men, but she hadn't seen the encounter. Kari finished her story then gave Jessie a hug and kiss on the cheek. "Could I get you and your friend's name and phone number? I'm sure Ashley would like to thank you both and the dog, as soon as she's able."

Taking an ever-present Curbside Counseling business card from her coat pocket, Jessie borrowed the policeman's pen and wrote on the back, then handed it to Kari. After giving Jessie another hug and kiss, Kari sat quietly with Ashley.

Police backed up as medical personnel formed pods around the injured. Ashley and two attackers were behind the building, and a third attacker in a parking lot just past the end of the building. Ashley, fully awake and talking, was taken to the hospital for further evaluation, though it appeared she only had some minor cuts and bruises. Kari rode in the ambulance with her. The other three would need extensive medical care.

A medic escorted Jessie back to her car to check on Harold. The front passenger side door was wide open, with Harold sitting in the fully reclined seat, sleeping soundly. Auggie, lying curled up but alert on the pavement by Harold's side, stood and moved to greet Jessie with tail wagging.

Jessie called Harold's name but got no response. She tapped his shoulder lightly but again, no response. Fearing he might be injured, she shook him forcefully and with panic in her voice said, "Harold, wake up!"

"I'm awake, I'm awake," Harold grumbled.

"Oh, thank god. Are you all right?"

Hand raised to shield his eyes from the bright light of the medic's flashlight, Harold rubbed his eyes and said in a groggy voice, "Why wouldn't I be?"

Except for a small bruise under his left eye, Harold appeared uninjured.

Before leaving, the medic said, "If the ones that got away have one-tenth the injuries of the guys we've got, they'll be showing up in emergency rooms around town before long. I'm sure we'll get them."

An old blanket Jessie kept in the trunk, came in handy to protect the back seat's upholstery from the blood on Auggie's fur. She'd wash him off as soon as they got home.

Asleep during the entire drive home, Harold woke as they pulled into the garage. After a yawn and a stretch, he said, "Sorry about being such a party pooper. Don't know why I got so tired all of a sudden."

Out of the car, Jessie called Auggie over to the hose hanging just outside the garage, "Well, I'd be tired too if I'd just got done beating the crap out of a twenty-year-old thug."

"What are you talking about?" Noticing the blood, "Oh my god, is Auggie all right?"

The hose sputtered then let out a constant stream. The bloodstains changed from red to pink then disappeared as they washed away. "Oh, come on now, Harold. Are you trying to tell me you can't remember what happened an hour ago?"

Convinced Auggie was unharmed, Harold walked to the back of the garage and sat on the wooden steps leading into the house. He fixed a blank stare on the floor. "The last thing I remember is letting Auggie out of the car and following him behind a building. Then I woke up here."

As Jessie told the story, she watched his eyes for a glimmer of recognition but saw none. "Well, maybe you hit your head. Do you have a headache?"

"No."

"Is your vision blurred?" Jessie persisted.

Looking around the garage, "No," he answered.

"Do you feel unusual in any way?"

"Just really tired."

"Why don't you go to bed? I'll finish drying Auggie and walk him around a little then we'll be in."

With a hand from Jessie, Harold got up and went into the house. She found him ten minutes later sprawled across his bed sound asleep, having only gotten as far as removing his shoes. She covered him up, gave Auggie a pat on the head, and closed the door.

The unmistakable smells of coffee brewing and bacon frying filled the house. Jessie blinked her eyes several times before her vision was clear enough to read the clock. Seven twenty-five. Drawn by the aroma, she shuffled down the hall tying the sash on her robe as she went.

"Good morning, Harold. How do you feel?"

"Great. And yourself?" Harold replied.

Grabbing a piece of bacon from a plate next to the stove, Jessie answered while chewing, "Good. Say, do you remember anything about last night?"

Harold was turning pancakes and stopped. "I remember

dinner and us talking about something in the garage after we got home but I don't remember anything else."

The phone rang, and Jessie picked it up on the second ring. "Hello."

"Good morning, Jessie. I hope I didn't wake you." It was Randy sounding very cheerful.

"No, we're all up."

"So, did you guys do anything fun last night, like say, kicking the shit out of five guys, saving two young women from being assaulted or worse in the process?"

"Sounds familiar to me but Harold doesn't recall any of it." Jessie watched as Harold tried in vain to get the lid off a jar of honey. "Hold on a minute," Jessie said to Randy.

"Harold, try running that under some warm water."

As Harold walked to the sink, Jessie said in a whisper, "Randy, I don't get it. Last night I saw Harold, flat on his back with no room to wind up, hit a guy so hard the guy landed ten feet away. He would have gone farther but a brick wall stopped him. This morning Harold can't get a lid off a jar. It's spooky."

"Do you think he's faking being weak now?"

"No."

"Well, that dog must be a little spooky too. The guy Auggie brought down at the scene was chewed pretty good, but three other guys ended up either coming to the hospital on their own or were brought in by family. There's blood all over around there. Are either of your housemates hurt?"

Jessie responded, "Harold has a tiny little bruise under his eye. Auggie doesn't have a scratch as far as I can tell."

"I can tell you right now the number of media people he'll be seeing at the dinner tonight just quadrupled."

CHAPTER 18

After a leisurely breakfast, their quiet morning was interrupted by a second call, this time from Yvonne. But the trio was on the road by noon. Retrieving Harold's tux and Jessie's dress, they were back home by two. The balance of the afternoon was spent on mundane housekeeping tasks and a long walk in the neighborhood. At five, Jessie excused herself to get ready. Harold started to prepare at five-thirty.

The limousine made its first stop at Randy Pepper's house at five-ten, then on to Bill St. James's hotel. At five-forty, Randy knocked on Yvonne Jackson's front door.

Opening the door Yvonne said, "My, don't you look handsome. Come in for a second while I get my coat."

It took longer than a second for Randy to plan a response as he looked at Yvonne. She was wearing a form-fitting, forest green, one-piece silk dress that displayed a discreet amount of both cleavage and leg. The view enhanced by matching high heels. Her jewelry consisted of a solitaire diamond necklace with matching earrings and a small tennis bracelet.

As Yvonne closed the door behind him, Randy took her hand and looked into her eyes, saying, "You're stunning."

Yvonne could feel the warmth in her cheeks as she blushed. They shared a soft kiss and a tight hug before leaving.

Auggie came to attention and barked once as the limousine pulled into Jessie's driveway. Harold was sitting in the living room and shouted down the hall, "Jessie, they're here."

"Invite them in. I'll be out in a second." Came the

muffled response.

Harold called from the front steps just as the chauffeur reached to open a passenger door. "Driver, tell the others Jessie wants them all to come in for a few minutes."

Through the open door, the chauffeur spoke to the closest person. Then, one by one, they stepped from the cavernous passenger compartment into the cool evening air. Inside the house, they exchanged greetings, compliments, and shared a laugh at Auggie who was sporting a white bow tie.

Unannounced, Jessie emerged from the hallway and the room got quiet. Her dress was a strapless beaded burgundy sheath with a matching bolero jacket. The hem brushed her ankles, while a slit to mid-thigh gave brief glimpses of flawlessly contoured legs. The package was complete when she flashed her smile.

Taking a half step forward, Bill was the first to comment, "I'm sure I can speak for the others when I say you look beautiful." Words of agreement from the others made the sentiment unanimous.

The smile broadened, and Jessie said, "In your company, I'm just a flower in a beautiful bouquet. You all look great."

She gave hugs and kisses to all the men. When Jessie got to Yvonne, she stopped three feet away, looked her up and down then said, "You're just plain hot." They laughed and hugged.

"Well, we better get going. It probably wouldn't be nice for the guest of honor and his entourage to show up late," Jessie said as Harold helped her with her coat.

During the ride into town, the privacy window between

the chauffeur and passengers was closed and the drapes pulled. Yvonne, Bill, and Randy all tried to pry every bit of information out of Jessie and Harold about the previous night's adventure. Harold was apologetic, "I know it happened because Jessie said it did, but I can't remember a thing. Same with the Corner Market incident." Behind a faint smile, Harold continued, "This afternoon I sat outside with Auggie for the longest time trying to figure out why I couldn't remember stuff. I didn't hit my head or anything. I have thought I might have multiple personalities and that one of them takes over in a crisis. That's the best I could come up with - I'm mentally ill." Jessie reached over to hold his hand. "I'm afraid the media people will be disappointed with my responses tonight."

Auggie was sitting on the seat, sniffing the air coming through the partially open window. "I wish he could talk," said Harold, scratching Auggie's head. "He could probably give a hell of an interview."

"I don't know why you can't remember, and I'm not going to guess," Yvonne said, "but, maybe we can guide you a little, kind of like preparing a witness for testimony in court. We could anticipate the questions you'll likely be asked and help you come up with answers that are direct enough to keep them happy, but vague enough so you don't have to lie."

After some encouragement from the group, Harold agreed. With Randy and Bill acting as reporters, Harold would attempt a response, then Yvonne and Jessie helped reword and spin the weak answers in historic political fashion. The Q and A continued until they were just blocks from the hotel where the event was being held.

While fiddling with some window controls, Harold

opened the sunroof and Auggie was quick to take advantage. Standing with hind legs on the seat, He was able to get his upper torso above the roof, ears flapping in the wind. Harold quickly joined him, and the others took turns as the car moved slowly through downtown traffic.

Media vans lined a side street next to the hotel. The fundraiser was to be held in the main ballroom. The media set up in a smaller conference room.

Everyone was back inside, and the sunroof closed as the limousine pulled into the hotel's driveway and stopped at the entrance. A uniformed doorman opened the door. Harold was the first out followed by Auggie. "I'm sorry, sir, but dogs aren't allowed in the hotel."

The others had gotten out and gathered around Harold and Auggie. With one hand on Harold's shoulder, and the other on Auggie's head, Randy spoke up. "I know you're just trying to do your job, but there are a couple hundred people here tonight waiting to meet this man and this dog. Please check before you make a terrible mistake. The name is Pearson, Harold Pearson."

With his back to the group, the doorman picked up a phone next to the door. After a brief conversation he turned around, his face was flushed. With a contrite tone, he said, "I'm sorry sir. Your party is expected. Please go in."

A woman dressed in a gray wool business suit with the hotel's logo embroidered on the left breast pocket hurried to meet the group as they made their way across the lobby. "Mr. Pearson?" she queried as she looked at the group.

Stepping slightly ahead of the others Harold said, "I'm Harold Pearson."

Extending a hand, she said, "I'm Sherry Conrad, the

hotel concierge. Please come with me."

She went down a hallway and into a room that was obviously an anterior room to a conference room. Voices and movement came from the other side of a heavy drape. "Everything is ready. Would you like me to announce you or do you want to just enter?"

Speaking to Sherry, but looking at Jessie, Harold said, "I was hoping Ms. Baker would enter with Auggie and me and do the introductions."

"I would be honored," said Jessie.

Sherry held the curtain back and the room got quiet. Jessie took the two steps up to the makeshift stage followed by Auggie and Harold. Clicking camera shutters drowned out all other sounds.

At the podium, Jessie looked out over thirty chairs, all full, with a good number of people lining the walls. "Ladies and gentlemen of the media, I would like to introduce two members of our community, who risked their own safety to help strangers not once, but twice. Anyone would be proud to be called their friend. Harold Pearson and Auggie."

Applause and another round of shutters clicking greeted Harold as he stepped to the microphone. He smiled the uncomfortable smile of someone unaccustomed to the spotlight, nodding his head in acknowledgment. Jessie saw his hands tremble as he adjusted his jacket. As the applause dimmed, Harold cleared his throat and started his brief speech. "I just wanted to say Auggie and I are happy we could be in a position to help some people, and because of us, they were not seriously hurt. As far as the men involved in these crimes who did suffer injuries, I'm sorry about that, and I hope you recover soon, but to use schoolyard vernacular: *You started it*."

With his last three words, the room erupted in cheers and laughter from the usually impartial reporters.

Hands went up and Harold's name was called from every area of the room. Jessie acted as moderator and selected questions for response. The preparation in the limo worked. Harold's answers were not challenged. Fifteen minutes later, and after answering several questions herself, Jessie cut in to say, "Sorry we have to leave you now, we've been invited to dinner."

Cameras clicked, and questions kept coming as Jessie, Harold, and Auggie exited the stage through the curtain. Yvonne, Randy, and Bill were ready with handshakes and hugs.

"Well done, Harold," said Randy. "Loved the line, 'You started it'. I'm going to recommend that be the unofficial motto of the Seattle Police."

CHAPTER 19

Sherry Conrad led the group through a service hallway that opened into the main hallway just outside the ballroom. She shook Harold's hand, petted Auggie, and said goodbye to the others. Several couples waited in line at the ballroom door, while tuxedoed ushers read invitations, checked seating charts, and escorted guests to their seats.

As the line shortened, Harold could see into the room. Three large crystal chandeliers, bulbs dimmed, provided the appropriate mood lighting. In a corner at the far end, a string quartet played soft classical music. A long table covered in white linens ran along the back wall. A small lectern, with a microphone protruding from the top, was centered on it.

The bulk of the room was filled with twenty round, white linen-covered tables. Each had place settings for ten people and a six-inch high, two-foot diameter floral centerpiece with three candles.

Serving stations lined the perimeter on two sides with a dance floor and bandstand making up a quarter of the room. Two-thirds of the available chairs were occupied, and a few dozen people moved from table to table, shaking hands and patting backs or trading hugs. Polite laughter came from everywhere.

Harold, Auggie, and their entourage were ushered to a front corner table. Four of the seats were already occupied. Jessie could make out Mr. and Mrs. Kim at a distance. It wasn't until they were nearly at the table, that she recognized Kari and Ashley, the two young women from last night. Both were attractively dressed and wore heavy make-up to hide cuts and bruises.

Being the only one who knew everyone else, Jessie made the introductions, including Auggie. The only part of him visible above the table was the top of his head.

Kari and Ashley started to cry as they walked around the table to hug and kiss Harold and Jessie. Kari said, "I don't know how to thank you for helping us last night." Hiking up her dress a little, she squatted to pet and hug Auggie, while his wagging tail pounded the wall, producing a sound like a bass drum. "Please tell me neither you nor your dog was hurt."

"We're fine and doing even better knowing you two are all right," Harold said.

With everyone seated, several different conversations spawned at once, most of them having to do with people at other tables. Leaders in business, local television personalities, city, state, and national office holders were here, all impeccably dressed.

Waiters made the rounds taking drink orders as the last of the chairs filled. The music stopped, and the Mayor of Seattle stepped to the podium and tapped a crystal water goblet with her fork. "Ladies and gentlemen, may I have your attention?"

The chairs of people not facing the main table were turned and the room got quiet. After a few half-funny jokes, the mayor introduced the first of several speakers. Each was mercifully brief and ended with a compliment on what a fine man the governor was, the good job he is doing, and how the public was lucky to have him running for another term.

On his way to the podium, the governor got a standing ovation, which he did nothing to discourage for a full minute. With a broad smile firmly in place, he finally motioned everyone to his or her seats. Taking note cards from an inside coat pocket he started a speech full of quotable lines about his successes and the shortcomings of his rival.

Auggie had been lying still, but attentive. As the recitation wore on he let out a yawn, audible to three-quarters of the room, rolled to his side, and closed his eyes.

Snickers filtered in from every corner, none louder than at Harold's table. Momentarily caught off-guard, the governor recovered by saying. "There's a Republican in here somewhere, and he's hinting I should wind this up." The laughter stifled moments earlier, rolled through the room. "But, before I go, I want to take a moment to publicly recognize someone whose exploits we've all been reading about. In a week's time, he and his dog were involved in two separate incidents that demonstrate the best in human nature and concern for your fellow man. Please join me in showing your appreciation to Harold Pearson and Auggie."

Leading the applause, the governor motioned for Harold to join him at the podium. Those at Harold's table were the first to stand and cheer. Service staff put down trays to join in the accolades. Harold was soon the only person still sitting. Frozen in modesty.

Like a scene from the Academy Awards, Harold accepted handshakes from the men and kisses from the women as he made his way to the podium, Auggie at his side. With encouragement, Auggie hopped into a chair between Harold and the governor, his head now even with their shoulders.

From a cubbyhole in the podium, the governor took out a dinner plate size, wood framed, chrome and brass plaque and a service dog vest. Several photographers rushed to the front and began taking rapid-fire photos as the governor put the vest on Auggie and handed the plaque to Harold as the two men shook hands. "Please accept these small tokens of appreciation from a grateful community, the vest will act as a key to the city, let me correct that, a key to the state, for Auggie, he's welcome anywhere," said the governor.

The applause roared back to life and from the audience came calls for 'speech'. Leaning forward into the microphone, Harold said, "Thank you" several times and, like before, nodded his head in acceptance. "Let me begin by saying no one in this room is more surprised than I am that Auggie and I are here." A glance at Jessie, then Harold continued, "We are here because a twist of fate put us in a position to help some wonderful people. There are people here tonight that help others every day, less dramatically but equally as heroic. To all those people, I say 'thank you'. To everyone else, I would ask that you be a little like them. Don't wait for fate. Give someone a hand. It may not always work out. You may even get burnt a time or two, but eventually, your help will make a difference to someone, and you'll be the hero. Thank you."

With a wave, Harold stepped back from the microphone. Shaking the governor's hand one more time, he motioned to Auggie and the two headed back to the table. Before sitting, he acknowledged the audience with a wave and a bow as the applause died off.

Back at the podium, the governor said, "Thank you Mr. Pearson and Auggie. Now enjoy your meal. There'll be dancing a little later."

In a flurry of activity, waiters had salads in front of everyone in minutes. The clinking of silverware against dishes competed with conversations to fill the room with sound.

Dinner progressed swiftly but none as fast as Auggie's. When the generous portion of steak was placed in front of him, he looked to Harold for permission and receiving it, consumed the meat in less than a minute.

Harold had iced tea to drink with his meal. Others at the table were sampling wines suggested by Bill St. James.

Just after ten o'clock, the dance band started playing a mixture of rock and roll from the sixties and seventies. Dessert over and tables partially cleared, couples drifted to the dance floor. Many women chose barefoot comfort over high-heeled style for dancing.

The first notes of a Beatles' song began, and Harold

stood, extended his hand to Jessie, and asked, "May I have this dance?"

"Yes, you may," came the response as she rose.

Yvonne and Randy joined them on the dance floor. Auggie jumped onto a chair so he could keep Harold in view from across the room.

Harold eventually danced with each woman at his table and several others including the governor's wife and a very attractive local television news anchorwoman. The crowd laughed as Auggie, on hind legs, dance alternately with Kari and Ashley.

On his way back to the table, Harold passed Jessie and Bill, hand-in-hand, moving in the opposite direction. Yvonne and Randy were sitting at the table, cheek to cheek, watching the festivities.

"Having a good time, Harold?" asked Yvonne as he sat.

"Yes, this is wonderful. Everyone else seems to be enjoying themselves too," said Harold.

Leaning slightly toward Harold to be heard clearly above the music, Yvonne said, "I'm so happy for Jessie. She works constantly and never seems to take any personal time. I don't know if she would have allowed herself to even go out with Bill if it weren't for this. I know she kind of likes him."

Across the room, Bill was holding Jessie close, looking into her eyes as they glided effortlessly around the floor, the perfect couple. Harold never responded to Yvonne's comment. He poured himself some wine, and then some more.

Auggie had come back to the table and sat with his head on Harold's lap. The others soon followed. The band was taking a break. When the Kims announced they would be leaving, Harold smiled politely while accepting another handshake and hug.

In the corner where the stringed quartet had been, a couple of news crews were doing interviews with whoever approached. The anchorwoman Harold had danced with earlier came to the table and sat in one of the vacant chairs and asked, "Mr. Pearson, could I get an on-camera interview?"

Harold started to speak but he wouldn't be heard. A roar like thunder shook the room. At the same time, a ball of flame appeared above the table illuminating the entire room for a few seconds.

There were screams and cries as people scrambled out of the area. Many stumbling and falling in the process as fire sprinklers activated, making the floor slippery. Decorations hanging from the ceiling were burning slowly, dropping embers to the floor, as the room emptied.

Randy raced to the podium and pleaded for a calm evacuation. A fire alarm had been pulled adding noise to the confusion. Bill escorted the women from their table out the main doors, coats over their head to protect from the sprinklers, through the lobby, and to the street. Randy opened a fire door on the other side of the room that led directly outside and shouted for people to take that option. Harold and Auggie helped others who had fallen or seemed confused by the situation or from drinking.

In the street, partygoers huddled with hotel guests and staff against the cold night air. Fire trucks were arriving, inching their way through the crowd. Firefighters leaped from the trucks, and ran to the main door, then dispersed inside after getting directions from their captain.

Police arrived too, blocking the street, and directing

traffic for those trying to leave the area. Statements taken from people in the ballroom were similarly vague.

Standing in the doorway, Randy looked back into the ballroom. It was empty of people now except for the two pods of news people who kept filming from the space in the corner they had been set up in earlier. He walked back to the table his party had occupied and looked around. Everything on, or directly above, the table was scorched. Several firefighters came into the room. A few pieces of smoldering linen were the only things needing attention. The sprinklers stopped, and lights flickered after being shorted out by the water. Some unseen person turned on the main lights, while Randy introduced himself to the fire captain and they conferred in the center of the room.

"I don't know how to explain it," Randy said. "There was a loud noise and this fireball appeared. It only lasted a second or two and then there was a second, much quieter, dull noise when fire disappeared. The second noise was pretty much drowned out by screams."

Righting overturned chairs as they began walking around the room, the captain said, "The first sound was most likely the main ignition. The next, I suspect, a small secondary ignition." Taking off his fire helmet and putting it under his arm, the captain continued. "We've seen fires at banquets before because someone put too much alcohol in some flaming dessert, but that doesn't seem to be the case here."

"No, dinner was over a half hour ago and we didn't have bottles of hard liquor at the tables."

"We're checking all the gas lines now and the fire investigation team will be here soon to take over. If there aren't any gas leaks, we'll probably be able to get people back inside in an hour or so."

Outside, hotel staff was passing out blankets. The valet parking operation had been moved across the street, where people, some calm and collected, some wet and angry, waited for their cars.

Randy found the others in the crowd. They were easy to spot, being the only group with a dog.

Huddled in a tight circle, they didn't notice the tall, heavyset man that had come over and tapped Harold on the shoulder. "Mr. Pearson?"

"Yes," said Harold as he turned to the voice.

Reaching out a hand the man said, "I just wanted to get an opportunity to meet you and thank you for your good works," as he stared into Harold's eyes.

As they shook hands, the big man used increasingly more force. Auggie reacted with a growl and Harold responded by applying a force of his own until the man's smile disappeared and an eye twitch, signifying pain, appeared. Then Harold said, "Thank you." And the two separated and the man blended back into the crowd.

"Does anyone know who that was?" asked Jessie.

"That's Keith Hart," said Yvonne. "He has a food distribution business and is an outspoken activist for the local Asian community. He's been to more city and county council meetings in the last ten years than most of the council members."

"I remember a couple of years ago he ran for some office but dropped out because of some questions about his financial statements," Yvonne added. "He's been kind of low key ever since."

The limo collected all of them before long. Yvonne told

the chauffeur, "Take us for a little drive."

Now comfortably inside, a quick damage assessment showed none were hurt and only Harold, Randy, and Auggie were significantly wet, having stayed back to help others. The passenger compartment filled with the musty smell of a wet dog. "So, Mr. Detective," Jessie said looking at Randy. "What the hell was that?"

Drying his hair with some hand towels from the limo's minibar, Randy said, "I suspect some kind of gas explosion. The centerpiece candles probably set it off. I have no idea what the source of the gas could have been though."

"Well, except for the last twenty minutes, I had a great time," said Jessie, "but I think I'll call it a night." Pushing a button above her head to activate the intercom, she called to the driver. "This is Ms. Baker, could you head to my house please."

"Yes ma'am," came the static-laced reply.

Harold and Auggie dozed during the trip. Randy and Yvonne whispered back and forth to each other, as did Jessie and Bill.

Gently shaking his arm, Jessie said, "Harold, we're here," as they pulled into her driveway.

Wiping his eyes with both hands, Harold looked outside first, then at the others. "Thank you all for coming tonight, that was fun."

"Thank you for inviting us to join you," said Yvonne.

Harold let himself out and called Auggie. He watched from in front of the garage as Auggie visited several bushes. The driver held the opposite door open for Bill, who in turn reached in to assist Jessie.

At the front door, Jessie unbolted the lock and stepped inside, Bill behind her. Harold walked to the front steps but waited while Bill and Jessie shared a kiss. Taking a legal-size envelope from his inside coat pocket, Bill handed it to Jessie then gave her a tight hug. On his way out, Bill shook Harold's hand and said, "Goodnight."

Harold merely smiled.

"Would you like a cup of coffee or anything?" asked Jessie as Harold and Auggie came in.

"No, thank you," came the reply, as Harold walked across the living room. Before going down the hall to his bedroom, Harold turned and with a quiet, sincere tone said, "You looked lovely tonight." Without waiting for a response, he continued down the hall. Jessie watched silently.

As she changed clothes, Jessie watched the news on her bedroom television. It was eleven-forty, but news crews were still covering the events at the hotel. The fireball had been caught on video by one of the cameras that had been set up to do personal interviews. Jessie ran to the living room and flipped on the television and her recorder. She recorded the fireball scene as the news station replayed it over and over along with comments from the fire captain and guests attending the fundraiser.

The cause of the fire had yet to be determined but people were being allowed back into the hotel. Other hotels in the area were taking the guests not comfortable staying in that hotel.

Jessie stopped watching television at midnight but lay in bed thinking about the evening. She didn't fall asleep until close to one a.m.

CHAPTER 20

Dressed in a bathrobe and sitting on an ottoman, her face two feet from the television screen, Jessie played and replayed the recording she'd made of the newscast the night before. Auggie trotted out, slipped his head under her arm, and planted a wet doggie kiss on the side of her face. "Well, good morning, Auggie." From the corner of her eye, she saw Harold and turned to face him. "Good morning, Harold. Say, I've got something to show you when you get back from taking Auggie out."

Behind a pained smile, Harold said, "I want to talk to you too. We'll be back shortly." With that, he put on the coat he was carrying and followed Auggie out the back door.

Coffee was done brewing by the time Jessie got back to the kitchen after changing into a heavy, long-sleeved sweatshirt and jeans. The clock on the microwave showed eight o'clock and the phone rang like it would eventually ring, several times an hour, for the rest of the day. Jessie listened politely and said, "Give me your number. I'll give Harold the message."

After the third call, she turned off the phone's ringer and let her answering machine pick up.

Barking from outside, brought Jessie to the back door. Harold and Auggie were making their way toward the house. Harold throwing and Auggie retrieving a stick as they walked. Once inside, Auggie made a beeline for his water bowl. Harold poured himself a cup of coffee and sat across from Jessie in the breakfast nook.

"Have a nice walk?" asked Jessie.

"Yes, not a lot of traffic, so it was pretty pleasant."

"Well, since you were gone, I've taken three calls from

television people wanting you to come for interviews."

Sounding perturbed, Harold asked, "How did they know I was here?"

"It didn't sound like they knew for sure you were here. They just wanted me to give you a message. It wouldn't take much of a detective to find you anyway. If anyone saw us getting into the limo last night, they could have called the limousine service to find out where you were let out. Or, maybe they got a guest list and called everyone from our table last night until they got a response."

"Well, I can't think of any good reason to do any more interviews. So, my answer will be no," Harold said emphatically. "Besides, I was going to ask you to get me a bit more of the reward money, so Auggie and I could leave. That's what I wanted to talk to you about."

"You don't have to go," Jessie said.

"I'm afraid I do, for several of reasons," Harold said as he stared into his folded hands. "First, this interview stuff may turn into a big mess and I don't want you to have to get involved in it. Your schedule is tight already. Second, Auggie and I have been here long enough. I feel like I'm taking advantage of you. Finally, you've been so nice, that I confused your concern for my well-being with love and began hoping for a romantic relationship. I realized last night that that is unrealistic, so it's better for me to leave now. There's no way I can start caring for you less, or differently."

Patting moist eyes with a paper napkin, Jessie swallowed hard then said, "I don't think anyone has said anything that nice to me in years. I don't know how to respond. Obviously, you took some time to think about this.

Please give me a chance to do the same."

"OK," was the response followed by a long pause. "What was it you wanted to show me?"

Now very animated, Jessie jumped to her feet and said, "Come look at this recording I made last night."

Motioning Harold to sit directly in front of the television, Jessie said, "Look really closely at the perimeter of the fire."

Harold shrugged his shoulders and shook his head. After several replays in slow motion, he said, "I don't know what you see."

Pressing the pause button, Jessie used her finger as a pointer against the screen. "The body of the fire is in the shape of a teardrop. The point of the teardrop is pointing right at you. Like you were a fire-breather."

"But I didn't do it."

"I agree you didn't do it. Intentionally. I watched the tape just before the fire. You hadn't put anything in your mouth."

"So, you seem to have a hypothesis. What is it?"

Auggie had come in and was sitting next to Harold. Jessie never took her eyes off them while she began to pace and began her theory. "In the last few days, I've seen Auggie do some truly amazing things that you can't explain. Two days ago, I saw you hit a guy harder than is humanly possible and shove a dumpster halfway across a parking lot with one hand. You can't explain that either. Hell, you can't even remember it. You might think I'm crazy, but I think, at times, you have super strength, like Auggie, and can breathe fire."

Jessie stopped pacing to watch Harold's face. He started to smile then said, "Yesterday I said I might be mentally ill.

If I believed you, I would have to be."

Hands on hips Jessie, leaned over until her face was inches from Harold's. "OK, Mr. Smarty-pants Genius. Let's hear your explanation again. Start with how Auggie can outrun a car, jump ten feet high without trying, and hit a solid wood door so hard it splintered."

Laughing, Harold said, "I don't know."

Sitting now, Jessie said, "So, hear me out. Maybe you got some powers the same way Auggie did and don't know it. You said yourself: you don't know what he's capable of. I think you're the same. The only difference is he seems to have his power all the time and you don't. Something triggers yours, maybe adrenaline, since you seem to have the power in an emergency."

"If that were the case, why would I be breathing fire last night? There wasn't an emergency until the fire, not before."

"Well, I don't have that figured out yet." Pausing to think, Jessie said, "If the trigger for your power is something else, maybe it gets switched on, then the crisis. You respond, then afterward the power is gone until it gets switched on again."

Harold didn't say anything and let Jessie continue. "After you helped Kari and Ashley you immediately went to sleep. Last night you slept all the way home. The only difference is you couldn't remember helping them, but you can remember last night."

Jessie got suspicious when Harold didn't say anything this time. "You can remember last night, can't you?"

"Well, I wasn't going to mention it, but I only clearly remember until just before the fire. I recall bits and pieces after that, but it's kind of hazy."

Jessie stood and walked into the kitchen. "That does it," she said. Returning with a legal pad and pen, she cleared a place on the coffee table. "We're going to sit here and write down every remote fact and scenario until we figure this out, even if it takes all day."

"You're being pretty optimistic thinking we can do this in one day," said Harold as he moved to sit next to Jessie on the couch.

CHAPTER 21

"We're going to start out with my theory that both you and Auggie have some kind of power," Jessie said. "With that in mind, the source would have to come from something you both had access to, like food, drink, or something in your environment."

As Jessie wrote her three possibilities across the page, Harold threw in another suggestion. "Maybe Auggie had the power from the start and I've gleaned whatever power you think I have from him."

"OK, we can add that one. Any other possibilities?"

Harold shrugged his shoulders. With that, the process of elimination started. They talked at length about places Harold and Auggie had been the last two weeks. All were readily accessible and public, except for Harold's living space. "But I've lived there about two years and didn't have any superpower before, that I know of."

"Sounds like that's not it," Jessie said," So, what have you two been eating and drinking?"

"Auggie eats dog food and leftovers. Nothing unusual, that I know about," Harold said smiling as he waited for the inevitable response.

Face scrunched Jessie looked at the dog and said, "Auggie, did you eat something disgusting?"

From the place across the room where he'd been laying, Auggie reacted to hearing his name by coming over and sitting on the floor between Harold and Jessie's legs.

While making circular doodles along the edge of the paper Jessie asks, "I wonder if it was the wine?"

"What wine?"

"Bill's wine. You said you drank some, did Auggie?"

Shaking his head no, Harold said, "He might have, but it couldn't have been much. I stopped him pretty quickly and the rest just soaked into cracks in the floor."

"It may not have taken much. How big was he at the time?"

Harold formed a rectangle with his hands, about six by twelve inches. "About this big."

"At that size, he probably weighed less than ten pounds. If he drank one-seventeenth of what you drank, he'd get the same dose of whatever was in it." Turning towards Harold, Jessie asked, "What happened after you drank the wine?"

"I don't remember clearly. I think I wasn't feeling well and had to lie down?

"So, you slept for a few hours?"

"No, the next thing I remember clearly is waking up the next day. Unless something else happened that I can't remember, I'd slept twenty-four hours."

Bouncing around like oil poured in a hot skillet, Jessie said, "I bet that's it. Did Auggie seem different?"

With a reluctant step to the obvious Harold said, "He was bigger than the day before."

"How much bigger?"

"Twice as big."

"Yes!" said Jessie, as she sprang to her feet, leaped over the coffee table, and began dancing around in front of the television. Auggie responded to the excitement by running circles around her. Barking nonstop.

Harold sat back and watched, a big smile on his face.

On hands and knees, Jessie playfully wrestled with Auggie, her hands full of hide, and his mouth full of sweatshirt. "I'm going to get you, Mr. Super Dog."

Eventually, Jessie let go her grip and rolled to a fetal position, a flaw in her attack. Auggie took the opportunity to grab the back hem of the sweatshirt and pull. In seconds, Jessie was helpless when the shirt was pulled inside out up over her head, her arms fully extended over her head, immobile. She was bare from neck to waist.

Sitting cross-legged in the middle of the room like an abstract painting of a tulip, she said from behind the thick material while struggling to get free. "Harold, I know Auggie can read your mind, and you told him to do this. So, stop looking at my boobs and get over here and help me before I smother to death, or your next twenty-mile trip into town will be on foot."

Auggie had stopped playing when Jessie sat up and was sitting at her side. Harold crossed the room to give him a pat on the head and a "Good boy." Looking down the cloth cylinder at the top of Jessie's head Harold said, "You, my dear, are in no position to be threatening your savior."

"OK. Please?"

Harold pulled the shirt to its intended position from behind while Jessie manipulated it over her breasts. Looking eye to eye at Auggie she said, "I'm not going to play with you anymore if you take my clothes off again." Tongue hanging out and nearly a grin on his face, Auggie sat clueless with tail wagging.

To the still smiling Harold in a playfully caustic tone, she said, "I hope you enjoyed the view."

"Yes, very much. Thanks for asking. Your breasts are beautiful. But I didn't have anything to do with it."

"Yeah right, Mr. Innocent. Maybe you'll forget this like you forget other stuff."

Already sitting back on the couch Harold said, "I hope not."

"Well, the peep show is over let's get back to work," Jessie said, straightening her clothes as she stood.

Harold told Jessie about Auggie's phenomenal growth over several days after drinking the wine, and examples of unbelievable speed and strength that appeared.

"Do you agree then that the wine is the most likely source of Auggie's power?" Jessie asked.

"Yeah, I guess so."

"So, if Auggie got power from the wine wouldn't it seem logical that you could also?"

Harold had leaned back, laced his hands behind his head and stared at the ceiling. Without looking down he said, "Maybe. But like you said before, Auggie obviously has power all the time. If I do have any supernatural power, it's only occasionally. How did you explain that again?"

Now it was Jessie's turn to lean back and stare, not at the ceiling, but at Auggie. "I think Auggie has power all the time because he's so young. Whatever was in the wine just became a part of him. I think that the power-generating element is in you, but not an integrated part of you. So, it needs a stimulant. If we can figure out what that catalyst is, we could test my theory."

Starting with a fresh page of paper, Jessie wrote the headings Corner Market, wharf, and hotel for each event where Harold had shown possible extraordinary strength or abilities. The page was divided into columns under each heading. Down the side of the page, she wrote each of the five senses along with food, drink, and time of day.

A check mark in each column for a positive correlation and leaving the space blank for no apparent connection, they discussed each possibility at length. An hour later, only three check marks appeared under all three headings. Evening, dim lighting and wine.

"It shouldn't be too hard to figure out if it's any these," Jessie said as she got up and walked out the back door.

As she headed to the barn, Auggie at her side, Harold had to jog to keep up. "What do you plan to do?" asked Harold as Jessie disappeared inside the weathered gray structure.

Without interrupting her task, Jessie said over her shoulder, "I'm going to give you some wine and tie you up with heavy rope."

A minute later Jessie came out with a coil of rope, like mountain climbers use, slung over her shoulder, and headed back to the house. "We'll try it now, outside, in broad daylight. If nothing happens we'll wait a couple of hours and try it again inside, in a dimly lit room, before and after you drink more wine. If we don't have a response then, we'll wait until later tonight for the final test. By ten tonight, we'll know if we're right". Dropping the rope next to a wrought iron patio chair, she said, "Make yourself comfortable, I'll be right back."

"I think she's a little batty, but she sure is pretty,"

Harold whispered to Auggie while they waited.

Video camera in one hand, a bottle of wine and a glass in the other Jessie came outside and continued with her master plan. Filling the glass, she handed it to Harold, stepped back and gave a short narrative to accompany the videotaping, including close-ups of the wine bottle, glass, and Harold drinking the wine. Placed on the window ledge, Harold centered in the viewfinder, the camera would catch any action.

Starting with his right wrist, Jessie firmly tied each of Harold's extremities to the chair. Confident that he could not easily free himself, Jessie held the glass while Harold drank. After the third glass, Jessie pulled over a chair of her own and watched for any signs of change.

Did he feel hot or cold?   How were his vision and hearing?   Any funny smells or tastes?   She peppered him with questions, but the answer was always the same. No change.

"I hate to throw a monkey wrench into your experiment, but I need to go pee," said Harold after sitting patiently for twenty minutes.

As she rose from her chair, Jessie asks, "Why don't you try getting loose on your own first?" But before Harold even tried, Jessie stumbled. He leaned forward and caught her, preventing a fall to the ground.

Looking first at his hands, then at the rope hanging limply from the now bent arms of the chair. She nearly screamed when she said, "Oh, my God, you did it!" Recovering her composure, "Quick, try your legs." With no visible effort, he freed both legs and stood. "It was the wine. I knew it."

She then stood by his side and flicked a lighter to life. Holding the flame, a foot in front of his face, she asks that he speak. Just like the night before, with barely two syllables complete came a ball of fire and intense heat that caused both to recoil. Even Auggie, who'd been quiet but attentive, leaped to his feet and backed up. "Take a deep breath and do that again."

The second attempt produced a small almost insignificant flame. "Well, Mr. Superman, what do you think now?"

"I'm going to need a shirt that says, do not expose to heat or open flame," said Harold stone-faced as they watched the remnants of a potted plant smolder.

"Yeah, and everyone else will need asbestos clothes." They exchanged a glance and then started to laugh. "Hey," Jessie said changing gears, "Let's see what else you can do. Maybe you're as fast as Auggie."

At a dead run, Harold and Auggie circled the barn and returned covering the two hundred yards in a dozen seconds.

"Well, you're definitely not as fast as Auggie but you're still probably faster than any man on earth."

Harold sat down hard on his chair and slouched a bit, watching Jessie in her now familiar three-stride pace. She was talking, as much to herself as she was to him, but Harold was having trouble concentrating. His eyelids were becoming heavy. He dozed off to sleep.

Two hours later, he woke up on the sofa. Jessie and Auggie staring at him from across the room. Sitting, he stretched, yawned, and returned the stare. "What?"

"You don't remember do you?" asked Jessie.

"Oh yeah, the experiment. How'd I do?"

Pressing buttons on the remote control, Jessie made the

television and recorder come on simultaneously. They watched the wine being consumed, ropes breaking, and fire coming from thin air, a spectacular run, and Harold sleeping in a chair. There was a pause, and then Harold was in the picture again, this time sleeping on the couch.

"You do have supernatural powers, like Auggie, that gets switched on after you drink. I don't know if it's just wine or if any alcohol will do it. For all I know, it's not the alcohol at all. It may be something else in wine. Anyway, you became very strong and could breathe fire." Harold listened calmly and without expression, as Jessie continued, "As you can see on the video, you seemed totally alert and oriented, but once you started using your powers, it wasn't long before you fell asleep."

When asked how he got on the couch, Jessie said she was able to wake him and have him come inside and lie down, but he was very groggy. Harold could add nothing to the mystery. His memory was totally blank.

The mere mention by Jessie about consulting a doctor got an immediate negative response. Jessie tried reasoning, "But what if having this power is harmful to you physically?"

"Then I just won't drink. No drinking, no power."

"You think you can quit just like that. No withdrawals, no DT's?"

"Yes."

"Well, I totally support your desire not to drink. Good luck."

On the end table beside her, Jessie took a three-page letter from an envelope. As she unfolded it, she said, "Bill gave me this last night. It's a list of the names, addresses and phone numbers of family members of the poison victims.

Only, one of them, a Joan Leahy, isn't a family member. She drank the wine and got very sick, nearly died, but recovered. I wonder if she has power too?"

They talked for a while and decided unless Joan agreed to multiple counseling sessions, there probably wouldn't be an easy way to broach the subject.

It was after one o'clock already. She had showered and changed into a business suit while Harold had been sleeping. Deciding first to see the families of the three young men who died in the building and offer her counseling service, she would see the others tomorrow. On her way back, she'd stop and pick up something for dinner.

"Do you remember what I said this morning about my feelings for you?" Harold asked as Jessie walked towards the door.

The question stopped her in her tracks. She turned slowly back to face Harold. So slowly, in fact, it was as if she were buying time to form a response. "I haven't forgotten. I promise we'll talk when I get back. Please don't leave."

CHAPTER 22

In a dirty, cramped office in the back of a large warehouse, nine young men were positioned randomly around the room. Some in chairs, others leaning against walls or sitting on the floor in front of, or beside, a large metal desk. Behind the desk, sat the man obviously in charge, just finishing a phone call.

Pounding fists on the cluttered desk, and cursing at the top of his lungs, the leader addressed his troops. "One goddamned defiant owner, now the whole operation is in trouble. Every time one of you goes into a shop, they're on the phone to the cops. I've got forty thousand dollars in food stamps I can't peddle, other merchandise I can't dump, and two of our guys in jail. All because of a stinking wino and his fucking dog." Face red as a beet and spittle starting to form at the corners of his mouth, he looked rabid as he continued, "You guys have made a shitload of money with me and haven't had to do much besides hassle some druggies, whores, and old people. Now you're going to have to earn it. I want those guys bailed out of jail first thing Monday. If they won't get on a plane out of town, I want their bodies dumped where they'll never be found. I can't risk them talking to the police."

Out of his chair now and making eye contact with each man in the room he said, "The wino's name is Harold Pearson. Everybody and his brother are fawning over him like he was the second coming of Christ. The only way I can get the shopkeepers back in line is to make an example of him. Find him and follow him. I want to know where he is every second of the day and who he associates with. When the time is right, he'll die very publicly."

The group filed out and talked amongst themselves briefly before driving off in several different directions. The office was quiet now. The leader sat back into his well-worn chair. It creaked and squeaked under his weight as he lit a cigarette and started to shuffle paperwork on the desk.

CHAPTER 23

House numbers were hard to find but Jessie finally located the one she wanted. The house was small but tidy with clean white walls, light gray trim, and mums blooming in pots on the porch, the yard well kept. It was the home of

Mary Stevens, the mother of Blue, aka Arron Stevens.

Jessie sat out front for ten minutes going over an introduction that she hoped would gain trust. Standing at the door, she took a deep breath and rang the bell. The woman that answered was probably Jessie's age but looked older, tired. She was short with a thick waist, but not fat. Her hair was auburn with solid gray roots. Her tone was pleasant, and she had a faint genuine smile.

Mary listened to Jessie without interrupting, then said, "I've been talking with my pastor at church and, although I'm heartbroken about Arron's death, I guess I'm doing OK. Thank you for coming, but I don't think I'll be needing your services."

Encouraged to hear she had sought out help, Jessie never-the-less wrote her cell phone number on the back of a business card and gave it to Mary. "Call anytime," Jessie said, though not believing she would.

The next address was a thirty-minute drive away. Jessie's mind wandered away from driving. She thought about Harold and Auggie, about supernatural power and how close to death they had probably come to achieve it. What would they do with it? They hadn't abused it so far. Quite the contrary, they had done nothing but good. What would she do if she had supernatural power? Could she resist the temptation to somehow benefit from it?

She pictured herself dressed from head to toe in form-fitting black spandex. Hiding in the shadows at night, ready to take on the pimps, drug dealers, and thugs who roamed the streets after dark. So deeply was she involved in her daydream, that she drove past the freeway exit she'd planned to take. The next exit proved to be equally as good and she was soon in front of the home of Gopher's, aka Jason

Nevers', parents.

Frank Nevers was cold and hard with nothing good to say about his son nor any appearance of sadness at his child's death. After only a brief discussion, he left the room to continue with a project he had going in the garage. Gayle Nevers apologized for her husband's behavior then went on to talk lovingly about her son, tearfully reminiscing about his few successes and downplaying his failures. She did accept a card from Jessie and gave assurances she would call. Jessie figured she would not tell her husband if she made any contact with her, and he would never ask.

It was only three forty-five, enough time to make one more contact. Fighting the almost irresistible urge to go straight to Joan's house, Jessie instead chose to visit the mother of Crazy Larry Jentzen. She lived in a notoriously bad part of town and Jessie wished Auggie were with her. The street had two abandoned cars, stripped to the frames sitting in the middle of the block. Just past those rusting hunks was the home of Connie Jentzen whose house looked as though little or no maintenance had been done to the exterior in decades.

Through a one-inch crack, Connie questioned Jessie. Satisfactorily passing the review, Jessie was let into the house. The interior was worse than the outside. With all the blinds or shades pulled, the house was dark. It reeked of stale beer and cigarettes.

Connie was in her late fifties but was trying, badly, to look younger. Blonde hair with dark brown and gray roots hung straight to her shoulders. Wrinkles around her eyes and across her forehead seemed to deepen with every passing second. She had on a low cut; overly tight top that strained with every fiber to contain her large breasts. Her shiny, blue nylon pants showed every curve, both good and bad. The four-inch high heels completed the trashy look. She was thirty pounds too heavy and thirty years too old to wear the ensemble.

"Did my lawyer send you?" asked Connie, as she sat on the arm of the couch and lit a cigarette.

"No, I'm being paid by the winery owner. But any discussion is purely confidential."

"In that case, you'd better go. I don't think my lawyer would want me talking to anyone from the winery. We're filing a wrongful death lawsuit against them for killing my son. He said I'm probably going to get millions."

Jessie looked around for a place to sit but decided it would be healthier to stand. "I was under the impression you hadn't had a lot of contact with your son for fifteen years or more."

Now defensive, Connie stood and pointed a yellow stained finger at Jessie. "Listen here, we may not have had much contact, but he was still my son, and I loved him. So, you go back and tell that rich winery owner to get out his checkbook. He's going to pay for my son's death."

Jessie tried again to talk but was cut off. "I'm expecting company soon. You'll have to leave now."

Ushered out the door without further conversation, Jessie sat in her car and wrote a half page note about the contact. About to leave, Jessie waited while a car parked in front of her. Two young men in their mid-twenties got out, each carrying a six-pack of beer and simultaneously flipped cigarettes into the street before heading up the walk. Connie greeted them at the door and, noticing Jessie still parked out front, stepped outside. She stood between the two and gave each an exaggerated, open mouth kiss. Looking directly at Jessie, Connie waved and laughed as she openly fondled the bulging groins, then they turned and went inside.

Three of six contacts made and only one reasonable possibility of a second meeting. Not a very good percentage. Hopefully, she would have better luck tomorrow.

Now Jessie's thoughts turned to Harold as she headed home. She made a mental list of his qualities. He was compassionate, thoughtful, intelligent, handsome and a superman who owned a super dog. Unfortunately, he was also ten years her senior, jobless, homeless and, despite his assurances, an alcoholic. She cared about him, but not romantically, and wished he would stay a bit longer. Understanding the heartache of unrequited love, she knew he would probably go. The leaving was going to be painful for both, just in different ways. She wouldn't admit it, even to a close friend, but she was frequently lonely and had been enjoying the company of Harold and Auggie and the excitement it had brought. She would be tactfully truthful when she spoke with Harold and hoped for the best.

Arms loaded with grocery bags, Jessie went into her house to find the table set and a meal already prepared. Whatever it was, smelled great. Explaining that he had scrounged through the cupboards and found plenty to make a meal, Harold put away the recent purchases while Jessie changed into her favorite sweats.

During dinner, she told him about the victim's families and her perception of what the three young men's childhoods must have been like.

He had worked on a project also, while she had been gone. "Since Auggie and I have these powers, we're going to need alter egos with appropriate names." Bending below the table, Harold sat up wearing a black mask over his eyes. With a deep voice reminiscent of a 50's television announcer he said, "Since my source of power is wine, I have chosen to become <u>Thunderbird</u>, valiant crime fighter aided by my faithful canine companion <u>Mad Dog</u>." A whistle brought Auggie into the room. He was wearing a cape and a mask of his own. "We will fight to preserve safety and freedom for everyone. But only after I get a few drinks in me."

"Oh, can I be the faithful trusted servant, slash sidekick?" Jessie asked, playing along with the routine.

"Absolutely."

They talked during the rest of dinner, while they were cleaning up and for more than two hours afterward. The conversation covered so many topics that it became clear to both they were saying a lot of unimportant things to avoid a significant subject.

After the longest pause in three hours, they started talking at the same time. Harold deferred to Jessie.

"First off, I want to say, from the bottom of my heart, what a wonderful person I think you are and what a joy it's been having you and Auggie stay here. I'm flattered that you care for me. But I don't have romantic feelings for you right now. Maybe if we were in a situation where we could go out on dates and get to know each other as individuals rather than me as a counselor, you a client, we could see where it goes. Right now, it would feel odd and be completely unethical for me to get involved with you. I hope this doesn't sound cold, I just want to be as truthful as possible."

She hadn't made much eye contact while she was talking but looked at Harold now. He had a pained smile on his face she was sure was for her benefit, not his.

Harold cleared his throat and reached out his hand. She met his touch half way and held on tightly while he spoke. "After I told you how much I cared for you this morning, then you left, I had time to think about it again. Other than my affection for you, I currently have nothing else to offer. If you will help me a little longer, I would like to get a job and a regular place to live. Then I'll ask you on a date like a normal person does."

"I'd be happy to help. Tomorrow we'll go online and see what kind of job prospects there might be available. I'll bet we'll find lots of possibilities. We can make you up a resumé too."

"We'll have to be *very* creative with the wording to explain the last fifteen years."

CHAPTER 24

The newspaper carrier's car hadn't made it to the next address before Harold was out the front door. It was only five forty-five in the morning and still dark outside. His shoes left a trail on the frost-covered lawn and his breath was a white aura around his head. He had gone to bed at ten but probably only slept four hours at best. Auggie was nearly invisible in the dim light as he ran around the yard expending some energy. Harold waited back on the porch for him but didn't interrupt the dog's pleasure by calling.

To the east were the first signs of a new day. In silhouette by the rising sun, Mt. Rainier was majestic. Her foothills bathed in red, her peak orange, giving way to clouds a brilliant yellow that met the dark blue sky. Had it been five years, or maybe fifteen, Harold couldn't remember the last time he'd seen the sun rise. He followed Auggie inside then leaned back out for one more look.

Much of the newspaper was put aside without a glance. Opening the business section to the help wanted ads, felt tip pen in hand to circle possibilities, Harold started the search. He wasn't going to kid himself. Even his previous stellar job performance wouldn't carry much weight considering the fifteen years since. He would have to hope for entry level.

Three times through the ads produced seven circles. Three of those were physical labor positions, but he noted them anyway because of the desperately worded nature of the ad. Ignored completely were the sales positions, which would require a large amount of interaction with the public. Those would be a last resort.

Resumés were next, but he would have to wait for Jessie to get up to help him with those. So, to advance the hour of her awakening, he quietly but methodically started breakfast, coffee first. The aroma filled the house and was too much for Jessie to resist.

She stood in the kitchen doorway, hair tossed, eyes not quite wide open, and said, "Good morning" mixed in with a yawn and followed by the moans accompanying a big stretch. Handed a cup of coffee on the way by, she headed for the breakfast table.

While eating, she flipped through the newspaper. She read Harold a follow-up article about the hotel ballroom fire. It said no source was found, the damage was minimal, and the investigation was continuing. Three pages later, a story about Jim Stacy facing five counts of involuntary manslaughter, other charges in the case were to be dropped, a trial date would be months away.

If he gets less than a year in jail, Jessie said, the reward money from the missing wine bottle Harold had given to the family might carry them through to his release.

Handed the help wanted ads, Jessie looked at the possibilities circled by Harold and borrowed the pen to circle a couple she thought would be good. They talked about each and ranked them in order by which Harold would prefer, and the likelihood he could be hired. An hour or so spent online produced other potential job opportunities.

Using templates on her home computer, Jessie made three different styles of resumés. Together, she and Harold made individual cover letters for each. Being well-dressed might get him in the door, but it would take a strong personal interview to get the job. He would start the search first thing in the morning.

The plan for the rest of the day was simple. Jessie wanted to visit the last three families from Bill's list. Joan Leahy would be last. Harold and Auggie would go along but wait outside considering Jessie's uneasy feeling during her meeting with Connie Jentzen yesterday.

It shouldn't take long, Jessie thought, since all three teenagers attended the same high school, they probably had lived reasonably close to each other.

During the drive, Jessie acted as a job interviewer and quizzed Harold. After several failed attempts to soften the fact that he hadn't worked in years, Harold decided to try the truth.

Skeptical at first, Jessie ultimately agreed that the sincere delivery was best. But she figured it would take a very compassionate or trusting personnel manager to give Harold any job of significance.

The first house she came to was Michelle's. The

neighborhood was upper class and the homes were attractive but not ostentatious. No one answered her knock, so she left her card with a note saying she would try another time.

Just two blocks further down the street was Mike's parents' home. His mother, Nancy Cabot was home alone at the time. She was trim and attractive. Her short brown hair the same shade as her eyes. She had on a long-sleeved white silk blouse, single strand pearl necklace and matching earrings, green plaid pleated skirt, and comfortable looking low heel shoes. She offered a hand that was soft, with perfectly manicured nails. The touch was cordial but cold. In a meticulously appointed formal living room. that probably didn't get used a dozen times a year, they sat opposite each other in uncomfortable antique straight-backed chairs. Jessie worked slowly to peel away layers of anger and sadness. Sporadically, Nancy would refer to something that would soon need her attention but did not stop the session. Tears formed when she spoke about the amount of traveling Mike's father did and how Mike had been not just the only child, but also a necessary companion against loneliness. Mike's father was a good husband and had been supportive as best he could. She had been thinking about looking for work but didn't have many skills. If she couldn't find something soon she would surely go crazy.

All Jessie could do was to move over next to her and put a comforting arm around her shoulder while Nancy sobbed like she would never stop. The two were soon hugging tightly. Nearly an hour had passed, and she apologized profusely for taking up so much of Jessie's time. Jessie tried to assure her that time was not an issue and she would stay as long as necessary.

Composed now, Nancy thanked Jessie and promised to

see her again. "Would it be all right if my husband was there also?"

"Absolutely," Jessie said as she gave her a card and phone numbers to call. "I stopped at Michelle's house but didn't get an answer. Do you happen to know when I might try them again?" Jessie asked.

A trembling lip preceded the tears. "Michelle's father made it clear at her funeral that he held Mike responsible for their daughter's death. He said Michelle wouldn't have even been there if it weren't for Mike, and although he knew my husband and I weren't responsible for what happened, he didn't want to have any contact with us." Wiping away tears she said, "I know it's just his way of dealing with her death, but it was worse than a slap in the face. Michelle's been over here a thousand times. She was a beautiful young woman that my husband and I were very fond of. We'll miss her too. As far as talking to them, I think the entire family went back east someplace for a while but I'm not sure."

"I know this is hard, but could I ask one more thing?"

"Sure."

"Has Joan Leahy contacted you?"

The question brought the first smile to Nancy's face since Jessie got there. "Joan's been wonderful. She comes by almost every day. She just lives a few blocks away and says she walks over for exercise. She calls on the days she doesn't come by. It truly is the one bright spot in all of this terrible mess, knowing she's getting better. I think she's going back to school soon."

They were saying goodbye at the front door when Nancy stopped in mid-sentence. "Say, that's Joan right there."

Three houses down on the same side of the street, Joan

was keeping a brisk pace towards Nancy's house walking with Harold and Auggie. Calls and responses back and forth across the lawn produced a meeting of the five halfway down the driveway. A round-robin series of introductions ensued. "Nancy, this is Harold and Auggie.

"They were on the news," said Joan, "They saved those girls the other day. When they walked by my house, I recognized them right away. He said a friend of his was visiting you, so I walked back with them since I was going to come to see you anyway."

They had a lively discussion like four old friends until Nancy noticed the time. "Oh my gosh, my husband's plane gets in at four and it's already after three. I've got to hurry. Goodbye, everyone."

She must have been sprinting because the garage door came up just moments after she went through the front door. She smiled and waved as she drove away. The car disappeared around the corner probably going a little too fast in the process.

Jessie introduced herself more formally to Joan. Harold and Auggie were going to stay at the car while Jessie walked Joan home.

"Auggie sure is a beautiful dog. I'd like to have a dog like him someday," said Joan.

Jessie was happy for the conversation starter. "He's a wonderful dog. I wouldn't mind having one like him myself, but I'd have to spend time in a gym first. He's so strong he knocks me down just playing sometimes. You seem to be doing well physically, you could probably handle a dog like him."

"Yeah, I feel pretty good most of the time now, but it's going to be a while before I can do sports again though."

"How about the rest of it. The psychological and emotional parts?"

"I have good days and bad days. My parents wanted me to see a counselor starting while I was still in the hospital, but I said no."

"Why?"

"I think it was just too soon."

"How about now?"

"They still want me to go see someone, but I was hoping that things would get better when I got back in school, so I've been putting it off. Seeing Mrs. Cabot every day helps. Yesterday, we went to Mike and Michelle's graves and cried for an hour. Afterward, we went and had ice cream. I don't know about Mrs. Cabot, but I felt better being able to share that with someone."

The quick pace had slowed to a stroll though neither was winded. "I'm sure she wouldn't mind me telling you," Jessie said, "but Mrs. Cabot says you're the bright spot in her day and she looks forward to seeing you. I guess Michelle's parents haven't been handling their daughter's death well and kind of took it out on the Cabots."

"Yeah, that was awful," Joan said. "My parents and I were standing with the Cabots at Michelle's funeral when Michelle's father came over and said some really hurtful things. For a second, I thought Mr. Cabot was going to hit Michelle's father, but Mrs. Cabot just took his hand and we all just left. Michelle's mom called me the next day to apologize, but I'm pretty sure she didn't call the Cabots."

They were in front of Joan's house now. They talked about how lucky it was that the last of the poisoned wine was found without anyone else being hurt and the reward money was donated to charity. Joan was going to school in the morning and said she was afraid of how the other kids would react. Some friends and sports' teammates had been to see her, so she hoped it wouldn't be too weird going back. No mention of any new or different physical abilities.

The conversation had come to a logical termination point and both had been fighting a chilly breeze by pulling up collars and shuffling their feet. Jessie, like with the others, handed Joan a card. "You can call anytime if you want but talk to your parents about it first. I'd feel more comfortable knowing they were OK with you talking to me."

As she backed up the driveway toward her house, Joan said. "Thank you, Ms. Baker. Say goodbye to Harold and Auggie for me."

Jogging back to the car got Jessie warm again, but she was still happy to find Harold had started the engine minutes earlier to heat the interior. They listened to the last quarter of a football game on the radio and Jessie remarked that they were getting by the stadium just in time to beat the traffic. The lead story on the radio news report that followed the game was about a lost nine-year-old girl who had been out hiking with her family on a popular local trail. She'd been missing three hours and searchers were racing against time to find her before nightfall when overnight temperatures in the area would be at, or below, freezing.

Jessie turned off the radio. The low-pitched drone of tires on pavement and Auggie's heavy breathing as he slept on the back seat were the only sounds. Traffic was heavy but moving well. The thick cloud cover was ushering in the dusk. "Do you think Auggie could find that little girl?" Jessie finally asked.

CHAPTER 25

"I think there are hundreds of dogs that could find the girl. But I don't think there are any who could find her faster," Harold said with a smile and then added, "How long would it take us to get there?"

"About forty-five minutes."

"Well, that's how long we have to figure out a way Auggie can help the girl without ending up on the front page again. Since it's being reported, there will surely be news crews at the scene. We can't let the super dog's identity slip out."

They talked about different scenarios and the responses to each. Everything would depend on the child's health when she was found.

At a grocery store along the way, Jessie bought a couple of cheap flashlights and batteries, some food and a child's plastic toy whistle. One more stop, at a discount store, to buy a pay-as-you-go cell phone, and they were off.

Channel surfing the radio, they heard two more reports about the missing child. Clouds had prevented the use of helicopters and the ground search was just getting fully underway with the arrival of volunteer help.

The leaves of summer were beginning to fall. The hills were splashed yellow and green with an occasional orange or red thrown in for good measure. The air had a pleasant musty fall smell. Sunset and darkness were not far away when they turned off the main road at a sign pointing to the trailhead. Pavement gave way to gravel and the road began to narrow. Jessie parked behind a line of cars that had pulled off along the road a quarter mile from the main parking area.

After a quick reconnaissance, Jessie came back to report a large van was in the center of the parking lot, it's back end, and the area around it for a hundred feet, illuminated by high-intensity lights on portable standards.

From this command post, a county sheriff was giving instructions to groups of four or five, many with dogs, and dispatched them up the trails. Each searcher wore heavy-duty clothing and hiking boots with lugged soles that made a crunching sound on the loose gravel as they walked. Most carried backpacks and some had rescue equipment like ropes and other metal climbing gear that clanked as they walked.

With a scarf wrapped around her head and partially covering her face, Jessie went back while Harold and Auggie stayed just off the road in the shadows. Hunched over a folding table making pencil X's in boxes on the map in front of him while static-filled voices flowed from a nearby radio, the deputy hadn't noticed Jessie. When a lull came Jessie spoke, "Excuse me, I was wondering who I need to talk to about helping to find the little girl?"

When he straightened up, he towered over Jessie. She figured six feet four at least. He looked her up and down quickly and said politely, "Thank you for your concern, but I'm afraid you're not really dressed for a search and rescue."

Still in her gray wool business suit and slacks under a gray wool coat and loafers, she definitely didn't fit the part. Squinting to read his nametag, Jessie said, "I know what I must look like to you, Deputy Wright, but some people consider me psychic. If I could just get a little information about the girl I might be able to help."

Another team of searchers arrived at the same time a raspy voice demanded concentration from the walkie-talkie.

With the officer's attention gone for the foreseeable future, Jessie looked around for another source of information.

Thirty feet away a young woman sat in the passenger seat of an older four-door sedan. The door next to her was open and a young man stood outside the car and rested his head on arms folded on the roof. In the back seat, a young boy about seven years old watched all the things going on around him in silence.

Waving to the young boy as she walked over to the car and getting a finger wave in return, Jessie stopped just short and ask. "Are you the parents of the missing girl?"

The young man turned around and answered, "Yes."

Up close, Jessie saw the desperate look on each parent's face. "I was hoping I could talk to you about your daughter."

"We'd rather not talk to the press right now if you don't mind."

"I'm not the press. I am a psychic and sometimes I can see things in my mind. I'd like a chance to try and see where your daughter is."

The couple looked at each other and Jessie saw a faint nod from the mother. "What do you want to know?" asked the young man.

Jessie found out the child's name is Tina. The family was halfway down the trail, returning to the car when the child went on ahead. Tina was not at the car when the parents got there, so they don't know if she got lost on the trail or was kidnapped from the parking lot.

"This is great. Just one more thing. Could I borrow something of hers for a few minutes?"

From between the front seats, the mother pulled out a fashion doll dressed like a ballerina, looked at it, hugged it and handed it to Jessie.

It was an old doll that had seen lots of use. A third of the hair was missing, its red lips and cheeks faded. Jessie nearly started to cry looking at it.

The sheriff deputy was giving instructions to a group of searchers as Jessie walked by. Trying to lower his voice so the parents wouldn't hear he said. "People on the trail have seen cougar tracks. Be extra careful."

Fighting the urge to run, Jessie held the doll away from her body in partially extended arms and slowly walked the parameter of the parking lot. With an occasional glance from the corner of her eye, she checked to see if her medium routine was drawing attention. Other than the parents, as far as she could tell, no one was watching. Keeping her pace as metered as a bridesmaid walking down the center aisle, she waited until she was out of sight of the parking lot and hurried to the still hiding Harold and Auggie. Had it not been for the glowing red eyes, Jessie might have walked right past them. It would be pitch black in an hour. Time was running out.

Auggie sniffed the doll while Jessie told Harold everything she knew about Tina and about the cougar. She hugged Harold hard and began to cry. "Please be careful," she said and squatted down to hug Auggie. "You be careful too, but please find this little girl."

They stepped from behind a massive fir tree and Auggie moved to the middle of the road. With nose held high, he made a series of widening circles, then started out in a quick trot down the road away from the trail.

"Harold, he's going the wrong way," said Jessie in near panic.

Shaking his head, Harold said, "No he's not. Trust him."

and started off at a jog after the dog, leaving Jessie at the car to wait for a signal.

Fifty yards down the road, Auggie headed into heavy brush following a barely discernible path. Unable to consistently stay on the meandering trail, Harold struggled to keep up through waist-deep ferns and chest high salmonberry bushes. Thorns left their mark on every exposed area of Harold's skin. Ahead he could hear Auggie pushing forward. Occasionally, he would catch a glimpse as the dog went over logs or stumps.

Out of breath, he called for Auggie to wait. It took several minutes for Harold to catch up. In a clearing, on a rise, Harold could hear water moving in a small valley below.

Not waiting for Harold's command, Auggie started out again, moving faster now, going downhill through the sparse underbrush.

The sounds of a river were louder with each step. Harold broke out of the trees at the top of a sixty-foot cliff, at the edge of a waterfall. He didn't know where Auggie was. Water crashing on rocks drowned out other sounds.

Along the river bank below, he could barely make out the form of a child in a yellow jacket huddled tightly against the rocks. Moving towards her from the trees was a cougar. From his position, Harold was helpless. The big cat was stalking, then charged at a dead run.

Auggie exploded from the dense brush in a hail of breaking branches and torn leaves. He met the cat in mid-air knocking it backward, and in the process, positioning himself between the cat and the girl. Recovered from the initial collision, the cougar advanced again. So did Auggie. Even the sounds from the waterfall couldn't obscure the sounds of the fight. Over logs and around rocks, the battle raged, Auggie constantly on the advance against a foe more than twice his size. Two long minutes later, a winner; when the cat ran for the woods and climbed mid-way up a maple tree and settled down to lick its wounds. Satisfied the threat was over, Auggie returned to the little girl.

In fear, both from being lost and witnessing the ferocious fight, Tina was afraid when Auggie approached and she moved closer to the river for safety. Keeping a comfortable distance, Auggie sat and raised his front paw as if to "shake". Combined with a wagging tail and a pitiful-sounding whine, the ploy worked, and Tina came away from the river to pet him.

Back in the woods, Harold made his way down the hill along the river's edge until he could see the girl no more than thirty feet in front of him. She appeared to be all right, Auggie on guard. Harold guessed they were less than half a mile from the parking lot as the crow flies.

From the shadows, Harold pulled a plastic grocery sack from inside his coat, wrapped it tightly around its contents and whistled just loud enough for Auggie to hear. Auggie left the little girl and moments later returned to her with the sack in his mouth. Inside was a bottle of water, some cookies, a plastic whistle, a flashlight, her doll, and a note that said, "Follow the dog and blow the whistle. Someone will come to help you."

Auggie took a slow deliberate path back toward the road while Tina held on to his collar. Like the note said, she blew the whistle frequently with Harold following just out of sight.

From the road, Jessie was pretty sure she heard the whistle but waited to hear it a couple more times before she took her cue. Using the new cell phone, she called 911 and asked to be put in touch with Deputy Wright, the search coordinator. She had information about the missing girl.

From a distance, she watched the deputy pick up the phone to answer then turned and walked back to her car. Using a slightly lower voice as a disguise Jessie said. "Walk slowly down the road and listen for a whistle. Follow the sound and you will find the girl."

"Who is this?"

"Never mind, just do what I say, and you'll find the girl. What have you got to lose?"

Slouched down in the front seat, Jessie could see several people walking toward her, Deputy Wright leading three others. Exactly where she expected, he held his hand up for silence, then they headed into the brush. Waiting a few minutes until they were well into the woods, Jessie started the car, turned it around and drove down the road. After making a sharp turn, she parked again, completely out of sight.

In the woods, Auggie and Tina had covered about half the distance to the road. Harold was still trailing behind. Beams of light flickered through the foliage, as searchers got closer. Tina saw the lights and blew her whistle even more.

Deputy Wright called her name.

Tina let go of Auggie's collar, and with hands cupped around her mouth and yelled, "Over here."

Twenty yards in front of her, the brush parted, and Tina was bathed in the bright light of powerful flashlights. She shaded her eyes to look for Auggie, but he was gone.

Cheers filled the air from all over the mountain as news filtered out that the girl had been found and she was OK. Parents and media waited anxiously in the parking lot, then moved at a dead run in unison when Deputy Wright, flanked by other searchers, carried Tina up the road and finally into her mother's arms.

Darkness came quickly, shielding Harold and Auggie from view as they stood at the edge of the road. He stopped for a moment to watch, then jogged down the road and around a tight corner. "She's fine," Harold said as he got into Jessie's car. "Let's get out of here." From his pocket, Harold removed a screw top bottle of wine and set it on the seat. "Thankfully, I didn't need this, Auggie did all the work."

As she started for home, Jessie said, "My heart's been going a million miles an hour ever since you left. I'm not so sure I can take being the faithful sidekick. I'll probably have a heart attack."

Jessie requested and received a minute-by-minute account of the adventure, culminating in the child's return to her mother. A brief examination showed Harold had suffered greater injuries tangling with berry vines than Auggie did in his life or death struggle with the cougar.

Both Harold and Jessie were animated during the drive as their bodies slowly returned to normal from the adrenaline high. Neither they nor Auggie had eaten since breakfast and it was nearly eight o'clock now. They discussed the possibilities and agreed on fast food. Auggie, the hero, had two triple cheeseburgers and a large order of fries. Together Harold and Jessie didn't eat as much.

A car was parked across the street from Jessie's house and two people got out when she turned into her driveway. Through the rear-view mirror, she could see a television station's logo on the car's side. Without hesitation, Jessie pulled into the garage and tapped the remote control to lower the door before the pair caught up.

First, there was knocking on the garage door then the front doorbell rang. "How could they know about us?" Jessie said as they walked through the house. "I didn't know anyone in the parking lot and no one saw you. The little girl was the only one that saw Auggie."

"This is what I was afraid of," Harold said as he got down on the floor next to Auggie. "If they report about Auggie and the cougar, people could start putting it together. Randy was already suspicious after the incident with the animal control truck's tire. He's a smart man, it wouldn't take much more information for him to figure it out."

The doorbell rang a second time and Jessie moved to answer it. "We can always refuse to talk or just lie. Let's just play it by ear."

On the other side of the door, a young man and woman in their early twenties each smiled through perfectly straight pearl white teeth. "Ms. Baker, we're interns at Channel Eight news," said the young woman, "We'd like to talk to Mr. Pearson about scheduling an appearance on the *Seattle Daily* program. We left several messages earlier today and just decided to drive out hoping to catch you home."

Behind a sigh of relief, Jessie said, "Just a minute."

Up from the floor, Harold drew his finger across his forehead and shook it, mimicking wiping sweat from his brow. He stepped to the door and smiled cordially. It was like looking into the faces of children on Christmas morning.

"I'm sorry to disappoint you, but I'm so uncomfortable speaking in public, I avoid it whenever possible. I'd just be too miserable, especially in front of a live audience."

The smiles hadn't faded yet when the young man spoke up. "Well, would you consider letting one of our show's hosts interview you one-on-one? It could be done anyplace you feel comfortable."

"Give me a couple days to think about it. I'll call back no later than Thursday. Do you have a card?"

Both fumbled through pockets, the young woman winning the race to get a card into Harold's hand. "Thank you so much, Mr. Pearson. We'll be waiting to hear from you."

Behind the now closed door, Harold listened for the car to start up and drive away. "Jesus, murderers aren't as paranoid as we are." They agreed that future adventures would include a well-planned and rehearsed alibi, just in case.

Jessie picked up a notepad and punched buttons on the answering machine to retrieve messages. There was a total of four messages left by the young interns who'd just left and several from the staff at other stations. Yvonne left a non-specific request for a return call. Bill St. James called to say he would be returning to his Eastern Washington winery in the morning and asked for the opportunity to buy Jessie breakfast before he left. Finally, a mother's admonition for not having made an obligatory call to worried parents.

At Auggie's insistence, Harold and the dog went for a trip outside. Jessie returned Bill's call. She told him about the contacts she'd made with the survivors and that Mrs. Jantzen promised a lawsuit. She would fill him in more fully at breakfast.

Just as she hung up, the phone rang. It was Yvonne. "Where have you been all day? My phone's been ringing off the hook with people wanting to talk to Harold. I was hoping for a little direction as to how I should respond."

Jessie told Yvonne about the interns at her door and the

multiple messages she had gotten also. "Just take names and give them to Harold. We'll let him deal with them."

When told Bill was going home, Yvonne said. "And you didn't even get a chance to do some naked wrestling with him, did you?"

"What makes you think I want to have sex with him?"

"Come on, Jessie. He's handsome, accomplished, intelligent, rich, and one more thing... I think you're probably as horny as hell. Should I go on?" Yvonne pressed.

"I'm no match in a debate with a lawyer. If he lived locally, it would be interesting to see what would develop. But I'm not into a one-night stand and I wouldn't even consider a long-distance romance. Those things never work out."

The conversation wandered from topic to topic for a while. Jessie talked about Harold's interest in finding a job and getting off the streets. Yvonne talked about her budding romance with Randy. It took all the willpower she could muster for Jessie not to talk about the evening's adventure and finding the little girl. By the time she got off the phone, it was too late to call her mother. She'd try first thing in the morning.

Harold had come back and just sat down to watch the news. The lost little girl was the main story. Jessie heard the lead-in and sat down to watch. With pictures of a tearful reunion on the screen, reporters told about a mystery woman, claiming to be a psychic, who took a doll from the mother and was not seen again. Phone calls soon afterward, possibly from the same woman, led searchers to the child, who now had the doll. On screen, the reporters talked to little Tina. She said she never saw a woman, that a black dog fought a cougar and then brought her a bag with the doll and some other stuff in it, including the whistle.

When asked how she got lost, Tina said she had gotten back to the parking lot and was walking around a bit waiting for her parents and brother to return. She saw a deer and fawn and followed them a little into the woods and got lost.

When asked to comment, Tina's mother said, "I want to thank all the people who came out today to help find my daughter. To the mystery woman, whoever you are and your dog, thank you so much. You probably saved my child's life."

Wiping away tears and blowing her nose, Jessie took a couple of deep breaths and asked, "It's worth it, isn't it, Harold?"

Not following the train of thought, Harold replied, "What do you mean?

"The planning, danger, and paranoia about being found out. Wasn't it all worth it, knowing we saved that little girl?"

"Yes, I guess it was."

CHAPTER 26

First thing in the morning, Jessie, as planned, called her parents. Thirty minutes of a guilt-heaped lecture from her mother about her lack of contact in more than two weeks ended with the promise to be a more considerate child. The five-minute conversation with her father consisted of apologies for her mother's overbearing diatribe and questions about the weather and her well-being. When Auggie crept into the room unnoticed and planted his wet nose on the back of Jessie's neck, she let out a squeal and said, "Auggie, stop that."

"Who's Auggie?" Her father asked in a stern tone.

Before Jessie could even answer, she heard the unmistakable sound of a phone being picked up. Her mother was listening in. "He's this young guy I met at the office who's been staying here the past week. He's a lot of fun and has energy to burn. He's such an animal, he wears me out in no time, but he can go on forever. Why just yesterday were we playing around in the living room, and before I knew it, he had me half naked."

Incapable of listening to any more, her mother's frenzied voice came on the line, "Jessie Baker, you stop this talk right now. You should know better than to say these kinds of things to your parents. Why in heaven's name do you have someone living with you anyway?"

The charade was up when Jessie, powerless to control her chuckles, just started to laugh. Several attempts to talk failed after only a few words. Excusing herself, she put the phone down and went to the kitchen, giggling all the way, to splash water on her face and took a few deep breaths. Finally composed, she was able to respond, "Auggie is a dog. He belongs to a friend of mine, Harold Pearson. He and Auggie are staying here," and with added emphasis for her mother's benefit. "In the guest room." Jessie waited for a second for the statement to sink in then continued. "Everything is perfectly all right. In fact, they're heroes. I went with them and some other friends to an awards presentation last Friday where they were recognized by the governor for their bravery. I'll email you the newspaper stories."

Without stopping for a response or a breath, Jessie's mother fired off questions. Basically -- who, what, where, when, and how that any good investigator would ask. To which, Jessie replied, "I'm sorry, Mom, but I really have to go. I have a breakfast meeting at eight. I'll fill you in later."

Not wanting to give her mother a chance to prolong the conversation with another layer of guilt, Jessie said goodbye to both parents and hung up. A quick shower and she was ready to leave but had to wait a few minutes for Harold.

Dressed smartly in new clothes, Harold looked every bit the part of a serious job seeker. In a briefcase, borrowed from Jessie, he had resumés, cover letters, and a county map with bus routes highlighted in yellow and Xs at his destinations. The plan was for Jessie to drop Harold off at the first business where he would be applying. From there, he would take buses to the others. They would meet later at Curbside Counseling, Auggie would spend the day with Jessie.

Painfully slow traffic gave Harold a chance to rehearse his presentation again. As they got closer, Jessie noticed Harold frequently stroking his pants leg to dry his moist palms. She offered a breath mint and a few words of encouragement when he got out of the car.

In the rear-view mirror, Jessie could see Auggie, chin on the top of the back seat, staring out the back window. He let out a sad whine as they drove away and stayed in that position until Jessie called him to the front.

Bill St. James was standing in front of the pancake house when Jessie drove past and turned in to park. She watched him walk around to the side of the building and waited until he got to her door and opened it. Together they went in and were able to get a booth next to the window where they could watch Auggie sniff the air through a partially open window.

The waitress was efficient and the cook fast. In less than fifteen minutes, the meal was in front of them. Jessie gave

Bill a nonspecific outline of the victims' family contacts and then tried to find out more about the wine. "Were you ever able to figure out what made the wine go bad, to begin with?" Jessie asked.

Bill put down his fork and took a drink of coffee. "Do you want the long version or the short story?"

"I'll go with the long version."

"Let me know if I'm talking down to you," Bill said. "It's actually hard for bottled wine to go bad. Recently in northern Europe, they found wine in a ship that sank hundreds of years ago. People that tasted it said it was very good. If it was good when it was bottled, about the only way wine can go bad is if it's corked."

"What does that mean?"

"Cork is actually the bark of a tree. Even with thorough cleaning, organisms can stay deep inside and, over time, get into the wine and spoil the flavor. It ends up smelling like a wet dog or rotting cardboard, though it's highly unlikely to become toxic. Since other bottles from the same barrel were good, my staff started looking at the corks."

"Was that it?" asked Jessie.

"They think so. Apparently, we ran low on corks near the end of a bottling run. A worker remembered seeing a box of corks in a storeroom and brought them out. They were cleaned and used. Unfortunately, he didn't tell anyone they had been in the shed with the fertilizers and pesticides for who knows how long. We think the chemicals may have been absorbed by the cork and thus couldn't be washed off. Those same chemicals reacted to the remaining yeast in the bottled wine to produce a toxin. The yeast consumed every bit of sugar in the wine creating a higher alcohol content."

"Did the same thing that happened to the people who drank it?"

"Probably. With all their blood sugar consumed, they eventually went into comas and died. The only reason Joan Leahy is alive is that she didn't drink much. But she might have eventually died, except we figured out the yeast was an anaerobe."

"You're over my head with that one."

"An anaerobic substance can't live in the presence of oxygen. Joan was put in a hyperbaric chamber and her body supersaturated with oxygen that killed the yeast. I don't know why he didn't drink any, but if Harold would have, he'd be dead. He's a very lucky man."

They finished the meal and nursed cups of coffee for another fifteen minutes. When it became evident to both that they were running out of small talk, Jessie quietly cleared her throat, straightened her spine, and spoke. "I've really enjoyed meeting and getting to know you some. It would have been nice if we lived closer and could continue seeing each other, but unfortunately, we don't."

"So, will phone calls or an invitation to visit Spring Rain be out of line?"

"I want to keep in touch and I'd love to visit your winery. But I want to do it as friends, not lovers."

"Well, I'll take what I can get. Who knows, people may stop drinking wine and I'll be out of business. Or all the drug addicts in Seattle will get straight and find jobs and homes then you'll be out of work. Then we won't have any reason not to get together."

In a mock toast, Jessie held her coffee cup and said, "Well, here's to your business's failure and my business's complete success."

Outside, after ten minutes of goodbyes, hugs, kisses, and promises of future contacts mixed together, they drove off in different directions. Jessie returned Harold's tux to the rental shop and paid for the extensive cleaning that would be required to alleviate smoke and water damage. After that, she drove to a waterfront park to let Auggie run. Even the playful pup couldn't lift the melancholia that began as an unblinking stare at the steel gray water. Her throat tightened, and her shoulders shook. Tears streamed to her chin, as Jessie was swallowed-up in waves of sadness.

She would be forty-two in a few weeks and, except for the last two weeks, had virtually no personal contacts. Oh, she knew people all over town. Friends from high school, business contacts, even former clients who had, with her help, gotten themselves together and improved their lives, but she couldn't remember the last time she had been on a date. She figured it was before her brother's death, about the same time as the last vacation she'd had that didn't involve a visit to her parents. Now, a very nice man with whom she shared a strong attraction just left town.

Trying to be honest with herself, she realized Bill would probably make a couple of trips back to see her. She would try and visit him also, but winter was coming. Snow in the mountain passes would soon make traveling difficult until spring. By then, he would get busy; she would go on as usual. Six months from now, the calls would be down to one a month or less and the visits would have stopped completely. Martyrdom had its price and she was growing tired of the cost.

She'd helped hundreds of people, maybe thousands. It wasn't her fault that her worthless, piece of shit brother killed himself. When was her turn? Just close the office, take a month off to travel and come back and find a job, any job, which didn't involve dealing with other people's problems. This wasn't the first time she thought about getting out, but she meant it this time. By the first of the month, she could be on some secluded moonlit beach in the Caribbean screwing some guy she just met and would never see again.

An intermittent electronic noise brought her back to the park in North Seattle. Her cell phone was ringing. She wiped her eyes, blew her nose, and cleared her throat before answering. In a voice still choked with tears, she said, "Jessie Baker."

It was the director of a downtown rescue mission wondering if Jessie could stop in and talk to a young woman that was newly homeless. The mission was between the park and the Curbside Counseling office. Jessie could stop by on her way back to the office.

Auggie had been sitting quietly beside her nearly the entire time and responded enthusiastically when Jessie picked up a stick and heaved it. Adding flare to the retrieval, Auggie jumped over the picnic table where Jessie was sitting and after grabbing the stick, made a wide arc at nearly full speed. He leaped from twenty feet away, and landed at a complete stop on the tabletop, claws making deep grooves in the wood, then dropped the stick neatly in Jessie's hand. Jessie threw the stick for Auggie a couple more times on their way back to the car. In the fifteen seconds it took Jessie to open the car door, Auggie chewed the stick into toothpick-sized splinters, then jumped from the heap of wood chips into the car.

Rush hour traffic was still heavy but thinning. Catching four green lights in a row, Jessie made good time and, with luck still on her side, found a parking space with thirty-two minutes still on the meter and just a half a block from the mission.

The mission was between an adult bookstore and a strip club. Both had neon marquees and large sidewalk signs that made the simple unlit "Rescue Mission" sign nearly invisible. All three buildings had the same basic exterior above street level. Three-story gray brick, the windows dirty, single pane, wood framed with peeling paint.

In front of the strip club, Jessie saw a brutish man trying to make eye contact with everyone who passed, encouraging them to stop in, or at least take a promotional flyer. "Jessie," he said as she walked by, "We've got a couple of new girls you should check out. They're not as hot as you but pretty nice. I'll get you in for half price."

When she first met him six months ago in the hospital, he was emaciated and nearly comatose due to a raging blood infection from a dirty needle. Now he looked like a healthy twenty-eight-year-old. He'd gained back his lost weight and then some, probably about two fifteen on his five-ten frame. "The offer is tempting, Willie, but I think I'd rather put my eye out with a broken beer bottle. Thanks anyway." Going on the offensive, she asked, "You still shooting up?"

"Nope, haven't done any since I started rehab four months ago, thanks to you."

"I'm glad. Why don't you do me a favor and find yourself a different job? You're plenty smart enough."

Sounding almost sincere, he said, "I plan to as soon as I get a little money ahead, but right now I'm having the most fun I ever had without being loaded. I get to see all the ladies, even backstage. Sometimes, I'll escort them home if you know what I mean."

"Well, don't stay down here too long or you'll never get out."

Feeling like his mother was chastising him, Willie changed subjects. "Nice-looking dog you got there."

"Belongs to a friend of mine, I'm just watching him. Well, take care of yourself. Stay clean."

Looking back from the rescue mission door, Jessie saw Willie hadn't missed a beat. He was holding the strip club door open to give a couple of guys a quick peek, sufficiently enticed, they went in.

In the mission director's office, Jessie got the story on her latest challenge. Brittany was a twenty-year-old who had followed her soldier boyfriend from Iowa to Washington. They lived together for a few months, but money was tight, and he was unhappy. Without telling her, he applied for and received a European assignment and left with only a day's notice. She couldn't make the rent payment on her own and had been evicted. She still had a job but would need a place to stay for a few weeks until she would have enough money to pay off a couple of debts then buy a ticket back to Iowa.

Not too hard, Jessie thought. Arrange a four-week stay at a women's shelter and a bus pass for commuting. With her connections, it would be simple.

"One more thing," Brittany said, almost as an afterthought, "I might be pregnant."

The complexity of the task shot up exponentially. She would need a confirmation test and a doctor visit if the test came back positive. Then a monumental decision, would she abort, adopt out, or keep the child? Any of the three choices led to another list of complications. What a mess.

Several rapid-fire phone calls later, Brittany was set up

with appointments at Planned Parenthood and the women's shelter. Jessie said she would be available if other problems arose, but if Brittany failed to follow up, even once, the help would stop. Tough love.

Back on the street, Willie waved but didn't say anything as Jessie walked back to her car. Only ten o'clock. In an hour, the lunch crowd would start filling up the club to eat bad food and watch girls like Brittany, who never got help, parade on stage in thongs and spiked heels. Today it would be harder to admit, but it was still worth the effort.

A bad choice of routes landed Jessie smack in the middle of a construction project where traffic ground to a halt. Front loaders and dump trucks lurched around in front of her while men and women in bright orange vests watched from several different positions. For a moment, she drifted back to the tropical island where she was being caressed by the strong hands of a faceless man until blaring horns from behind commanded attention and action.

The Curbside Counseling office wouldn't be open for a couple more hours. She'd do a little paperwork, send off newspaper stories about Harold to her mother, then sit back in the chair with her feet on the desk and take a fifteen-minute power nap. Maybe even walk Auggie around the block before opening. But first, she had to make a phone call.

She was put on hold, forced to listen to bad elevator music consisting of instrumental renditions of classic rock-n-roll songs, for ten minutes before finally getting connected.

"Detective Pepper."

"Good morning, Randy. It's Jessie Baker, I was hoping to weasel a favor out of you."

"Sure, what can I do for you?"

"I was wondering if you could use whatever resources are at your disposal to find Harold's son? I tried several times using the Internet but didn't get anyplace."

"Well, I'd be happy to give it a shot. What have you got for information?"

Reading from a thin file folder, Jessie told Randy everything Harold had told her and the little extra she was able to gather on her own. It really wasn't much. The most current information was over fifteen years old and that trail dead-ended in Winslow, Arizona.

After Harold's wife died, his sister-in-law took in his son, and they continued to live in the San Francisco Bay area. About six years later, his brother-in-law was killed in a traffic accident. Two years after that, the sister-in-law remarried and moved with her new husband and Harold's son to Arizona. Harold had gone to Winslow but didn't have his sister-in-law's new name, and even though it's a small town, he couldn't find them. He really had no firm proof they were even still there at the time. His son would be twenty-eight. His name is Steven Preston Pearson.

"Well, that's all I have except for some old addresses and phone numbers of other relatives. I'll just email those." Jessie said.

"I suspect if I mention Harold's name to my captain, he'll let me have half an hour of computer time. It shouldn't take much longer than that. Are you going to be in the office later?"

"Yeah, I'll be here until ten. I suspect Harold will be here around six. He's out job hunting."

"Really? Good for him. Well, I'll try to have something for you later today."

The small radio in the corner of her cubicle was tuned to a classical music station with just enough volume to cancel out street noise and other miscellaneous sounds. With her high-backed swivel chair rocked as far back as it would go, Jessie put her feet on her desk and dozed off, Auggie on the floor beside her.

CHAPTER 27

The receptionist was young, attractive, and efficient, juggling phone calls while working on the computer and directing people as they came through the door. She smiled at Harold and mouthed "one second", while she finished a call. He asked for and received directions to the Personnel Department and a "good luck" as he walked down the hall.

The secretary in Personnel wasn't nearly as nice. Barely looking up from her desk, she handed Harold a clipboard with the company's standard employment information sheet and pointed to a row of computers where he could sit to fill it out. Looking it over, Harold figured it wasn't a lot different from what he would be required to do if he applied at some fast food restaurant.

Form completed and returned with his resumé, Harold watched as the secretary stapled the papers and phoned to someone else that an applicant was present. Before long, a young man Harold guessed to be about thirty-five came down a short hallway, picked up the paperwork and said, "Mr. Pearson?"

He introduced himself as Jeff Collingsworth and together they walked to a back office. "Are you the same Harold Pearson that was just on the news last Friday?" he asked while pointing Harold to a chair directly in front of his desk.

"Yes."

"That was a nice thing you did helping those people."

"Thank you. I was glad to do it."

Collingsworth got quiet while he read through Harold's resumé. It didn't take more than thirty seconds for the dreaded question to be asked. "There doesn't seem to be any job history for many years. What have you been doing?"

Though the answer was well rehearsed, Harold still fumbled with his words a bit before he got started. "After a family tragedy, I quit my job and began traveling up and down the west coast. I've been in Seattle a couple of years and now want to reestablish myself."

With nary a raised eyebrow, Collingsworth continued, "The position you're applying for is an entry level architectural engineer. Have you done anything to keep current in the field?"

"I was able to keep current on the literature at the public library. As for technical aspects, I routinely have gone to the university's computer lab to familiarize myself with the applications of some of the newer engineering programs." Harold even impressed himself with how intelligent he sounded. Especially, since he was stretching the truth a bit.

"This company is in the second year of a multimillion-dollar, five-year contract to do seismic safety retrofitting on city and county-owned structures. Any thoughts on that?"

"Your company must have made a great presentation to get the contract in the first place. As far as the retrofitting, it's long overdue."

Collingsworth asked a few more questions, answered several, and then gave Harold a quick tour. Back at the personnel office waiting area, they shook hands then Harold said. "I planned on applying for several other positions today. Would you be honest with me and tell me what you think my chances are?"

Over Collingsworth's shoulder, Harold watched as the surly secretary, who had been writing, stopped but didn't lift her head.

"Your frankness is refreshing, Mr. Pearson considering the usual 'yes sir', brown-nosing I usually get. So, I will be equally as candid. It was reported on the news that you were a homeless transient. I suspect that's close to the truth. Even though you present yourself well, that's a huge hurdle to overcome. I will recommend you for a second interview done by the technical staff. But I must admit it would be very unlikely that you will be hired."

The anticipation of rejection never has quite the same effect on your psyche as the real thing. Standing outside, Harold looked over his bus route map then started the three-block walk. Head up, he went over possible scenarios to be played out in other personnel departments. It always came out the same, and he couldn't blame them. No work history, no job.

The bus had a total of ten passengers, counting him. An elderly woman sat two rows behind the driver and a young man in the last row. Others sat randomly alone or in pairs. Harold chose a seat six rows back and stared out the window at nothing in particular. He thought about Auggie and then Jessie, caught himself smiling and felt invigorated in his effort to find work. His stop was the one after next, so he moved to the aisle seat in anticipation.

The bus rocked and lurched on its way through traffic

and the young man who had been sitting in the back made his way forward, balancing himself by holding on to the backs of the seats as he walked. He stopped just behind the woman apparently ready to get off at the next corner.

As the bus slowed and turned toward the curb, Harold saw a box cutter drop into the man's right hand, while his left reached for the strap of the handbag draped around the woman's neck. Harold stood just as the bus came to a stop and the door opened. In one lightning move, the young man slit the strap and lunged for the door, purse in hand.

Leaning over the rail at the front of the bus, Harold was able to reach out, grab a handful of dreadlocks and pull. Off balance, the young man lurched backward, striking his head on the bus doorframe. Harold repeated the action two more times before shoving the man forward with enough force to send him sprawling.

Screams echoed from inside the bus when the woman realized she'd been robbed. The driver was on the radio calling for the police. On the sidewalk, Harold stood on the cut strap, briefcase raised above his head ready to deliver a blow if necessary.

With his clandestine plan exposed, the young man scrambled to his feet. Harold told him to "forget it when he looked down at the purse. Brakes squealed, and horns blared as he made his escape dodging mid-block traffic, crossing the street, and disappearing around the next corner.

Sirens were converging from several directions. In minutes, police would surround the area. Harold tossed the purse to the bus driver and without a word walked away at a pace just shy of a jog. Half a block later, he went into a department store then exited a few minutes later on a side street from the lower level parking garage, crossed the street and when into a coffee shop. Going directly to the restroom, he occupied a stall for almost twenty minutes, using the time to curse himself for nearly becoming another news item, before coming out to read a newspaper and nurse a cup of coffee.

He watched from the corner of his eye, as a bicycle patrol officer came in, got a coffee, and chatted with a cute waitress. Having already paid, Harold got up and walked out, took a quick look in both directions and, not seeing any unusual activity, was on his way.

He was unsuccessful getting even a preliminary interview at the next two businesses to which he applied, having to settle for just dropping off his resumé. The next business on his list was an hour's bus ride counting two transfers.

A pair of mischievous toddlers bounced on the seat in front of him and stared while jabbering away in a language only their mother could translate and respond to. Though not going very fast, when the bus suddenly braked to avoid people in the crosswalk, the youngest child nearest the window, lost his grip. He reeled backward and sideways, striking his head on the window. The resulting wailing waxed and waned for fifteen minutes, though other than a bump on the head no real damage was done to the child.

As he passed on his way to get off the bus, Harold noticed the now-silent child apparently nursing from a well-concealed breast, while his mother sat with eyes closed, the second toddler sat quietly manipulating a small toy car.

~*~

Ashcroft Architecture and Design was housed in what was once a large two-story single-family home. Probably once isolated, the area zoning had changed to allow the current six square block business district to develop. The house itself was well maintained. A concrete walkway bordered with well-kept shrubs led from the front door down a gentle slope to a parking area along the side that could accommodate three or four cars where a garage had previously been. A meticulously maintained twenty-year-old Mercedes sedan was the only car there. An attractive carved wood sign in the front yard announced the business.

Harold took three steps up to a large covered porch that ran the length of the front of the house. A hanging wooden swing at one end helped the building keep its homey quality. A gold-colored plaque on the front door advised visitors to *Please Come In*. Standing in the entryway, Harold was looking down a wide hallway with two open doors on the right side, on the left one closed door and a stairway to the second floor, beyond that what was once, and may still be a kitchen. He could hear a radio playing in a back room and smelled coffee, but no one was immediately apparent.

"Anyone around?" Harold finally asked.

Shadows from inside the room crept towards the furthest doorway on the right. A wheelchair, deftly powered by a slightly built gray-haired man in his mid-seventies, turned into the hallway, and approached. Crisp white shirt, dark paisley tie, and navy pants over black wing tips. Old school business attire.

"Good afternoon, Harrison Ashcroft here. How can I help you?"

Harold introduced himself and said he was responding to an ad for an architectural engineer.

As he began to rotate his wheelchair, Ashcroft said, "Well, come on back, Mr. Pearson. Let's talk."

Harold followed him to a room that was much bigger than he expected. Books took up one wall with a drafting table and two desks at one end and a small couch and two chairs at the other. A computer on one desk was running a state-of-the-art architectural program Harold had seen in the engineering department at the University of Washington.

Directed to the most comfortable chair, Harold sat and started to go through his briefcase for a resumé. Ashcroft wheeled to a position directly in front and four feet away and said, "Never mind the paperwork for now. You can leave it with me before you go."

Ashcroft began to ask questions; sometimes very technical. Harold found himself to be comfortable with the more specific questions and Ashcroft seemed to be satisfied with the answers.

"Let me tell you about the business," Ashcroft said in a change of pace. "I started this company almost forty years ago. It was a family business. My wife and son both worked here. My wife passed away two years ago, and my son decided last year to retire at fifty-two and moved to Arizona. He wanted me to go with him, but I wouldn't have anything to do there, so I gave him my blessing and sent him on his way. I have a daughter and her family still here. My granddaughter is still in high school and comes in and works some but she's a very busy young woman."

He paused briefly to offer Harold coffee then continued when Harold declined. "I specialize in designing upscale custom homes. I do at least two a month. With all the computer millionaires around, business is booming. Here you would answer your own phones, do your own typing, and get your own coffee. I work weekends only when I have to, and the client pays dearly for it. Any questions, Mr. Pearson?"

At that moment, the phone rang, and Ashcroft wheeled himself to the closest desk to pick it up. Harold looked around the room, then watched as Ashcroft propped the phone receiver with his shoulder and unrolled a twenty-page house blueprint he had removed from a cubbyhole beside the desk. A builder was obviously questioning a design component. Ashcroft handled him perfectly.

He had only been here twenty minutes, but Harold felt very comfortable in the home-like setting with the amiable, straightforward Ashcroft. He felt compelled to be brutally honest.

Phone call complete, Ashcroft came back over, "I got a twenty-nine-year-old builder trying to tell me my design is flawed. Turns out he put a wall in the wrong place. I swear you'd think that someone building a five-million-dollar house could find a builder that could read a blueprint." They both chuckled, and Ashcroft asked, "Well, did you have any questions?"

"Before we go any further, I want you to know that although at one time I was a very good architect, for years I've been nothing more than a transient. I collapsed after a personal tragedy and am just now trying to reestablish myself." Harold watched for any sign of a response but saw none. "I would love to come work with you, but you'll certainly be taking a big chance that other agencies would never even consider."

"Now it's my turn for a confession," Ashcroft said, "I recognized you from television the minute I saw you. I told myself right then if you mentioned helping those people, even casually, I wouldn't consider you. I didn't want someone around who would try and profit from a selfless act of heroism. To your credit, you said nothing about it. So, leave your resumé. If everything on it checks out, you've got a job. Give me a call, say Wednesday."

Out of his chair like a shot, Harold thanked Ashcroft with the exuberance of a teenager and started toward the hall.

"Your car isn't out by mine. Where'd you park?" Ashcroft asked.

"I don't have a car. Frankly, I don't even have a driver's license. I took the bus."

"Well, you're going to have to get your license back and get a car to work here. We do a lot of driving."

"I'm sure I can do that."

"Good. By the way, you never asked what the position pays."

Excited about the possibility of a job, Harold realized Ashcroft was right. "OK, what does the job pay?"

"You'll start with a salary of eight hundred a week and a ten percent commission on each project you finish. After you get established, you'll be on straight commission."

Harold had to work hard to stay composed when Ashcroft added, "My last year's net was two hundred eighty-five thousand and I turned down a lot of work I couldn't get to."

"In light of my background, that would be more than generous. Considering the pay, I'm surprised every architect in town doesn't want to work here."

Ashcroft chuckled, "The good ones look at this place and

drive by without ever coming in, not much prestige here. The bad ones, I either offer a very small starting salary, or I don't offer a job at all. You're only the third person to get a salary offer. Of the other two, one was only a junior in college who at the last minute told me he could only do about fifteen hours a week depending on his class schedule. The last showed up with short spiked blonde hair and three or four prominent facial piercings. I could handle that, but she had a know-it-all attitude that pissed me off. I felt insulted talking to her, so I offered her a salary that was equally insulting out of spite. In retrospect, it was a childish thing to do. Thankfully, she didn't take it. Hell, she'd probably sue me if she heard what I just offered you."

Harold could hear callused hands rubbing lightly against the chair's wheels as Ashcroft followed him down the hallway toward the door. With one hand on the knob, Harold turned to thank Ashcroft. To his surprise, Ashcroft had stopped ten feet away and was in the process of standing. With a shuffling gait and a pain induced wince, Ashcroft managed the last ten feet and shook Harold's hand.

"Wondering about the wheelchair?" Ashcroft said. "I took a fall recently and bruised my hip. I have to limit my walking whenever possible for a month or so. Hopefully, I'll be back playing tennis at the gym soon. Until then, I'm limited to swimming a couple days a week."

Final greetings said, Harold only got to the sidewalk before stopping to look back at the house that might soon be his place of employment. Satisfied he had committed every detail to memory he started toward the bus stop. The ride back into downtown was exhilarating.

CHAPTER 28

The short nap Jessie had planned lasted half an hour and would have been longer if the phone hadn't rung. She let the answering machine pick up while she stretched and worked the kinks out of her neck. It was just noon and the classical music she had been listening to on the radio gave way to the news. She wasn't paying attention until a story came on about an attempted purse-snatching on a city bus that was thwarted by a middle-aged rider who then left the scene before the police could interview him.

"Was it Harold?" Jessie asked Auggie. A bobbing head and wagging tail his response. "Did he break his promise and have a drink. In that case, he might be sitting in some doorway in his new clothes by now sleeping. Maybe it wasn't him at all. Some other well-meaning man could have done it. The only way to know would be to go look."

Jessie figured Auggie could find Harold in a heartbeat if he were sleeping it off someplace. She grabbed her coat. At attention since Jessie first started talking to him, Auggie was eager to do whatever it was she was planning to do.

The phone rang again, and Jessie waited for the answering machine to pick up, so she could hear who was calling. Nancy Cabot, the mother of Michael Cabot, one of the teens that had died, was leaving a message.

"I just dropped my husband off at the airport again," she said in a tone that sounded forlorn, "and was driving around aimlessly. I was thinking about stopping in to see you. I see by your card your office doesn't open until two."

From the background noise, Jessie guessed Nancy was calling from her car. Able to pick up before Nancy finished,

Jessie said. "Hello, Nancy. I'm not busy right now why don't you come on over. Where are you now?"

"I think about two blocks away. I'm not exactly sure where your office is."

Jessie gave directions and walked outside, cordless phone in hand. Nancy pulled up a few minutes later and they laughed at seeing each other while still on the phone. A car was just pulling out of a space just down the street and Nancy held up traffic waiting for the spot.

Auggie, nose to the pavement, made slow circles around Jessie but stopped to look at her when she said, "If I don't hear from Harold by the time Nancy leaves, and there's still time before the office opens, we'll go drive a bit."

"It's not much," Jessie said as they walked through the waiting area. "But it's functional."

"How many people do you see in a day?" asked Nancy.

"On an average, I'd say eight to ten and maybe twice that many phone calls. The only services we provide are referrals to homeless shelters, battered women's shelters, food banks, drug centers, and places like that. When the office isn't open, we take turns stopping at the shelters and missions a couple times a day."

Jessie offered a chair then, instead of going behind her desk, turned another chair to face Nancy and sat.

Nancy took off her coat, slipped it over the back of the chair then asked, "Who is 'we'? You seem to be the only person here."

"There is a couple of part-time paid staff, but I sent them to a conference in Portland. Mostly this place runs with volunteers. UW, Seattle U., and City University all have social work programs. So, every fall, I train a half-dozen interns and we manage to get through until spring. Training will be starting this week."

"Is this something you think I could do?"

"Of course, you could. The only requirement is wanting to help someone and being able to dial a phone. But I need to warn you; a lot of the clients that come in are very marginal in personal hygiene and social skills. Even some of the higher functioning ones have chosen lifestyles that many people find highly unusual all the way to disgusting," Jessie said.

"Like what?" asked Nancy in an apprehensive tone that wasn't there a second ago.

Jessie began to rattle off a list like naming flavors at an ice cream shop. "Well let's see, we have your alcoholics, drug addicts, hookers, and transvestites. Some are heavily tattooed or have multiple piercings in places you can see, and in other places, you don't want to. Then there are the mentally ill or recent parolees, maybe a homeless preteen, senior citizen, or any combination.

It doesn't take long before what shocks you most will be when a normal-looking person comes in. Most of the time when that happens it's because they have the wrong address."

"You seem to handle it well."

"Believe me, I certainly didn't start out this way. I was scared out of my mind most of the time for the first six months. I think the turning point for me was when I looked at them less and started listening more. I realized they are someone's parent, child, brother, or sister and were asking me for help."

Buoyed, Nancy asked, "When can I start?"

"If you have time, you could hang around here for a

while today and if that's not enough to scare you away, tomorrow evening a new training session starts."

For more than an hour, Jessie talked about typical problems she dealt with and flipped through the Rolodex explaining the resources available to solve each one. "Sometimes you won't have an answer or at least one that's acceptable to the person. Like one time a young girl came in, said her mother was a drunk and her father was sexually abusing her. I wanted her to tell the police, get her into a foster home or a shelter, then start counseling, but she was too afraid of what would happen. She had other siblings at home."

"What did you do then?" Nancy asked.

"Wrote down all the information for her, told her she could come back any time and said goodbye."

"Why didn't you just call the police?"

"I do that and pretty soon no one will come here. I just have to hope they eventually take my advice."

Nancy had gotten quiet and Jessie felt the need to lighten the mood. Walking to a large folding table that served as a break room Jessie hugged the coffee maker. "This is one of the most important tools in the office. If you can make a decent cup of coffee, you will earn the undying admiration of clients and staff."

A key turned in the lock and the door slowly opened as the key was being removed. Jessie stood on tiptoes to see over the office's partitions. Auggie sprang to his feet and went to a place six feet from the door. Ears at attention, hair raised, and a soft low growl coming from deep in his lungs, he became an immovable force. "Holy shit," Yvonne Jackson said in a startled yell when she stepped into the office to face him.

Nervous laughter followed after Auggie recognized Yvonne and trotted over with tail wagging to welcome her and receive a pat on the head in return. "You scared the crap out of me."

Jessie and Nancy had come up from the back. Jessie asked, "So, how do you like the new security system I had installed?"

"Very effective," Yvonne said, "But we're going to have to put a shower in the bathroom and have extra clothes on hand, so people can clean themselves up if he greets everyone like he did me."

"Nancy Cabot, this is Yvonne Jackson, the best lawyer in Seattle and my very good friend."

As they shook hands, Jessie added, "Nancy is considering becoming a volunteer."

"We'd be thrilled to have you," Yvonne said.

"Well I really haven't been out of the house much, so for me, it's kind of intimidating," Nancy said.

"Jessie's the best at finding people's strong points and putting them to good use."

Yvonne walked to the back, hung up her coat and poured herself some coffee. Jessie had turned over the OPEN sign in the window, then she and Nancy sat across the desk in Yvonne's cubicle and the three talked for ten minutes before the first client contact came by way of a phone call.

It was a request from a local hospital's social worker for an emergency housing referral. A quick flip of the Rolodex and Jessie was able to provide the necessary information. The phone rang intermittently for the rest of the afternoon. Yvonne and Jessie alternated taking calls while Nancy listened.

The first walk-in client came just after three. He was in his late twenties, tall and gaunt. Brown eyes set deep and surrounded by dark brown circles, collar length auburn hair thin and greasy. Several layers of clothes could not hide the emaciated frame. Just inside the door, he slumped into one of the chairs, dropping the backpack he carried beside him. Auggie watched without reaction.

Jessie had stood to look over her cubicle wall when the door opened, then came out to meet him, with Nancy right behind.

"Bret," he responded when Jessie asked his name.

"How can we help you?"

He started to talk but began to cough forcefully as he buried his face into the bend in his left arm. He pulled a ragged blue handkerchief with crusted blood on the edges from an inside pocket to cover his mouth.

Composed he started again. "I got your card from a bulletin board at the bus station. I just got in from California and ran out of money. I'm trying to get to my family's place on Mercer Island."

"I could call and see if there is someone there to come pick you up?" said Jessie.

He looked on the verge of starting another coughing spell but was able to suppress it. "I don't think that would be a good idea. You see they are very religious and ultra conservative. Twelve years ago, when I told them I was gay, they insisted I go to this residential program sponsored by the church to get myself straightened out so to speak. When I refused, they basically disowned me."

Done with her phone call, Yvonne was listening from the hall. Nancy had taken a seat beside Bret while Jessie sat on the coffee table just in front of him. "So, if you believe you're not going to be welcome, why contact them now?" Jessie asked.

He seemed to be deteriorating before their eyes as he struggled for breath to continue. "I'm dying, I have hepatitis B that isn't responding to medication."

Trying to maintain eye contact, Jessie said bluntly, "If your plan is to show up to get sympathy or to fling some guilt, it will probably work by the looks of you. But, if you want to mend some fences why don't you let me drive you to the hospital? Get some treatment and a few regular meals in you. When you're stronger, I'll help set up a meeting if you still want to do that."

He looked like he had fallen asleep but when his already closed eyes shut even tighter and a tear escaped from each corner, Jessie knew Bret was listening.

Even from just two feet away, Jessie barely could make it out when he said, "OK."

Motioning Nancy to follow, Jessie walked back into her cubicle. Yvonne joined them. "I'm going to take him to the hospital. As soon as we leave, get some detergent, and thoroughly clean the chair he's in and everything within ten feet. I'm a little concerned that his cough might be TB. I'll be back soon."

Bret waited inside while Jessie got her car then summoned him with a tap on the horn. Nancy helped him out and watched as the car moved out of sight.

Yvonne was already wiping off the furniture with heavy-duty disinfectant. Nancy put on a rubber glove and helped. "Jessie sure is direct with people," Nancy said.

"It's a very valuable tool around here. If you're not direct, you end up spending hours listening to stuff you have no control over. I'm not saying a person's history isn't valid. Broken families, sexual assaults, and physical abuse -- any of it may play a very strong role in why someone comes in. But they need long-term counseling for those things, and we don't do that. Here we don't look for the cause of a situation. We look for a solution to a current, short-term problem," Yvonne responded. "Ninety percent of the time the problem is one of the big four: food, shelter, clothing, or medical attention."

As if on cue, each of the next four phone calls fell roughly into one or more of the big four groups providing emphasis to Yvonne's statements.

Just after four, Jessie got back and filled the others in while completing the client contact form. Bret would probably be hospitalized for several days. Jessie would follow up daily.

Auggie began pacing from Jessie's side to the front door and back. With each trip, he would stop briefly and stare intently at Jessie. "You need to go outside?" she asked after Auggie's fourth trip.

A single loud, sharp bark was the response, and a race to the door the result when she picked up his leash. "Be back in a minute," Jessie said while being dragged by her wrist out the door.

Half a block away, a bus pulled to the curb and Harold stepped off, called, and waved to Jessie. She let go of the leash and watched the squatting Harold get planted on his butt when Auggie failed to brake completely before contact.

"So, how'd the job hunting go?" Jessie asked as she helped Harold up from the sidewalk.

"Good I think. I have to call back in a couple of days, but I think I might have a job."

"Oh, that would be wonderful. Tell me about it."

As they took a leisurely walk, Harold told every detail about his meeting with Harrison Ashcroft in the unassuming little house. The excitement caused him to talk much faster than usual. Jessie wasn't sure he was even stopping to take a breath.

When the story finally concluded, Jessie reached to take Harold's hand and said, "I have a confession to make. About noon, there was some trouble on a city bus and some guy in a suit carrying a briefcase broke it up. I thought you might have had something to drink again. I was nearly out the door to go look for you when I got a phone call and needed to stay at the office."

Taking a quick look around to be sure no one was within earshot Harold said. "Now I have a confession. That was me, but I didn't have anything to drink."

Frozen in her tracks, Jessie slapped Harold on the shoulder and in mock anger asked, "Are you all right? Were you going to tell me about it?

"I'm fine, and sure I was, but the possibility of having a job was more significant to me than breaking up a pathetic attempt at a purse snatching."

Jessie hugged Harold tightly and kissed his face. "I didn't mean to take anything away from your good news. Please believe me, I couldn't be happier for you."

They started walking again and didn't speak for several minutes until Jessie asked, "Do you have power now, without drinking, like Auggie?"

"No, no extra powers. Hell, I damned near dislocated my shoulder messing with that guy."

"Do you think anyone recognized you?"

"I can't say for sure. I think only the driver, an elderly lady, and the purse-snatching little weasel got more than a cursory look at me. I don't think the lady got more than a side view, and the little weasel was probably too panicked. That just leaves the driver. Just hope he hasn't been reading the paper or watching the news much lately.

Say, how would you feel about teaching me how to drive?"

"I've seen how white-knuckled you get on the freeway so that might be quite a challenge but I'm up for it."

Back at the office, Harold told Yvonne about his possible job but said nothing about the bus incident. Later, on their way home, Jessie pulled into the nearly empty high school parking lot and Harold drove a car for the first time in fifteen years.

CHAPTER 29

Skies were threatening rain in the morning as Jessie, Harold, and Auggie left home. She would be doing her regular routine with Auggie in tow. Harold was headed for the library to look at architectural design books and magazines. He had noted the computer design program Harrison Ashcroft was using and would try to locate information on that as well. They'd meet around noon at Curbside Counseling for lunch.

Having dropped Harold off, Jessie was cruising the block by the office looking for a parking spot, when her cell phone rang. Caller ID said it was Yvonne.

"Good morning, Jessie. is Harold with you?"

"No, just dropped him off. Why?"

"Well, it's a good news, bad news kind of thing. Randy

thinks he might have found Harold's son, but the guy said he doesn't want any contact with Harold."

"I'll be in the office in ten minutes. Have Randy call me there. Let's not tell Harold until I have a chance to talk to the guy myself. Maybe I can change his mind."

Randy's call came minutes after Jessie got to the office. It all seemed to fit. Steven Preston Pearson had the correct birth date and background. Jessie could understand him not wanting to speak to the father who had virtually abandoned him after his mother died. It would certainly take some finesse on her part to overcome a couple of decades of animosity.

"So, Randy, how'd you find this guy so fast?"

"Well Jessie, sometimes it's who you know. In this case, I know a guy that works in the benefits office at the Fort Lewis military base. Just so happens Harold's boy was a soldier. Got out a couple of years ago on an honorable medical discharge. He's living in Ashland, Oregon with his wife and son."

"Why the medical discharge?"

"My contact didn't say, and frankly, it's none of my business."

"You're right, not mine either. So, how about an address and phone number?"

After going over a couple dozen scenarios in her head Jessie made a phone call. Normally self-confident dealing with family issues, Jessie was dry-mouthed, with sweaty palms, and hands trembling with nerves. She wanted so much for this to turn out well for Harold.

The phone rang several times before an answering machine picked up. She hung up without leaving a message.

An hour on the computer spent typing, revising, and retyping, produced what Jessie thought was a first-class letter to Steven Pearson. She had printed it out and was just about to seal it in an envelope but stopped. She wouldn't go behind Harold's back.

Jessie tried to busy herself with putting together information packets for the evening's training session, but time still crawled. Harold came in at twenty to twelve and was met at the door by a bounding dog and Jessie just ten feet inside. Smiling, she watched as Harold fawned over Auggie and when Harold looked up she moved forward and gave him a hug.

Hand-in-hand, Jessie led Harold to her cubicle and sat down next to him.

"Not that I'm one to complain about hugs and hand-holding, but I am a bit suspicious. What's up, Jessie?"

Looking straight into his eyes, Jessie said, "Randy found your son, but he doesn't want to talk to you right now."

Nothing was said for several minutes. Harold mainly looked at the floor; Auggie moved over and put his head on Harold's lap, and Jessie stared at Harold.

"It's been so long, I'd half given up ever finding him. I feel a little numb." After another pause, "Did he say he didn't want to speak to me right now or ever?" Harold finally asked.

"I didn't actually talk to him, Randy did. But what was told to me was, never."

Another silent period, then Jessie said, "I wrote him a letter saying what a wonderful person you were and how you'd been trying to find him for several years, but I didn't mail it. Even though everything I said is true, I think you need to write the letter, not me. You can use my computer if you want."

"Thanks for the offer, but I think a paper and pen is the way to go. It's been impersonal for too long."

"One other thing, there's more than just your son involved. It seems you're a father-in-law and a grandpa to a boy."

A smile broke across Harold's face followed by a nervous chuckle then he joined Jessie in full-blown laughter.

CHAPTER 30

The trainees started to arrive at quarter to six and by ten after, the few meager chairs were filled, and several people were standing along the back. Eleven trainees in all, this was one of the better turnouts for new staff and interns Curbside Counseling had had in the last couple of years. Nancy Cabot sat front and center.

Experience told Jessie several wouldn't be back for a second day and half the remainder wouldn't make it through an entire college semester. The training wasn't complicated or particularly hard, turnover was almost exclusively the result of bad interactions between staff and clients. She'd put in whatever effort was needed to keep all she could.

The first day was given to outlining the services Curbside Counseling offered and the general nuts and bolts of the office. Tomorrow trainees would be assigned one on one with a trainer and schedules arranged. After two hours, Jessie called it a day.

Harold borrowed a stamp and dropped the letter to his son in a mailbox just down the street from the office. Jessie drove until they were a few blocks from home and Harold white-knuckled it the rest of the way.

Safely in the garage, Jessie joked, "You're some superhero. Scared shitless doing what every sixteen-year-old in the county begs for the chance to do. You'd better hope all the bad guys have the sense enough to find you because I just can't see you speeding after them like you see in big budget action movies."

The balance of the evening was quiet and uneventful for a change. Goodnights were said, and the lights were out by ten thirty.

~*~

Harold and Jessie had both been up for more than an hour the next morning when Jessie's cell phone rang. Yvonne was calling. She cut off Jessie's small talk early and got right to the point.

"I was going over files to prepare for Jim Stacy's trial when I came to the folder with the autopsy reports on the kids that died. According to this report, all the deaths were from heart failure. Like their hearts got slowed to a point that they just stopped. The blood work is all screwed up too. I'm going to have to find a doctor to explain some of this stuff to me. I'm just telling you this because I wanted you to be sure Harold didn't have any of that wine, although I'm not sure what he could do at this point if he did."

Jessie was dying to tell Yvonne the whole story but had to settle for, "I'll talk to him again, but I think he's fine."

"So, how'd it goes telling Harold his son wants nothing to do with him?" Yvonne wanted to know.

Walking back to her bedroom to get out of Harold's earshot, Jessie said, "He took it as well as you could expect and then sat down for more than an hour hand writing a letter to his son. Mailed it and didn't say anything else about it the rest of the evening. I figured I'd give him a little space and maybe let him start up any other conversation."

Yvonne let out a sigh and said, "I sure hope this turns out well for Harold. Seems like he's due for something really good happening in his life."

"Well, say a little prayer for him then because he has to call back today about a job that he seems really excited about," Jessie said.

"Say, I have to be down by the convention center at noon today. I'm helping one of the women in our office finalize her divorce and her husband's lawyer's office is in the 2 Union Square building. We just have to get signatures on the final paperwork, so it shouldn't take very long. If Harold gets the job, text me and we can all meet and do lunch, my treat."

"Sounds great Yvonne, but I won't mention anything to Harold until he has an answer."

"OK, catch you later and all my best wishes to Harold, bye."

Back in the kitchen, Jessie could hear Harold talking on the living room phone and tried to eavesdrop on the conversation with little success. Her heart started to race when she heard Harold say, "Wonderful, see you in two weeks." Then hung up.

Grinning ear-to-ear Harold came into to the kitchen, "You're looking at an almost employed new man. I have to take a drug test, which I am not at all surprised about, then start in two weeks."

Jessie was crying and hugging Harold as hard as she

could. "It couldn't have happened to a more deserving person. I'm so happy for you."

Auggie was bouncing around the room like a kangaroo on a pogo stick and making sounds like he was talking.

Looking Jessie in the eyes Harold said, "I've only known you a short time, but I've seen you crying at least a half a dozen times. What's up with that?"

After wiping tears, blowing her nose, and taking a big cleansing breath Jessie said, "I think it's the job. I don't remember being an emotional kid but coming in contact every day with human tragedy and having to remain stoic and professional, I just have this release when I get away from all that."

"Well I've seen tears when you're happy and tears when you're sad and I never want to be the cause of the sad tears."

"You and Auggie have been such a wonderful addition to my life I can't be anything but happy. Speaking of happy, I told Yvonne you were in line for a job and she said she would buy lunch downtown if you got it so, I'll text her and tell her she's on."

An hour of practice driving in the local area showed Harold becoming more confident on the road but still no match for Seattle traffic.

"Do you want to come with me while I make a few stops before lunch?" Jessie asked during the drive into Seattle.

Looking out the window with Auggie's head on his shoulder, Harold responded," It's a nice day so I think Auggie and I will walk a bit and just meet you and Yvonne. Thanks, by the way for setting me up on your cell phone account. I really do need to become savvier about these things."

"Well that's a three-year-old phone but it should do fine

for the time being. Where do you want me to drop you off?"

Harold thought for a few seconds, then for no particular reason said, "Seattle Center. I'll have plenty of time to walk to Union Square to meet you later".

Jessie smiled and thought how fun it might be just to wander the city without expectations or appointments. "Remember, you're famous now so people might approach you just to say hi, take pictures of you and Auggie or want their picture taken with you."

"Another good reason to get off the front page of the newspaper and stop being the lead story on the local news," Harold said staring at his shoes and shaking his head.

Harold and Auggie got out of the car at a stoplight and Jessie watched them until they rounded a corner. She made some of her usual stops and checked in with her staff at Curbside Counseling. She had to give the Cliff's Notes version of why the office had a new front door and called the hospital to check on Rhonda Jean and the young man who she had taken to the hospital days earlier. Both were doing better though not quite ready for discharge.

The lobby at the 2 Union Square office tower is a cavernous display of marble and granite with rows of escalators leading to the elevators of the fifty-six-story structure. Harold was outside and turned Auggie loose to greet Jessie when he saw her coming up the stairs from the street.

Already wearing the service dog vest the governor had given him, Auggie, Jessie, and Harold entered the building unchallenged. Yvonne was standing at the top of the escalators and waved to get their attention while she spoke to Jessie on the phone to help triangulate their positions.

"Jill, my co-worker slash client is already waiting for me in the law firm reception area. You should come with me and see what life looks like for the people at the high end of the legal pay scale," Yvonne said.

Jessie ran her fingers down the arm of Yvonne's jacket. "Is this new?"

Yvonne smiled. "No, I've had it for a while, but leather seems to have gone out of style. Don't see a lot of people wearing it anymore."

"Well, it looks like it was tailored just for you. It fits perfectly." Yvonne just smiled.

The elevator ride was so smooth you could barely tell that you were even moving. When the doors did open, they were greeted by a ten-foot high translucent glass wall etched with the firm's name, which was just the last names of several people, in twelve-inch-tall letters to the left of glass and brass doors. Behind the reception desk was another wall, this one of fine wood, which again had the firms name in even larger letters. The chairs were leather, very comfortable and most likely very expensive.

At the reception desk, an attractive woman was wearing a company lanyard around her neck announcing her name as Lisa. She greeted them with a broad smile as she took their names, offered refreshments, and made the appropriate phone calls.

Yvonne and Jill Adams were escorted to an unseen meeting room. The receptionist had said Jill's soon-to-be ex-husband had not arrived yet but was due any time.

Moments later, the elevator doors opened and an impeccably dressed man stepped out and looked in each direction down the empty hallways. He was wearing an expensive suit under an unbuttoned knee-length tan camel hair coat. His hands were firmly in his pockets and he pushed the door open with his shoulder.

The hair on Auggie's back was up and he let out a low growl as the man passed. The receptionist said, "Good morning, Mr. Adams. They're waiting for you in the conference room."

He didn't wait for her to lead the way and instead walked with a stiff, somewhat awkward gait, quickly passed her without a word. She followed, almost running to keep up.

"What was all that?" Harold asked Jessie.

Auggie stood and started pulling against his leash. "I don't know but I'm with Auggie. I have a bad feeling about this."

CHAPTER 31

"He's got a bomb," Lisa said in near panic as she ran toward the door. Harold grabbed the hysterical woman before she could leave.

"Who's in the room with him?" Harold asked.

"Mrs. Adams, your friend, his lawyer, Mr. Brand, and Kayla the recording secretary. He shoved me back into the hallway when he got into the room and I could see him open his coat with lots of different stuff hanging from it on the inside. He has a gun too," she said crying.

"I need you to be very brave and do a couple of things. Jessie will help you. Call into each office and tell your coworkers to get out. Tell them there's a gas leak near the conference room and they should avoid it. Can they all leave without going past the conference room?"

Composing herself she said, "Yes."

"Good, tell them to do that. Start with the offices closest to the conference room and work your way out. Can they get to elevators other than the ones right out here?" Harold asked pointing out the glass doors.

Again, she said, "Yes."

"Great and have them tell anyone they see in the halls, just in case someone isn't in their office."

It only took a few minutes and she put down the phone. "That's everyone."

"Perfect. In a minute, I'm going to pull the fire alarm to empty the rest of the building, so it's going to get noisy in here. Now I want you to get out yourself and call 911 on your way down. Tell the dispatcher it's not a fire, so we don't have firemen clogging up the stairwells. Can I get back there without being seen from the conference room? I'm assuming it's all glass like everything else?"

"It is glass, but Mr. Bland's office is right next to it and his office has a connecting door. You can go out the main doors and down the hallway to the right. Take the first door on the right and that hall goes right by Mr. Bland's office. His name is on the door."

Harold pushed the button for the elevator and when the doors opened he took Lisa's hand. "You've been wonderful, now get out of here and make that 911 call."

Turning to Jessie, he just winked, grabbed her by each shoulder looked straight into her eyes and said, "You too, darling." And gave her a gentle push into the elevator. As the doors closed, he pulled the fire alarm.

In a mini-fridge behind the reception desk, Harold found bottled water, small cans of various sodas and what he had hoped to find, airline size bottles of wine. He took a pocketful and headed to Bland's office, Auggie on his heels.

A few stragglers were still in the process of leaving their offices, and Harold held the door and told them to head for the far elevators. Phones were ringing randomly, and emergency lights illuminated the passageways as Harold moved down the hall his back to the wall. Bland's office was unlocked. He gingerly tested the doorknob connecting to the conference room and found it unlocked. From the other side of the door above the relentless ringing of the fire alarm, Harold could hear shouting from whom he assumed to be Mr. Adams.

"No one should be surprised, I told this bitch exactly what would happen if she ever tried to leave me. You all seemed to be on her side, even my own lawyer, so fuck all of you. I got arrested for hitting her one lousy time, spent a couple nights in jail, then got threatened with a restraining order. My boss wouldn't listen to my side and fired me because of the jail time. This divorce settlement will just about wipe me out and my lawyer tells me to sign it. Frankly, I have nothing to lose so if I'm going to hell, I might as well take all of you with me."

Several people tried to talk at the same time, but over all of them all that could be heard was, "Shut up!"

Auggie growled and Harold turned as the door to Bland's office slowly opened. Jessie put her head in and whispered,

"What's the plan, Superman?"

"Oh Jessie, please get out of here," Harold whispered back.

"Yvonne is truly my best friend and I want to help. Besides I'm the trusty sidekick of our trio. You can't do this without me."

"I'd love to just throw you over my shoulder and put you back on the elevator kicking and screaming, but I don't want to waste the time. So, if you're going to stay and have an idea of how I might be able to see into that conference room I'd like to hear it."

While Jessie thought, Harold removed everything from the top of Bland's desk and as quietly as possible and laid the desk on its side, with the desk's top facing the connecting conference room door.

"Give me your phone," Jessie said.

In seconds, Jessie had her own phone connected with Harold's and was video streaming the inside of the office.

"I'll crawl down the hallway and hold the phone out, so you'll be able to see into the conference room. I'll have my earbuds in, so you can tell me which way to angle the phone to see what you need."

Harold shook his head no. "Too risky. Adams has a gun and you could get shot if he sees you."

The fire alarms stopped, and everything was quiet except for talking coming from the other side of the door. A phone rang, and it was clear from the half of the conversation they could hear, that Adams was talking to the police.

"Listen, asshole. You are not in charge. I am, so don't give me any of your hostage negotiation bullshit. I've got enough C4 to take out this entire side of the building. If I hear the elevator doors, people moving in the halls or even a glimpse of anyone, I'll blow this place and everyone in it to bits. You got that? If I want to talk to you again, I'll call, but until then, if this phone rings again, someone will get a bullet in the head."

Harold looked at Jessie. "OK, we'll try it your way, but if he comes towards you or even raises his gun, I want you to run as fast as you can out of here. Don't stop, no matter what."

The picture Jessie sent was better than expected. Harold could see everyone had been zip tied to chairs and blindfolded. Sitting on the large conference table close to the connecting door, what appeared to be explosives were wired and taped together with blinking lights on the top. Having used her hat to prop her phone in place, Jessie was back at Harold's side looking at the video.

"We're going to need a diversion. Go back out as quietly as you can and get the fire extinguisher by the elevators. Get two if you can find another one. Hurry," Harold said.

While Jessie was gone, Harold took the oversized trashcan from under a paper shredder, partially emptied it and filled it with water from the sink in Bland's office lavatory and set it next to the connecting door.

Lugging two full-size extinguishers, Jessie came back breathing hard.

Harold pulled the safety pins from both extinguishers then set one by the connecting door.

"This is it. Last chance to back out and I wish to God you would because here's where it could get very bad," Harold said with tears in his eyes.

Jessie kissed him softly and said, "I'm exactly where I want to be. Let's go save my friend."

"I'll go through the main door with my extinguisher going and try and draw Adams' attention." Pointing to the connecting door, Harold said, "Watch the phone, as soon as you see me inside the door you fire off your extinguisher and come through this door. Tell Auggie, *get him,* as soon as you open the door. Keep the extinguisher high to use as a shield, spray the retardant around the room for cover and grab the bomb. Bring it back here and submerge it in this trashcan then run. It's up to Auggie and me to do the rest."

Harold cracked open the tops of several of the mini wine bottles and downed them one after another. Jessie took one for herself.

Adams had been on a nonstop screaming diatribe about every perceived slight or show of disrespect he'd had in his entire life and as Harold and Jessie listened, it seemed like he might be running out of steam. Then the phone rang.

"I told you not to call. What the fuck is wrong with you people?" Adams yelled into the phone.

After a brief pause, "Hello Ma, what bar did they drag your sorry ass out of, or were you in the drunk tank so you'd be easy to find? Did you tell them you and I aren't exactly on speaking terms? Never mind, let me talk to the cop.

I told you what would happen if this phone rang again. Maybe you need to see the results of your stupidity up close. How about I send one of these lawyers out the fucking window down to see you? I'll let you know which window to watch."

Half a dozen gunshots followed by a chair thrust through the floor-to-ceiling window sent shards of glass raining down on the street fifty stories below. Harold had picked up his extinguisher and was out Bland's office door. Yvonne was thrashing side-to-side and her chairs wheels squeaked as Adams pushed it across the room.

As the white fog of fire retardant filled the conference room from two directions, nearly everything became invisible. Adams got off a couple of random shots before

Auggie started an attack that would be both exquisitely painful and mercifully short for Adams.

Yvonne's chair teetered for a long two seconds on the window's edge before starting to fall.

Harold lunged, then held on with both hands to the collar of a nearly new leather jacket as the chair dangled outside, below the window ledge. With no way to brace himself, Harold could not pull her back; all he could do was hold on. Arms burning from the strain, he fought to maintain his grip.

Then he felt tightness around his waist and a cold nose on his low back as Auggie, fresh from the fight, gripped Harold's belt in his teeth, planted his feet and pulled.

News cameras focused on the woman strapped to the dangling chair did not capture the arms keeping Yvonne suspended or help explain how she was pulled back into the building.

Everyone and everything in the room was almost completely white as the last of the fire retardant settled. Everyone seemed OK, except for Adams who was balled up in a corner, hands, and wrists grotesquely mangled. The gun was well out of his reach, not that he would have been able to use it. There was no sign of any kind of detonator device. It had been a little over an hour since the whole thing started and now it was over.

Jessie had strained to watch the foggy cell phone picture from the reception area and was walking briskly toward the conference room as Harold staggered out on trembling legs.

"Call 911 and tell them everything is OK, but Adams will need a paramedic. I want to get Auggie and myself away from here before they come. I'll call you later to tell you where to pick me up. Go see Yvonne," Harold whispered as he walked by only stopping to pick up the cell phone they had left in the hallway.

"What should I say about all of this to the police?" asked Jessie.

"I don't know. Be creative and vague. Hell, tell them you did it."

Taking one of the far elevators to the tenth floor, Harold took the stairs down two more floors. Walking the deserted halls, he found an unlocked janitor's closet, locked himself in, created a makeshift bed and laid down.

It was after four when he woke to the sounds of people in the halls. Using supplies he found, he cleaned himself and Auggie the best he could, waited until he couldn't hear any activity and walked out on still wobbly legs. Obviously, police had cleared the building of any lingering threat and people were being allowed back in their offices with a great story to tell.

Harold tried, unsuccessfully, to walk quickly but his legs would or could not respond. He felt disoriented and couldn't formulate a plan. He managed just a few blocks and sat in a doorway as the phone in his pocket began to ring.

CHAPTER 32

Jessie was on the floor hugging and kissing a still-bound Yvonne, when heavily armed police entered the room. Jessie complied with the order to get face down on the carpet and stayed motionless until the hostages in unison yelled that she was not the threat and that it was Adams, in the corner bleeding, who started the entire chain of events.

While one group of paramedics attended to Adams,

others were cutting zip ties, offering oxygen, and assessing minor wounds.

Bomb squad personnel pushed a cart carrying the remnants of the bomb down the hall and announced the area to be completely safe.

One by one, the hostages were led to different areas to be interviewed by detectives. The stories were very similar including the ending when they heard gunfire, Adams screaming in pain, one or more people moving around the room then quiet and Jessie entering the room.

The story Jessie relayed was vague indeed. She told detectives she had been hiding, waiting for a chance to help her friend, and only started back after she heard gunfire.

Yvonne was unable to say what or who kept her from falling or how she was pulled back into the building. Jessie had whispered to her during the hug not to mention Harold and Auggie and Yvonne complied.

Ultimately, all four hostages declined further medical treatment and were free to either face the horde of reporters or attempt a stealthy escape.

Both Jessie's and Yvonne's cars were at a nearby parking garage, which on a normal day would just be a short walk. Trying to avoid the media they took multiple detours to find a door not being staked out by reporters.

Sitting in the quiet of Jessie's car Yvonne finally asked, "Did Harold and Auggie do all of that?"

Smiling Jessie said, "With a bit of help from yours truly."

"Who saved me? No way could all hundred and twenty-five pounds of you hold me and a twenty-pound chair dangling free outside that window, let alone pull me in."

"I don't know for sure, but logic tells me it was Harold. Auggie was busy with Adams."

"So, why didn't you want me to tell the police about them?" asked Yvonne.

"I don't know how well you think you know Harold, but he hates the spotlight and notoriety after years of being all but invisible. He can't wait to get off the front page of the newspaper. This is obviously going to be the lead story on every station in town and will most likely show up on the national news as well. For him this is awful."

Yvonne asked, "Where are they now? I was supposed to buy lunch to celebrate his new job. Now I have to add saving my life. I'll be buying them and you meals forever."

Jessie got quiet for a moment then said, "I don't know. Harold said he would call and tell me where to pick him up. I want to give him a little bit longer but if he doesn't call by five, I'll call him."

Looking down at deep bruising on Yvonne's exposed wrists Jessie asked. "Did the zip ties do that?"

"Yes, but oddly enough in a good way. When I was dangling outside that window I was being held up because Harold or someone was holding my jacket collar. If my hands hadn't been zip tied to the chair I would probably have just slipped out of my jacket and fallen."

After going through the entire series of events that she was a part of in detail, Jessie said a tearful goodbye to Yvonne.

CHAPTER 33

Staring at the phone as it rang several times, Harold finally remembered how to answer, "Hello."

"This is Jessie. Are you and Auggie OK, and, where are you?

"Auggie's perfect. I, on the other hand, feel like shit but I guess I'm alright. I'm on Seneca Street a few blocks south of the convention center, but I can't tell you exactly where."

"Stay where you are. I'm not far. I'll be there in just a few minutes. Watch for me."

Rain started to fall, and by the time Jessie pulled up to the curb in front of Harold, it was coming down in torrents. Auggie leaped in with his usual agility. Harold was moving like an eighty-year-old. Jessie audibly gasped looking at Harold's pale, gaunt face.

"Oh my God, you look terrible. We're going to the hospital."

Shaking his head no. Harold said, "I need some food. Auggie is probably starving too. It doesn't matter what we get. Just pull in to the next open drive-thru you see."

With the seat fully reclined, Harold dozed off and was sleeping soundly when Jessie pulled into a burger joint. The barely functional speakers sent cryptic messages in both directions. Awake, Harold added orange juice to the order Jessie had already placed. In the far corner of the parking lot, Harold drank the juice in one breath, then consumed the food. Within twenty minutes, he looked and sounded much better.

As with previous adventures, Harold was not able to recall the events past the point where he went into the conference room. When Jessie told him about saving Yvonne, Harold just shook his head in amazement.

The events of their day were consuming the airtime on local radio stations as expected. In one interview, Lisa, the law firm receptionist, named Harold and Auggie as having been at the scene. She'd recognized them from previous television stories. Police could neither confirm nor deny that they had been there. They were not in those offices when police arrived and hadn't been seen leaving in the building in the immediate aftermath of the event.

"Well, I suspect that Auggie and I are in for another round of incessant media scrutiny after this little episode," Harold said staring at the floor mats.

Reaching over to touch his hand, Jessie responded, "Do you want to have another group gathering like at the banquet, minus the fire sprinkler event of course, and get it over all at once, try to avoid them for a while, or take them on one at a time."

"I think I'd like to sleep on it and see what the coverage is tomorrow or even the next day before I decide. This isn't going to be pleasant for you either. We've been linked together. Hell, maybe somehow, we can generate some funds for Curbside Counseling out of this mess. Maybe I should get an agent or at least an official spokesperson."

The ringing phone was Jessie's, and Randy Pepper's picture appeared. "Don't lie, are they with you?"

"Well, hello to you too," Jessie responded.

"Sorry to be so abrupt, but apparently, you told a little fib to my coworkers today and encouraged Yvonne to omit some important stuff too. I want to get the real story. But more importantly, I wanted to be sure you are all safe and thank you for saving my girlfriend."

In the background, Yvonne's voice said, "So, I'm your girlfriend now. That would have been nice to hear before I was dangled out of a fifty-story building, but I guess I'll take it anyway."

"We're all fine, but I suspect that my house is completely surrounded by media. Any suggestions for a hotel to hide out in?" Jessie asked.

"Why don't you come over here. I can put all of you up until another story takes over the news cycle. We can arrange a midnight run to your house for clothes and other stuff tomorrow."

Harold shrugged and agreed with an affirmative nod and Jessie got the address.

The drive was quiet for a while before Jessie broke the silence. "You looked exceptionally bad when I picked you up. I'm not kidding either. I would have taken anybody who came into my office looking like you did straight to the hospital. The only other time I've seen you after one of your little adventures was when you and Auggie helped those two girls, Kari and Ashley. Then you just came to the car and took a nap and by the time we got home you seemed fine. Why do you think this time was so much worse for you than before?"

Harold had been lying with the seat back and eyes closed but not sleeping. "I'll have to take your word for how I looked. I know I felt terrible and I'm still not a hundred percent. Guessing, I would say it has to do with the time between meals and blood sugar. Today I had breakfast early, and we were planning to go to lunch, so it had been four or five hours since I'd eaten. When Auggie and I helped Kari and Ashley, you and I had just come out of a restaurant and there was no planning involved. This time the planning and execution were over a relatively long period of time in a very tense atmosphere loaded with adrenaline. Maybe I was already burning through my body's sugar stores before I even went into the conference room."

"Well," Jessie said, "if you're right that would mean you were very close to dropping into a diabetic coma. Before, you would sleep afterward, and your blood sugar would stabilize. This time it didn't. I know people can die in those cases."

"Well, either I have to give up the superhero stuff, which would be fine with me, or I have to have some sugar with the alcohol I drink. Another other option would be to hang out with dull people like architects and building contractors, so I won't get into these messes."

CHAPTER 34

Randy lived in a quickly gentrifying area south of downtown Seattle proper. His house was a beautifully remodeled home, originally built in the late 1940's with three stories including the small attic bedroom. A full, unfinished basement added even more usable square footage. It had taken years of nights and weekends, but Randy had done virtually all the work himself.

The rain's intensity had decreased but was still falling when Jessie parked directly behind Yvonne's car on the street. Auggie bounded out with his usual enthusiasm and proceeded in short order to take a massive dump on Randy's well-manicured lawn then water multiple pieces of ornamental shrubbery.

"I should have seen that coming," Harold said while looking through his pockets for a doggy do bag. "He's hardly been out since noon and it's what, about seven-thirty?"

"Close, it's a quarter to eight. Why don't you let me take care of that and you can go in and get comfortable?" Jessie offered.

"Thanks, but I want to take care of Auggie considering how he looks after me and everyone else for that matter. Do you happen to have anything in your car we can use as a toy to throw for him?"

The only thing Jessie could find was an empty water bottle, which lasted a mere four throws before it was all but destroyed.

It was obvious by the weak throws and halfhearted interest that Harold was tired. Jessie finally used a bit of force in her voice to make him relent and go inside.

Randy and Yvonne met them at the door and proceeded to give them a tour of the house.

The inside was as clean and neat as the outside with refinished hardwood floors stained to match the fireplace mantel and sweeping banister. Crown molding in each of the high ceiling rooms added to the classic style. The original but rewired light fixtures finished off each space. The kitchen was completely updated with an oversized stove, new appliances, new cabinets, and granite countertops.

Harold took in all he saw, asked questions only an architect would ask, and complimented Randy on his workmanship and choices.

As they all moved toward the living room, refreshments were offered and declined and they each settled into comfortable furniture.

Without a bit of hesitation, Randy asked, "The beginning and ending I've gotten from Yvonne. What I would like to know more about is the middle part that lasted, like, two minutes."

Jessie and Harold exchanged looks and then Jessie told nearly the whole unvarnished truth, avoiding mentioning Auggie's atypical abilities. She told about the cell phone video and the planning, but she didn't know what happened between the time she put the bomb in the trashcan and Harold meeting her in the hallway. It was clear that Auggie was the source of Adams's injuries, and that left Harold as the only person able to help Yvonne.

"I'm afraid I can't add much to the storyline," Harold said, "The last thing I remember clearly is going into the conference room with the fire extinguisher going. It does seem obvious that I had to have been the one holding on to Yvonne and pulling her in. If that's true, then I would be the second happiest person, Yvonne being the first, but that is purely speculation. I truly don't remember. Sorry."

Crossing the room, Yvonne straddled Harold's legs, bent over, and while holding his face with both hands, kissed him then hugged him tightly. She whispered 'thank you' in his ear, then moved to the floor to repeat the hug, kiss, and thank you with Auggie.

Randy asked, "Have either of you seen the news reports and video? It's dramatic, to say the least."

"We heard on the radio that the receptionist named Harold and Auggie but nothing besides that," Jessie said.

"Well, after I made a call to my office to tell them I was alright, and I would be taking tomorrow off, I called my mom then Randy. I had to turn my phone off after that. It was going off nonstop. I checked just before you guys came, and my message inbox is full," Yvonne said.

It didn't take much scrolling through the television

stations to find one that was replaying the day's events. Seeing Yvonne hanging out the window was terrifying to watch even with her sitting ten feet away.

The police chief and mayor were making statements then taking questions. Harold and Auggie came up multiple times but the answer was always the same, "We have not had a chance to interview Mr. Pearson but hope to contact him soon."

On another channel, they saw Mr. Bland, his note taker Kayla, Jill Adams, and Lisa the receptionist, relaying their stories and answering questions. Lisa told the assembled media that when she and Jessie got on the elevator, Harold seemed totally in control and that he and Auggie had remained at the law office. Jessie had gotten off the elevator two floors down and headed toward the stairs. The others agreed that blindfolds kept them from seeing who came into the room and no one entering the room had spoken. They said they did not see a dog and any other noises were drowned out by Adams' screams. They all had been aware of random movement in the room, then Jessie arrived just seconds ahead of the police.

Two other stations were showing the same news conference and repeating the same information. Randy turned off the television.

Looking at Randy, Harold said, "Not that I don't like being in all your fine company but I'm really tired. Would you mind showing me to a shower then a bed?"

As a group, they toured the second floor. Harold and Auggie would share a room on one side of a bathroom and Jessie's room would be on the other. The master bedroom was on the opposite end of the hall with its own private bath.

Randy provided Harold with a T-shirt and sweatpants to wear. Yvonne came up with something similar for Jessie.

After a shower and one last trip outside for Auggie, Harold said his goodnights.

The discussion taking place in the living room meandered from different aspects of the day, then finally centered on how to help Harold navigate what would surely be an avalanche of media requests. Jessie would have her own cross to bear as far as media, thus would be of little help. Yvonne offered to act as a spokesperson until Randy pointed out that she too, as much as Harold, would in great demand. "You can't be seen by millions of people tied to a chair and dangling out of a window fifty stories high, escape death and not have people wanting to talk to you."

A statement would need to be given to the police about Harold and Auggie's role in the rescue. The same statement could be altered and presented to media outlets either at a press conference or simply as a press release. But it would all have to wait until morning as Jessie said, "I'm running out of gas myself."

After her shower, Jessie stepped into the hall and marveled at how quiet the house had become. Stopping in front of her bedroom door, she turned and went to check on Harold. Stretched out on the floor beside the bed with Harold's hand draped over him, Auggie lifted his head to recognize Jessie then laid back. They both looked peaceful, but Jessie felt a maternal pull that compelled her to watch Harold for a little while. Across the room, an antique rocking chair provided a comfortable observation site. It was just past eleven, with eyes too heavy to keep open, that Jessie slipped under the covers next to Harold and fell asleep.

A familiar cold, wet nose planted squarely in his ear,

brought Harold to attention. Awake, he did not move or even slightly stir. He felt Jessie's outstretched arm across his chest and smiled to himself as he listened to her slow rhythmic breathing. He would happily have stayed there indefinitely had it not been for Auggie's impatience that had escalated to insistence, most assuredly being driven by his need to visit the great outdoors.

Sliding awkwardly sideways, Harold exited the bed, took a loving look at the sleeping Jessie, then quietly gathered his things. The ritualistic morning dog routine started with a bit of outdoor playtime before heading in for food.

The smell of coffee pulled Harold to the kitchen. Yvonne, with both hands wrapped around her mug, sat on a counter stool watching as Randy arranged pans on the stove in preparation for making breakfast.

"Good morning, Harold. How are you feeling?" Randy asked.

"Very good, thanks. How about you, Ms. Jackson? Are you OK today?

"My wrists are a bit painful, but all things considered, I'm doing great, thanks to you and Auggie."

"Speaking of Augie," Randy said. "I went out last night and got a bag of food. I don't know what you normally feed him. I hope he'll eat it."

Harold laughed, "I'm can't imagine it will be a problem. He is not what you would call a finicky eater. Watching him eat is comparable to watching a black hole in space consume a solar system. Nothing escapes."

With that, Harold filled a medium size mixing bowl and placed it on the floor next to a bowl of water. All the food and half the water were gone in seconds.

Coming into the room, even with no makeup and hair tousled, Jessie still looked beautiful. "My phone is screaming at me to respond and half the calls are from my mom, so I turned it off. I'm not going to even try to have a coherent conversation until I get some coffee in me."

Cup in hand, Jessie headed toward the living room to make the requisite calls, the last being to her parents.

"What on earth have you gotten yourself into now?" Her mother said before even a hello. "Deranged men with bombs and guns throwing your friend out a window. You're going to give me a heart attack."

"Well, first off we're all fine. Thanks for asking, but you're being a little overdramatic. It was only one deranged guy with one bomb and one gun and he didn't throw Yvonne out the window he just pushed her chair in that direction," Jessie said nearly laughing.

Her father, as usual, was listening in on an extension, and asked in a clearly concerned tone, "Are you really alright?"

"Yes, dad, my friend, Harold, and his dog Auggie, were there and everything worked out fine. I didn't get a scratch."

"Is this the same guy that was staying at your house? Is he the one that's bringing this madness into your life? I've never felt comfortable with your choice of jobs working with all those street people and now this," her mother said almost crying. "And that dog. Ever since I saw your name on television yesterday, I've been reading those newspaper clippings you sent and stuff on the Internet about this Harold Pearson and Auggie and how that dog is somehow capable of extreme violence. I don't want him to turn on you."

"I hope you read the part where he has only attacked

bad people who were hurting other people. When I'm with them, I couldn't possibly feel safer."

The conversation devolved into an uninterruptible speech until Jessie finally broke in. "Mom, I totally understand your concerns and I will try my best to keep myself safe. Love you both, bye."

Plates of food were being dished up, and Jessie got in line for her portion. Yvonne was grinning like a maniac and looking back and forth between Harold and Jessie. Harold was not paying attention, but Jessie noticed and finally said, "What?"

"While you were clearing your phone messages, I was doing the same. One of the messages I had was from Bland's law firm. I called back and was immediately transferred to one of the senior partners. He wanted to know how I was and if I knew how you guys were. I was vague about both of you and myself. He was extremely sorry about what I had been through and offered to pay any medical bills that may arise and hinted at a payment for emotional distress. These guys are thinking like the lawyers they are and trying not to get sued, Yvonne said.

Jessie added, "I bet there are a dozen personal injury lawyers with either cards sticking in my front door or just parked along the street in front of my house right now. You guys are next."

Shaking his head, Harold said," No good deed goes unpunished."

Staring at her plate while her mind raced through possibilities, Jessie finally asked, "Is this something we want to tackle as a group or individually?"

"I don't want to tackle it at all," Harold said. "Yesterday

may have been the last day I get to walk down the street anonymously for a long time and I can't buy that back."

Finishing his meal quickly, he excused himself and went upstairs. Jessie followed fifteen minutes later and found him in the rocking chair by the bed his belt in his hands.

"Look at this," he said. Holding the belt out.

"What am I looking at?"

"Teeth marks. I may have been the one holding Yvonne but there is no way I could have pulled her in. It had to be Auggie."

Tossing the belt on the bed, she sat on his lap and pulled his head to her chest. "None of it would have happened and they all could have died without your plan. Together we saved everyone, and you and Auggie specifically saved Yvonne. So, do me a favor, and for just one minute stop feeling sorry for yourself and sit back. Don't think about anything else and reflect on the number of lives that were impacted yesterday. Not just the people in that room, but their parents, sisters, brothers, husbands, wives, children, boyfriends, girlfriends, and co-workers to name a few. It's all because you decided to make a difference and Auggie was there to help you."

"What was I thinking when I told you to move that bomb? It could have had a motion sensor or a pressure switch that would have set it off. I could have gotten you killed," Harold argued.

"Well, thank God, that Adams was not as diabolical a bomb designer as you would be. Even with everything we are going to have to face media wise in the next couple of days or even weeks, I, personally, am happy to be alive and I want you to be happy too."

Taking his hand from her thigh and sliding it under her

shirt and onto her breast, she whispered in his ear, "Randy and Yvonne left for a while, please let me make you happy."

CHAPTER 35

Heavy-duty lawn trash bags full of hastily picked clothes were being hauled in by Randy and Yvonne and dropped at the bottom of the stairs. Pointing to two bags, Randy said, "Harold this is your stuff." Then to Jessie, "Your stuff is in those three overstuffed bags. Should be enough to get you through for a while."

"It wasn't as bad as we thought," Yvonne said. "Only three cars in front of your place, two from the media and one unknown. My house had five. I was hiding in the back seat, so I had to get the breakdown from Randy, three media, and two unknowns. Don't blame me for any of the clothing choices. Randy used his badge to go in and out. No telling what's in these bags. Could be just socks and underwear for all I know."

"Thank you both I'm sure it will be fine. Hopefully, it will just be a couple of days and we can try to get back to something resembling normal," Jessie said.

With the clothes put away, the group assembled in the living room and in relatively quick fashion, the decision was made to have one big media meeting that Jessie, Yvonne, Harold, and Auggie would attend. A discussion ensued over what to do, if anything, about a possible monetary settlement with the law firm.

"I say we have a meeting with them and listen to what they might offer. Once we hear what they are proposing we can decide," Yvonne said.

Jessie agreed and added that there should be no threat of a lawsuit and each person would decide individually what to do with any money each received.

Harold was quiet through most of the discussion but finally said. "If I get anything, I hope it's enough to buy a decent used car, assuming I haven't been fired already. The guy that hired me seems very fair but low key. All this attention might be a deal breaker."

"I don't recall much about this kind of civil and personal injury stuff from law school and I don't have any outside experience. My guess, based on how prestigious that firm is, they would be an offering something in the six-figure range to all of us, you two for saving everyone and me for the emotional distress of hanging outside that window. We'll sign non-disclosure agreements, they'll split the cost with their insurance company and everyone will walk away happy," Yvonne said.

"Before you all start spending that money, there is still some other business to attend to." Pointing to Harold and Jessie, Randy said," You two need to go down to the police station and make a revised formal statement or in Harold's case initial statement, to fix the fibbing that went on yesterday. You could announce a time for your press statements after that. Maybe that could even happen later today to get it over with. They have conference rooms set up for news people if you want to have it there."

With a unanimous agreement to meet at the police station at 2 p.m., the group dispersed. Harold and Jessie took Auggie to an off-leash dog park for a long overdue period of prolonged exercise. He chased old tennis balls with gusto and literally ran rings around everyone and everything in the park. The rain was intermittent, and they managed to avoid most of it. Back at Randy's house, Auggie got hosed off and dried.

The drive into downtown provided Jessie and Harold an opportunity to coordinate their stories and fill in the blanks in Harold's memory.

Several media trucks were unloading equipment as Jessie, Harold, and Auggie walked in. The news conference started at 2:30 p.m. with multiple variations of the same questions directed at each person. Were you afraid? Did you know it was Harold that pulled you in? Why get involved? How did you get out without the police seeing you? Three times in a short period, you were able to help someone, how do you think that happens? An hour later, much to everyone's relief, it was over.

Like the day before, airwaves were consumed with the story and follow-up reports. The rescue was reenacted in some detail with footage of the actual conference room thrown in. The video of Yvonne hanging out the window was trending on social media. The hostages were mainly unhurt as were their rescuers. Adams would be in the hospital for several more days following surgery to repair his hands and forearms. Once transferred to jail, he will be charged with four counts of attempted murder.

"Any chance you could take a couple of days off?" Harold asked a bit sheepishly during the drive back to Randy's house.

"Maybe, did you have something in mind?" Jessie responded with a hint of mischief in her tone.

"I was thinking we might go hide out on one of the San Juan Islands."

"That actually sounds fun. Unless you have someplace

already in mind, I know a place on Orcas Island that has nice little rental cabins right on the water. I could try and arrange something when we get back to Randy's."

"Could you try and make it for tonight?"

"Boy, you are anxious to get away from here," Jessie laughed.

"Not just away from here, but away with you."

CHAPTER 36

Pacing around the desk and screaming at a subordinate, made the warehouse office echo with rage. "That asshole is on every fucking channel twenty-four hours a day now. I'm caught holding thousands of dollars in food stamps debit cards that are going to expire all because of him and his goddamned dog.

The cops are poking around the edges of my business, my network is breaking down, and there he is waiting to get a medal wrapped around his neck. It's only been a couple of weeks and this operation that took me years to put together is falling apart. Even the legal stuff I do is going down the tubes. The shop owners have almost completely deserted me and even the druggies and hookers have stopped doing business with my guys. I hoped things would just go back to normal in time, but it's just gotten worse. Well, I've had it. I want everyone here now."

They started coming in slowly, but it took less than an hour to fill the little office. There was a total of nine young men ranging in age from late teens to late twenties. Although primarily Asian, there were also two Hispanic and one black in the group. They all came well-dressed and had arrived in late model sports cars. The hierarchy was well established.

There were only three chairs in the little room, one behind the desk belonged to the boss and the other two were occupied by his longest-serving lieutenants. The others were relegated to sitting on the floor with their backs against the wall or leaning against filing cabinets or doorframes.

"The Hawks have a home football game on Thursday night. The cops will be busy managing all those people and traffic. That's when we grab this guy Harold Pearson. Until then, I want you guys to break into teams and follow him 24/7. When I say go, whoever is watching him at the time, will grab him and anyone who's with him at the time and bring them here. I don't want anyone left around who could call the cops. Any questions?"

From a corner, a voice asked, "What about the dog?"

"Bring him if you can, but if not, kill him, don't waste a lot of time."

CHAPTER 37

The ferry ride from Anacortes into the San Juan Islands was wonderful. Dressed in heavy winter coats, Jessie and Harold were leaning on the deck railing and looking out over the beautiful blue water that was quickly fading to black with the setting sun. In the distance, the outlines of islands came into focus.

The wind created by the movement of the ship caused Auggie's ears to flap as he too looked over the railing. After a brief walk, around they retreated to the warmth of the enclosed deck.

Sitting quietly hand in hand for a significant length of time with the drone of the ship's engines as a backdrop,

Harold broke the silence. "I don't want in any way to jinx my extremely good fortune, but a couple of days ago you were very convincing when you said you didn't have feelings for me as a lover. This morning you were as sensual and passionate a partner as any man could hope for, then this afternoon, you agree to go away to a secluded island with me. So, I'm curious, what changed?"

Turning to face Harold, Jessie squeezed his hand in both of hers and looked directly into his eyes. "Last night, I watched you while you were sleeping, and I felt an all-encompassing warmth for you. Knowing how you unselfishly risked your life for Yvonne and the others and even tried unsuccessfully to save me from myself just filled my heart. That's why I got in bed with you last night. This morning, seeing you so despondent about the amount of media coverage we will likely be facing, I felt the desire to make love to you, both out of gratitude for what you've done and the hope that you would look past the next couple of weeks and see the exciting possibilities of the future."

Standing, Harold pulled Jessie to her feet, brought her close and kissed her deeply. Then whispered into her ear, "If you are in my future, I can't help but be excited."

The island was quickly coming into view and the overhead speakers blared the request that people disembarking at Orcas Island return to their vehicles. Descending two flights of stairs then weaving around bumper-to-bumper cars, Jessie yelled, "Catch," and threw the keys to Harold as they reached her car. You can practice driving all you want while we're here. Not much traffic on an island."

Racing across the beach with abandon, Auggie swam aggressively for any thrown object. Trying to avoid the violent shaking and subsequent drenching that followed each trip out of the water, Harold and Jessie tried to run away from the wet dog with little success. They entered the cabin with Harold and Jessie only slightly drier than Auggie.

The cabin was just as Jessie remembered from childhood when the family would come for a week every summer. One main room served as living room, dining room, and kitchen. She could have sworn the same linoleum was on the floor and laminate on the countertops from three decades earlier. A small bathroom and small bedroom rounded out the amenities. Steps from the water at high tide, the sound of the surf would rock Jessie and her brother to sleep each night as they lay in sleeping bags on the floor in the main room.

A freestanding wood stove in the corner had been prepped to start with kindling and paper already in place and a generous supply of extra wood sitting beside it. Jessie started the fire and added a nice big piece of hemlock once the kindling was burning well. In the shower, Harold washed the sand and salt water off Auggie and dried him as best he could. The shower was a small rectangle and it got even smaller when Jessie stepped in.

Pulling her close, Harold ran soapy hands up her arms to her shoulders then down her back. Turning her around he started at her waist and moved his hands up until her breasts were cupped in each hand as he kissed her neck. Her nipples hardened against his touch.

"I really need to shave my legs. It's been a while and they're like coarse sandpaper," Jessie said while grinding her hips against his groin.

"If you trust me with the razor, I'd love to do that for

you. Put your foot up."

Back to one wall and her foot against the other Jessie enjoyed the warm water as Harold meticulously ran the blade first from ankle to knee then onto her thigh.

Taking his eyes off her toned leg for the first time in minutes, Harold asked, "How far up do you want me to shave?"

"You can go as high as you want as long as you're careful. Just keep in mind that a slip up might seriously curtail some activities."

The water temperature was slowly dropping as Harold's sensuous task finished. In minutes, the water was seriously cold, and they raced out of the shower to stand in front of the now blazing wood stove to dry off.

Progressing no further than the nearby couch, they entwined and, as they would do multiple times over the next two days, worked hard to please each other.

For Auggie, the experience of being at the cabin was like a child's Christmas morning. His exuberance seemed boundless as he showed flashes of his amazing abilities with every trip outside. Watching his joy brought joy to Harold and Jessie.

While on the island, no mention was made of the tempest that awaited them, but during the ferry ride home Jessie scrolled through texts and tried to prepare Harold.

"Yvonne has done three more interviews, one local and two for national news outlets. She says each time our names were brought up, but she didn't answer any of those questions. Her phone is only ringing ten hours a day now so that's an improvement. We'll have to hone our interviewing skills just in case we can't avoid them."

As if on cue, Jessie's phone rang, and the number and

identification were from a local television station. She let it go to voicemail and then turned off her phone.

Poking at the screen of his phone, Harold was able to find one of the national interviews and they huddled close and watched Yvonne's performance. "Well, she sure is photogenic," Harold said at the end.

The drive south toward Seattle was uneventful and the conversation light. It was almost eleven when Jessie turned the last corner onto her street. Only one car was parked in front of her house as they pulled into the garage. It was a smaller white sports car with two people inside and it had driven off by the time they had gotten into the house. Relieved, they unloaded dirty clothes, leftover food, and miscellaneous mangled dog toys.

Never having been in Jessie's bedroom, Harold took a quick look around. Like everything else in the house, the room was neat and clean. More of her brother's paintings were on the walls. There were some framed family photos and a small television on a dresser across from the bed. A comfortable-looking overstuffed chair and matching ottoman were in one corner with a reading light above it. On the nightstand between the chair and the bed, was a current best seller with a dog-eared page mid-way through.

The attached bathroom was all tile with a big walk-in shower at the far end, toilet in its own nook and a large two sink granite-topped vanity.

Slipping under the covers, Harold watched from across the room as Jessie brushed her teeth while standing at the bathroom sink. The white nightshirt she was wearing came just to mid-thigh and rode up considerably higher as she bent over to rinse her mouth. Seeing him out of the corner of her eye, she purposely dropped her toothbrush and proceeded to bend even further to pick it up. When she turned to face him again, he smiled and said, "Thank you."

CHAPTER 38

"That's brilliant!" Harold said in all sincerity when Jessie suggested they offer only phone interviews to the media. Take it or leave it. "We could knock out several in the next hour or two and maybe get off the hook for some of this mayhem. Do you want to do them together or separate?"

Jessie answered, "Let's do them together. It might turn out to be fun, although I'm not betting on that. Finish your breakfast and give Auggie a good run and I'll make a list of who to call."

"I don't know if they will, but how do you want to answer if they ask if we're a couple?"

The question didn't catch Jessie completely off guard. In fact, just an hour ago, before Harold woke, she had been lying in bed thinking about that very thing but had not come up with a satisfactory answer. She'd only known Harold and Auggie for a couple of weeks and they had only been intimate for a few days. "Do you by chance have a suggestion?" she asked after an agonizing half-minute.

"I think we could stretch the truth a little bit and say something like, we've been friends for a while but are just starting a relationship and leave it at that."

"Sounds better than anything that has gone through my mind, so if it comes up, we'll go with that."

The first call went to the local NBC affiliate. The news producer pushed hard for an on-camera interview but finally relented when faced with a take it or leave it. After about five minutes of set up time, the familiar voice of an on-air reporter started asking questions. The answers were pleasant and brief with few if any follow-up questions. In fifteen minutes, they were on to a second call, this time to a local newspaper. As hoped, they managed to make it through their list in less than two hours.

"Well," Jessie said while stretching out on the sofa, "I'm glad that's over with. What's on your agenda for the rest of today?"

"I want to get that drug test done, so hopefully the results will get to Mr. Ashcroft before the weekend. I called him earlier to see if he might have had a change of heart about hiring me after the whole bomb in a high-rise incident."

"What'd he say?"

"Frankly, he asked better questions than the reporters we just talked to. I gave him a bit more detail but didn't mention that I couldn't remember most of it and almost died in a janitor's closet. He was cool about it but hoped my heroic adventures would be winding down soon. I assured him I hadn't gone out looking for trouble and also hoped that my life would settle down. Oh, one other thing. It turns out Joan Leahy is Ashcroft's granddaughter. Small world."

Jessie stood and moved toward the bedroom. "Did you tell him we've met her?"

"He already knew. Joan told him about walking with Auggie and me."

"That can't hurt being on good terms with your boss's granddaughter."

"Changing the subject, unless you already had a lab picked out, I know some people at a lab that we use frequently to see if our clients are maintaining court-ordered sobriety. I'm sure you could just walk in there with no problem."

Following Jessie down the hall, Harold said, "Sounds great. After I get that done, I could show you where I've been living the last couple of years if you're still interested in seeing it."

"I'd love that, and you said before it wasn't far from the office. I really should go to work for a while first though since I've been gone for days. You could hang out with me or walk with Auggie, then we could see your space after."

"Although I think it's supposed to rain all day, I think I'd like to wander a bit and maybe stop by your office about four."

"Done."

Unrelenting rain crippled the drive toward Seattle. Standing water on the freeway made traction dicey at times and spray from big truck tires frequently made seeing the lane markers impossible. Off the freeway briefly, Jessie drove to the lab and waited with Auggie while Harold had his blood drawn for his drug screening. Freeway traffic had only mildly improved in the intervening half hour but was at least moving when they proceeded.

Once on city streets, Jessie trolled for street parking for ten minutes before deciding on a parking garage four blocks from the office. Huddled together under the same umbrella they walked to the office and parted with a kiss.

Three staff members were manning the phones when Jessie walked in and each ended their calls quickly and hurried to Jessie's cubicle for hugs and to hear the amazing tale first hand. The story Jessie told was essentially the same as the one she had given at the police station to the news media two days before and only slightly different than the one Yvonne had told the day before when she had stopped in at the office, but no one cared. The rest of the workday for Jessie consisted of paperwork and taking her turn answering phone calls.

The first in-person visit to Curbside Counseling didn't happen until three-forty when Nancy Cabot and Joan Leahy came in together.

"My husband got tickets to the game months ago but was called out of town on business and I didn't want them to go to waste, so I called Joan," Nancy said.

Joan supporting a wide grin said, "I know it's a school night, but this game has been sold out for months. My dad was so jealous that I was getting to go. We just stopped in to see for ourselves that you were OK and be sure Yvonne, Harold, and Auggie were OK too."

"Well, I'm glad you did stop. And yes, Yvonne, Harold, Auggie, and I are all fine. I'll tell them you stopped in."

"My grandfather says he offered Harold a job. I sure hope that works out. He could surely use the help. I had no idea Harold was an architect."

"I think your grandfather made a great choice and he'll be really happy with Harold's work. Go enjoy yourselves and eat some of that decadent stadium food I've heard about," Jessie said walking them to the door.

A steady stream of foot traffic was moving past the office as people headed to the game due to start at five. Nancy and Joan stepped into the crowd and were out of sight quickly.

With just two blocks to go, Nancy pulled Joan aside. "I don't think I can wait to get to the stadium, I need to stop and pee. Let's go to that bar across the street."

The place was packed shoulder-to-shoulder with revelers getting primed for the game. Multiple televisions were showing the same station covering the pre-game show. Joan waited just inside the door while Nancy snaked her way through the crowd and took her place in a slow-moving line outside the women's restroom.

Overly loud music mixed with a hundred voices made a conversation nearly impossible. People were forced to lean over and speak directly into the ear of the person standing or sitting next to them. Joan watched with a smile as testosterone-fueled men strutted and estrogen-filled women preened in the newest mating rituals.

Out of the crowd, two young men approached Joan, one carrying a bottle of beer in each hand. Holding out a bottle he leaned in, "Hello, I'm Jason and this is Vince. Would you like a beer?"

"No, thank you," Joan replied trying to maintain her smile.

"Come on, baby. Just one then I promise we'll leave you alone."

"No, thank you. I'm just waiting for my friend and then we're going to the game."

They moved to put her between them and pushed against her with increasing pressure.

"A beer at the game is five bucks and you can have this one for free."

"I don't drink, but thanks anyway. There's my friend," Joan said stepping toward Nancy.

In full view, Nancy immediately realized Joan's predicament and reached out for her hand. "Let's get going I don't want to miss the kick-off."

One of the guys was now blocking the door, and the episode continued. Looking Nancy up and down, Jason said, "You didn't say your friend was a hot cougar. Why don't you both stay and have a beer with us? You have plenty of time."

Not responding, Nancy and Joan pushed between the men and just reached the door when a hand forcefully fondled Nancy's butt in the same manner and at the same time as Joan was being assaulted.

"Get your fucking hand off me, asshole," Nancy said, before delivering a forceful face slap to Vince.

Joan's response was to whirl, grab a handful of Jason's shirt and without thought, hesitation, or effort throw him high across the room. During his flight, two ceiling-mounted television sets and the only security camera were destroyed, before he landed on a pool table thirty feet away.

Not waiting to see the damage, Nancy and Joan left and moved into the crowd quickly. Minutes later they were standing near the stadium gate. "Oh, my God. Where did, 'get your fucking hands off me, asshole,' come from? I've never even heard you say darn before and that slap was impressive. You might have broken his jaw," Joan said laughing.

"Hanging out at Curbside Counseling with strong women who don't take any shit like Jessie and Yvonne might have rubbed off on me a bit. But, I'm not the one who threw a guy across a bar with one hand. Where did that come from?"

Looking down at her still trembling hands Joan said, "I don't know. I think it must have been a combination of fear and an adrenaline rush like when a woman lifts a car off a child in an emergency.

I hope those guys aren't badly hurt. Do you think we should go back and wait for the police?"

"Well, let's see. We could go back and tell our side. Then they would tell their side, assuming either one of them could even speak, and we'd have a fifty-fifty chance of going to jail. Or, we could go enjoy the game and take our chances. Do you even think that they're likely to admit to having their butts kicked by a forty-five-year-old housewife and a seventeen-year-old high school girl?" Nancy said, grinning.

"When did you become such a rebel? If he were here now, Michael would be proud of you. Let's go to the game."

CHAPTER 39

During his walk, Harold had been recognized several times and engaged in small talk with people who would not have given him the time of day three weeks ago. It was in that environment of uncomfortable social connections, that Harold had the uneasy feeling of being followed. With little more than a block to go before he was back at Curbside, he turned quickly to scan the swarm of people walking behind him towards the stadium. No face was familiar, and no one made significant eye contact. A half-block ahead, he saw Nancy Cabot and Joan Leahy wave goodbye to Jessie as they left the office.

Auggie looked like a dog at those agility trials weaving through poles as he dodged people's legs to get to Jessie after Harold had let him off the leash. Seeing him coming, Jessie braced for impact but this time Auggie was able to come to a nearly complete stop and Jessie was able to remain upright.

Reaching for her hand, Harold smiled broadly and kissed Jessie lightly. "Wasn't that Nancy Cabot and Joan I saw leaving?" Harold asked.

"Yes, they just stopped by to ask if we were all OK and to say hello. They're going to the game."

"Not wanting to project or anything, but with Nancy's son's death and her husband on the road a lot she would be a prime candidate to start a downward spiral like I did. I'm glad she has Joan around and is interested in volunteering here."

"I am too. If she can stick it out a few weeks until the creepier aspects of the job become less creepy, I think she'll be great. She seems more confident and more powerful every day. I'd love to be able to get her into a paid position even if it's only part-time." Jessie said with a smile.

"I have confidence that you'll work your magic and make it happen.

So, ready to go visit my previous humble abode? After that, we can grab some dinner. I'm already starving."

"Sure. Come in a minute while I let them know I'm leaving and grab my coat.

By the way, I got a call from Bill St. James. He saw Yvonne's video and was checking to see if we were all OK. It was nice to talk to him."

"Yeah, that was nice of him to call," Harold said through a forced smile.

Police and medical vehicles, sirens blaring, tried their best to zigzag through traffic and dodge the occasional jaywalking pedestrian as they moved past Curbside towards the stadium.

"Gee, the game hasn't even started yet and already an incident. I suspect those guys are in for a busy night. Glad we're going in the opposite direction." Harold said with a head shake as he, Jessie, and Auggie headed out.

Rain, heavy at times, over the last twenty-four hours had given way to a mostly clear sky. The sun, still perched well above the Olympic Mountains, would fall behind them in less than an hour and trade its place in the sky with a beautiful crescent moon.

The walk was quick and as they approached the entrance to the alley, Harold asked, "Are you by chance claustrophobic?"

"No, not at all. Why?"

"We'll be going into some small poorly lit places and I just wanted to check. Going to see my space isn't worth a panic attack."

With a broad grin on her face, Jessie said, "This is starting to sound exciting. Let's go."

Halfway down the alley, Harold had that feeling of being watched again and looked back but saw nothing. Now standing next to the grate, he motioned Jessie to one side, found his hidden pipe and slid the grate out of the way.

"Oh, my God, don't tell me you live in the sewers," Jessie said pretending to be disgusted.

"If by chance, I did live in the sewers first, I would never admit it and second, I would never take you there. This is a storm drain. If you listen, you can hear water from all the rain we've had heading out to Elliot Bay. Where we're going is more than ten feet above that and reasonably dry."

Shining his flashlight down, Harold could see the plank still in place and with a makeshift harness and rope he had fashioned earlier in the day, lowered Auggie. Harold climbed down himself then shone the flashlight for Jessie. Once she was in, Harold climbed back up to replaced grate and then the tour commenced.

"How did you find this place?" Jessie asked excitedly while looking at the old storefronts before walking into Harold's living space.

"I'd seen some old maps and taken the Underground Tour and was fairly certain something had to be here, so I took a chance on coming down that manhole and found this. That was almost two years ago, and I've been here ever since. The Underground Tour goes down a passageway just on the other side of that wall." Harold said pointing to a brick wall at the far end of the room.

They walked through the connecting tunnel to the makeshift bathroom then back to his space, there holding up his hands Harold said, "Well, that's it. You're the first and only person to be given this exclusive opportunity to view the home of local Seattle hero, Harold Pearson."

Sitting on the bed, Jessie unzipped her coat, unbuttoned her blouse, and said, "I'd like to tip my tour guide if your company policy doesn't forbid it."

"I know the company president personally and he encourages the staff to take tips, so he can keep the wages low."

The next hour was filled with both passion and playfulness followed by a brief nap.

While dressing, Harold asked, "What are you hungry for?"

"I just got what I was hungry for, now I have to think about what I want for dinner," Jessie said with a big grin. "Frankly, whatever is close and quick. It's almost seven already."

At the top of the ladder, Harold listened for any sound. Hearing nothing, he moved the grate with arm and shoulder as usual and stepped up into the alley. Jessie was right behind him and took his outstretched hand. As she stood up, four young men appear from the shadows, each holding a gun.

Pointing his gun into the drain, one of the men asked," Where's your dog, Mr. Pearson? He down there?"

The answer came like a bolt of lightning when Auggie appeared just long enough to get the man's gun hand in his jaws and pull the assailant into the abyss without ever having touched the ground.

From the drain opening, came screams, sounds of a scuffle, then the sound of large objects splashing into the churning water far below. Then silence.

Pointing a gun at Harold's head, the apparent leader of the group asked, "Where does that water come out?"

"I don't know for sure, but I think about a quarter of a mile out towards the middle of Elliot Bay," Harold said while holding Jessie tightly to his side.

"Any chance someone might survive that?"

"Again, I don't know. Even if he did manage to make it to the surface, out there the water is probably only forty-five degrees. He would get hypothermia and drown in a very short time. The police have rescue boats. If you call them now, maybe they can help."

With little more than a shrug, the answer was plain. "No cops. The boss wants to see you. Let's go."

Looking at no one in particular, he continued, "Put that grate back and push that dumpster on top of it just in case. We don't need any more fights with that dog if he's still down there."

Two cars were parked side-by-side just inside the alley facing out and as the group approached the trunks sprang open remotely.

Trying his best to stay calm, Harold said, "I don't know what this is about but if it has to do with me, there's no reason to take her. Why don't you let her go?"

"She goes, so shut up and get in the trunk or I put a bullet in her head right now."

Able to kiss Jessie, he whispered, "*Stay strong.*" Before being forced into a trunk, Harold's wrists were duct taped together. Jessie was also bound after getting into the other trunk.

The sound of a high-performance muffler made listening difficult, but at a brief stop, he heard, "Yeah, we got him and his girlfriend, but I think Von is dead. The dog got him, but I think the dog is dead too. We'll be there in fifteen minutes. Be ready to open the door." Harold's mind raced. Was Jessie OK? Could Auggie have survived? Why were they being taken?

After a series of intermittent stops and starts, the car's engine was turned off and the trunk opened. Aggressively pulled to his feet, Harold could see he was in a large, poorly lit warehouse that reeked of noxious chemicals. At one end was a small office. Its back wall looked solid, the other three walls were glass mid-way to the ceiling. He could see Jessie already seated and restrained.

"Can you tell me what this is about?" Harold asked again.

"Just sit your ass down and shut up. When the boss gets here, he'll tell you what he wants you to know." Came the reply as Harold was forced to sit and have his arms tied to the chair.

As six young men milled around not far from the office

door clearly waiting anxiously, the tension became palpable.

"Darling, I have no idea what this is about or what I might have gotten you into and I'm having trouble coming up with a plan. All I can say is I'm sorry for whatever this turns out to be and I love you." Harold said in a whisper.

"I can't even imagine that anything you might have done has brought this on," Jessie said while trying to hold back tears.

The sound of a large bay door being opened on poorly lubricated tracks echoed throughout the building. A car came speeding in and slammed on its brakes creating a different echo.

Looking into the group of young men, the driver yelled as he exited his car, "Where is the mother fucker?"

Several men pointed at one time to the office, and someone said, "He's in there, Zak," and the group parted as he passed between them. Without another word, he walked in, stood directly in front of Harold, and began a savage beating.

Jessie screamed and begged as blood began to flow freely from Harold's nose and mouth. A large cut opened above his left eye adding to the blood that was now being sprayed liberally around the room with each strike.

Stopping to catch his breath, Zak said, "That guy your dog killed tonight was my best friend. If I didn't need to keep you alive until the boss gets here, I'd beat you to death right now with my bare hands." Looking at Jessie, he continued. "I usually wouldn't hit a woman, but if you don't shut the fuck up right now I'll make an exception. Shut up!" he said as he left the room.

Slumped in the chair nearly unconscious, Harold could only mumble a barely audible, "Yes," when Jessie asked if he was awake. It was several more minutes before he could raise his head off his chest.

Spitting blood to clear his mouth, Harold was finally alert enough to talk. "The only chance we have is if I can somehow talk them into giving me some alcohol. Maybe then I could hold them off long enough for you to get out. Whatever I can do won't last long. I haven't eaten since breakfast."

The sound of the bay door opening again, pierced the relative quiet as yet another vehicle came in. It was not a small sports car like the others, but a big black premium SUV with windows tinted to make seeing inside impossible. With the back door held open, a big lumbering figure emerged, walking nonchalantly into the office, and sat behind the desk.

"Well, Mr. Pearson we meet again. My, your face is a mess. Appears you've had a disagreement with one of my employees. Does it hurt as bad as it looks?"

"Now that you mention it, I am in a bit of pain. If I could get a little something in the way of alcohol to drink it might help," Harold said trying to speak clearly.

"Why not? We're not going anywhere soon. The Hawks just won the game with a field goal as time expired and so the drunken partiers are jamming the streets. We've got at least an hour to kill, so to speak." Looking out the door, he said, "Someone get a bottle of wine out of the back for Mr. Pearson."

Turning his attention to Jessie, he continued. "Ms. Baker, as beautiful as ever I see. Glad you didn't have to suffer like Mr. Pearson. You look confused. You do know who I am don't you?"

"I know you're Keith Hart. I just don't know why we're here."

"Well, you're here because you happened to be with Mr. Pearson when I told my men to pick him up. All day long, it was just him and his dog wandering around the city. Then fifteen minutes after I tell them to grab him, he hooks up with you. Unfortunately, bad timing for you.

I am intrigued about this sewer you two disappeared into for over an hour. I just told my guys to wait, figuring you'd come out eventually. Besides, they didn't want to go down there anyway."

"You said you've met me before, but I don't recall it," Harold said.

"Clearly I didn't make as big an impression on you as you did on me. We were out on the street after that banquet where you and your dog got that cheesy award for being heroes. Your handshake nearly broke my hand. How is your dog by the way? I heard he went for a swim in the bay with one of my employees."

A tear rolled down Harold's cheek at the mention of Auggie, but he didn't respond to Hart.

"Now, let's get to why you're here. I had a thriving business pushing drugs and managing hookers, but my primary income came from providing local street people with needed cash or drugs in exchange for their food stamp debit cards. I also had agreements with several local merchants to cash in those cards for a nice profit in exchange for nothing happening to their stores. But, since the day you and that dog interfered with one of my negotiating sessions, my entire enterprise has been compromised. Hell, I have a half dozen coke whores with their brains totally fried that are refusing to work for me.

Until now, fear was my primary negotiating tool and I lost it. You're here to help me get it back. I'm planning on making a short video of your death to show those reluctant to work with me what happens when I'm crossed. You see, it's just business. I sent one of my associates to get a couple of burner phones to make the recordings. He should be back soon."

"Think I could get that drink while we're waiting?" Harold asked calmly.

"Sure, let me see what's holding that up. Do you prefer red or white wine?"

"Red I think, so if any gets spilled it will blend in with my shirt."

"Well said, Mr. Pearson. Red it will be."

CHAPTER 40

The violently churning water in the storm drain mixed with various types of rubbish and moved relentlessly towards the bay. Air pockets formed briefly where secondary drains merged with the primary pipe but were gone quickly as the volume and speed of the water increased. With three hundred yards remaining, there were no more secondary pipes and no more air pockets. Heavy steel bars in place to keep debris from entering the bay were spaced closely enough to trap bigger items, including the body of a young man and the plank Auggie had ridden like a surfboard to that point but were just wide enough for Auggie to pass through. Aided by the water's flow and an outgoing tide, Auggie quickly cleared the pipe's end and swam sixty feet to the surface with ease.

From the pier, people pointed down at what they thought to be a harbor seal moving towards shore. In the dark, it was impossible to make any other assumption. Climbing large boulders at the water's edge to the parking lot near a ferry dock, Auggie shook himself off then headed back into the city.

In minutes, he was back in the alley, his alley, the one that led to his home. The dumpster was still in place over the grate. Nose in the air, he moved to track whatever faint scent existed. On the street, it mixed with a million other scents until it was gone. His pace was quick, and direction deliberate. At Curbside Counseling, he scratched and barked at the door incessantly.

Yvonne interrupted a phone call to open the door. Auggie moved through the office checking each cubicle and communal space without acknowledging her. Back at the door, he started barking again and could not be quieted or consoled until the door was opened for him and he was gone into the night.

~*~

"Hi, baby. What's up? Randy asked in a pleasant tone.

"I think something's wrong," Yvonne said clearly upset. "Auggie was just here and it seemed like he was looking for Harold and Jessie. When he didn't find them, he wouldn't stop barking. I swear, I think he'd have gone right through that door if I didn't open it. He took off towards the stadium. I called both Jessie and Harold's phones and got nothing. I tried to text, but I don't think that was delivered either. I've never seen Auggie like that. I'm scared."

"Keep trying to call them and I'll be over as soon as I can. I'll make a request for patrol officers to report in if they see Auggie but not to try to stop him; just let me know where he's headed. Everyone on the force knows what he looks like."

Blaring car horns mixed with drunken shouts as the celebration moved from the stadium to the streets. There were no visions, sounds, or scents to follow but somewhere deep inside, Auggie knew the direction he had to go, and he was relentless. Leaping cars and dodging people, he became an unstoppable force on a mission.

The first report from the street, got to Randy as he turned his truck into the freeway. A patrol car had just been seen Auggie trotting briskly down the center of 1st Avenue South past the stadium then turning east onto South Holgate.

~*~

The little office was getting smaller by the second, as Zak and several of his crew came in. After removing the cork from a bottle of cheap wine, he moved behind Harold and said, "The boss wants you to have some wine. Hope you like it, asshole."

Grabbing a hand full of hair, he snapped Harold's head back and emptied the bottle over his face and into his mouth. Standing back, he laughed with the crew as Harold coughed and gasp for breath. On his way out the door, Zak added, "It's almost time for the movie to start. See you then."

Alone again, Harold asked Jessie, "I count about eight including Hart. How many do you think there are?"

"I think eight is about right, but it's a big building and I don't know if there are others we haven't seen. Were you able to swallow enough?"

Turning as best he could to face Jessie, he responded, "I don't know how much is enough, but I did get some. Promise me right now that if I can get us loose you'll get out. I mean it.

If you're not going to promise, don't say another word to me."

"I love you."

"I love you too, that's why I need a promise."

"I promise."

The bay door opened again to let another car enter. Hart was standing in the middle with all the others around him. Too far away to hear, Harold and Jessie could only assume the burner phones had been delivered. Zak and two others headed to the office.

Sitting on the desk, Zak lit a cigarette and blew smoke toward Harold's face while Jessie was being untied. "The boss doesn't think you should have to watch the rest of this. Yours will be lots quicker and less painful, just not here."

Harold took a deep breath, winked at Jessie then, as Zak inhaled on his cigarette, Harold exhaled forcefully. The momentary fireball engulfed Zak and started a wall calendar, some file folders, and other miscellaneous papers on fire. Breaking free, Harold grabbed the gun from Zak's waistband with his left hand while simultaneously striking with a perfectly placed right fist. That punch crushed Zak's jaw and propelled him against the back wall with enough force that a protruding coat hook caused instant death when it impaled him just below the skull. The others scrambled from the room as Harold and Jessie hugged on the floor.

Putting the gun in Jessie's hand, Harold said, "I'm going to try and get their attention away from that bay door. Pick your time and make a break for it. Shoot if you have to, but don't stop. When you get outside run until you're exhausted, then hide."

Multiple bullets shattered the office glass walls. After a brief moment of quiet, Hart said. "I don't know how you managed to get loose, but if you come out now, I promise you'll both die quickly. If we need to come in, Ms. Baker will get to watch you die slowly and painfully. Then she'll be locked in a room and used by my crew indefinitely. Your choice."

"One of your tough guys is already dead. I don't think all those pussies you have out there would be able to handle me, you included, so come on in," Harold said with the most bravado he could muster.

"I have a better idea. It's kind of small in there. How about we put down our guns and then you come out. We'll see if you're as tough as you think you are," Hart replied.

Rising just high enough to see over the jagged remains of glass, Harold said, "Deal, put them down and step away, fellows."

All eyes turned to Hart. When he nodded, guns and several cigarettes went to the ground, and seven nameless young men started a slow robot-like advance across the cavernous building. A couple looked side-to-side trying to get an indication of what an attack plan might be. The rest stared straight ahead with deadly intent.

As Harold stood fully erect, Jessie couldn't help but notice a tremor in his legs. Looking down, he smiled. "This is it, darling, at the first sound go. Don't wait and don't watch just get to that door open it and run."

~*~

Randy was just inside the Seattle city limits when he got another call. Auggie had been seen again, he was heading south again, deep into the industrial area at a dead run. The patrol car had tried to keep up but lost sight of Auggie in heavy traffic. The freeway exit to that area was just ahead.

~*~

Moving well clear of the office, Harold positioned himself in a corner, his attackers fanning out to cut off a potential escape. The first brave soul to charge started from twenty feet away but missed with a wild swing. Harold landed a solid punch to the midsection that drove the young man first to his knees then face flat on the concrete, blood streaming from his mouth. The remaining six charged in unison.

Punches rained down that were individually ineffective but cumulatively began to extract a toll.

The previous wound above Harold's left eye reopened sending out a stream of blood that severely limited his sight. Only able to connect randomly and with rapidly fading power, Harold managed just one more significant punch, a perfect upward strike to a nose that drove cartilage into the brain. Now exhausted, Harold's arms were restrained, and he was pummeled relentlessly. Gunfire was the last sound he heard before losing consciousness.

Jessie hadn't gone much of the sixty feet she would need to cover to get to the bay door before Keith Hart started shooting. Each shot was slow, deliberate, and increasingly more accurate. Without aiming, she returned fire while running as fast as she could, eyes fixed on the door. Her shots shattered car windows and flattened a tire. Her last shot ricocheted off the floor and into the gas tank of Hart's SUV creating an expanding pool.

After what seemed like an eternity, Jessie grabbed the door handle and pulled. The heavy door squeaked and groaned then rolled opened just far enough, but not soon enough. The bullet struck her left thigh from behind shattering the bone. The force of the impact buckled her knees and sent her sprawling to the ground just outside.

Putting his gun in his waistband, Hart looked down, "It didn't have to be this way, Ms. Baker. It could have been quick and nearly painless, but I guess you're one of those people that won't accept the inevitable." Scanning the darkness and only seeing a truck trying to make a U-turn halfway down the block, and a distant nondescript red glow, he continued, "Well, let's get you back inside before someone sees us."

CHAPTER 41

Only someone with a radar gun could have known that Auggie was going over fifty miles an hour when the top of his head struck Hart's sternum. Most of Hart's ribs shattered on impact, with the resulting bone fragments forced deep into his heart and lungs. Airborne, his now deceased body came to rest embedded in his SUV's back window.

Nearly unconscious from pain and blood loss, Jessie smiled when a wet nose touched hers, "Get 'em Auggie," she whispered. But he was already gone.

The man standing closest to Harold's nearly lifeless body was the first to encounter Auggie. Slammed to the ground, he was all but decapitated from a single bite to the throat. As the realization of what just happened penetrated their consciousness, the remaining four scattered and ran for their lives. Sprinting to try and retrieve a gun was fruitless when Auggie easily caught one from behind, shook him violently like a cheap dog toy before launching him thirty feet to the roof where he dangled briefly on a truss support before falling head first to the concrete. Another man, who was quickly cornered, flailed his arms and legs in defense only to have them mauled to the bone or broken. Kellen and Lee were the only two left.

Looking down from what he believed to the relative safety of an eight-foot-high stack of shipping pallets, with an iron pipe in hand, Kellen saw nothing but bodies; some mangled, all covered in blood. He heard nothing but the moans of those not dead or unconscious. The fire Harold had started in the office from one deep breath, had grown and now lapped at that room's ceiling tiles. The smell of gasoline overtook the usual stench of noxious chemicals. He knew he had to get out but didn't know how.

~*~

With his windows down, Randy slowly trolled the nearly deserted and poorly lit streets hoping for a glimpse of a black dog. Cutting through an alley, the sound of muffled gunfire got his attention. Turning onto a street, he heard one more shot, coming from behind him, that was significantly closer and louder. Driving over the curb to complete his U-turn, he only passed four buildings before he saw a body illuminated by a stream of light coming from a partially open warehouse door. After a quick phone call for help, he approached cautiously, gun in hand. The smoke and the stench of gasoline and random chemicals rolled from the open door. From inside, came blood-curdling screams from the victims of a violent attack.

Jessie moaned in pain as Randy gently lifted her leg to wrap his belt around her thigh and tightened it firmly. He asked, "Jessie, can you hear me?" but got no response. "Help is coming but I need to get you away from this building." Sliding his hands under her shoulders, Randy sat her up then dragged her to the street. In the distance, sirens were convening from several directions. Multicolored strobe lights appeared from each end of the block and bright headlights bathed the scene with light as he sat with Jessie's head in his lap.

~*~

Managing to escape Auggie's initial attack, Lee had run, then crawled to stay out of sight until he could get into one of the cars. From there, he'd watched as Auggie wreaked havoc and knew without a doubt he was no match for that dog. But, laying not twenty feet away were several guns, so he decided to take a chance. As quietly as possible, he opened the car door, got his right foot firmly on the floor then ran. Barely slowing, he scooped up two of the guns then after three long strides, jumped from bumper to hood to roof of the SUV.

Auggie had been making slow deliberate circles around Harold but stopped and watched as Lee made his mad dash.

"Shoot that motherfucker or we'll never get out of here," Kellen yelled.

With a gun in both shaking hands, Lee fired repeatedly and missed. Hot spent casings were landing harmlessly on the SUV roof, but one bounced off. Landing in the pool of gas, it ignited flames that instantly moved fifteen feet in every direction. Lee was trapped.

As the paramedics moved in, Randy left Jessie to huddle with other officers and firefighters. "I smelled phosphorous when I was by the door. We might have to pull back and treat this like a meth lab. The whole place could blow." When the gunfire started again from inside followed by an enormous fireball they scrambled behind vehicles for cover.

Tapping Randy's shoulder, a paramedic said, "The lady wants to talk to you."

Taking Jessie's hand and getting a faint squeeze in

response, Randy put his ear to her lips. "Harold and Auggie are in there. Please help them."

Kissing her cheek, he said, "I'll try."

Inside, the gasoline fire had reached two other cars. Outside, thick black smoke billowed from the door, carrying with it the stench of burning tires. From thirty feet away, firefighters aimed water at the door while others prepared to enter the structure. Pleas for help from inside were drowned out when tires began to explode, sending out flaming pieces of rubber which started fires in other locations.

Watching helplessly, Randy couldn't believe his eyes. Moving against the force from two high-pressure fire hoses, Auggie was backing out the door pulling Harold's unconscious body. Breaking through the line of firefighters, Randy was first at Harold's side.

Unresponsive and unrecognizable with a thick layer of caked blood covering his swollen, battered face, Harold was gently placed on a stretcher and wheeled to a waiting ambulance.

With Auggie as his passenger, Randy followed the ambulance to the hospital calling Yvonne on the way.

Liquid gasoline burns but gasoline vapors explode. As the last of the gas drained from the SUV, the remaining fumes in the tank exploded. Lee was thrown from the roof of the SUV into a now raging inferno. On fire and disoriented, he batted at the flames but could not get up. Kellen jumped from the stack of now burning pallets but was struck mid-flight by multiple pieces of shrapnel from the SUV explosion. He died soon after hitting the floor.

Firefighters' attempts to get inside the building were repulsed by more explosions and a toxic cloud. Establishing a defensive parameter to protect surrounding structures, they hosed down the outside walls while the fire raged inside. It would be two days before the first investigator would get inside.

CHAPTER 42

Awake for a few minutes, Jessie still needed time to clear her head. Opening one eye a sliver, Jessie looked around her hospital room. Mom, Dad, Yvonne, Randy, and even Bill St. James talked quietly. Oxygen delivered by tubing in her nose was making her mouth dry and nose itch. Her left leg was elevated, immobilized in a long leg brace, and suspended in a medieval-looking traction device. IV bags dripped multiple fluids into both arms. Wires from her chest led to a monitor above her head that beeped in a steady rhythm.

"There sure are a lot of flowers in here. Did I just win the Kentucky Derby or something?"

Everyone stopped talking and looked at her. "That figures," her mother said in an exasperated tone. "She almost dies and the first thing out of her mouth when she wakes up is something smart ass."

Laughing, everyone surrounded her bed. Her mother held one hand and Yvonne the other. They asked how she was feeling. "OK, I guess." Also, if she was in any pain. She replied, "A little, not too bad." Then several questions came at once. But she had a question of her own, "Are Harold and Auggie OK?"

The room got quiet and Yvonne's grip tightened. Randy spoke, "Auggie's fine. His fur was singed a bit is all. He's an amazing dog."

"And Harold?" Jessie wanted to know.

Randy paused for a deep breath. "Harold took a serious beating. His jaw is broken in two places and plus some other facial fractures. He has some internal injuries too. I don't know about all of that."

Crying, Jessie asked, "Is he going to be alright?"

"The doctors don't know for sure yet. He had surgery to relieve pressure on his brain and stabilize some of the facial fractures. All his vital signs are stable, but right now he's in a coma."

"Is he here, in this hospital?"

"Yeah, in intensive care."

Sitting up, she looked at Yvonne. "I have to go see him." Not waiting for a response, she turned to her mother and repeated, "Mom, help me. I have to go."

Touching her right foot to get her attention, Jessie's father cut in, "Sweetie, listen to me. It's Saturday morning. You've been all but comatose yourself for one whole day. You've had four units of blood because you lost more than half yours and had a broken femur from a gunshot wound that they repaired yesterday. When the doctors say it's OK, I promise I'll take you to him myself, but not yet."

"He doesn't have anyone. Will one of you go sit with him?" Jessie implored.

"We've been taking turns," Yvonne said. "Someone is there all the time, twenty-four hours a day not counting Auggie. The only time he leaves is to pee and poop and he's back. I don't know what army it would take to keep him out."

Clearly relieved at the thought, Jessie laid back. "You're all here. Who's with him now?"

"His son and daughter-in-law."

"Oh, my God. That's great, but how did they find out?"

"Well," said Randy. "That was me. In cases where a person isn't able to give consent for a surgery or any procedure for that matter, the hospital has to contact the next of kin. Since I had his information, I called his son and told him the situation. He gave the consent the hospital needed and then when I got back on the phone, I told him all the wonderful things his father had done just in the short time I've known him, including saving Yvonne. He'd seen that news video of her hanging out of the window and was already planning on reconnecting with his dad. Apparently, Harold sent him like a ten-page handwritten letter full of contrition and asking for forgiveness. So, ten minutes after I got off the phone with him, he calls back wanting to be sure he knew which hospital and asking to meet up. He and his wife, Carla got here this morning at about eight. They seem very nice. Horrible set of circumstances to walk into though."

Tears streamed down each cheek as Jessie lay back with eyes closed taking slow, deep breaths.

"Are you hungry? Can we get you anything?" asked Yvonne.

"When you say *anything,* would that include a nice burger and fries? Jessie said through a grin.

"Well, you probably have a diet restriction. I can go ask."

"Chocolate, if pudding is the only option."

A knock on the metal doorframe got everyone's attention.

"Hi, Jessie, can we come in?"

"I don't know. Who are you?"

"These are the doctors that fixed your leg honey,"

Jessie's mom said.

"This is Dr. Hamm, he's the orthopedic guy that repaired your femur, and I'm Dr. Richmond. My specialty is vascular surgery. I repaired your femoral artery." Feeling Jessie's left foot, Dr. Richmond continued. "We're just checking to see how you're doing. The color in your toes is good and you have good pulses, so we'll keep watch. But for my part, it looks good."

Dr. Hamm asked, "Can you rotate your ankle?"

Eight pairs of eyes fixed on Jessie's left foot as it made a slow circle.

"Fine, that's good for now. The bullet broke your femur cleanly. I put a rod down the center of the bone which is standard practice for a mid-shaft femur fracture." Pointing to the traction he continued. "We have your leg elevated to decrease swelling."

"What kind of recovery time am I looking at?" Jessie asked.

"Eight to ten weeks until you're walking without crutches or a cane."

"How soon can I be out of bed?"

"I'll have physical therapy get you up in a chair later today, then have you practice using crutches this afternoon if you're doing OK. Unless you have a problem, or some other doctor has issues, I could look at sending you home Monday."

"My friend, Harold Pearson, is in ICU. Could I go see him later?"

"That will probably be alright IF you do OK sitting up. Your blood counts are still on the low side. I don't want you passing out and taking any kind of fall."

While Yvonne followed the doctors out to ask about food, Bill St. James brought up logistical issues. "I don't remember how your furniture looked but we can rearrange stuff so you can get around easier." Pointing to Jessie's thigh he continued, "You're going to need alterations done to some of your wardrobe to accommodate all that hardware."

"Your father and I can run out and buy three or four pairs of sweatpants. I can take out the side seam and put some Velcro in a couple of places. That should work," Mrs. Baker said.

"We need to find your car too," added Randy.

Food in hand, Yvonne returned with a tray full of juices and pudding cups. "Sorry kid, it's a soft diet to start with and advance as tolerated to solid food."

One pudding cup and a juice box into her first meal, Jessie stopped eating, laid back, and closed her eyes. "I'll try some more a bit later. I'm not really hungry right now."

Clearing his throat, Randy said, "Let me start off saying there is no rush, Jessie, but as soon as you feel up to it, I need to get your account of what happened. The coroner has nine bodies he needs to explain."

"Ten," Jessie said without opening her eyes. "I'm pretty sure there's another body in the storm drain system somewhere between Pioneer Square and the middle of Elliot Bay."

"I guess I'd better go make some phone calls and get someone to look into that. I'll stop back later. Bye, everyone."

Taking Jessie's hand again, Yvonne said, "Looks like you're getting tired and it's time I took my turn with Harold, so I'm going to take off. All our numbers are on a pad on your nightstand. If you need or want anything, have a nurse call one of us."

"Kiss Harold for me and tell him I'll come to see him soon."

"I will."

The room got quiet. Mr. Baker and Bill took a walk, first to see Harold, then outside for some fresh air. Mrs. Baker sat in a marginally comfortable chair at her daughter's side and Jessie fell asleep.

Her mother was dozing, her father and Randy watching a college football game minus the sound, so no one noticed when Jessie's hands started to twitch. Everyone noticed when the twitching turned to jerking, then violent thrashing and finally blood-curdling screams at the top of her lungs. A good portion of that floor's hospital staff crowded into the room to find Jessie's parents trying to control each arm and Randy attempting to protect her fragile left leg. Alarms from the cardiac monitor and IV pumps were going off adding to the chaos. Then, with one last vicious jerk, Jessie woke up and began to sob uncontrollably while her mother lay across her chest hugging Jessie as hard as she could.

Alarms silenced, nurses assessed IV sites, cardiac monitor leads, and leg traction before leaving. Randy typed a message into his phone then watched from the foot of the bed as the room calmed.

"I was back there, back in that warehouse watching Harold being beaten and I couldn't do anything," Jessie said when she was finally able to speak. "Now Harold is still fighting for his life and I'm helpless again."

Wiping Jessie's face with a damp washrag, Mrs. Baker fought back tears. "You've spent most of your adult life helping people. People that much of society completely ignores. Now you're in a tough spot. Helping, the very thing that you do best, you have to hand over to other people. Not only that, but you have to accept help too. No one knows better than me, how hard that is for you. I can't begin to imagine what you and Harold went through, but your father and I will be here to help both of you for as long as it takes."

"All this is so expensive too. I have some insurance, but Harold has nothing. He's supposed to start a job next week and who knows about that now. Then he'll have this enormous bill hanging over his head forever."

"Let's not worry about that right now. Just focus on getting both of you better first," Mrs. Baker said.

Sounds that usually accompany a potential disaster, came from the hallway when the elevator doors opened releasing the tornado that is Auggie. Unable to maintain traction on the tile floors, he careened into various people and things, slid sideways while trying to stop at Jessie's room, regained direction and momentum then launched himself from just inside her door landing perfectly in the place on Jessie's bed that Mrs. Baker had just been occupying. With what appeared to be a smile on his face, he stared at Jessie momentarily before flopping across her chest to deliver a not so subtle face washing. For the second time in ten minutes, multiple machine alarms brought staff.

While relative quiet was being restored, Jessie treated Auggie to a world-class belly rub with hugs and kisses thrown in. "Mom, this is the deranged killer you wanted me to be careful around."

"I had the good fortune of meeting Auggie in Harold's room yesterday. I saw then his quiet solemn devotion to Harold and now his poorly contained exuberance and affection for you. I believe in my heart he would never intentionally hurt you but a fifty-pound dog leaping and jumping around like he does could indeed seriously hurt you. So, the mother in me still very much wants you to be careful around him but for a totally different reason. He could nearly beat you to death just with that wagging tail of his."

Peeking in from the hallway Yvonne asked, "Is it safe to come in here yet?"

"Thank you for bringing Auggie. I know all of you said he was fine but it's great to see him for myself." Jessie said.

"Well, Randy sent me a text saying it might be a good time for a visit. I had no idea he would go flying down the hall like he did when I said, *Go find Jessie*. If I'd had a leash on him I'm fairly sure I would have been polishing the hall floors with my butt while he dragged me to your room." Stepping back towards the door and motioning to someone unseen, Yvonne said, "Jessie, I brought someone else to see you. I'd like you to meet Steven and Carla Pearson. Harold's son and daughter-in-law."

With hand extended, Steven crossed the room and shook Jessie's hand gently. "So nice to meet you, Ms. Baker. Randy told me you were the driving force behind locating me. Thank you." Stepping aside, he continued, "This is my wife, Carla."

"Please, call me Jessie. I couldn't be happier to meet you both. When your dad wakes up, he'll be thrilled too. As I recall, you have a child."

"Yes, Kenny. He's at home with Carla's parents. I didn't know what to expect when we got here and generally hospitals are no place for children anyway."

"Well, welcome to Seattle. How long can you stay?"

"I'm flying back home to Ashland on Wednesday. Steven is going to stay a little longer. We drove so he doesn't need any kind of flights or reservations," Carla said.

"Do you have a place to stay?"

"Randy has been kind enough to let us stay at his house."

Jumping off the bed, Auggie walked to the door then looked back. He let out a gentle whine with a meaning that was clear to Jessie. He wanted to go back to the ICU.

Yvonne offered to be the escort and since Bill was currently with Harold, he could look after Auggie if need be.

"Come right back," Jessie said.

"Is that as painful as it looks?" Steven asked pointing to Jessie's left thigh.

"I'm sure it will be eventually, but one of these IV machines is giving me a morphine drip so, for now, I'm happy. I get to be out of bed soon, so we'll see what happens then.

Tell me about your dad. Any change?"

"About an hour ago Dr. Thompson, the neurologist, was in and did some testing of his reflexes and looked at lab work. After that, she said she felt like his reactions were more brisk and his intracranial pressure, whatever that is, was back to normal. So, she felt like those were all positive signs. He still doesn't have any voluntary movement though," Steven said, trailing off at the end.

"I'm seriously going to try to see him later. I just have to show that I can tolerate being up before they'll let me take a wheelchair ride."

"I will totally understand if you say no, but would you mind telling me what happened to you and my father?"

Mrs. Baker intervened quickly. "If that could wait a day

or so, I think it would be better."

Reaching for her mother's hand Jessie said, "Randy has been waiting patiently to hear the story to file a police report and I suspect inside all of you are dying to know."

Yvonne had just stepped into the room. "Great, my lawyer's here. Could you close the door please?"

"What's going on?" Yvonne asked.

"I was just going to talk about Thursday. Say, could you call Bill? He can listen on his phone."

An electric motor hummed when Jessie activated the control to raise her head to be more upright, but she had to recline back down when a bolt of pain ran from her left hip to her toes.

Gleefully, she told in detail the adventure of descending into the storm drain and going back in time a hundred years and how Harold had managed, with lots of ingenuity, to make that small space quite comfortable. But the smile left her face and tears began to form with the first mention of contact with their captors, the first death and the thought Auggie had been killed. Barely maintaining her composure, she was able to continue until she began to describe Harold's first beating.

The small bedside tissue box emptied quickly as the women openly sobbed, while the men tried unsuccessfully to hold back tears.

Repeating Keith Hart's reason for their abduction and his intent to kill them, Jessie said that at that moment she believed they would soon be dead.

Giving no explanation of exactly how Harold had managed to get free and overpower one of the men, she told of bullets peppering the office and glass shards raining down while they hugged on the floor.

"He made me promise I would try to escape, handed me the gun then taunted Hart into disarming his men. When he stepped out of that office, I'm sure he believed he would be killed but that was the only chance I might have to get out and I almost made it too. I have no idea how Auggie survived the storm drain or how he found us miles away, but just as Hart reached to drag me back into the building, Auggie slammed into him like a runaway freight train, then went in to find Harold. I vaguely remember Randy putting something on my leg but that's it." Smiling at Randy, Jessie continued, "So, the award for saving my life has to be split three ways. Harold got me to the door, Auggie stopped my attacker, and Randy stopped me from bleeding to death."

"Well," Randy said while moving to take Jessie's hand. "Harold and Auggie have saved more people from death or severe injury in the last few weeks than seems humanly or dogly possible. I cede my third of the award and any rewards that may follow, above and beyond a kiss, to them."

"Thank you for telling us, Jessie. I appreciate it. But now I think I'm totally pissed at my father," Steven said while shaking his head.

The room went silent. "How could you possibly be mad at your father after hearing that?" Jessie asked.

"My father has set an impossibly high bar for all other husbands and boyfriends to achieve. How do you compete with a guy who figuratively gave up his life because he loved my mother so much and now literally offered his life for someone else he loves?" Steven said with a smile.

"How do you compete indeed?" Bill thought to himself hanging up the phone.

"There are millions of ways to show love that don't

involve near death experiences. I'm essentially an atheist, but I do believe that if you do kind things without the expectation of a reward, like sitting in an ICU with someone that is unconscious who you barely know or maybe have never even met, good things will come to you." Activating the bed control to lower her head, Jessie finished, "I'm getting tired and I want to try and rest again before they come to get me up."

Hugs and handshakes went around the room and as they turned to leave Jessie added, "One more thing. I don't know who's going to be with Harold, you guys seemed to have that all figured out. But I just want to warn whoever that is, if I find out he moved so much as a little toe on his own and you don't come and tell me, three months from now when my leg is healed I'm going to track you down and kick your butt. No exceptions for family or best friend."

CHAPTER 43

The physical therapist was gentle and efficient when helping Jessie to the chair and it felt good to be unencumbered by the wires and tubes.

"How long have you been out of bed?" her mother asked.

"About twenty minutes I think. If I'm still doing OK at three, the nurse said they could cover my leg in plastic wrap and take me to a shower room. That just sounds heavenly. A couple of days of lying in bed and my hair is an oily mess and I smell like road kill."

"I brought you some tops and a couple pair of sweats with the leg seam opened and Velcro strips added, so you'll have something to wear after your shower."

"Great, I want to be wearing street clothes and feel kind of normal when I go to see Harold. Besides, when they get me up on crutches I won't have to be gimping down the hall with my butt hanging out."

"I talked to Randy and Bill a bit ago," her father said. "They found your car and took it to your house then Feng Shui'd your furniture a bit."

"Look who's upright," Yvonne said cheerfully while giving Jessie a hug. "You look great. How do you feel?"

"That first move out of bed was painful but once I got settled I feel fine. I'm anxious to get moving."

"Well, rein in those horses, Calamity Jane. I figured you'd need something to do that didn't involve a lot of movement and had nothing to do with work, so I brought you a couple of boxes of thank you cards."

"A couple of boxes seems like overkill. There's maybe ten flower arrangements here."

"Well, there's twice this many flowers in Harold's room and then there are these," Yvonne said while dumping half a paper grocery sack of letters on Jessie's lap. "This is what came to the hospital and to Curbside just today. Randy said your mailbox at home is stuffed too."

"This is crazy. I don't even know this many people."

"They're not all for you, I've seen a few addressed to Auggie. Harold has a full bag in his room too. Steven and Carla are going through those and reading them to him. Some of them aren't even local. They're from people all over just wanting to wish you well."

"So, are you going to tell me what this is all about?"

"The bulk of the news about Harold, Auggie, and you aired yesterday while you were still asleep. Those reports went over everything that the three of you have been involved in since the Corner Market incident. Frankly, each event is worthy of praise, but my God, when you string them all together it's impressive as hell. I was there for the biggest one and I may not show it but I'm still so awestruck and grateful for what the three of you did for me and the other people in that room, I almost cry just thinking about it," Yvonne said,

"How does a news report turn into hundreds of cards and letters?" Jessie asked.

"Do you remember Ashley and Kari, the girls from down by the waterfront?"

"Yes."

"They were being interviewed again for this new story and were crying because you and Harold were hurt and said they planned on sending get well cards and suggested everyone else do the same. I suspect this is a drop in the bucket compared to what you'll get next week."

"Well, everyone take a handful and we'll take turns reading them. I don't have anything planned until three."

"We should tell her about the flowers too," Mrs. Baker said.

Looking at her mother Jessie asked, "What about the flowers?"

"This room isn't nearly big enough to hold all the flowers you've gotten. We picked a few nice ones or ones from people you know and had the nurses spread the rest around. This floor has thirty rooms and I know for a fact that they all have at least one bouquet plus the nurse's station and break rooms. I took pictures of all the arrangements with a close-up of the cards. We can work on that later."

"Was it the same for Harold?"

"Yeah, pretty much, give or take a few."

"Oh my gosh. Well, let's get at it. These cards aren't going to read themselves."

The feelings expressed in the cards ranged from a simple "get well" to several pages of heart-wrenching stories of love and loss. By the time three o'clock rolled around, Jessie had laughed or cried a dozen different times reading or hearing those sentiments and was more than ready to get off the emotional roller coaster and take a break.

While the nurse wrapped her leg in cellophane, draped a light flannel blanket around her, and assisted her to a wheelchair, Jessie asked, "Yvonne, will you come to help me if I promise not to soak you?"

"I would only come if you promised because even though you're just this side of a train wreck, I still don't think you can be trusted with running water."

Back thirty minutes later, smiling and looking fresh wearing the altered sweatpants and a bright violet T-shirt, Jessie had another request. "Dad, you said you would push me to ICU when I got the green light. We just saw the doctor in the hallway and he said yes."

Chuckling, Mr. Baker said. "OK, Sweetie. Let's go."

With her mother on one side and Yvonne on the other, Jessie was greeted with smiles and good wishes from the staff. The elevator ride was quiet and while they waited at the door to be buzzed into the ICU, Mrs. Baker squeezed Jessie's hand.

The entire back half of Harold's room looked like a florist shop. Floor to ceiling, wall-to-wall beautiful arrangements filled the room with color and fragrance. On one side of the bed, Carla was reading get well cards pulled from a bag by her feet, while Steven appeared to be dozing in a chair next to her. Auggie was sprawled on a dog bed between them and sprang up to greet Jessie. Carla tapped Steven awake and they too came over.

Machines of various types and sizes, all with blinking lights, dominated the other side of the bed and connected to Harold with a series of wires and tubes.

Covered by a crisp white sheet with nothing more than his head exposed, Harold looked small. Deep bruising covered the small area of his face not bandaged. A thick blue hose delivered oxygen to a small tube protruding from the base of his neck.

Sliding her hand under the covers, Jessie found Harold's and grasp it firmly but got no movement in return. "I guess I've been extremely naïve or maybe in denial. In my mind, I pictured him looking relaxed like he was asleep in a lawn chair on some beach and I could just roll in here and wake him up. This isn't even close."

A voice from just outside the room said, "I know it looks bad, but believe it or not I've seen worse."

Moving in to face Jessie, "Hi, I'm Roberta Thompson, Harold's neurologist. I'm guessing you're Jessie Baker. So nice to meet you."

"Well, doc, I'm a good news-bad news kind of person. I'm looking at a lot of bad news. Tell me what the good news is and feel free to exaggerate a little to make me feel better."

"I won't have to exaggerate much. His internal injuries and facial fractures have all been treated and are stable. He has a couple of broken ribs on each side that we need to be mindful of but won't be treating. We had to do the tracheotomy, so we could have a decent airway before the surgeries. He's breathing on his own and the trach can be plugged as soon as he's awake. We've kept him heavily sedated until we could get him stable. He's being slowly weaned off the sedatives and pain meds now and had a brain scan this morning that was essentially negative. This is absolutely not a vegetative state; he could wake up at any time. That said, he could come to with some physical or cognitive limitations. On that, we'll just have to wait and see."

"Is he in pain?"

"Probably not much right now since he's essentially motionless, but considering his injuries when he does start moving, he'll most likely have some pain."

"One last thing, can he hear us?"

"Research says yes, and in fact, people respond more quickly and can even recall what was said, if the voice is familiar."

"Thank you so much, Dr. Thompson."

"If anyone sees any change, just let the nurses know and they'll call me."

"We will."

Steven and Carla joined Mr. and Mrs. Baker on a trip to the hospital's cafeteria for lunch. Yvonne took Auggie out for a walk.

Pulling Harold's hand to her chest and leaning in close Jessie said, "I need you to wake up for me, so I know you're going to be alright. Since my voice is the most familiar to you, I'm going to sit here and talk non-stop until you wake up and tell me to shut up. You, Auggie, and I have things to do but none of it can happen until you're out of this bed."

Startled, Jessie looked down at Harold's hand. "Did you just pinch my nipple?"

Watching for the faintest finger movement, she saw none. "Come on, Harold, don't mess with me this is too important." Still nothing. Moving his hand so her nipple touched his thumb, she said, "OK, you perv. Is this how you intend on communicating?"

There it was, another pinch. "I'll let you get away with it for now because you saved my life, but if I find out you're using this on any other woman you'll be sorry. You got that, Thunderbird? One pinch for yes and two for no?" One pinch.

"I want to see what else you can move. Start up from your toes and move any joint that you can."

Toes, ankles, knees, fingers, wrists, elbows, and shoulders all moved at least a little.

"Can you see clearly?" Two pinches.

"Can you see at all?" One pinch.

Back from her walk with Auggie, Yvonne found Jessie kissing Harold's hand and crying then guessed.

"Oh, my god, Harold. Are you awake?"

One pinch. "He says yes," Jessie said.

"How do you know I didn't see anything?"

Shaking her head Jessie explained, "I think he must have some brain damage. He only answers yes/no questions by pinching my nipple."

"One minute out of a coma and already thinking about sex. I don't think he's any more brain damaged than any other guy."

Moving as slow as a snail, Auggie moved first to the bedside, then gently onto the bed until he was stretched out next to Harold. Equally as slow, was the movement of Harold's hand until it came to rest on Auggie's head.

"If we got a pen and paper do you think you could

write?" Jesse asked. One pinch.

"Yvonne, would you see if the nurses have paper and a pen before I end up on the maternity ward looking for nipple cream? Also, ask them to call Dr. Thompson."

"I don't know how much you were able to hear before. Do you know that your son Steven and his wife Carla are here?" One pinch.

"They're very nice. I kind of think he looks like you, or at least what you looked like a few days ago. I liked your face before, but if it's different when all these dressings are off, I'm hoping the plastic surgeon had George Clooney in mind when he was working." Hard pinch.

Propping the writing pad on a pillow, Yvonne moved Harold's hand into position. *Are you and Auggie OK?* He wrote.

"I have no idea how he managed it, but Auggie saved both of us and never got a scratch. I got shot in the leg and am looking at eight weeks of rehab, but all things considered not bad." Jessie responded.

"Are you in pain? Do you need anything?" Yvonne asked.

My pain is tolerable. I would like to sit up higher, get the tube out of my penis, get the tube out of my neck, and drink a really good chocolate milkshake in that order, Harold wrote.

Activating the bed controls, Yvonne raised Harold's head until he waved his hand. "We'll have to wait for the doctor to write orders to grant your other wishes."

I hope she's not a man-hating sadist hellbent on making me suffer and beg. I want to go back to the Yes/No questions.

"Oh, my God," Jessie said. "Who's the sadist now?

Sorry, but you've evolved from that primitive form of communication and I don't want to see you regress."

The number of visitors to Harold's room swelled well beyond what the hospital usually allows in an ICU setting when Steven, Carla, Jessie's parents, and Dr. Thompson all returned at the same time to join Yvonne, Jessie, and Auggie.

Looking at Jessie, Dr. Thompson asked, "Forty minutes from unconscious to awake and communicating. That's wonderful. What did you do to get this kind of response?"

"A tiny fraction of what I was prepared to do. He's a terrible negotiator," Jessie replied with a smirk.

Handing the paper with Harold's request to the doctor, Yvonne said," I told Harold you're the genie that might grant his wishes."

"Well, since you've shown you can express yourself, yes, the catheter can come out," Dr. Thompson told him.

"I'll call the pulmonologist and have him do a quick assessment. I suspect that he'll plug the trach or just remove it and then you'll be able to talk.

We'll try you with sips of water and if you swallow OK then liquids will be fine. Might as well get used to drinking your meals with a syringe since your jaw is wired because of the broken bones. As far as finding a decent chocolate milkshake, good luck.

Finally, I see you have a concern that I might have sadistic tendencies. As a matter of fact, I do but the Hippocratic Oath means I have to totally suppress them."

After a quick exam, she continued, "If your other doctors agree, I think we'll get you out of bed later today and walking tomorrow. The sooner you're up and moving the less likely you'll get pneumonia and the sooner we can move you to a regular floor and closer to being out the door. I'll check back before I go home but this is all good news. Bye, everyone."

"Now that you're awake, I think we should do formal introductions." Pointing to the foot of the bed Jessie said, "That distinguished older couple are my parents, Betty and Michael."

"I don't know how we could ever possibly repay you and Auggie for saving our daughter's life. Thank you and we hope your recovery is quick and uneventful. I'm going to put off giving you a big hug for now but once you're healed I will. We're going to stay in Seattle to help both of you any way we can," Betty Baker said with her husband nodding in agreement.

"The handsome couple standing next to my mom is Steven and Carla Pearson."

Gingerly, Steven took Harold's hand and leaned in for a gentle hug, then Carla did the same. "We have a lot to talk about and I truly don't know where to start. Carla and I are going to be here a few more days, so we'll have some time to figure it out."

Being surrounded by all you wonderful people is the perfect way to wake up from this nightmare. Thank you all for being here and looking after Auggie. Harold wrote.

For the better part of an hour, questions came to and from Harold, only interrupted briefly by other doctors' visits and the nurse twice. That second nurse visit was with a request, "Jessie, your doctor would like to see you in your room."

In an upbeat tone during the elevator ride, Jessie commented to no one in particular, "It might sound weird coming from someone in a wheelchair who just visited someone in ICU, but this is one of the best days of my life. I know there might be setbacks, but right now knowing he's better just makes me happy."

Her doctor's visit was brief and all positive. Soon after that, the physical therapist was back, this time with crutches.

"You can put your foot down for balance but don't put much weight on it."

Jessie was moving with some confidence after a trip around the unit and some practice in the stairwell going up and down stairs. Ten feet from her room's door, she smelled the unmistakable scent of Thai food and went in to find a buffet had been arranged. "Look at this, and from my favorite restaurant too," she exclaimed.

"You have Yvonne to thank, she called in the order. Bill and I just picked it up on our way," Randy said.

"Seeing all this beautiful food makes me feel bad for Harold, knowing he can't eat any of it."

"Well, we also got the order for a decent chocolate shake and dropped that by his room before coming up. The nurses were in the process of getting him into a chair. Frankly, I'm amazed he can even move, considering it's been less than forty-eight hours since Auggie dragged him out of that building."

The meal progressed quickly with entertainment provided in the form of some of the funnier cards and letters. It eventually became clear to everyone Jessie was winding down.

Looking squarely at Jessie, Bill said, "I'm amazed at how well both of you are doing. Seeing that you have all this help available, I think I'll head back home in the morning. I'm still dealing with the fallout from the bad wine, although my insurance company says negotiations are going well."

"It was very nice of you to come and the offer of help is greatly appreciated. Thank you."

"Your mother and I are going to take off too. Neither one of us has had much sleep the last two days, so we're going to go home, stretch out, and get a decent night sleep now that you're clearly much better. That doesn't mean we don't want you to call if you need anything or if you want us to bring anything when we come back in the morning," said Mr. Baker.

Jessie replied, "Absolutely, go get a good night's sleep."

"You seriously need to take a nice nap. Randy and I are going to take off for a bit, but we won't be gone long. When we get back I'll give you a ride to ICU," Yvonne said while gently stroking Jessie's hair.

Yawning and struggling to stay awake, Jessie said, "Don't let me sleep for more than an hour. I want to see Harold before it gets too late."

"OK, get some rest."

It was just one hour later when Yvonne and Randy got back to find Jessie not only awake but heading toward the door. Exasperated, Yvonne said, "Jessie, I love you, but sometimes you don't have the patience of a two-year-old. Sit down and wait one minute until I find a wheelchair. Randy, take those crutches away from her."

Sitting in a chair watching television with Steven and Carla, Auggie at his feet, Harold waved weakly as Jessie rolled in. Frail-looking and still connected to some machines it was, nevertheless, an improvement. A bandage at the base of his neck had been added to the ones that covered much of his face. The nearly empty milkshake cup sat on a bedside table next to his chair. Mustering a volume just above a whisper, he managed a quiet, "Hello," to everyone and was greeted warmly by everyone in return.

After answering multiple questions about how he was feeling, and his pain level, Harold had a question for Randy. "Did anyone else survive the warehouse?"

"No. Part of that building was being used to cook meth and those chemicals are both toxic and explosive. Once the fire got into that area, it became too dangerous for firefighters to go in. The heat got so extreme that it melted the metal walls and even weakened some of the support structures. Most of the roof eventually collapsed. All the bodies have been removed, but determining the cause of death, making positive identifications, and notification of next-of-kin might take a while. City workers did find the body Jessie said was in the storm drain system. He's been identified, and his family contacted."

"What an incredible waste of life."

"I agree," Randy said.

"Jessie, do you think Mr. Ashcroft will hold that job open for me a bit longer? I'm fairly certain I won't be able to make it to work a week from tomorrow," asked Harold.

"Is that Harrison Ashcroft?" Carla asked.

"Yes."

"You got a card from him. I remember because he has an unusual name. We can look through the bag, but as I recall it said something like, "Give me a call when you're up to it and we'll set up a new start date. No hurry," Carla recited.

"That's great. I'm really looking forward to working with him," Harold said with a bit of spark in his voice.

For the visitors, the anxiety and dread that had produced episodic levels of stimulation somewhere between a double shot latte and adrenaline were turning to relief and calm. Waiting to speak with doctors after surgeries and nights with restless sleep in bedside chairs gave way to exhaustion. Yvonne would take Jessie back to her room, then stay one more night with Harold and Auggie. Everyone else would leave the hospital for a quiet bed and a good night sleep.

Awake and dressed when her breakfast tray arrived, Jessie ate heartily. Individually, her doctors stopped in and after brief discussions deemed her fit for discharge.

Ambulating using crutches and without an escort, Jessie arrived in the ICU just in time to greet an upright Harold. Holding firmly to a walker, he labored with each step down the hallway while a staff person on either side protected him from a possible fall.

"Well, what do you think? Not bad for a ninety-year-old," he said in a voice that was slightly stronger than the night before.

"I'm very impressed. Does this mean you'll be getting out of ICU soon?" Jessie asked.

"The orders have already been written to move me upstairs. I think we're waiting for a room to become available on the neurological floor."

"That's wonderful. Boy, it's going to look like a float in the Rose Parade when they try to move all your flowers to a different room.

I'm being discharged as soon as my parents show up to claim me. I figured I'd go home for a while then come back later."

"Would you take Auggie with you and have someone get

him out for a good run. He's outside on a walk with Yvonne now but he really deserves some exercise. He's been so good here. I'm so proud of him.

Also, when you come back will you bring me some street clothes and another milkshake? I figure if I start looking the part maybe I can get out of here too."

"Sure, anything else?"

"I don't think so."

Comfortably back in bed, Harold watched with some amusement as Jessie first sat in the chair, then had to use both hands to raise her left leg and rest it on the end of the bed.

Sporting his happy face, Auggie trotted in and greeted both Jessie and Harold before flopping down on his dog bed. Yvonne was just behind. "Well don't you two make an attractive couple. I need a picture of this," she said while positioning her phone, "Smile."

"I'd have you send that to me, but I don't have a phone right now. I'm getting discharged, so I'll stop and get us a couple of new ones later."

"Glad you're doing well enough to get kicked out of here. Steven and Carla should be here soon. I'm going home for a shower and a nap, then I'm going to poke my head in at work. Call me later if you get a new phone."

Extending his hand, Harold said, "Yvonne, thank you for hanging out with Auggie and me. Uncomfortable chairs and odd noises all night long are not conducive to good sleep."

"Truly, it's the least I could do to repay you for everything you've done for me and my best friend. Thank you," Yvonne answered.

Fifteen minutes later, when a nurse followed by two young men pushing wheelchairs came in, the relative quiet ended. "Harold, we're ready to move you upstairs, and Jessie your family is upstairs loading up your stuff now. Instead of going back to your room, we'll just take you to the front door from here."

After moving to the wheelchair, Jessie held Harold's hand firmly. "Well, you may be on your own for a while. I'll be back before three. Call if you think of anything else you want. Auggie, let's go for a ride."

At the door, Auggie turned back and gave a little whine. Wishing he would stay but knowing he should go, Harold said softly, "It's OK. Go with Jessie and I'll see you later."

The back end of the SUV was crammed full of flowers, bags of letters, and a sack of clothes. Jessie stretched out across the back seat and Auggie managed to find a reasonable spot on the floor.

"Comfortable?" Mr. Baker asked before closing the back door.

"Yes. This is fine. Say, there's a cell phone place not too far from the house. We need to stop and get Harold and me new phones."

"You're just getting home from the hospital. Can't that wait a few days?" Mrs. Baker asked in her concerned mom voice.

"I really do feel pretty good and it will only take a few minutes. Then right home after that, I promise."

In the garage two hours later, Jessie's father helped her out of the SUV while her mother carried in bags containing two new cell phones, some new loose clothes for Harold, a toy to throw balls and three cans of new tennis balls for

Auggie.

Unceremoniously dropping the bags on the kitchen counter, Mrs. Baker said, "I know I shouldn't be surprised that you're back into helping mode already. You can't manage to take one hour, let alone one whole day for yourself."

"I love you for saying that because I know in my heart you just want to be my mom and look out for me. But if our roles were reversed and you were the one that has a broken leg and it was Dad who was still in the hospital, what would you do for him? Can you truthfully say you'd take a day off for yourself?"

Moving to embrace her daughter, Mrs. Baker whispered, "Don't throw out some hypothetical to try and trap me. Of course, I'd do anything I could for him."

"See, I'm just trying to be as loving a person as my mom."

Once out of the car, Auggie raced around familiar territory with reckless abandon. Mr. Baker threw tennis balls until arm fatigue won out. Back inside, Auggie polished off a bowl of food in his usual fashion then tracked Jessie to her bedroom and stretched out.

A ringing doorbell heralded the arrival of several hundred more get-well cards in a large box.

Refreshed after sleeping three hours in her own bed and eating food from her own kitchen, Jessie took a quick call from Harold, then joined Auggie in the back of the car anxious to leave. The drive to the hospital was interrupted by one stop.

With forty dollars' worth multiple flavors of milkshakes in hand, the Baker family followed Auggie as best they could on a new floor and to a new room. As expected, Auggie was already on the bed next to Harold when they caught up.

When Jessie came in Steven, Carla, Yvonne, and Randy, all crowded around Harold's bed, parted like the Red Sea, and watched for her reaction.

"Oh, my God, I can see your face," Jessie exclaimed joyously.

Lines made prominent by various thickness and colors of stitches crossed Harold's face, thick black above each eye, thin blue along both cheekbones and nearly invisible white on the left side of his jaw. Deep bruising covering nearly his entire face was in diverse stages of retreat.

"We were just trying to count all the stitches but couldn't agree on a specific number, but the consensus is somewhere between forty-five and fifty. Harold says there are more inside his mouth so for the sake of accuracy we should round up," Yvonne said matter-of-factly.

"This sounds like some morbid game my daughter would come up with. Is she rubbing off on all of you?" Mrs. Baker joked.

"It was Harold's idea. He figured instead of us all looking at him and wondering, we would just try and count stitches as a group project. And now we know if anyone asks."

"I still think it's morbid, but that is a lot of sewing."

"Move over you two," Jessie said to Harold and Auggie as she sat on the edge of the bed then rotated and carried her left leg up until she was also lying on the bed.

Mr. Baker passed out milkshakes and straws with a couple to spare. "Enjoy."

Looking at Yvonne, Randy said, "I think this might be a

good time to tell everyone some good news."

"The law firm whose window I was dangling out of a week ago, called today. They've offered to cover the first $100,000 of each of your medical bills. Since Jessie has some coverage, I asked if they would just make it $200,000 total and they said yes.

Also, I may have mentioned in one of the interviews I did, that Harold was going to be starting a new job and needed a car. Yesterday, I got a call from one of the bigger local dealerships. Harold, when you're ready you can pick any used car or truck from their lot that you want. They'll even pay for the taxes and license. Randy and I drove by this morning. There are some really nice cars and trucks there."

"That's just so wonderful I can't believe it," Jessie said while Harold hugged her tightly.

"You interrupted, I'm not done," Yvonne said while tapping on her cell phone. "Someone started a GO FUND ME page for both of you. I'm looking at it right now and there's a shade over $1.2 million in it."

"Someone will have to explain that part to me. I have no idea what you're talking about," Harold said in all seriousness.

"Stories about worthy causes are put out on the Internet and people can donate to them if they choose. The money could come from 1 person, 20 people or 1.2 million people. Anyway, the money is yours to do as you wish."

"Unbelievable."

"Since you three look comfortable, your mother and I are going to head out to do some shopping. We left Arizona in such a hurry we didn't have time to plan or pack well. We'll be back around eight. Call if you need anything," Mr.

Baker said.

"You can spend the rest of the evening planning how to spend a million bucks. The four of us are headed out to dinner, then Randy and I are going to take Steven and Carla on a little tour," Yvonne said.

Alone, Harold asked. "Did you bring it?"

Taking a half-empty bottle of wine from her purse, Jessie said, "Yes, but I don't even know if it's any good. I opened it weeks ago and it's been in my fridge ever since. Are you sure you want to try this?"

"I've had a lot of time lying in bed to think about it. Seems like every drink I've had in the last couple of weeks has been followed by a need to use my power. So, I just want to see if anything happens after I drink a couple ounces and do nothing. Grab my syringe."

"How will you know if it helps?"

"Walking. I was up using the walker an hour ago and got winded just getting to the end of the hall and back. It's only 3:30; I want to try again at 7:30 before your parents get back."

While musing about possible ways to spend large amounts of money, both came to the realization that they had very few wants. Another secluded cabin vacation was high on a very short list.

Sporadic naps, occasionally interrupted by a very tolerant nursing staff who chose to ignore any hospital regulation about two people and a dog in one bed, made the time go quickly. At 7:25 Jessie got to her crutches, Auggie jumped down, and they accompanied Harold as he walked confidently a hundred feet to end of the hall then back pushing the walker.

"Well, Harold you don't look winded now. Do you feel

better?" Jessie asked.

"Yes, I really didn't lean on the walker at all. Let's go again without the walker."

Having watched from the nurse's station, Dr. Thompson agreed. "I don't know exactly what kind of magic you have Jessie, but it seems like whenever you're around he does much better. I'll have physical therapy do another assessment in the morning, but it looks to me like you're doing well enough to go home."

After several more trips down the hall, Harold and Jessie were back in his room. "I want you to take the wine home with you but leave me a couple of ounces. I'll wait for a bit and drink it before I go to sleep and see what happens overnight."

"I want you to be seriously careful with this Jekyll and Hyde experiment. This has been an awesome day, don't get greedy and blow it."

"This is the best I've felt since I've been here, but I agree, I don't want to overdo it and have some weird unintended consequence. Maybe I'll just have one ounce of wine and get some sugar in me too just in case."

All three were back in the bed like they'd never moved when Jessie's parents returned. Particularly animated on the ride home, Jessie relayed Harold's improvement and the possibility of discharge although the topic of wine consumption didn't come up. "We need to get out my blender and go shopping tomorrow for fruits and veggies to make smoothies. Harold's got at least a month of drinking his meals to look forward to."

"Will you at least let me do that shopping for you?" her mother asked in a frustrated tone somewhere between sarcasm and sincerity.

Choosing to hear sincerity, Jessie responded, "Yes, please. We'll put together a list in the morning."

By the time the phone rang at 7:25 a.m., Jessie had already taken Auggie out, fed him breakfast, showered and was mid-way through her own bowl of cereal. "Good morning, baby. What's up?"

Sounding concerned, Harold said, "About my experiment, I have some good news and some bad news."

"OK, good news first."

"You won't believe your own eyes, the nurses here sure don't, but every bit of swelling is gone from my face and more than half of the bruising is not just faded but totally gone. Oh, and I don't have any discomfort at all from my broken ribs either and my vision is perfectly clear again."

"That's wonderful. So, what's the bad news?"

"How am I going to explain it to the doctor. Or do I just play stupid?"

"There's no way to explain it without going all the way back to the beginning. Then you might have to give up Auggie's secret too, although that one's already on thin ice to anyone who watches him play for five minutes. I think you go with, it's a miracle because that's the story we're going to have to tell everyone else who's seen you in the last four days."

"The physical therapist just left after giving me her blessing. I'm just waiting for the doc now. I'm fairly sure the nurses called her right after they saw my face."

"Call back with any updates, but I'm planning to be there to pick you at 10:00 unless you say otherwise."

Carefully looking from several angles, Dr. Thompson shook her head. "I thought the nurses were exaggerating when they told me about your overnight improvement, but I guess not. This is amazing. How do you feel?"

"Pretty good. I'm walking even better than yesterday. I don't have any real pain and you would know if I have any neurological signs to be aware of," Harold said trying to show little emotion.

"I've never seen healing happen like this. Have you been taking any herbs or potions I should know about?"

"No, just milkshakes. It must be because I have a good doctor."

"I totally agree about that, but I wish I knew what physiologically happened, so I could try and duplicate it. There are a lot of very sick people here and in every other hospital around the world that could benefit from some extraordinary healing. Anyway, we're going to miss you, your entourage and all the wonderful flowers but I guess you're free to go. I'll get the paperwork ready."

"Is it a go?" Jessie asked before saying hello.

"Yes. I'll be totally ready when you get here. I think I'm going to leave most of the flowers here. Then this floor will look like the ICU and the orthopedic floor."

"I just talked to Steven. He wants to pick you up, maybe go for a little drive. You two have a lot of catching up to do and won't have much time face-to-face. Since you're doing so much better, Carla canceled her flight and she and Steven are driving back to Ashland in the morning."

"It was good of them to drop everything to come to see me, but they do have a child and I want them to be better parents than I was so it's best that they go."

CHAPTER 44

After a quick double take to be sure he was in the right room, Steven could only say, "Wow, the difference from yesterday is incredible. Not only is the swelling and bruising better but the wounds where you have stitches look like they are almost totally healed too. What'd they do?"

"Nothing different. The doctors don't know how I healed so fast overnight either. I just did." Changing the subject, Harold asked, "Did you have a plan of someplace to go?"

"Not really. Do you have someplace in mind?"

"How about Mt. Rainier National Park. It's less than two hours from here."

"Are you sure you're up for that? It will make for a long trip on your first day out of the hospital."

"I really feel good, but we can always turn around if we need too."

With flowers, letters, clothes, and a few miscellaneous things loaded into Steven's car, they headed out hoping the cell phone's GPS directions they were getting were accurate. After a brief silence, Steven asked, "I was little when mom died, and I don't remember much. Can you tell me about her?"

The most vivid memories Harold had, were of his wife and those times. With the seat partially reclined, he closed his eyes and talked lovingly about his wife, their new baby, and her tragic bout of cancer in great detail. He was still talking when they stopped at the park entrance.

Over the next two hours, they took pictures of meadows and waterfalls and selfies with Mt. Rainier in the background on a beautiful fall day. On the way home, Harold asked

Steven a question he partially dreaded the answer to, "What was your childhood like?"

"What I remember most was being afraid a lot. Maybe it was feelings of abandonment or the fact we moved several times, but I just never felt safe, if that's the right word. I joined the army right out of high school to be in a tightly controlled environment and got trained to work on heavy equipment. I'd probably still be in, but a hoist chain broke and dropped a 5000-pound diesel engine on my leg. I was in and out of the hospital for eight months with non-healing bones and reoccurring infections. They eventually gave me a medical discharge and a 50% disability. I still limp a bit, but it hasn't stopped me from doing anything really. The only good thing that came from that was meeting Carla. She was a civilian employee working in the office where the army helps to transition injured soldiers to other jobs. She helped get me a job at the Oregon State DOT maintenance shop in Ashland then came with me. We had Kenny two years ago," Steven said.

"Initially, Randy said you didn't want to have any contact with me, and I don't blame you one bit for that, but you came and have been very nice to me and my friends. What changed your mind?"

"Three things. First, I felt the letter you sent was sincere and you weren't asking for anything. Second, those news reports of you risking your life to help people were very compelling. But most importantly, I wondered how I would react if something were to happen to Carla. I can't say for sure that I would be able to handle it any better than you did when mom died. You're flawed just like everyone else but not evil. So, here I am."

"Thank you for the leap of faith," Harold said, touched.

"So, a month ago you were living on the streets and now you're almost employed and have a beautiful girlfriend. How did that meteoric transition happen?"

"It absolutely started when I found Auggie. Having him around gave me something significant to care for and care about. He stopped my slow but inevitable decline. In the long run, he probably saved my life. Then five days ago, he literally did save my life.

Jessie has lifted me up. She made me want to be better and to think about how exciting the future could be, especially if she's in it."

"You have Jessie and Auggie, I have Carla and Kenny and we have each other. I think we're extremely lucky guys," Steven remarked.

"I couldn't agree more."

Standing in her garage, watching Steven and Harold unload the car, Jessie asked, "Where'd you guys spend the day?"

"Mt. Rainier. It was beautiful up there. Have you been there lately?" Steven responded.

"It's probably been ten years but as I recall it was beautiful. I need to get out of town more."

With a hug, Harold said, "You will."

"If you're both doing OK physically, I was wondering if you would come to Ashland for Thanksgiving. Auggie, your parents, Yvonne, and Randy. You're all welcome. You don't have to answer right now but please think about it."

"Have you talked to Carla about this I wouldn't want to cause a family issue?"

"It was her idea."

Harold answered, "I look forward to meeting my

grandson, so I hope we can work this out."

Hugs, handshakes, and sincere promises to keep in touch were exchanged and Auggie got a good whole body rub before Steven headed out.

"From the looks of it, the day with your son went well," Jessie said from her new favorite position stretched out on the couch with her left leg resting on the back.

"Seems he's turned out to be a very fine young man in spite of me. I seriously need to send a nice letter to my sister-in-law for doing a decent job of raising him.

On a vaguely related topic, when we talked about that GO FUND ME money yesterday, I really didn't have many thoughts about how to spend it, but if you agree I think I would like to use some to pay off Steven and Carla's mortgage."

"You absolutely should, it would be a wonderful Christmas present. You could tell them at Thanksgiving."

"We have a few weeks to work that out but I'm leaning that way.

Where are your parents, I figured they'd be here?"

"They went home about ten minutes before you got back. I almost had to do handstands to prove to my mom that I was safe to be left alone," Jessie chuckled.

With a playfully evil tone, Harold said, "So, it's just you, me, and Auggie. No doctors, nurses, or visitors to interrupt anything we might want to do."

"I totally get where you're going, and I absolutely want to play but we're expecting guests. Nancy Cabot called; she and Joan asked to visit. They should be here soon. Then after they leave, I have a job for you. My legs need to be shaved again."

"And I thought today couldn't possibly get any better."

Racing to the door, Auggie started barking about the time Nancy turned on to Jessie's street and a full thirty seconds before she turned into the driveway. Once outside, he ran to the car, waited patiently for Joan to get out, then gave and accepted kisses.

"Come in, make yourselves at home. Can I get you anything?" Jessie said.

"You're the ones just out of the hospital. Is there anything we can do for either of you?" Nancy replied.

"No, we're good. Nice of you to stop by."

"We're only going to stay a minute. We thought about coming to the hospital but decided to wait until you were discharged. Yvonne kind of kept us up on how you were doing. To be home already after what you two went through is amazing. Auggie looks as healthy as ever."

Watching Joan and Auggie wrestle on the floor, Harold laughed, "Unlike me, he's kind of indestructible."

"To tell the truth, we kind of have an ulterior motive for coming. Joan and I were in a little altercation the night you two here hurt. We didn't go the police and Joan has been super paranoid about it ever since. I'm not completely comfortable about it either and didn't know who to talk to. I remembered you offered us counseling services and even though this doesn't have anything to do with those poisonings, I just trust your opinion."

"I think I should leave," Harold said while struggling a little to stand.

"Why don't you stay and give us a second opinion. You've had more than your share of events recently where people were injured and you're not in jail."

"OK, but I'm working for free and you're going to get

what you pay for from me."

The wrestling complete, Joan was still sitting on the floor petting Auggie when she looked at Jessie and started the story. "Remember we saw you at Curbside on our way to the game?"

"Yes."

"Well, we stopped at a bar a couple of blocks from the stadium, so Nancy could pee. While I was waiting for her by the entrance, a couple of guys started to hassle me a little. When Nancy got back, we tried to leave, and they blocked the door and grabbed our butts when we pushed by. Nancy slapped one guy and I don't know how, but I threw the other guy across the room. There was only a little blurb about it in the paper and on the news. I tried to call the hospital to find out if the guy was hurt badly but he only said his name was Jason and that didn't get me anywhere. I don't know if that was the right hospital or if it was even his real name."

"Well, I do have contacts in the police department. I could call tomorrow and poke around a bit and let you know what I come up with. In the meantime, I don't want you two to worry about it. Defending yourself from an assault is not a crime."

"Thank you. We should be going and let you guys rest."

"Joan, could you do us one favor?"

"Sure. What?"

"Neither of us is in any shape to handle Auggie. There's a high school about a mile from here with a multi-sport athletic field. Could you take Auggie there and give him a good run? Say, twenty or thirty minutes. Harold can go to show you where it is. Take my car. Nancy can keep me company until you get back."

"OK. Sounds fun."

Right behind Harold as he got his coat from the hall closet, Jessie excitedly said, "You heard that, right? She threw some guy across a bar. She might have power like Auggie. I was thinking you could watch her move and maybe have her do running or jumping and see what you think. If it turns out she is powerful, we're going to have to tell her and her parents."

With true sadness, Harold said, "Frankly, I hope she doesn't. Her life was devastated once when her friends died. What would it be like for her if she had to carry this secret the rest of her life? Or, God forbid, it got out."

"First things first. Go see if she has the power then we'll have to decide what to do."

Daylight was fading fast and the track surrounding the football field was deserted. Auggie retrieved tennis balls with his usual gusto. Walking the perimeter, Harold and Joan talked in generalities.

"As I recall you are quite an athlete. Have you started back in practices?" Harold asked.

"I really like sports and I'd be running cross country now, but mom wants me to take it slow and not overexert myself. Speaking to someone who just got out of the hospital, you know how everyone wants to help you and do the right thing, but they don't always listen to you. I just really feel like running sometimes just to clear my head," Joan said obviously frustrated.

"Well, I can't run but it seems like that's all Auggie can do. Why don't you take a jog around the track with him? It's just a quarter mile so I doubt it could hurt you."

"OK, but I haven't run for more than a month so I'm not expecting much."

Randomly picking a starting point, Harold said go and checked his watch. She was moving like he'd expect any fit teenage girl could for the first hundred yards but after that, it was obvious that she was picking up speed. Auggie was pacing her at a jog, which for him was still faster than most dogs and she was pushing to keep up. Down the backstretch, Joan seemed to kick into another gear. Running even with Auggie, she looked fluid and comfortable. When she crossed in front of Harold, she was barely breathing hard. It had taken just under forty seconds.

"That felt amazing. How'd I do? Was I under a minute thirty?"

"Yes, you were definitely under. Let's try something else."

Walking to the football goalpost, Harold pointed up. "The crossbar is ten feet. Can you jump and touch it?"

"I'm not much of a jumper. You can ask the volleyball coach. A volleyball net isn't even eight feet and I can barely touch the top of that, but I'll try."

Two quick steps preceded her leap. "Oh, my God, I was two feet above that bar. Even an Olympic men's high jumper couldn't do that. What's going on? You brought me out here because you either knew or suspected something, so tell me."

"What I'm about to say is going to sound completely crazy but you have to hear me out. About the quarter mile you just ran, you did that in less than forty seconds and weren't breathing hard. Essentially, if you ran four laps you probably could have done a two-minute mile. That jump was at least eight feet high from just a two-step start. The story about throwing a man across the bar, it's a part of this. I believe there is only one other creature on earth that could possibly do what you're capable of and that's Auggie. Some of the things I've seen him do, I know are impossible, but he does them with ease and you have a couple of things in common. You are both young and both drank a little of that tainted wine a few weeks ago and didn't die. Unfortunately, I can't explain any of it biologically. I also know this is a lot to take in and process. Jessie is the only other person that knows, and she might be a better resource than me about most of this."

"I don't know what to say, it does sound crazy. Is this permanent?"

"Don't know?"

"Can anything bad happen to me? Should I go see a doctor?"

"Sorry, but again I don't know about any possible ill effects you might have. I have this power too but not nearly as strong and only for brief periods of time after which I've gotten very sick. Auggie has his power all the time and seems totally fine. I will tell you the concern I have about telling some vet about Auggie is that it gets out that he's a super dog and the next day someone from the Pentagon or the CIA is at my door wanting to take him to clone or do experiments on."

"What do you think I should do?"

"Nothing until you get a chance to talk to Jessie privately then you can decide. You could do other experiments to find out what your abilities might be and if they have any limits, but you've got to stay under everyone's radar.

If what I suspect is true, you could go to the next Summer Olympics and set an unbeatable world record in every track and field event, both men's and women's, and not break a sweat., I know this is a huge secret to keep but for Auggie's sake please don't tell anyone. Ultimately, your parents should know but not yet."

Staring at the front of the car with a grin on her face, Joan asked, "We know I'm fast and can jump really high, let's see how strong I am. How much do you think the front of this thing weighs?"

"A mid-size SUV with 4-wheel drive, I'm just guessing but at least 2000lbs." Stepping back Harold added, "Remember to lift with your legs."

Metallic groans come from springs and shock absorbers when the front tires leave the ground. Smiling while holding the bumper waist high, Joan started laughing when it was above her head with one hand.

Easing the vehicle back down Joan wondered. "Guess I'm pretty strong too. Why haven't I noticed this until now?"

"Another thing I don't know. Maybe it was because you hadn't tried. You said your mom has really wanted you to limit your activity."

The short ride back to Jessie's was taken up by a series of relevant questions with "I don't know" as the answer.

"Do you think you could come back on Saturday and talk with Jessie or would you rather we meet you someplace?" Harold asked as they pulled into the driveway.

"Saturday would be great. I'd prefer to come here just so we don't have a chance of being overheard. I'll text Jessie and work out a time."

~*~

"There they are," Nancy said as she stood and reached for her coat. "It was wonderful to see you and know you and

Harold are on the mend. Everyone at Curbside has stepped up and from what I can tell the place seems to be running smoothly. So, take your time and get healed."

"Thank you for coming," Jessie said while sharing a hug. "I'll be back to work before you know it."

Waving goodbye from the front door, Jessie couldn't even wait until the car had left the driveway before she started quizzing Harold. "Well, what's the verdict? Is she super girl?"

"Definitely yes," Harold said as he dropped into one of the overstuffed chairs. "She's fast. She did a quarter mile in forty seconds without much effort then lifted the front of your car over her head with one hand."

"What did you tell her about it?"

"Everything I could without sounding like a crazy man. She's going to come here on Saturday to talk then decide what to do. What I know about the inner workings of a teenage girl, you could put in a fortune cookie with room to spare. That said, the more I think about it, the more convinced I become that this power will turn into a terrible burden for Joan.

She did ask a couple of things I hadn't spent much time considering. She wanted to know if this was permanent and if she could become ill. It could be that it will wear off in time and we know from my experience it can make you sick."

Pondering the thought for a moment, Jessie said, "True, it could wear off, but she might just keep getting stronger too."

"Well, at the same time my mind is racing, my body is seriously running out of gas. I want to get another shot glass of wine, take a shower, and go to bed. I promise I'll do an exceptional job of shaving your legs tomorrow."

CHAPTER 45

"I didn't see a bit of bruising, do you?" Harold asked as Jessie surveyed his face.

"Nope. Looks completely healed as far as I can tell. We should probably go see some doctor and have these stitches removed before your skin heals right over them."

"It would probably be better to take them out ourselves, rather than have another doctor question my speedy recovery. Do you have a small pair of scissors and tweezers?" Harold wanted to know.

"Yes, but I've never taken out stitches before."

"If you've taken a stitch out of fabric you have all the necessary skills to do this."

Rummaging through the vanity drawer, Jessie retrieved the tools, smiled sweetly, and said, "Alright here we go, but I don't want to hear any whining if I hurt you."

When Jessie said, "Done," Harold came back with, "Forty-eight. I was counting. I had forty-eight stitches."

"I bet by tomorrow even where the stitches came out will be healed over. I doubt you'll even have visible scars in a few days. Let's take the dressing off your neck and see how that looks."

The adhesive perimeter of the dressing had done its job and Jessie had to pull hard, first with tweezers, then with fingers to get it off. "I don't know why I'm surprised considering all your other wounds, but it's totally closed. I swear, it was at least two inches across and now I can hardly see it."

Looking in the mirror, Harold smiled. "Sorry, darling,

but apparently the plastic surgeon didn't know what George Clooney looks like, so you're stuck with Harold Pearson."

"Well, fortunately, that was my second choice so I'm happy."

Having watched intently, like he knew every word of what was being said, Auggie's attention diverted to an itch. Rolling onto his back he moaned, wiggled, and squirmed his way across the bedroom carpet stopping just outside the hallway door. Satisfied he trotted back to his observation post sporting his omnipresent happy face.

Smiling, Jessie said, "How could anyone not love him?

Say, if you still want to do my legs or even do me, we'd better get with it. I have my first physical therapy appointment at noon. Mom is going to drive me in, so she'll probably be here by 10:30."

Shower, shave, and romantic interlude complete, Jessie was putting on her usual t-shirt and sweats and humming a favorite tune when she stopped to ask. "I was wondering where that desire to shave my legs came from? It seems a bit unusual."

The question caught Harold a bit off guard. He was quiet for a moment then came over to sit on the end of the bed next to Jessie. "The last couple of months before my wife died she was very frail and could only either lie in bed or sit in a chair. I tried my best to anticipate her needs because she rarely asked for anything. The one thing she did like was having smooth legs. I don't know why that was important to her but if I'm guessing, it was because she had lost all the other things that she considered feminine. Her hair was gone from chemo. She only weighed 90 lbs. and she was totally dependent. So, every other day when I would help her shower I would shave her legs even though I'm fairly sure her hair had stopped growing. It was the closest thing to being intimate and sexual that we could do and somehow, she got a sliver of joy from it. I understand if you want me to stop knowing that it's a remnant of that part of my life."

"Absolutely not. I want you to keep shaving me because frankly, that's one of the most romantic stories I've ever heard. If it brings you some bit of pleasure or comfort I'm all for it."

Wrapping Jessie in a total embrace, he kissed her then whispered in her ear. "Only a tiny percentage of women would hear that story and respond with acceptance such as that. Thank you."

While tying Jessie's shoes, Harold made a request, "When your mom does get here, I'm going to stay in the bedroom. You can tell her I'm still sleeping. I think it's a bit too soon for people to see my miraculous recovery."

"Do you what us to stop and get you anything on our way back?"

"Yes, about five hundred in cash. While you're gone I'm going to call around and try and find some doctor to take these wires out of my mouth. Unless you what to do it?"

With a definitive, "No!" Jessie made herself clear. "Pulling stitches wasn't too bad, but I'm not fishing around your mouth with a pair of pliers and wire cutters. Sorry. Have you already conjured up some story to tell a doctor?"

"Unless you can think of something better, I was going to say that I live in Europe and had been in a car wreck 2 1/2 months ago. I'm in the States on business and will be here for several more weeks. When they see my face is all healed they'll probably believe that."

"How do you even know your jaw is healed?"

"I'm just going by the rate of all the other healing. I'll insist on an x-ray first if they don't suggest it. Getting my meals from a syringe is getting tiring."

"I don't know if telling a convincing lie is something to be proud of, but we've sure have had a lot of practice lately and we seem to be getting good at it."

Laughing, Harold pointed out the irony, "I just heard a car pull in. If that's your mom get ready to tell her the 'he's sleeping" lie. You'll have to think up another one for when you get back, so she won't come in and hang out. You can text that story to me just in case I need to hide out."

Looking through a slight opening in the drapes, Harold watched Jessie and her mother drive off. "OK, Auggie, let's go for a nice walk then I have to make some phone calls when we get back."

The text was nine minutes old when Harold noticed it.

Jessie: *Told my mom that you have a sensitivity to noise and light that sometimes creates headaches. Be home in ten minutes.*

Auggie's bark signaled Jessie had probably turned onto the street and time was short. Grabbing an ice pack from the freezer and a dishtowel off the kitchen counter, Harold turned out the lights, flopped onto the couch, covered his face totally with the towel and ice then waited.

"Hello, Harold," Betty Baker said in a near whisper.

"Hi. Excuse me for not getting up."

"Oh, please stay comfortable. Jessie told me about your headaches. I'll just drop off a couple things and be out of here and let you rest."

From the kitchen, Jessie and her mother whispered considerately for a few minutes. Saying goodbye, Jessie waved from the front door while speaking over her shoulder,

"You can come out now, she's gone."

Tossing the ice pack on the coffee table Harold said, "Thank God. My face was freezing. How'd it go at physical therapy?"

"Good. I can start putting more weight on my leg and use the crutches just as support. I might be able to go to a cane in another week or ten days. Have any luck finding a doc to take out those wires?"

"As a matter of fact, I got very lucky. Talked to a doctor in Bellingham. He had a cancellation for tomorrow at ten. Said it would take about a half hour if the x-rays were OK. I told him I didn't have insurance and he agreed to $650.00."

"Bellingham is a little over an hour from here. We could drive up today and wander around a bit. It's a nice town.

What name did you give him?"

Harold chuckled. "I didn't have a name picked out in advance and the first one that came to me was Lou Reed."

"Like the singer?"

"Yeah."

"I guess that's as good as any for the hour or so you'll need it."

"What about a disguise?" Jessie asked.

"The story about light sensitivity sounds good. I'll use that and try and wear sunglasses as much as possible. For a few weeks, I'll have to fake having my jaws wired when I'm around people."

Auggie seemed to be dozing, but when Jessie suddenly became motionless and quiet he moved to her side. She responded with a pained smile and gave him a pat on the head. Harold too moved to sit next to her and waited another silent minute before asking. "What's wrong?"

"It just occurred to me, this morning I joked about becoming professional liars but it's true. Just about everything we do has to be cloaked in a lie. It's insidious. I didn't think about it much at first when we were just trying to protect Auggie. But now we're hiding that plus your amazing healing and adding Joan's abilities to our list of things to be concealed. The worst part for me is lying to my parents and Yvonne. Hell, I even got Yvonne to lie about you and Auggie being in that law office."

"I have to admit I've spent so much time trying to concoct these narratives that I wasn't paying attention to the corrosive effect they can have. I mean, I knew right off the bat handing this burden to Joan was going to be difficult for her. But I didn't see what it might be doing to you. For that, I am truly sorry."

"It's not like we planned for this to happen, it just did and now we're stuck with it."

"I just remembered what a beautiful, brilliant woman once told me when I was terribly depressed about losing my anonymity and having to face the media and even the general public. She said something like, 'Be happy to be alive and look to see all the wonderful things the future can bring if we can just get through the next couple of weeks.' Well, I believed her then and I believe her now. We just have to stay off the front page until we approach something that looks like normal."

On her feet, Jessie smiled down at Harold. "That was good advice. I think I'll take it. Come on, let's pack some bags and go to Bellingham."

"While you're loading up, I need to give Randy a quick call," Jessie said to Harold while tapping on her phone's screen.

"Hello, Randy. Do you have a minute to talk?"

"Sure, what can I do for you, Jessie?"

"I need a favor. Last Thursday there was a fight or something in a bar a block or so from the stadium. One guy whose name I think is Jason might have been hurt. I was wondering if you could find out the extent of his injuries and if there is any pending police action."

"My God," Randy said behind a laugh. "What are you into now?"

"I can't say much about it. One of my counseling clients gave me some information during a session and I'm just trying to follow up."

"Don't even tell me you're seeing clients. You've been out of the hospital for only two days."

"It was a short visit. What do ya say?"

"OK. I'll poke around a bit and let you know. How are you guys doing?"

"Really well. Think you and Yvonne could come for dinner Friday?"

"I'm good for it. Do you want me to talk to Yvonne or will you?"

"I'll text her. Thank you so much. Bye."

~*~

Traffic was heavy but moving well and the trip was uneventful. "Let's track down this doc's office then we can get a hotel someplace close," Harold said checking addresses while Jessie took direction from her phone's GPS. "There it is, the new looking place on the right."

Four stories of red brick, marble, and smoked glass

made a fine presentation. A large sign listed several different medical practices. Harold would be seen on the third floor.

Two blocks away, on the same side of the street, an older but well-kept motel called The Drifter advertised a vacancy with pets' welcome. The room was typical. Two queen size beds, tv, internet, and a full-size tub/shower. It looked clean and smelled like the ocean breeze air freshener hanging on a string in the little closet.

Though close to the center of town, the distance was too far for someone on crutches. A three-minute drive put them in the downtown core where late day mid-week traffic was minimal, and parking was abundant. They walked a few blocks in each direction, got ice cream, and were back at the motel by 7 pm and asleep by 10 pm.

Up early, Harold showered and managed some tasks before he sat on the edge of the bed to stroke Jessie's bare back and speak softly, "I think I'm all set. Auggie had a nice walk and all my stuff is in the car already. I'm just going to walk from here. If I get there early hopefully, they can get going sooner and we can be on the road. Remember, when you come to pick me up to ask for Lou Reed. Check out time here isn't until noon so no need for you to hurry. I'll call if anything comes up."

"OK Lou, go take your walk on the wild side. See you later."

The doctor's entire staff wore matching navy-blue scrubs with the clinic name stitched into the left breast pocket. The receptionist was a pretty twenty-something with perfect teeth and hair. "Good morning, Mr. Reed. I have some paperwork for you to fill out then I'm to send you to x-ray. The doctor will see you later."

As hoped, ten minutes after returning to the reception

area from x-ray, Harold was led into an office where Dr. Glenn was staring intently at his computer. "Come in and have a seat, Mr. Reed. When did you say your accident was?"

"August 10th."

"So, that's around ten weeks. Well, I'm not positive I can even tell where the breaks happened. Looks totally healed to me, so let's get that metal out of your mouth."

"Can't happen soon enough for me."

Groggy from sedation and drooling from the effects of local anesthetic, Harold's speech was less clear than when he walked through the door. "Hi Jessie, this is Lou you can come pick me up. You'll need to come in to sign some discharge stuff and pay the bill. Apparently, I'm under the influence and therefore, not responsible."

"Well, from the sounds of you I agree. Be there shortly."

Paperwork complete, Harold, who was busy giggling about something not apparent to anyone else, was taken by wheelchair to the car. Once outside, he took a couple of deep breaths, wrapped his arms around Jessie and in a voice intended to be a whisper said, "I really love you."

"My little drunk Romeo, I love you too. Now get in the car."

Comfortable in the reclined seat, Harold was asleep before Jessie even got to the freeway and slept most of the trip, waking only long enough to restate his love. Once home, he managed to only get as far as the living room couch where he slept the rest of the afternoon.

Disheveled and disoriented, Harold stumbled into the kitchen. "What time is it?"

"A little after six," Jessie said trying not to laugh.

"What day?"

"It's still Thursday and for future reference, you're an incredibly lightweight when it comes to narcotic sedatives."

"You'd think all the drinking I did would have made me immune to sedatives but apparently not."

"Well, before you fall asleep again would you like something to eat?"

"A big juicy steak sounds great but if you have any soup that would be fine too."

"How about tomato soup and a toasted cheese sandwich?"

"Sounds wonderful."

When an unblinking stare did not produce results, Auggie barked and Harold complied with a trip outside for a few minutes playing fetch and wrestling until Jessie yelled the food was ready from the back door.

Becoming curious while watching as Harold gingerly nibbled at his sandwich, Jessie had to ask, "Does it hurt to move your jaw?"

"All the Novocain has worn off and I keep expecting it to be at least a little uncomfortable, but it feels OK. It's just weird not having eaten anything solid for a week. This is probably the perfect first meal. Thank you."

"Speaking of meals, I want to have Yvonne, Randy, and my parents over for dinner tomorrow."

"Are you sure that's wise considering my current perfect state of health or did you come up with some way to explain my incredible recovery?"

"I haven't, but I also don't want to avoid them for the two months it would take if you healed normally. We can be totally honest saying we don't know how your extremely unusual healing occurred but we're very grateful. We won't say anything about Auggie, Joan, or even you after a glass of wine."

"If there's anything we can do to lighten the load that keeping these secrets has placed on you, I'm all for it. I trust you and you trust them and that's good enough for me."

"Starting next week, I think we should just go about our daily lives. You go start your new job. I'll go back to work and after a few days of people seeing us, it will just seem normal."

"I never thought normal and average could sound so good."

"When you're done eating why don't you take Auggie for a nice walk. I'll clean up the kitchen and meet you in the bedroom. Using these crutches makes my back and shoulders ache. I could use a massage."

"After I finish with your back, can I do your front?"

"Yes, I insist."

CHAPTER 46

"How long have you been up?" Jessie asked Harold while pouring a cup of coffee.

"An hour or so. I slept plenty yesterday and I was wide-awake at five. What would you like for breakfast?

"I'm not really hungry. Just some fruit and cereal for me."

"Have you decided on a dinner menu for tonight or are we ordering take out?"

"I was thinking I could buy the main course and dessert then whip up a salad and some other side dish. Anything sound good to you?"

"Lasagna, garlic bread and gelato," Harold suggested.

Jessie marveled, "Wow, you sure came up with that in a hurry."

"If you'd like something different that's fine."

"No, that actually sounds good. I haven't had Italian in a while and I know a nice family-run place that I like."

"Other than food shopping do you have anything else on your agenda for today?" Harold asked.

"Later this morning, I want to make a few phone calls just to be sure there aren't any fires that need to be put out at Curbside, but after that nothing really. How about you? Anything you need to get done?"

"I'm going to call Mr. Ashcroft shortly and be sure it's still OK to start on Monday. If that's a go, then I'd like to buy some more new clothes. Maybe later we could drive by that car dealership that offered me a car and check out the possibilities although my knowledge in that area is severely lacking."

"I've had the same mechanic for twenty years. He's a really nice guy. I could give him a call and maybe he could meet us there or we could pick him up."

"That would be awesome. One last thing, I checked that GO FUND ME site. Our total as of an hour ago, was $1.54 million. I don't know the mechanism for turning off the spigot but that's a gift I'm already painfully uncomfortable receiving."

"I didn't know it was still accepting donations. By all means, we'll get that stopped."

"What time did you tell everyone for dinner?"

"Six, so if we're out of here by ten, we should be back in plenty of time."

"Auggie and I are going to go for a walk around the neighborhood. Mr. Ashcroft should be in his office by the time we get back then I'll be ready."

~*~

"Good morning, Harrison Ashcroft."

"Harrison, this is Harold Pearson."

"Harold, great to hear from you. How are you doing? My granddaughter Joan said she saw you the other day and thought you were doing much better than expected," Mr. Ashcroft said.

"I am doing well. So well, in fact, that I would like to start work on Monday like we originally planned," Harold informed him.

"There's no hurry but if you think you're up to it that would be fine with me. I have a couple of small home addition projects I've been putting off that I could give to you to start out."

"I'm excited at the possibility. Thank you again for the opportunity."

"You're welcome. Have a nice weekend and I'll see you Monday at 8:30," Mr. Ashcroft offered as the call ended.

~*~

Staring into the mirror while putting on the last of what little make-up she wore, Jessie noticed Harold out of the corner of her eye. "How'd it go with Ashcroft?"

"Wonderful. I start Monday morning. How are things at Curbside?"

"From what I hear, Nancy Cabot kind of jumped in with both feet. I talked to three different staff members and each one said she's been fabulous, taking calls, running errands, and doing follow-ups. I really have to get her on the payroll."

"Seems to me that Nancy is at Curbside for the same reason you started it. After suffering a terrible loss, you a brother and she a son, you both decided consciously or unconsciously to channel that grief into something positive," Harold surmised.

"You can be very insightful at times and it's a wonderful trait to possess. I hope you're right and that working at Curbside helps her fill the void."

"Did it help fill the void for you?" Harold asked.

"It took a while, but the gratification that comes after one of those rare instances where something I've done truly changes someone's life for the better helps immensely."

"I hope you count Auggie and me among those lives you changed for the better."

"And I hope you know how much the two of you have helped fill the void," Jessie assured him.

"I'm seriously fighting off the urge to shit-can today's agenda and pull you back in bed, so we either need to get going or get naked," said Harold, grinning.

"Let's get to it. The more tasks we get done today, the fewer we'll have to do tomorrow and Sunday. Where do you want to go clothes shopping?"

"Someplace with fairly good quality stuff that's also likely to let Auggie come in without giving us disapproving glances or a downright refusal. I am really at your mercy since I haven't shopped for dress clothes in almost twenty years."

"OK, I think I know where we'll go. While you're trying on clothes I can order the food and call my mechanic about looking at cars with us," said Jessie.

The clothes buying went quickly with Harold as the model and Jessie providing input with either a brief nod yes, or a head shake for no. In a little over an hour, they walked out with two three-piece suits, several pairs of slacks, dress shirts, a sports jacket, and new shoes totaling $1500.00.

When Jessie pulled up in front of the car lot, as promised, her mechanic, Colin, was there to meet them. When she stepped from her car, he wrapped her in a bear hug. "I was thrilled you called, Jessie. The local news had everyone at the shop so worried about you," Colin declared.

"Thank everyone for their concern and thank you so much for taking the time to come over. Colin, I'd like you to meet Harold Pearson and Auggie. Harold, this is Colin Keller, the best mechanic in King County."

Grabbing Harold's hand with gusto, Colin gave a firm handshake and followed that with a head pat for Auggie. "You two have been amazing the way you've been helping people left and right. How can I help you today?"

Looking out over row after row of various cars, trucks, and SUVs, Harold said, "As I understand it, I can pick any used car in the lot, but I really don't know much about them. I want to get a good solid vehicle that gets decent mileage, has a high safety rating, plenty of room for a rambunctious dog, is easy to repair, and inexpensive to maintain."

"You're asking all the right questions. Let's take a look at the options."

While Colin, Harold, and Auggie walked the rows stopping at various times for a closer look at different possibilities, Jessie went inside and was ushered to an office where she waited only briefly before the manager arrived. A short conversation confirmed the free car offer. Once a choice was made, the paperwork could be completed in a day and the car picked up the next. All that was requested was that Harold and Auggie have pictures taken while accepting his choice.

A half dozen test drives later and with Colin's blessing, Harold picked a 2018 SUV with only 8500 miles and an intact new car smell.

"I think you'll be happy with this, Harold. It was nice to meet you," Colin said with a parting handshake.

Harold replied, "I really appreciate your input. Thank you."

Unusually animated during the drive to pick-up dinner, Harold talked about the possibility of going hiking or camping once Jessie's leg was healed.

"Hey, City Boy, where did all this outdoor nature stuff come from all of a sudden?" Jessie said with a chuckle.

"Three of the best days of my life in the last twenty years were the two days we spent in that cabin and the day at Mt. Rainier I spent with my son. I guess I just want to recreate those feelings," Harold said while reaching over to hold Jessie's hand.

"Well, just remember, I don't heal like you and Auggie. It will be at least six more weeks before I might be able to do even simple hikes and by then we'll be in the middle of winter."

"Isolated cabins are still a possibility until then," persisted Harold.

"Yes, they are," agreed Jessie.

Feeling emboldened knowing that in less than twenty-four hours he would own a car, Harold drove with confidence from the grocery store to the restaurant then home. Quickly unloading packages, he and Auggie left for a walk that morphed into a run that covered more than five miles.

"What can I do to help?" Harold asked when he saw Jessie preparing food.

"I'll finish this if you could set the table. Then I think we're ready," Jessie said before a brief pause at her task. "Do you want to wait until everyone's here to come out and show your unbelievable recovery or pretend that there is nothing unusual and see how long it takes for someone to say something?"

"I think pretending there's nothing unusual sounds more fun, but I can't imagine your mom lasting more than five minutes before she'd have to say something," he answered.

"You're being awfully generous to think she could go five minutes."

"Well, I met her less than a week ago when I was coming out of a coma, so I'm basing my guess on limited contact."

Auggie's bark provided an advanced warning that someone had turned on to the street and Harold sent him out to be the official greeter. From the window, Jessie watched, and as if coordinated, her parents' arrival was followed within seconds by Randy and Yvonne.

At the door, Jessie welcomed each with a hug and kiss, and led them through the living room to dining room and finally to the kitchen. Positioned to see everyone's reaction, Jessie tried desperately not to show any emotion.

Harold, head down while taking garlic bread from the oven, said hello to everyone over his shoulder then turned to face them while he, too, tried to keep a straight face.

"Oh, my God, how is that possible?" Betty Baker said the second she saw Harold while pushing past her husband for a better view. "A week ago, you were unrecognizable and now it looks like nothing ever happened to you."

"I have no idea how I managed to heal so fast and so completely. I checked the internet and there are people that heal very quickly. Luckily, I guess I'm one of them," Harold said.

"Even bones? Your mouth wires are gone," Randy noticed.

"Apparently so. I had x-rays before the wires were removed and the doctor couldn't even find where my jaw had been broken."

Now face to face with only inches between them, Betty asked. "What did the doctor say about it when you got your stitches out?"

"She was as surprised as you are. Isn't that right Dr. Jessie?" Harold said looking at Jessie.

"You took all those stitches out?" Betty asked Jessie.

"I made a simple comment that he should get them removed before his skin heals over them and he talked me into taking them out. It wasn't very hard."

Picking up a plate, Yvonne started to uncover and dish up food. "I don't mean to be rude, but I didn't get much of a lunch break and I'm starving. Harold, could you cut me some of that bread?"

Once introduced, the subject of food brought everyone to the table and questions about Harold's recovery deceased. Dinner progressed quickly and by 8 pm the guests had gone. Harold was putting away leftovers and loading the dishwasher while Jessie sat on the kitchen counter eating remnants from the gelato container.

"According to Randy, Joan will be relieved to know the guy that she threw across the bar ended up with a broken arm and broken nose. He was out of the hospital by the next day. He couldn't explain what happened and didn't want to press charges. Because there were no reliable, sober witnesses, no real investigation was done, and the case was closed.

Speaking of Joan, she texted me that she wants to come over at 10:00 o'clock tomorrow morning. I said OK, so we have until then to decide what to say to her," Jessie said between bites.

"I think we tell her everything we know for sure and anything we suspect might be true and hope for the best." Harold said with a slight shoulder shrug.

CHAPTER 47

"Get your muddy paws off me, you silly mutt. Don't you know enough to get in out of the rain or do you just not care?" Joan said as she pried a dripping wet Auggie off her lap, so she could get out of her car.

"Good morning, Joan," Harold said from the garage while he begged the overexcited Auggie to stand still long enough to be dried off. "Here's a towel. Sorry about the mess he made of your pants. Go on in and with any luck we'll be in soon."

Looking at what clearly had been freshly washed jeans minutes earlier, Jessie just shook her head. "Jesus, that dog can make a bigger mess in two seconds than a room full of toddlers can make in a month. Let me wash those for you."

"Any other day it wouldn't matter much but I'm meeting

my mom for lunch and a movie later so I'm going to take you up on that offer," Joan said.

"Let me get you something to change in to. How's your blouse?"

"It looks alright but just in case could you give me a T-shirt or something to wear until I'm ready to go."

"Smart girl. Now you're catching on."

Finally, with everyone comfortably settled in the living room, Harold spoke first. "I am curious Joan, have you tested your abilities at all?"

"Yeah, I've done a few things. I went into the high school's weight room and bench-pressed 300 lbs. without much effort, swam four lengths of the school's pool on a single breath and ran a mile in under two minutes and it felt like I was jogging. Those are just some of the physical things I've tried. My vision is so good I can read a magazine from across the room or see a small bird in a tree two hundred yards away. And I hear everything, even things I'm not supposed to like my parents having sex. I have to wear my noise canceling headphones to bed to drown out that and all the other stuff I can hear. You know how they say long distance runners get an endorphin high, well when I'm being really active it's totally euphoric. Whatever I'm doing I just want to keep going. It's exciting and scary at the same time."

"That explains Auggie's insatiable desire to be in motion. Have you noticed anything negative at all?"

"No, but that's the scary part because you said you got sick when you have power."

"This is some of the stuff we need to talk to you about," Jessie said. "Harold is different than you and Auggie. He only has a fraction of your abilities and only if he drinks some alcohol first. Even those powers are limited by his blood sugar. His body doesn't seem to have the capacity to maintain his blood sugar levels and he passes out basically from hypoglycemia. Using the running analogy, you've heard about marathon runners 'hitting the wall' twenty miles into the race. Well, Harold hits the wall then the wall falls down on him. You and Auggie never get anywhere near the wall in the first place."

Noticing Auggie destroying a chew toy that was marketed as indestructible, Joan smiled and asked, "All this is because of that wine?"

"We're pretty sure about that. It's the only thing all three of you have in common. You drank a little wine straight from the bottle and nearly died. When Harold and Auggie drank their wine, it had been open and exposed to air all night. It just made them fall asleep for a whole day.

There's no way for us to know if it will wear off or you'll get stronger, or if it will shorten your life, make you immortal or have you popping out super babies. As far as going to a doctor is concerned, I couldn't even guess who you might see that would be able to diagnose and advise on a condition that has never been documented outside of superhero comic books."

No one spoke for almost a minute before Harold broke the silence, "Eventually when more and more weird things started happening you might have figured some of this out on your own. I can hide my power by not drinking. Auggie can't hide his very well, so we try to be careful when there are people around. You have the biggest secret anyone could ever imagine and for that I'm sorry."

Harold continued, "Right now the three of us are the only ones who know. If you decide to tell your parents, and

I'm not saying you shouldn't, that would make five and if you see a doctor then the number of people who might see that chart goes through the roof. My only request is that you be very, very careful who you tell. Don't bring up Auggie or me and give us a heads' up if you do tell someone, so we can be ready just in case anything comes back to us."

"I'll be careful. I promise," Joan swore.

Moving over to give Joan a hug, Jessie said, "I mean this in all sincerity. If you want to talk about any of this at any time day or night call me. OK?"

"OK."

"I do have a bit of good news. I talked to my contact at the police department. That guy you threw across the bar ended up with a broken nose and a broken arm but was out of the hospital the next day and didn't want to press charges so nothing to worry about there," said Jessie.

"That's both a big relief and a warning to me to not let my power to get out unexpectedly. Although, I hope he learned a lesson about assaulting women."

"Any other questions we can try and answer?" Harold asked.

"I noticed you seemed to be completely healed. Is that a part of all this too?"

"Yes. Open wounds and broken bones fully healed in a week. We've just been telling everyone I'm a fast healer and leaving it at that."

"One last thing. Do you think I'm bulletproof?" Joan asked.

"I think it might take a lot to harm you, but I don't think for one second that you can't be seriously hurt or killed by a bullet or a thousand other things."

"This sure gives me a lot to think about. It's hard to

imagine what my parents would do if they knew about all this. I'm sure my mom would be on the phone to every doctor she could think of to try and be sure nothing bad was going to happen to me. My dad would probably be a bit more pragmatic as long as I wasn't showing any bad side effects. For the time being, I don't think I'll tell them. I'll be eighteen in a couple weeks and legally an adult if that makes any bit of difference to anyone if this gets out," advised Joan.

"Oh, I just thought of one other thing you should be aware of if you're around an open flame. You might be able to breathe fire. I've done it three times. The first was an accident the second a test and the third on purpose. I don't know if I can do it because I need to have alcohol in my system or it's just another piece of the pie. We haven't tested Auggie," Harold told her.

"Now that's just cool. I could go to a Halloween party as a fire-breathing dragon."

"Yeah and burn the house down. I'm talking flamethrower type fire. You'd better find out for sure before you go to blow out the candles on your birthday cake and torch your house."

"On that happy note, I'm going to put your pants in the dryer and make some hot chocolate. Anybody else want some?" Jessie asked.

At the dining room table, Joan poked at the marshmallow floating in her cup. "If a hundred people in the world had this power, I wonder what percent of their first thoughts would be 'how do I monetize this?'"

"A big proportion I suspect," Harold said while wiping the foam from his upper lip. "The possibilities are endless. Someone like you could be the best stuntwoman ever. Or, maybe you could star in an outdoor adventure television show.

On the humanitarian side, you could go someplace where there was just an earthquake and pull hundreds of people out of the rubble all by yourself. But to really cash in the big money would most likely come from pharmaceutical or genetic engineering companies who would be willing to pay a million dollars apiece for vials of your blood or tissue samples. If they could replicate what you have, they'd make billions and you'd just have to hope they act responsibly. Of course, the Pentagon would love every soldier to have power like you. You're holding Pandora's Box," Harold went on.

Sensing the heaviness, Jessie stepped in. "We're getting a bit dark with that analogy. Let's lighten up a bit. What movie are you and your mom going to see?"

Smiling broadly, Joan had trouble answering without laughing. "The new superhero movie where beautiful young people save the planet."

"Well, just remember it's entertainment; not research."

As the conversation evolved into more traditional topics like school and jobs, Joan excused herself and returned in now clean clothes. "Thank you both so much for this. I don't know what I would do if I didn't have you to talk to," Joan said.

"You're totally welcome. Call any time and if you ever need a partner for a brisk twenty-mile run you can always come to pick up Auggie. Say, do you have enough time to drop us off in town? Harold is supposed to pick up a car," asked Jessie.

"Sure, if we could leave in the next ten minutes or so."

True to their word, the dealership had the car Harold had chosen sitting directly in front of the main showroom doors. Inside some staff came over for pictures with the local hero and his dog while Harold signed multiple lines of a six-page document. Moving outside, Harold sat in the driver's seat and accepted the keys from the dealership owner with a handshake while a professional photographer took nonstop pictures. In a mercifully short forty minutes, Harold, Jessie, and Auggie drove off in the lot.

"Well, darling, it's one o'clock on a rainy Saturday afternoon. Is there anything you'd like to do?" Harold asked.

Sliding her hand across his thigh and onto his crotch, Jessie gave a gentle squeeze. "At some point, we're going to have to plan another press conference. We need to thank everyone for all the cards, flowers, money, and well-wishes. But today I say we go to the store and get some fruit and veggies and a whole bunch of junk food, stop and get four or five movies from one of those vending machines, and spend the rest of the weekend not doing a damn thing. Our new normal lives start Monday morning."

"Sounds perfect right Auggie?"

"Woof!"

About the Author

After a 33-year career as a registered nurse I retired and decided to try and finish this novel I started more than 20 years ago. I hope everyone enjoys it and I receive the feedback I need to continue with the obvious follow-up book.

Fortifiedbook1@gmail.com

12269746R00191

Made in the USA
San Bernardino, CA
10 December 2018